*Keep reading – and
enjoy!
Rachel Starr
Thomson*

Burning Light

Book Two of The Seventh World Trilogy

Rachel Starr Thomson

LITTLE DOZEN PRESS

Burning Light

Published by Little Dozen Press
Windsor, Ontario, Canada
http://www.littledozen.com

Copyright 2009 by Rachel Starr Thomson
Visit the author at http://www.rachelstarrthomson.com

Cover artwork and design by Deborah Thomson
Copyright 2009

All rights reserved. No part of this publication may be reproduced, stored in a retrieval system, or transmitted, to any form or by any means, electronic, mechanical, photocopying, recording, or otherwise, without the prior written permission of the publisher.

ISBN: 978-0-9739591-3-0

Table of Contents

Prologue

It was cold in the shadow of the pine trees. The moon was shining, but only a few brave slivers of light found their way through the woven canopy of long green needles to the bank of the stream where Nicolas Fisher sat. The air smelled of heavy snow, the first of the year in Galce—a thick, swirling snow that blew down from Fjordland in the far north and swallowed the world in white.

Nicolas was watching the water.

He had not been watching it long. For hours he had listened to it running over rock while he thought of other things, other places; of a black river in the City of Bridges, of a girl he loved, who was still there.

He thought of these things, and breathed the air that had lately drifted over the northern mountains, and he was not sure when he noticed that the water was running uphill. Yet noticed it he had, and now he could not take his eyes from the sight of it, black and silver in the moonlight, calmly doing what it could not do.

He reached down, touched it, and jerked his hand back. The water was warm. Its warmth ran up through his fingers, into his hands and arms, and his skin tingled.

It was then that he heard the voice.

He heard it first as a barely perceptible change in the

water's flow. A deepening—then a shimmering echo as though something had cried out far away, and the stream had carried the musical cry up into the forests of Galce.

As Nicolas listened, the echo became a whisper, and then a call.

Come for me, the voice said. *I am the prisoner River-Daughter, yearning to be free. Come for me. Set me free.*

He closed his eyes while the words swirled through his mind. Another voice mixed with the first—a young man's voice. His own. It repeated the words urgently before the running of water drowned it out. *Come for me. Set me free.*

"Where?" Nicolas asked, the sound barely escaping his lips.

Follow the stream, the shimmering whisper answered.

A moment later the deepening became shallow again. The whisper was gone, and with it the echo. The stream was running downhill, as though it were a normal stream without any voice beyond that of rapids rushing over mossy stone.

Nicolas stayed by the stream for a little longer. The form of a great black bear melted out of the pines and stood by him, snuffling. Nicolas stood and stretched his legs. He buried one hand in the fur of Bear's neck.

He said nothing, but together they started to walk. Downstream.

And the snow began to fall.

1

Trouble Afoot

NICOLAS TURNED fitfully in his sleep. His small fire had nearly burned itself out in the night, and only a few small embers still glowed. The cold of the ground was seeping up through the thick green woolen blanket Nicolas was wrapped in. It was making its way through the bundle of rags he used as a pillow, up into his ears and his head until all his dreams were white and grey, snow and fog and endless skies.

Something nudged his booted foot, once, twice, and harder. He opened his eyes and blinked away the frost from his lashes. With a grunt, he pushed himself up, pulling his foot away from Bear.

"And where were you all night?" Nicolas asked. Bear moved closer, and Nicolas leaned on the animal's bulk as he rose and stamped his feet on the hard earth. "Eh?" Nicolas prodded. Bear grunted once.

"That's no excuse for leaving me out in the cold," Nicolas said. "I could have used that fur coat of yours."

He rubbed his hands together and blew into them. His breath formed small clouds in the air, and he grimaced. "I swear it's getting colder every night. At least we're headed

south. This stream seems determined to take us all the way to
Italya."

Something in Nicolas's eyes glinted. He added, with a hard
smile, "They say Athrom is never cold. Too many dragons
there to keep the city hot. Too many snakes to coil around you
and keep you warm. Isn't that right?"

Bear snuffed and looked away. Nicolas put a sympathetic
hand on Bear's shoulder. "I know," he said. "I never wanted to
go to Italya, either."

He lifted his head, and the nearby sound of a brook met his
ears. "But what choice does he have, who follows?"

Nicolas sighed and looked around his little campsite. He
stamped on the last few living embers, threw the wool blanket
around his shoulders like a cloak, and pulled a loaf of bread out
of his pillow. Breaking off a piece, he returned the bread to its
bundle and tied the whole thing to his belt. Bear was already
walking toward the stream. Nicolas quickened his pace to catch
up.

The brook ran down through the forest and became a wide
creek running through open fields. Nicolas and Bear left the
cover of the trees to walk among tall field grasses and reeds,
bent, brown, and patched here and there with snow. The fields
stretched out for acres, intersected with lines of tall trees,
stripped to elegant skeletons by the northern winds. On the
horizon, smoke rose from half a dozen small cottage chimneys.
A deeply rutted road came to run alongside the creek.

Nicolas stepped gladly onto the road, grateful to get away
from the burry tangle of the fields, but as the sole of his foot
touched the track, a scream rang in his ears. The scream was
torn from a milieu of other sounds to give warning to the

young man who could hear. It sounded and was gone, but it left echoes like the ringing of a great bell.

"Go!" Nicolas commanded. Bear loped across the field as Nicolas threw himself into the tangle of weeds and snow. The muted green of his woolen blanket, spattered as it was with mud, sank inconspicuously into its surroundings. He lay beneath it and waited, watching the road. His fingers reached through the scratchy wool to the smooth tip of his short sword and rested there.

Nicolas lay on the ground for twenty minutes while his body soaked up dampness from the ground. His muscles tensed, cramped, and yearned to move. He had nearly given in to his own urge to jump up when sounds once more reached his ears —nearby sounds this time. The jangle and stamp of approaching horses mingled with rough voices and the pitiful crying of children. A gust of icy wind blew the blanket back slightly from Nicolas's head, and he realized that the wool had muffled the noise, or he would have heard it earlier. The approaching company was very close.

In a few minutes they were passing along the road in front of Nicolas's eyes. His fingers tightened around his sword. Beneath the dirt on his cheek, his face tightened with anger.

High Police, marked by their black and green uniforms and silver insignias, were herding a band of Gypsies down the road. There were only a few men among the captives, and these were battered and bloody. The others were women and children— about twenty in all. Even these showed signs of mistreatment. Bruises marked their pale skin. One woman cradled a broken arm. Their clothes were filthy, and the children staggered with hunger and exhaustion. The High Police, riding well-fed horses, prodded the band on with spears and swords. Their eyes were hard.

It was all Nicolas could do to remain hidden, although he knew that he would die instantly if he dared go to the captives' defence. He swallowed a cry, and his eyes burned with unshed tears. There were babies among the captives—tiny infants too small to do anything but cry. Their cries reached Nicolas with all the pain of a dagger twisting in his stomach. All his life he had been able to hear the language of the small ones, even of the unborn. What he heard from them now was nearly too much for him. The raw, heartbreaking awareness of want, of loss, gnawed into his soul.

The band had nearly passed by when a tiny child lost his grip on the shoulders of his mother, who had been carrying him on her back. The little one slipped to the road with an exhausted cry. One of the Gypsy men darted toward him.

"Get back," commanded the captain. "Leave it alone, I say."

The man ignored him. He picked the child out of the mud and handed him tenderly back to his mother. She took the emaciated little form in her arms with a choked sob. Scarcely had the man given the child over when a kick to his jaw sent him sprawling in the road. The captain, his face red with anger, glared down at the man from the top of his horse. He raised his spear and aimed it at the Gypsy.

One of the women in the band screamed. The spear flew at nearly the same instant. Perhaps the scream had unnerved the captain, for his aim was off. The spear missed the man's heart, but pinned his shoulder to the ground. The Gypsy did not cry out, but a deep groan emitted from his throat. The captain dug his heel into his horse's side and spun around.

"Move out!" he commanded.

Most of the band had already gone down the road. It did not take long before the captain had driven the last few captives to catch up with them. When they had gone far enough, Nicolas dashed from his hiding place and knelt beside the man on the road.

The Gypsy was not old, but the stubble on his chin was grey. He looked up at Nicolas with eyes glazed with pain. He opened his mouth to speak, but sobbed instead.

"It's all right," Nicolas said, knowing that the angry tears in his eyes—tears that still would not fall—belied his words. "I'm a friend. I'm going to help you."

Nicolas looked around as though he might find a cure lying beside him. His eyes fell on the stream, and he jumped up and untied a few rags from his bundle. When he had soaked them so that they ran with water, he brought them back to the man and made him drink.

As Nicolas squeezed out the last few drops, the man clenched Nicolas's arm with his free hand. He shook his head as he looked into Nicolas's face, his own twisted with pain.

"I don't want to die," he said.

"You aren't going to," Nicolas answered. He heard Bear behind him on the road. They could carry the man together, he and Bear. He caught sight once more of the chimney smoke on the horizon. Surely someone would help.

He started to his feet, intending to pick the man up with him, but the sight of the wooden shaft protruding from the Gypsy's shoulder stopped him short. The spear had gone all the way through into the ground.

The Gypsy followed Nicolas's eyes. "Pull it out," he rasped.

"I can't," Nicolas said, but the man's grip tightened and stopped him from saying more.

"Pull it out," said the man again. "You can't leave me here!"

Nicolas stood up resolutely and took hold of the spear. He closed his eyes and pulled with all his might. The man screamed. When his voice gave out, he was unconscious. The spear had not come free. Nicolas drew a deep breath and pulled once more, placing his foot on the man's chest. This time it pulled free easily. Blood flowed after it. Nicolas pulled rags from his belt and staunched the flow as best he could, but the rags turned dark red before his eyes as blood began to seep through.

Nicolas got down on the road and placed the man's good arm over his own shoulder. He hoisted him up on his back with a grunt, his legs shaking as he stood. The man was taller and bigger-boned than Nicolas, but he was lighter than expected. Nicolas remembered the half-starved appearance of the other Gypsies in the captive band and wondered how much weight this man had lost in the last few days.

Carefully, Nicolas lifted the man onto Bear's back. He wiped sweat from beneath his eyes with his shirtsleeve. When he drew his arm away, he could smell the blood that streaked his own face. He pointed toward one spiraling ladder of smoke in the distance.

"There," he told Bear. "That's where we're going."

Nicolas threw his blanket over the man, and they left the road, trusting to instinct to lead them along the fastest route. Nicolas walked close by Bear, supporting the wounded man and holding him steady. He stumbled across the uneven ground, but they made good time. The sun was high in the sky when they reached a small cottage with a thatched roof. A small stone pathway, meticulously laid, led to the door.

The door was made of rough, solid oak, and it stood up firmly under Nicolas's pounding. No sound could be heard from the other side except that of a fire crackling and the meow of a cat.

Nicolas knocked harder and leaned up against the door in exhaustion. "For stars' sake!" he shouted. "I know someone's in there! Let us in, please. There is a wounded man with me!"

"And you'd do well to be quiet about it," said a sharp voice from behind.

Nicolas spun around, hand on his sword. He found himself facing a stolid man with a haystack of straight blond hair and a face that had been old since childhood. The man was holding a scythe, and while his expression held no welcome, neither did it threaten. There was, in fact, very little about the expression to suggest that anything was out of the ordinary. It was sour, as is the face of a man who has found children throwing tomatoes at his newly whitewashed fence.

The farmer cast a long glare on Bear and his cargo, then stepped forward and thumped the wooden door with a gruff, "Open up, it's me." He turned to Nicolas. "You'd better come in. Leave the beast outside."

The door was opened by a girl of about sixteen. Her demeanor could not have been more unlike that of her father: she was quaking all over with fear. Her hair was the same haystack yellow, though most of it was tied back in a kerchief. She held a large wooden spoon, which was dripping with whatever concoction was cooking over the fire. The only other

9

inhabitants of the room were three cats: two calicos and one hideous orange.

The farmer pointed to a cot in one corner of the room. "Get that ready," he told his daughter. "Man's wounded."

She hurried to obey while Nicolas lifted the Gypsy and carried him into the cottage. The girl cleared a few odds and ends off the cot, and Nicolas laid the wounded man down on it. The man groaned but did not open his eyes. A dark red stain had seeped through his clothing and spread all over his chest, neck, and shoulders.

Nicolas saw the farm girl shudder and turn away. Her father stood for a moment in thought, and then snapped, "Go get an old sheet and rip it up. He needs more bandaging." The girl fled the room, and the farmer dropped into a chair beside the cot. He sat regarding Nicolas sternly.

"You can rest up here," he said. "Get going as soon as you can."

"But this man—" Nicolas began.

"Can't stay here," the farmer interrupted.

"Can you tell me where to find a doctor then?" Nicolas asked.

"No," said the farmer.

Nicolas drew a breath and wished for patience. "I have to find someone who can take care of this man," he said. "Can you help me at all?"

"Ain't no one," the farmer said. "No one round here 'd touch that fellow."

"Why?" Nicolas exploded. For the first time he thought he saw a glimmer of fear in the farmer's eyes as he motioned for Nicolas to hush.

"High Police is after the Gypsies," the farmer said. "Clearing them out of the country. You help one, you might as well be a Gypsy yourself."

"Better a Gypsy than a coward," Nicolas snapped.

The farmer hung his head slightly but said nothing. After a while he drew himself up and said, "Now, that ain't called for. We took in your friend and we took in yourself, though you look Gypsy enough to cause a heap of trouble. We took you in, and we'll feed you and let you rest your bones, and that's a deal better than anyone else in these parts 'd do for you."

"I'm sorry," Nicolas said. "I thought human life might mean something to you. You're not the High Police, after all."

The farmer leaned forward suddenly and said in a whisper, "Only one place you might find shelter. They say there is hope in the City of Bridges."

"Pravik?" Nicolas asked, feeling hope drain out of him at the name. "I can't go to Pravik." His throat tightened at the thought of the ancient city of the Eastern Lands.

"It's far, I know," said the farmer. He leaned even farther forward. "But they say the High Police is scared of it. They say something happened there . . . something magic and terrible. Who knows? But every Gypsy on the road is headed for Pravik, with everyone else who wants freedom. They never come back, those who go east. All that comes back is rumours."

Nicolas sat with his head in his hands. Something magic. Something terrible. When he closed his eyes he could still see the otherworldly warriors, creatures of darkness and creatures of light, as they battled over the City of Bridges. He could still see Maggie running along the castle wall. He could hear her singing; could see her weeping over the body of the man she loved.

He drew in a deep breath and looked up at the farmer. "I can't go to Pravik," he repeated. "Do you know anyone who is going there? Anyone who can take this man with them?"

The farmer hesitated. "I can find—maybe I can find—a man to help you. A doctor of sorts."

"Thank heavens," Nicolas breathed. "Can we stay here, then—until the doctor can come?"

The farmer gave a short nod. "My daughter won't like it. Thinks the High Police are right. She never liked Gypsies. Can't say I ever minded 'em, except when they stole my cabbages."

He stood and paced the length of the cottage, ending at the door. He didn't turn around, but Nicolas heard him say, "Had a bird with a broken wing once. Didn't turn that out until it got healed up, and birds have ruined a heap of cabbage."

Nicolas smiled at the farmer's broad back as he pushed out the door and banged it shut behind him.

The farmer's daughter reappeared a few minutes later, trailed by all three meowing cats. She handed Nicolas a roll of clean bandages, newly torn, and went to stir her cauldron without a word. Nicolas watched her for a moment and turned to his charge. He changed the bandages tenderly, grimacing at the blood that still flowed from the wound. How much blood could one man stand to lose?

The cats circled the girl's feet as she worked at the fire, yowling piteously. "All right, then," she told them. Nicolas heard the edge in her voice. She ladled stew into three battered wooden bowls and set them on the floor. The smell of meat and vegetables sent a pang of hunger through Nicolas. He looked up from the unconscious Gypsy to see that the girl was watching them. She turned away quickly when he looked at her.

"You won't be staying long?" she asked, her voice muffled as she turned her back.

"Long enough," Nicolas answered. "Your father's gone for a doctor."

The girl's face flushed angrily, and she turned around again. Nicolas was taken aback at the hostility in her eyes.

"A doctor for that?" she said, motioning toward the cot. "We'll be driven out of town when the magistrate finds out."

"Why?" Nicolas asked. "What have the Gypsies done?"

"Does it matter what they've done?" the girl asked. "They're Gypsies."

Nicolas bit his tongue to keep back a harsh retort. How could such a young girl be so full of hatred?

"Did you take him from the High Police?" the girl asked. She did not wait for an answer. "Every day the police bring more Gypsies through. They won't stop till every one of them is gone from the country. Them and the queer folk, what hears and sees things that aren't there."

Nicolas's head shot up at the girl's words. "Queer folk?" he asked.

"You know," the girl said. Her eyes were shining, and her voice had lowered. This was gossip of the first order. She wiped her hands on her apron as she spoke. "The High Police offer rewards for them, but they ain't easy to find. They keep themselves hidden. They could be anybody. Him—" she said, pointing at the Gypsy on the cot, "or you even, or me."

Nicolas tilted his head and said, "Are you one of them?"

"No!" the girl pronounced. She giggled. "Of course not. I was only making an example."

"But how do I know you're telling the truth?" Nicolas asked, rising to his feet. The girl backed up a little, the first hint of alarm beginning to show on her face. "As you said, the Gifted keep themselves hidden. You might be lying to me. You might have said what you did to throw me off and keep me from suspecting the truth."

The girl's face was white. She shook her head vehemently. "No, I was only *saying* it—to show you how it could be anybody. I was only saying it."

Nicolas sat back down abruptly and leaned back with his arms folded across his chest. "You should be careful what you say," he said.

The girl turned back to her stew, but she was unsteady on her feet. It was obvious that Nicolas had disconcerted her.

A groan issued from the cot. Nicolas was at the man's side in an instant. The Gypsy's eyes were open, and he spoke with great difficulty.

"It is dark," he said.

"It is evening," Nicolas told him. "The sun is beginning to set."

"No," the Gypsy said. He shook his head with painful slowness. "There is no more evening. Only night."

Nicolas leaned over the man, and the smell of blood filled his senses. He took the man's hand and gripped it tightly.

"The day is coming soon," he whispered. "Night can't last forever."

For a moment the man was silent, and Nicolas feared he had lost consciousness again. Then without warning the Gypsy cried out. His whole body shook with the effort.

"Where is the sun?" he cried. "Blackness has swallowed the sun!"

Nicolas raised his face to the window. Setting sunlight glinted on the tears in his eyes. "It is shining even now," Nicolas said.

"Not for us," said the Gypsy. He closed his eyes and lay still, though his blood-stained chest still rose and fell with laboured breathing. Nicolas felt the eyes of the farm girl on them: disdainful eyes. He felt suddenly trapped, closed in. His eyes searched the room for a way of escape.

No, he told himself. *Don't run. There is no reason to run.*

There was a pounding on the door, and Nicolas's heart beat as hard as the fist on the door. He recognized the voice of the farmer through the wood. "Open the door, fool girl. It's me!"

The farmer's daughter moved quickly to the door and unlatched it. The farmer entered, stamping his muddy boots on the floor. There was another man behind him, a thin, gangly form wrapped in a slick black cape.

At the sight of the newcomer, the farmer's daughter turned red with anger. "Father, no!" she said. "How could you bring him here?"

"Hush, child," the farmer answered. "Leave my affairs to me. You stick with your stew pot!"

The girl turned away, breathing hard with indignation, and snatched up her wooden spoon. Stew spilled from the pot as she stirred. It dripped on the fire and hissed loudly.

The thin stranger moved to the cot and knelt beside the wounded man. Long fingers inspected the bandages and the wound. The stranger pursed his lips.

"It is bad," he said. "But perhaps it can be healed. And then what? What is this man's life worth if he recovers?"

"It is worth as much as mine," Nicolas said. He searched the stranger's face for some hint of his sympathies, but the thin, dark face was enigmatic.

"And where shall he go?" asked the stranger. "He is not safe here."

The farmer spoke in his gruff voice. "I thought you would take him to Pravik with you."

"He would slow me down on the road," said the stranger.

"Guilt will slow you down if you don't take him," Nicolas said.

"Will it?" asked the stranger in surprise. "Why should it? This man is no concern of mine unless I make him so." He placed an almost skeletal hand on Nicolas's shoulder. The expression in his strange amber eyes was still unreadable, though his words were kind. "Do not worry, lad. I shall make him so."

"You will take him?" the farmer asked.

"Indeed," said the stranger. He stood, and his cape parted, revealing clothes stitched in amber thread. For an instance Nicolas seemed to hear voices speaking in a language he could not understand—an ancient language, long dead among the peoples of the Empire. But something made him think that he was imagining it.

"Who are you?" Nicolas asked.

The man regarded him with one sharp eyebrow raised. "Good question," he said. "I am someone who, as of this moment, is on your side. Assist me; I cannot take this man to my carriage alone."

Nicolas stood immediately. Together the two men carried the wounded Gypsy out of the cottage. The thin stranger was surprisingly strong. He carried the wounded Gypsy's head and shoulders with ease. The road was dark. Night had fallen so quickly that Nicolas had not noticed it in the cottage, but now his eyes strained to see the path in front of him. He heard a grunt behind him, and Bear's nose nudged the small of his back.

They came to a stand of trees. The stranger whistled a signal. A black carriage drawn by one white horse pulled out of the stand to meet them. The stranger and Nicolas eased the Gypsy onto the seat of the carriage.

Nicolas touched the Gypsy's head in an awkward gesture of farewell. He climbed out of the carriage and started back down the road with his head low. The voice of the stranger stopped him.

"And how long will it be till we see you in Pravik?" he asked.

Nicolas turned. "Never," he said. "I am heading the other direction. Into Italya."

"Come now," said the stranger. "You have the look of one who has listened to the stars. And you have defied the High Police by taking in a Gypsy. I am quite sure that I will see you in Pravik."

"What is in Pravik that cannot be found on the roads?" Nicolas asked.

"Strength worth exploring," replied the stranger.

"How do you know that?" Nicolas asked. "No one knows what happened in Pravik. Only that the High Police are afraid to go there."

"I do not know it," the stranger said. "I feel it. Come, wanderer. Join me." He looked away from Nicolas and said, half to himself, "Sooner or later we must take sides."

Nicolas lowered his head in the darkness and felt Bear by his side. "My future lies in other places."

The thin stranger cocked his head. "You are afraid of Pravik?"

Nicolas shifted his weight. "I am not afraid of anything."

"That is very foolish of you," the thin man said.

"Good speed, sir," Nicolas said. He began to turn away.

The thin man bowed his head. "And you. My thanks for the traveling companion you have brought me."

Nicolas felt a wash of guilt. "No, it is you who should be thanked. Without you this man would die."

"And with me he shall live," said the stranger. An odd light in his amber eyes testified to thoughts Nicolas did not wish to know. "And will he thank me for that?"

With those words the man climbed onto the carriage seat and took the reins in his hands. Nicolas stood and watched the black wheels turn after the white hooves for some distance, and then he put a hand on Bear's shoulder and started back down the road for the farmhouse. The night was cold. An icy rain had begun to fall, and Nicolas had no wish to sleep out of doors. If the farmer did not welcome his return, he would take shelter in the barn.

The farmyard was quiet when Nicolas and Bear stepped into it. The house seemed to have gone to sleep. No lights shone in the windows; no sound came from within. Even the cats were silent.

"Looks like it's the barn for us," Nicolas said to Bear in a low voice. He started to walk toward the shelter, but Bear would not move.

"Let's go," Nicolas said. He took another step toward the barn and froze.

Something had moved in the shadows.

Nicolas turned on his heel and ran. The farmyard erupted with police. Their silver insignias flashed in the moonlight. Nicolas raced through the yard, leaping obstacles where he found them. In the road he skidded to a stop and turned once more. He had heard the sound of hooves pounding the road ahead of him.

He looked wildly around, and his eyes fell on the door of the cottage. The farmer's daughter stood in its frame, next to a tall police captain with his arm around her waist.

Nicolas turned away from the road and ran to the west. Shouts filled the darkness behind him. He knew he had been seen, but he did not care. He shouted to Bear, and the faithful beast ran in the other direction. High Police fell away as Bear charged into their midst, roaring as only a bear can roar.

Nicolas reached a fence and hit the ground, rolling under the rails. He gained his feet again quickly and ran through the barren fields with the High Police close behind him. The cold air burned as he sucked it into his lungs; the icy rain stung his face. Ahead he could hear the rippling of the creek as it splashed over rocks. There, Nicolas knew, lay his only chance to hide.

He flew over the ground until his legs gave way. He rolled into himself, arms clutching his knees. He turned over and over, and just before hitting the creek, he clutched at the

brown reeds to slow himself. He came nearly to a stop and then
dropped, almost silently, into the water.

Muddy water filled his nose and ears as he sank, one, two
feet under. Dirt and pebbles showered the water above him as
the High Police skidded to a stop at the bank of the creek.
They were looking for him; looking around—but they did not
look down into the reeds and the mud and the water.

Nicolas gripped rocks and weeds at the bottom of the creek
and let out a little air, desperate to keep from floating to the
top. The water was crushing him, the lack of air was crushing
him; crushing his heart and his lungs. He would drown
himself. He would die waiting for them to leave.

The world was blacker than it had ever been, but Nicolas
did not know if it was black because he was under water and
the night was dark, or because he was already drowning. He let
out more air and knew that soon he would have to breathe in.

He thought he heard Bear roaring and water rushing over
stones. Then it was Maggie he heard: singing, talking to him by
a campfire on a warm night in the fall. That night, too, he
should have drowned. He heard laughter and horses and stories
in a Gypsy camp. He heard a captive woman on the road to
Italya screaming out against horror. He heard the thin dark
stranger say, "Sooner or later we must take sides." He heard
nothing.

And then he heard a voice, clear and strong. It rushed into
his nose and ears and mouth and lungs even as the water
rushed in. The voice said, *I still await you. Your journey has
not ended. Wake up, Nicolas Fisher. Your story is not over yet.*

2

Snow and Roses

MICHAEL O'ROARKE stood on the prow of the longship as it cut its way through the blue waters. His eyes swept the mountains on every side, following the cliffs to the high summits white with snow. The sense of awe that filled him was oppressive, and yet it set his heart free to fly to the topmost peaks of Fjordland.

He tore his eyes reluctantly away when the longship's captain joined him. The captain was a big man, tall and broad-shouldered. His chin was covered with a neatly trimmed beard of gold; the ends of his mustache extended far below his beard. He smiled when Michael turned to greet him.

"Na, don't look at me," said the captain. "Keep your eyes on the mountains. I will not steal such treasure from any man's eyes."

Michael turned his eyes up once again. Cold air rushed past his handsome face and through his dark red hair. The air was exhilarating. It did for Michael's lungs what the mountains did for his heart.

A young man joined them at the front of the ship. He leaned over and spat into the water. His dark eyes, set deeply in his face, hardly seemed to notice the beauty around them.

"Weeks on the sea," he grumbled, his voice, like Michael's, heavily shot through with the accent of the Green Isle. "And now we have reached the land, and still we're on the water. Is there no place in Fjordland for a man to walk that doesn't buckle and heave under his feet?"

"Patience," said the captain. "We will reach the land soon."

"I don't suppose you Fjordlanders have drink in this country of yours?" the young man asked.

"The best," said the captain, his blue eyes twinkling. "Soon you will forget all about ships and the sea."

"There, Michael!" said the young man, slapping his friend on the back. "Does it not do you good to hear that?"

Michael smiled and turned on his friend. In a moment he had wrestled him into a headlock. He held the young man's head so that his eyes looked up at the blue sky beyond the crags of the mountains.

"Stocky, a baser man than you I have never known," Michael laughed. "How can you think of drink while you pass through the country of heaven?"

Stocky squirmed free and shook his head, rubbing his neck gingerly. "Eh, Michael, you've lost none of your strength at sea."

"I will need it to climb those mountains," Michael answered. He raised his eyes once again. He did not look back at the sound of the captain's voice.

"I wouldn't try it if I were you. The winter mountains of Fjordland are not friendly to strangers—nor to their own born children. Stay on the lower slopes, Green Islander."

Michael did not reply.

Twenty minutes had passed by the time the longship finished its journey up the fjord. They docked the ship at a small harbour and trudged up the slopes to a little valley where a village lay under the snow. The houses and shops were built of grey stone and thatched with straw. Small mountain ponies with long, shaggy hair blew frost clouds from their nostrils and nibbled on stray bits of thatching. There were few people in sight, though Michael could feel curious eyes on him from windows that were mostly covered for the winter. Smoke rose from the houses through small round holes in the thatching.

The captain and his sailors led the way to a long stone building with a high roof of logs and thatch. They ducked through a low door into the dark interior. Michael stepped inside and breathed air thick with cedar smoke. The floor of the tavern was dirt, and three fire pits burned brightly along the length of the hall. Men sat around the fires, laughing and drinking ale from large wooden cups. Stocky brightened at the sight. He followed the sailors to the bar, behind which were six enormous ale vats. Oven-heat wafted from alcoves at one end of the hall, and the smells of hot meat and bread mingled with the smell of smoke.

Michael stayed near the door. He heard a fluttering of wings above him and looked up curiously to the rafters, where dozens of tiny brown birds flitted from place to place. The twigs and straw of their nests stuck out from the joints of the rafters.

Michael looked back down when he became aware that someone was walking toward him. The man's long grey hair was braided, as was the beard that reached down past his chest.

His skin was rough and weathered from years spent in cold, salty air. His eyes were a startling blue.

The man appraised Michael quickly and said, "If you're not Thomas's son, these eyes have lost their power over the years."

Michael smiled warmly, for he was sure he knew who was addressing him. "I am the son of Thomas O'Roarke," he said. "And I think I recognize my father's friend. You are Kris Jarald, are you not?"

Kris threw his arms around Michael and crushed him to his chest. "I am Kris of the Mountains, as you say. And I welcome you."

Kris released Michael and looked him over at arm's length. "You look like your mother," he said, "as she looked when last I saw her. She carried you in her arms then."

The big man took Michael's arm and steered him toward an empty space near the central tavern fire. "Come," he said. "There is time for business later. Now you will tell me of your home."

Michael sat down on a cedar-log bench. The smoke from the fire stung his eyes and made the room waver like a heat mirage, though the air outside was numbingly cold. The room was close and stuffy, but the wind occasionally found its way through cracks in the door, cutting through the tavern with icy precision.

"What news of the Green Isle?" asked Kris.

"I hardly know," Michael answered. "It has been three long months since my feet walked its lovely ground."

Kris took a swallow of ale and peered at Michael over the top of his cup. His voice lowered. "Do my roses still bloom in the Isle, Michael O'Roarke?"

Michael looked into the Fjordlander's intense eyes and whispered, "Aye, that they do."

"Then tell me, son of my friend, why have you come to see Kris of the Mountains?"

Michael reached into his coat and drew out a yellowed piece of paper. "Years ago you promised this land to my father," he said. He unfolded the paper to reveal a land deed. "I've come to claim it."

"It's yours," Kris said. "But why now, lad?"

Michael looked away for a moment. The smoke stung his eyes. "There is trouble in the Green Isle," he said at last. "It is perhaps time for your roses to come home."

"The Clann O'Roarke would not leave their land for any small reason," Kris said. "Your father would not leave, though I all but begged him to."

"Many do not want to come," Michael said. "And I will not force them. But I am the head of the clann now. I must do what I think is best."

Kris leaned forward. "Why do you think it best that you leave?" he asked, gently.

"There are strangers in the Isle," Michael said at last. "They do not wish to be seen, but we see them. They wear black robes and move among the High Police, commanding the forces of the Empire."

"They are looking for those who are Gifted?" Kris asked.

"Yes," Michael answered.

"For this reason Clann O'Roarke will leave their home? Is the threat to you real?"

Michael closed his eyes and thought of the small ones, the four little cousins he had left behind. "The spirit of my father

25

runs deep in the clann. The blood that flowed in him flows also in us. I am not Gifted—we older ones are safe—but the children show signs. I do not know what time will reveal in them. It is enough that the black strangers have returned. I fear they will take the children away."

"Do you have children, boy?" Kris asked.

"No," Michael said. "We have remained largely isolated since—since it happened. Our family has not grown. But the little cousins are under my protection. I must bring them away from the Green Isle."

"So you would bring them to the Northern Lands for safety," Kris said. He looked into his ale cup and shook his grey head. "You cannot, Michael. The black strangers ride here as they do in the Isle."

"How can it be?" Michael asked. "Are they everywhere?"

"They have always been everywhere," Kris said. "But we have not seen them until now."

"Surely in a village like this . . ."

"It is safe? Don't think it. They are looking for something, and they will not leave until they find their quarry. To bring Gifted children here would only cause them to take renewed interest in our mountains."

Outside, a sound of hooves arose. Kris raised his head. "Come and see," he said.

Together they went quickly to the door, ducking low under the stone. A party of High Police was riding down the main village street. Their southern horses towered over the native ponies of the fjords. Michael's eyes were immediately drawn to two men riding with the police. Both wore black cloaks. The taller of the men turned and scanned the roadside, and Michael thought that his eyes lingered on him for a moment. He was young and strikingly handsome, but Michael shuddered at his eyes.

"They call him the Nameless One," Kris said quietly.

Stocky staggered out of the tavern door and stood by Michael. He made a face at the black-robed riders and the soldiers that followed them.

"The creatures are everywhere these days," Stocky said. He spat into the snow. He smelled like ale and smoke.

Michael looked down at the deed in his hand, and oppression fell on his head. He crumpled the deed suddenly and shook his head. "We will leave soon," he told Stocky. "We're going back home."

Stocky's mouth dropped open. "Back on the boat?" he said. "We've only just arrived, man! You'd have us go now?"

"No," Michael said. "Not quite yet." He lifted his eyes to the snow-streaked slopes. "Not until I have climbed the mountains and seen what my father once saw."

He felt a heavy hand on his shoulder. Kris's eyes were gentle and troubled. "Careful, son of my friend. Take care that you do not break your heart on the northern cliffs. The mountains have made many a man, but they have broken just as many."

* * *

For Stocky's sake Michael hired a band of experienced men to accompany them on the mountains. They set out together early the next morning under a heavy grey sky. Kris went with them, watching Michael carefully. The young clann leader had

27

drawn into himself. He said very little as they hiked up the steep sides of the northern heights.

Michael trudged forward silently, every step full of determination. The weight of responsibility was heavy on him. His troubles loomed like the mountains before him, and he knew he must conquer them or die trying. His worry and despair focused themselves on the peaks they traversed, high sentinels of rock and snow. Could he only reach the top of a single peak; could he stand at the highest height of the far north; then he might see what his father had seen, might hope as his father had hoped, and nothing in the Green Isle could defeat him.

The sun failed to lighten the world as it rose, disappearing instead behind ever-greyer clouds. Snow began to swirl around them, drifting in strong blasts of wind. Short-lived flurries swallowed them entirely, the guides disappearing ahead of the little band only to reappear when the wind died down. The snow vanquished place and time, and for a moment Michael found himself alone.

The wind in his ears echoed from the past. As a child Michael had begged his father to tell of the time when he climbed the highest mountains in Fjordland. Michael would lay by the fire while his father told the story, and he would shiver when the winter wind blew through the crack under the door. The power of his imagination would transform the gentle wind of the Green Isle into the fierce gales of the far north; and Michael would lay in bed afterwards and dream of climbing the mountains with his father beside him—up to the mystery that waited at the top of the world.

Up to the vision that had changed his father forever.

Michael stopped his forward motion and let the snow drift around his booted feet. His heart beat hard and fast. For a single moment he had felt as though his father was there—as though he could touch him. He lifted his face and let the cold bite at him. The clouds had cleared in one place, just enough to show the sheer, snowy side of a mountain.

The others were far ahead, pushing their way around the cliff. Michael took his eyes from them and looked up to the waiting height.

The day was half-gone when Kris realized that Michael was no longer with them. He gave a shout, and the party stopped their trek. The leaders turned their heads to look back, but they saw only the broad back of Kris of the Mountains as he left in search of the Green Islander. The wind was beginning to howl, bringing with it snow in earnest.

"The snow will fill in Michael's tracks," Stocky said, dark with worry. "He'll never find him!"

"Kris of the Mountains could follow a flea through a snowstorm," said one of the Fjordlanders. "Do not worry your head about it." But the man could not help but lift his head to the peaks and the falling snow, and Stocky saw the worry etched across his face.

* * *

Ice and wind whipped Michael's face as he clutched the face of the cliff and slowly pulled himself higher. The sky had grown black with clouds; snow blew around him in every direction. Michael could see neither where he was nor where he was going, but he continued to move upward, driven now

29

by desperation as much as determination. His eyes searched the rock face above him for some glimmer—some sign—anything.

The storm lashed at him. He clung to the rock and closed his eyes against its ferocity. He would die in Fjordland, he thought, and Clann O'Roarke would have a new leader. It was best. For a moment he thought that his father would take good care of them; then he remembered that his father was dead—that the same death stalked them all.

Awareness was fading from Michael's mind. A sudden sharp need to survive drove into him. He had to keep moving, or he would freeze there on the cliff face and become part of the mountain; someday someone would climb up the cliff and go over him without even knowing. He moved one stiff foot and one cold hand. In horror he felt the rock slip away. He was falling. Was it light he saw above him? He reached up as he fell.

Michael fell for what seemed like a long time, and then he hit rock and heard a horrible breaking sound. He knew it was his own body that had broken. Pain shot through his eyes and blinded him. He could see nothing but blackness in a world that was deathly white. He tried to move, and pain took him like a torturer. He screamed out. Just before his mind slipped away from him, he thought he heard the answering shout of Kris of the Mountains.

The mountain had defeated him.

* * *

Kris of the Mountains carried Michael on his broad back all the way to the village. Stocky followed close behind, tears in his dark eyes. They pushed through the blizzard most of the night and reached the tavern just as the veil of snow began to thin and reveal the light of early morning.

Kris laid Michael down on a cedar bench beside one of the fire pits and called for help to revive him. Stocky knelt by Michael's head and called his name while the men of the village tried to wake him. Word of the injury spread quickly, and the tavern filled with the curious and the concerned. Men, women, and children surrounded the makeshift bed where Michael O'Roarke lay dying.

Kris retreated from the crowd and stood against the wall of the tavern, his massive arms folded across his chest. There were tears in his eyes. The lines of his mouth betrayed the suffering of a stoic. Michael would not recover, and Kris knew it. He had carried the young man through the mountains; he had felt Michael's body move and bend as it should not; he had felt the heat of fever come and go. The young chieftain's body was broken. There could be no healing now. Only pity for Stocky kept Kris from ordering the would-be physicians away: the Green Islander must be allowed to feel that he had done his best for his chieftain.

A real doctor arrived. He was making his rounds of the small villages along the fjords. He inspected Michael quickly and stood, wiping his hands on his pants.

"There's na good for it," he said. "The young man will not last till evening."

At these words Stocky put his head down on the bench in front of Michael's closed eyes and wept.

The back of the tavern stirred as the door opened and a howling wind rushed in, cut off abruptly as the door shut again. Kris heard murmurs of wondering surprise from the villagers. Women gasped and whispered thanks to the stars. The mountain man lifted his grey head.

A young woman was moving gracefully through the crowd in the tavern. The villagers fell back from her approach like floating petals before a swan. She was indeed much like a swan, possessed of an unearthly beauty that quieted all around her. Pale hair fell in waves to her waist, glinting now silver, now gold in the light of the fire pits. She wore the simple clothes of a peasant; her dark cloak, lined with sheepskin, was patched and frayed. A silver chain-link belt around her slender waist contrasted sharply with the poverty of her garments. Tucked into the belt was a pink rose. The scent of it mingled with the cedar smoke and perfumed the tavern. Its petals were bright and new.

She reached Michael's side, and for a moment she lifted her violet eyes to the dark corner where Kris stood. She bowed her head slightly, and he bowed his; and then she knelt at Michael's side and touched Stocky's shoulder gently.

He started. His tear-stained face filled with awe at the light that seemed to shine from the girl's face. Slowly, without protest, he moved away from his friend and chieftain and joined the people of the village in watching.

The girl bent her head until her face nearly touched Michael's. Cascades of her hair fell around him. Her forehead creased with sympathy and pain, and then slowly, tenderly, she touched him. She put her hands behind his neck and laid her head on his chest, and the villagers heard her whisper, pleadingly; but to whom she was speaking or what she was saying they could not make out.

Then she stood and smiled down at Michael, and without a word she turned to go. She had not yet traversed the length of the tavern when Michael draw in a strong breath and let it out again in a rush. The villagers exclaimed and gathered around him, the girl momentarily forgotten. Michael gasped again for breath, and his eyes opened. He sat up just in time to see the young woman disappear through the door of the tavern.

Stocky fell on his knees beside Michael. "Stars bless you," he said. "Michael! We'd given you up for dead."

Michael looked at Stocky as though he had never seen him before. "What happened?" he asked.

"You fell in the mountains," Stocky said. "You broke your own back like the fool you are, and your father's friend carried you all the way home. You were going to die, Michael."

Stocky stopped and looked up at the tavern door. A cold draft reached his face.

"You would have died," he said. "That girl healed you. If I hadn't seen it with my own two eyes . . ."

Stocky turned to Kris at the same moment that Michael looked to him. Kris stepped out of the shadows and drew near the fire pit.

"Her name is Miracle," he said. "She does not often come down to the village. No one knows what brings her."

"She comes when we are in need of healing," said an old woman. "She healed myself when I was sick of the cold and ready to die."

"It was her hands made my crop grow after a fire destroyed the fields," said a young farmer.

"She grows roses in the dead of winter," said another.

Michael was no longer listening. He strode for the door, breaking into a run before he had reached it. He had to say thank you, he told himself—he could not be so ungrateful as to let her go without thanks. Or, whispered his heart, so cold as to let her go before he had clearly seen the beauty he had only just glimpsed in the doorway.

The High Police were in the street.

Their horses formed a circle around Miracle. The animals stamped their hooves and tossed their heads impatiently. The cruelly handsome young man in black, the Nameless One, smiled down at his captive.

Michael rushed forward with a shout. The heads of the police turned, as did Miracle's. She ducked beneath the neck of the one of the horses and ran. The circle broke. The soldiers rode after Miracle, with the Nameless One at their head. Two soldiers spurred their horses in Michael's direction. He reached for his sword and found that it was not there.

One of the soldiers slashed at Michael's head with his spear. Michael ducked away from the blow and grabbed the shaft, wrenching it from the soldier's grasp. He spun around and let the spear fly. It lodged itself in the leg of the soldier who had come up behind. The man cried out in pain, and his horse bucked. He lost his seat and fell to the snowy road.

Michael turned his attention to the first soldier once more. He dodged the man's sword easily. In one fluid motion he mounted the horse behind his startled enemy. Michael grasped the man's sword arm at the elbow and twisted until the sword dropped in the snow. With a heave, he sent the soldier flying after it. Michael dug his heels into the horse and galloped after the rest of the High Police.

He rode into their midst, yelling and brandishing a spear that had been tied to the horse's saddle. He was faster and stronger than the High Police. He knocked two off their horses using only the shaft of the spear—but he was too late. The Nameless One had caught Miracle. He held her tightly in front of him on his horse. He turned to face Michael, eyes were glittering dangerously. He held a knife at Miracle's throat.

"There is no need for either of you to die, foreigner," he said. His accent was that of Fjordland, but lighter and more refined than the villagers'. "Throw your spear down and go back to your ale."

"What do you want with her?" Michael demanded, breathless from the fight.

"What do *you* want with her?" the man in black returned. "I have as much right to her as you do. More."

"You have no right to take an innocent woman," Michael said.

"I have every right, Green Islander," the Nameless One answered. "I have orders from the Overlord of the Northern Lands himself. Turn around. Go back to your tavern. Better yet, go back home. You have no business here."

Michael only tightened his grip on the spear. As he did so, Miracle stiffened. The knife at her throat pressed harder, and the man in black smiled.

"Go ahead," he said. "Attack me. Attack my men. Beat them all, as I have no doubt you can. The moment you move, I will kill her."

Michael turned anguished eyes on Miracle. Her violet eyes met his beseechingly. He understood what she wanted. With a broken heart he dropped the spear, point down, in the snow.

35

Once again he met Miracle's eyes, and without saying a word, he poured out a promise to her. She gasped suddenly as the knife pressed harder. The point drew a single drop of blood.

"Ride away, foreigner," said the Nameless One. "I am tired of you."

Michael lowered his head and reined the horse around. Slowly he rode away, toward the tavern, and did not look back. Something in the snow near the tavern door caught his eye. He dismounted and bent to pick it up, and a thorn pricked his finger. Miracle's rose. His heart quickened. Rose-grower—like his father. His finger bled, and he looked at it as though the blood would give him answers.

He felt a hand on his shoulder, but he did not look up. "I let them take her, Kris," he said.

"You could not have done more," said the grey-haired man.

"I will do more," Michael answered. "I am going after her."

"Yes," said Kris. "And I am going with you."

Stocky left his place in the half-open door of the tavern and joined them. He placed his hand on Michael's other shoulder.

"I'll be with you too, Michael," he said.

Michael attempted a smile. "That I know, Stocky," he said. "You are always with me."

They wandered into the street; the three together. Michael cradled the rose in his hands, looking to the horizon where she had gone. Stocky stood by him, fidgeting a little, biting his lip with a million things he wanted to say and knew he shouldn't. Kris stood behind them with his arms folded.

After a moment he spoke. "They are going to the castle of Ordna," he said. "The ancient stronghold of the Northern Lands."

"The Overlord is there?" Michael asked.

"No doubt," Kris said. "And many men in black robes, or I am greatly mistaken."

"Who are they?" Stocky asked.

Kris tightened his mouth. "They are Blackness," he said at last. He turned and wrapped his cloak of skins around him. "Come, Michael," he said.

"But the tracks lead this way," Michael said.

"You are not ready to follow them yet," Kris answered. "Soon."

"The tracks will disappear."

"Kris of the Mountains knows the way," Kris said. He was already walking away from the village, up to the mountains. Michael lifted his eyes to the heights. He tightened his hold on the rose without thinking, and drew in a sharp breath as the thorns pierced his hand.

* * *

They wound their way up a mountain track silently. Stocky tried more than once to break the quiet and draw his companions into conversation, but neither wished to speak. Kris led them stalwartly, disdaining even to turn around and look at the Green Islanders who walked behind him. The rose in Michael's belt released its dangerous perfume as he walked, still feeling the sting in his hand. He thought of beauty and the mountains.

The track led them far off any road. They journeyed through the snow for miles, lost in their own reflections, passing under a craggy overhang of rock until the smells of cedar smoke, porridge, and horse dung met them. Kris stepped into a cleft in the rock and disappeared. Michael and Stocky followed him, wondering, into a dark cave.

In a moment Kris lit an oil lantern. A warm glow illuminated the dry place where they now stood. A fire pit lay near the door of the cave, where the floor was more dirt than rock, and in a corner nearby, a heap of animal skins and furs served as a bed. On the other side of the cave was a pen built of logs and rope. It housed a small black mountain pony that stared at the newcomers out of huge marble eyes. In the joints of the pen was a scraggly nest, and perched above it was a small brown bird like those Michael had observed in the rafters of the tavern.

Kris dug into a small recess in the rock and pulled out loaves of bread and a skin full of water. He handed them to Stocky, instructing him to wrap the bread in some rough cloth that hung over a well-carved wooden chair. A moment's groping in another recess brought forth heavy northern swords, of sufficient length and weight to be worn on the back and not at the side of a warrior. Michael took the one handed to him with gratitude; he unsheathed it and swept a wide arc in the air. The sword fit his hand well.

"Here, lad," Kris said, holding another one out to Stocky.

Stocky shook his head. "The weight of the thing will knock me over! The small swords of the Green Isle are quite good enough for me." He wore two at his side. He drew them and whipped them deftly around in the air.

Kris nodded. He strapped an enormous sword onto his own back and hung an axe at his side. He pulled a heavy wooden spear with an iron tip from the hole in the wall and passed it to Michael.

When they had armed themselves sufficiently, Kris opened the door of the pen and led the black pony out. He and Stocky loaded the shaggy creature with food, water, and cloaks and blankets of animal hide.

When they emerged from the cave, the sky was grey with clouds. The temperature had dropped. Only Stocky seemed to notice the cold.

They followed another obscure path, the Green Islanders trusting that Kris knew where he was leading them. They went up for a long time, all in silence. Only the sound of their breathing and the occasional neigh of the pony broke the stillness of the mountains. At last they reached the top of a ridge. Below them, the ground dropped into a small valley. A lone house of stone huddled against the ridge.

Kris looked down on it for a long time, weighing something in his mind, before he turned to his companions and said, "Come."

Gingerly they made their way down the steep ridge to the valley floor. Michael slipped once, and Stocky created a small avalanche of snow as he trod, but Kris and the pony did not seem to disturb the snow at all.

When they were within eye-level of the stone house, Michael caught his breath at the sight that greeted them. Snow lay thick on the ground, just as it did everywhere else, but up from the white blanket grew bushes and vines, green as though it was the height of summer. Roses were in full bloom, their scent intoxicating. Their soft pink petals sparkled with a dusting of frost.

The snow was deep, and Michael's feet were heavy as he followed Kris to the front door. The mountain man did not knock. As he pushed the oak door open, such a fluttering of wings arose from within the house that Michael wondered if he had disturbed the nesting place of every bird that ought to have flown south.

In the hearth, embers were still glowing, and plants and flowers graced every window ledge. Vines climbed around the frames of the windows and door. Birds—so many of them!—perched in the thatching and over the hearth, on the sparse furniture and in every cranny of the rock walls. A white dove landed on Kris's shoulder and cooed softly.

A whine greeted them, and a grey dog jumped up from its place in a corner and limped to Michael. Its leg was tightly bound where a wound had been incurred. Michael stood still while the dog approached him—something was strange about the animal. He realized suddenly that this was no dog, but a wolf. It nudged the rose in Michael's belt and whined again.

Stocky said what Michael knew and did not utter: "This is her house, isn't it?"

"Yes," said Kris.

"Why have you brought us here?" Michael asked.

"It was on the way," Kris answered. His eyes met Michael's without flinching. "And I thought you should see . . . some of what she is."

They did not stay long. Kris stamped out the embers in the hearth and placed the dove on the mantle, stroking its feathers lightly. They turned to go, and the wolf limped after them.

"Go back, boy," said Michael. "Stay."

The wolf looked at him reproachfully. "All right then," Michael said. "Come along. But you mustn't slow us down. Understand?"

The wolf ran its tongue over sharp white teeth and whined.

"He understands, Michael, well enough," said Stocky. "Look at that, would you?"

They closed the oak door behind them. Michael would have pulled it tight, but Kris stopped his hand.

"The birds may want to fly again before she comes back here," he said. "Leave it open a little."

The dove began to mourn as they headed back up the side of the mountain ridge: three men, a black pony, and a limping grey wolf.

3

Alone and Not Alone

THE CITY OF ATHROM sprawled like a great cluster of jewels over
the flatlands of Italya. Its wide streets were made for pageantry
and parade, made to showcase the colour and splendour of a
man who ruled the world.

Lucien Morel, Emperor of the Seventh World, was a man
on whose brow the Jeweled Crown of the Empire rested
uneasily. His thick black hair was greying at the temples; his
face, handsome and strong in its lines, was too pale. When he
was angry or nervous or excited—when he felt any emotion at
all—the little finger on his right hand twitched.

Lucien Morel stood on a small marble bridge in the garden
of his villa east of Athrom. A brook flowed under the bridge,
very close, he thought, to the soles of his feet. He stood on the
bridge with his hands on the rail, and his finger tapped the
marble. A servant, short and balding, stood at a respectful
distance. He stayed close enough to see if the Emperor needed
anything, but far enough that he could not hear Morel
muttering to himself.

"Hundreds of them," said Lucien Morel to no one in particular. "Thousands. All over the Seventh World. A plague on them all." He sniffed. "They are a plague."

The water under his feet seemed to rise. At least, he thought it had risen. Just a little. Half an inch. Heavy rains in the north would do it. Make it rise like that. He swallowed. His finger twitched hard, jerking itself nearly out of joint.

"It can't go on like this," he said. "My father should have done something. My grandfather. Should have tamed them, made them settle down. Made them pay taxes and pay homage and pay!" He slammed his fist on the rail. "Too late now. Now it's my job, and there are thousands of them. Too many to tame. I'll have to. Have to . . ." He glanced at the water. "Kill them."

He shuddered. His finger twitched. He sounded like Skraetock when he said things like that. Ruthless, cruel things. He sounded like Skraetock and his black-cloaked cronies.

He hated them.

The word *hatred* ran through his mind. He stiffened and looked around. He saw his servant, pudgy and balding—harmless—standing in the shade. He relaxed. Skraetock was gone. He and—that other. They had gone north, after one of their prized "Gifted Ones."

Lucien Morel wondered how many of the black-cloaked men there really were. He had never seen more than a few at a time. That was enough, he thought; enough to be too many. They were worse than the Gypsies. But you couldn't kill them, no matter how much you wanted to.

"Mannish!" he called.

The servant snapped to attention. "Sir?"

"Do you like Gypsies?" Morel asked.

Mannish concealed his surprise well. "No, sir," he said.

Morel leaned over the rail and muttered, "Just as well nobody likes them."

The river swirled blackly under his feet. He looked down at it and tried to catch his own reflection, but the water would not form his face. It kept swirling, eating away at his lines. He was cold, he realized. His finger was not twitching. It was frozen.

He was afraid. He hated water. He hated rivers, and brooks, and streams. He hated them because they hated him.

He could not tell anyone that. They would think he was crazy.

The Emperor of the Seventh World turned and left the bridge. His servant followed a respectful distance behind him.

* * *

Nicolas stayed off the road as much as he could. The road belonged to the Empire, and the Empire had gone mad. The High Police rode under the direction of the men cloaked in black, the Order of the Spider.

In the forests of Galce, off the roads, life continued as it had for hundreds of years. The trees lived their long lives and the insects their short ones, and no creature complained of its lot in life. Nicolas needed the steadiness of the wilderness as much as he needed its beauty—as much as he needed the secrets which the forest might reveal unexpectedly, in a white flash as a deer bounded from a clearing, in the discovery of red winter berries growing even in the snow.

There were times when Nicolas thought he would never go back to mankind. He knew how to survive in the wild. Why should he ever leave it? As a child he had often stared wistfully out at the edges of the meadows where the Gypsies camped. The trees on the other side, guardians of the deep forest, seemed to challenge him to step into their realm forever. When the Gypsies would stay by the edge of a lake or at the mouth of a cave, young Nicolas would shiver to think that he could dive into the water if he liked, or disappear into the cave, and never come back again. Then the Gypsies would speak of him only in rumour and legend, as they spoke of all the world's mysteries.

But in the end, Nicolas could never bring himself to truly disappear. Even now, as he wandered the forests of Galce, loneliness began to gnaw at him. Its touch was no less painful for its familiarity. Bear was with him always, his faithful companion, and the creatures of the wood spoke many things to his listening ears, but there would always come a time when Nicolas could not be separated from his own kind anymore, a time when his physical ears longed to hear greetings and the sound of his own name. So he would go back to the Gypsy camps or the Galcic cities to pretend that he was normal and accepted as other people were. And he would stay until the old wedge of his differentness, his Giftedness, drove itself between him and his kind once again.

He often thought of Maggie as he and Bear made their way to the southern border of Galce. When he had first found her in the streets of Calai, he was on his way back to the forests. But she had stopped him. He had gone back for her, and not only because she was in danger. Something in her had made him go back. He could have entered the world of men and never left it again if she would have stood by his side. But she did not. The eyes of another man captured her heart, and when he died her heart was buried with him.

When Nicolas had last spoken with Maggie beside the body of the Eastern rebel whom she loved, he had felt himself once again driven from the world of men. He had gone into the forests and buried himself there, nursing the hurt that even now festered inside.

From that time till this he had returned to the world of humanity only three times. Once, he had gone to supply himself with clothing for the winter. Another time he went to listen to the rumours concerning Pravik that swept the Eastern Lands and the provinces that bordered them. He kept himself quiet as the words were repeated, over and over, that all who knew what had truly happened in Pravik had afterward disappeared. Lastly, he had gone to deliver the wounded Gypsy into the hands of someone who could care for him. The horrible vision of the captive Gypsies on the road and the farm girl's whispered threats to the "queer folk" had distanced Nicolas even more.

But he could not avoid the road forever. The brook led him out of the mountainous forests and into the Galcic flatlands near the southern border. Here, the brook ran directly alongside the road. To make matters worse, the plains offered no hiding place.

The snow was sparse on the flatlands, and Nicolas was soon covered with mud from the soles of his boots to his knees. The lonely road wound its way through uninhabited wasteland. No bird flew in the wide empty sky; no sound broke the stillness of the day.

"What is this?" Nicolas said suddenly, and stopped. He had reached the beginning of a wooden fence, cracked and covered with dead brown lichen, that ran for miles between the road and the brook. It began in the middle of nowhere, and Nicolas could not see any reason for its being there.

"Do you suppose there used to be farm fields here?" Nicolas asked. "What think you, Bear?"

Bear only grunted and kept on going.

"All right then, don't comment," Nicolas said. The fence managed to keep his interest for a while, but soon the sight of it became as monotonous as the mud of the road and the sound of the brook.

It caught his interest again six miles or so down the road, when he saw the markings.

The tiny symbols had been carved into the wood only recently. Their lines stood out clean and pale on the dark fencing. Nicolas ran his finger over them. Gypsy markings. He read their story silently. A warning to other Gypsies: a warning, and a remembrance.

Bloody the road where hearts sicken and die. Treachery stains the road. Here the free have fought; here the free have fallen. Sing for them, fight for them. Vengeance is his who will take it.

Nicolas came to the last symbol and opened his eyes wide in surprise. It was a signature—one that he knew. Carved into the fence was the emblem of a small bird surrounded by a wreath of leaves. It was the mark of a Gypsy clan whose numbers had dwindled over the years: the mark of the People of the Sky.

At that moment Nicolas heard the keening of a hawk overhead; and from a high willow tree, rising like a lone soldier on the barren plains, came an answering whistle. He jumped to his feet and whirled around to face the tree. A tiny gust of wind blew in his face, carrying the smell of pipe tobacco with it.

The long hanging branches of the willow parted, and a young Gypsy woman emerged. A purple scarf adorned her head; tarnished gold earrings decorated her ears. Her deerskin boots were muddy and patched. She smiled at the look on Nicolas's face. The branches parted again, and the Gypsy girl's cousin, a young man smoking a pipe, stepped out.

Nicolas said the first thing that came into his head, which was, "What are you doing here?"

"Is that the best welcome you can give?" Marja asked, folding her arms. "Come now."

"I'm sorry," Nicolas said. "I didn't expect to see you."

"Obviously not." Marja smiled. "It is good to see you too, Nicolas Fisher."

"My question stands, though," Nicolas said. "What are you doing here?"

"We're Gypsies," Marja said. "We wander. Remember?"

"But you're here alone," Nicolas said.

"Hardly," Marja answered. "We are with you."

Nicolas shook his head. "Where are you going?"

Peter the Pipesmoker took his pipe from his mouth. "With you, I expect."

Nicolas choked. "You can't come with me!" he said.

"We don't have anywhere else to go," Marja said. "We've run away, Nicolas; and since you are the best runaway we know, it's good that we've met up with you. We'll go wherever you're going."

"I'm not sure where I'm going," Nicolas said. "But you can't come with me. I'm on a—I have something important to do."

Marja raised a pretty eyebrow. "Last time you went questing, you had a companion with you."

Nicolas reddened. "That was different," he said. "Where are the Major's Gypsies? Why don't you go back to the band?"

"Because we can't," Marja said.

The blood drained from Nicolas's face. "Why?" he whispered. "Where are they?"

"There isn't any more 'they,'" Peter said. "Just us, and I, and you. The band has broken up."

"The High Police," Nicolas began.

"No," Marja cut in, holding out her hand as if to stop him. "They did not reach us. We eluded them for over a week, traveling into the Eastern mountains. But you cannot hide an entire caravan easily. The Major ordered us to disband so that each family and individual could seek safety."

"Most are headed for Pravik," Peter said. "A caravan could never get past the soldiers around the city, but there are ways in for smaller groups."

Nicolas leaned against the fence. He felt as though the breath had been knocked out of him. "And you?" he asked. "You're a long way from Pravik."

"The People of the Sky do not do well underground," Marja said. She saw Nicolas stiffen with alarm, and she smiled.

"Don't be afraid—the secret of Pravik is not known to the world. Your friends are still safe in the catacombs. The Gypsies have used the undercity for centuries, whenever we had need of it. It was not hard for us to guess the means of the mysterious disappearances in the City of Bridges. But most of the world does not know."

Nicolas relaxed and leaned on the fence again. "You could be in danger out here," he said. "The Empire does not look kindly on Gypsies these days."

Marja's dark eyes flashed. "The Emperor cannot bear to see any in the Seventh World free," she said. "But some of us will never be enslaved."

Nicolas looked down at the fence, and his eyes fell again on the markings. "You made these," he said. "What happened here?"

Marja was silent a long time. When Nicolas looked up, he saw tears running down her face. "The High Police herd our people like cattle over the roads," she said. "And when the horns of the oppressed gore their oppressors, blood is spilled."

"We saw a band of captives on the road," Peter explained. His pipe was back in his mouth, and he puffed out smoke between words. "There were a few boys who tried to fight. We saw it all from up in the willow tree."

For the first time Nicolas thought he saw a red tint in the mud. His face paled.

"The police slaughtered them," Marja said. "They believe their injustice is hidden from the eyes of the world. But I saw it."

The tone in her voice was unmistakable: Marja would see to it that many heard what the High Police had done. There was nothing of the passive witness in Marja. Every atrocity she witnessed became a weapon in her hands. Nicolas could imagine her in the light of a hundred campfires, telling the story of what she had seen—inciting others to vengeance with her words.

That night, Nicolas, Marja, and Peter made a fire of willow branches in the road. Nicolas leaned against a fence post. Peter rested on a rock a good way back from the fire, his face in shadow, his features lit every few minutes as he puffed on his pipe. Marja sat in the road, wrapped in her faded red coat. She played with a jeweled dagger as she spoke. The light glinted off its golden handle and sharp blade, off the gold of Marja's earrings and the bracelet on her wrist, off the deep black of her hair.

"The Major has convinced many a Gypsy to go to Pravik," she was saying. "I think he plans to join the rebels there. When next they move, he will fight alongside them."

"Then the Ploughman has a worthy ally," said Nicolas.

Marja's eyes flickered to Nicolas's face and back to her dagger. "And where are you going?" she asked. "Surely you could use allies of your own."

"I am going to Italya," Nicolas told her. She looked up, surprised, and laid the dagger in her lap.

"Then of course you can't go alone," she said. "The Emperor's own province is no place to go without friends."

"It is no place to take friends, either," said Nicolas.

"Why are you going?" Marja asked. She leaned forward. "What voices have been calling to you?"

Nicolas looked away from her abruptly.

"I have always known you were Gifted," she began.

51

He held up a hand to stop her. "Marja, I don't—"

She cut him off. "I am not your enemy, Nicolas!"

He hung his head. "I'm sorry."

She did not answer. When he looked up, she had turned her head and was gazing away over the snow-covered flatlands.

"I have heard a voice," he said at last, slowly. "A voice that calls me south."

"Does the voice command you to go alone?" Marja asked.

"No," he answered.

"Then don't."

He looked up and met her eyes.

"We are your friends," she said. "Your family. All your life you've run away from us. Let us run with you this time."

Nicolas swallowed and turned away. The light of the pipe brightened Peter's face and then cast it into shadow again, but in the brief illumination Nicolas saw the concern of a true friend. He turned back to Marja and nodded without looking at her.

"Come with me then," he said. A sharp pang filled him as he said the words—whether of relief or misgiving, he could not tell for sure.

* * *

That night as Nicolas slept, his dreams came not in pictures but in sound. He thought he heard the far-off notes of a song, but the more he strained to hear it, the more indistinct and distant it became. He reached for it, as though a song was something that could be taken in hand, but it was far from his grasp. He thought he heard himself sigh, then realized it was not he who had done so—something else had sighed, something great and infinitely sad. Something that was all around him.

A rhythmic striking intruded on his dream. He woke up and opened his eyes. In the dying firelight, Marja was sharpening her dagger on a flat rock. The metal blade sparked on the stone. She was humming to herself. Nicolas fell asleep again with the sound of her voice in his ears.

He heard no other songs that night.

* * *

Iron-hubbed wheels left the snow crushed and bruised with soot as the black coach rolled over the high mountain roads to the fortress of Ordna. Half a dozen soldiers on horseback accompanied it. Black paint covered the windows. The interior of the coach was lit only by a single candle. It swung and jostled in its glass lantern case.

Miracle gazed at the black windows as though she could see through them, while the candlelight traced a mad dance over her face and hair and dark cloak. The man across from her watched her silently, his face shrouded in shadows and nearly covered by a black hood.

Hours passed in darkness. The candle had nearly burnt itself out when the coach pulled to a stop. Miracle looked away from the window, turning her face to the door as it opened on a grey world. Cold air invaded the stuffiness of the coach and stabbed her lungs. She ignored the pain and breathed deeply. In a moment a second black-cloaked man climbed into the coach. Once again the door shut; once again all was darkness.

The candle wax shrank away from the flame until the last of the wick flickered and died, and the coach became as dark and as silent as a tomb. The men said nothing, but Miracle's captor did not take his eyes away from her.

The coach pulled once more to a stop. This time, the wheels jarred over rocky ground. The muffled sounds of horses were heard inside the coach. The coachman talking with the soldiers. There was some dispute. It was settled quickly, and one of the harnessed horses neighed.

Someone yanked the coach door open. A cold wind bore the fading light of evening in with it.

The black-cloaked men descended from the coach step, and a young soldier ordered Miracle out. She stood, head bent under the low coach door, and the soldier took her hand to help her down. She smiled at him gratefully. He blushed and turned away. She saw the light of shame in his eyes.

They had stopped to make camp for the night on a graveled circle of flat ground beside the road. Beyond the small camp, the ground sloped down, dropping suddenly in a sheer cliff overlooking a small valley. The mountains around the valley thrust their peaks high. On the other side of the road was a wall of rock. Only the road, stretching out of sight around bends in either direction, offered any hope of escape.

The coachman tended to his horses while the soldiers unfurled sleeping rolls and built a fire. The black-cloaked men stood apart, watching with their arms folded deep in their sleeves. A soldier, wearing a captain's insignia, seized Miracle's arm and threw her to the ground. The cold rocks skinned her palms, but she made no sound.

"Sleep there," said the captain. Miracle sank down and wrapped herself in her patched cloak. She closed her eyes. The voice of the Nameless One, the man with the cruel smile, was easily recognizable. "Be easy with her, Captain. There is no call to batter the girl before she reaches our master."

"The Overlord of the Northern Lands cares nothing for the health of the strange ones," the Captain returned.

"I do not speak of the Overlord," answered the Nameless One, icy with disdain. "You would do well to respect your true masters."

Late in the night, when the moonlight broke through the clouds in frosted rays, Miracle rose soundlessly from her place by the fire. High Police lay all around her. She held her skirts and stepped over one of them without a rustle. The coach horses stood by the wall of rock across the road, neck to neck. One, a chestnut gelding, turned its massive head at Miracle's approach. She murmured soothingly to it and stroked its neck. It whinnied softly and pushed her shoulder with its nose. She froze as someone in the camp stirred, but all fell quiet once again.

She took hold of the horse's bridle and led it away from its fellow, whispering to it as they went, and with a practised spring she seated herself on the animal's back. The gelding moved uneasily beneath her. Once again she stroked his neck, and touching his sides with her heels, she spurred him back the way they had come.

After a time the wall of rock gave way, and they left the road. The horse stepped carefully down the boulder-strewn hillside into a small glen, where a frozen stream lay across their path. The gelding was skittish before the ice, and Miracle dismounted. She would leave the animal—she could traverse the steep places of the mountains with more ease on her own feet than on those of a horse, and she would not be so easy to follow. She removed the bridle from her companion's head. His breath was hot on her hands.

The ice held steady under her feet as she crossed it. The snow crunched, and the bare trees cast strange shadows in the glen. With the stream behind her, she turned her eyes back to the place she had left. The gelding had not moved. She would have turned to go, but a movement caught her eye. A black-cloaked figure stepped out from the shadows behind the horse.

"Come back with me," he said. Miracle felt relief at the voice. It was not her captor who spoke. Neither threat nor cruelty lay beneath his words. It was the young man who had boarded the coach on the journey. Miracle felt the presence of the stream between them and the nearness of freedom beyond it. She held her head high.

"Why should I?" she asked.

"Because if you do, I will not tell my companion that you tried to run away," he said.

"I am still running away," she said. "You have not captured me."

"I am only a few steps away from doing so. And if by some power you elude me, my companion will find you. I do not want that to happen."

Miracle stood still on the mountainside, the moonlight flashing silver in her hair. Her enemy did not move. She looked away from him, turned, and began to climb up the slope. Once again his voice arrested her.

"Please," he said. "Please come back with me." He stretched out a hand to her. Even in the moonlight she could see the ugly black mark that sprawled across his palm: the bulbous body and skeletal legs of a spider.

Dawn was beginning to streak the sky when they returned to the camp. The black-cloaked young man rode the gelding; Miracle walked alongside it. The soldiers and the coachman still slept, tightly rolled in their blankets, but the fire was already blazing. Beside it stood the Nameless One. His arms were folded. Miracle felt his eyes on her as she entered the camp and sat by the fire.

Her friend said nothing as he left the gelding and joined them. He sat between Miracle and the Nameless One's cruel eyes.

"Wake the camp," the Nameless One ordered.

Miracle watched as the young man who had brought her back held his tattooed hand over the fire. In a moment he turned his hand up. Blue flame arose from his marked palm. He closed his fist around it. Tongues of fire licked out between his fingers.

With a smile, he opened his fist. Sparks of flame shot from his hand, lighting on the faces and hands of the soldiers. They awoke with shouts of pain and anger. Miracle saw burns forming on their skin. The captain jumped to his feet and strode to the fire, his face red.

"It is late," said the Nameless One. "Next time do not allow your men to be so lazy. Nor yourself."

The captain bit back a retort. His eyes opened wide at the sight of the black-cloaked young man still playing with the fire in his hand.

The Nameless One crossed to Miracle's side and sat down so close that she could feel his breath. "You see," he whispered, "we are also Gifted. You are one of us." He touched the back of her neck. The tips of his fingernails felt like claws. She pulled away from him, and his face darkened.

"Be careful," he said. "You do not want to make an enemy of me."

Miracle forced herself to look at him. "Better an enemy than a friend," she said.

For a moment his face twisted, but the lines of anger resolved themselves into a smile. She cast her eyes down as he leaned over her. His mouth was at her ear.

"We shall see," he said.

The young man near the fire pulled each of his fingers into the palm of his hand, and the flames he had conjured went out. The spider was blacker and deeper in his hand than before; the touch of the blue fire had brought it to life. He stood abruptly, coming near and laying his hand on Miracle's shoulder.

"Will you look over the soldiers before we leave?" he asked the Nameless One.

Miracle did not look at the man beside her, but she felt displeasure from him. He stood up and moved away from the fire, casting a glance back that made her shudder.

"Thank you," she said.

Her rescuer did not answer. Impulsively, she looked up at him. "Do you have a name?" she asked.

"I did once."

She tilted her head. "Once?"

The young man nearly smiled again, but this expression was bitter—caustic. "Every day the Order takes a little more of it from me," he said. "I am less and less who I was."

"Who were you?" she asked.

"My name was Christopher Ens," he answered.

Miracle looked over her shoulder at her captor. He was upbraiding the captain in a low voice. "And he?"

Christopher's mouth hardened. "He has no name," he said.

"You have a master in Ordna?"

"Adhemar Skraetock."

"Are you supposed to tell me this?" Miracle asked.

"No," Christopher said. "You are to know nothing more than the master himself tells you."

"Then why do you answer my questions?"

"Because it does not matter. If you join us, you will learn our secrets. If you do not, you will never tell anyone else."

Miracle shivered and looked down at the dirty snow beneath her feet. "Would your master kill me?"

Christopher smiled grimly. "One way or another."

The coach was ready. The High Police mounted their horses. Miracle entered the tomb-like coach with the men of the Order. Christopher sat beside her; the Nameless One across from her once again. The candle had been replaced, and Christopher lit the new one. Miracle did not see where the fire came from.

They did not talk as they rode. As before, Miracle kept her eyes on the black window. She reached up and laid her fingertips on the painted pane, and there they stayed for hours. She knew that the Nameless One's eyes were on her, but she would not look at him. If Christopher was watching her, she could not tell.

The coach slowed its pace until every rock in the road felt like a mountain beneath its wheels. Christopher swept his eyes through the dark interior of the coach.

"Something is wrong," he said.

The door opened, and the captain peered in. "Bandits in the cliffs, sir," he said. "They have been watching us for miles."

"Kill them," said the Nameless One.

"They outnumber us," the captain answered.

"You are the High Police," said the Nameless One. "Soldiers of the Emperor himself. Kill them."

"Yes, sir." The captain spurred his horse ahead. The Nameless One fixed his eyes on Miracle.

"Get out," he said.

"There will be danger," Christopher protested.

"Yes." The Nameless One smiled. "Get out."

Miracle obeyed. They stood in the center of a narrow pass. The High Police had arranged themselves all around the coach, swords drawn. The snow crunched as Christopher and the Nameless One landed on the ground on either side of her.

The cliffs erupted with yells, and arrows pelted down. Miracle breathed in sharply as a soldier in front of her fell from his horse, the tip of an arrow showing through the skin at the back of his neck. The bandits leaped onto the horses of the police and drove axes into the soldiers' skulls. The police fought back with expert skill, fighting until the snow ran red.

Miracle covered her face with her hands and turned her back to the carnage. The Nameless One grabbed her arm and spun her around. He tore her hands from her eyes, his own flashing with vicious joy.

"Look on me!" he cried. "See how it ends!

He raised his tattooed hand to the sky and shrieked with hatred and exultation. The air took on visible substance and twisted. It seemed as though the cliffs shattered. Tortured cries filled the air.

When the Nameless One lowered his hand, the air became invisible again. The cliffs could be seen to stand as before. The pass was silent. Soldiers, horses, and bandits alike lay dead in the snow, their faces twisted with horror, blood running from their mouths and ears and eyes.

Miracle looked wildly at the Nameless One. His eyes burned blue like the flame Christopher had played with at the camp. The fire burned into her. She tore her gaze from him, and it fell on the black-cloaked figure that lay at her feet. Christopher.

She dropped to her knees in anguish beside him. The laughter of the Nameless One filled her ears.

"You are very alone now," he said.

She closed her eyes and tried to stop her ears against him. Beneath her hand, Christopher's chest rose and fell. Blood gurgled in his throat.

"Why don't you heal him?" said the Nameless One. "You have seen my power. Now let us see yours."

Miracle did not look up. She touched Christopher's face. His blood was warm and sticky and black on her fingers.

"I give you back your name, Christopher Ens," she whispered, so low that even she could barely hear the words. "If you live, if you rise from this place, know that your life is reclaimed."

She closed her eyes tightly and moved her lips without sound. As she breathed in, the power within her rose to meet the air. It flowed gently through her, through her fingertips, into the body before her. Christopher opened his eyes and stared up at her.

A black-booted foot nudged the side of Christopher's head. "Get up," said the Nameless One. "We are still half a day from Ordna."

Miracle rose. The staring faces of the dead seemed to cry out to her. Tears filled her eyes, and she took a step toward a young bandit near her. An iron grip on her arm stopped her.

"You cannot raise the dead," said the Nameless One. "Come. The master awaits."

The coach horses had been spared, but they left the coach behind. Christopher loosed the horses from the harness and mounted one. The Nameless One forced Miracle to mount another, and he swung himself up behind her.

He leaned forward and whispered, "Well done."

Nothing stirred in the pass behind them.

4

A Heartbreaking Pang for Freedom

NICOLAS FOLLOWED the brook over the border into Italya late in the day. The flatlands stretched away behind the travelers. Before them, the road rose and fell over gentle hills.

The wind whispered in Nicolas's ears. He heard voices in it, but could not make out words. Sighing voices—dying voices. Voices from his dream. His heart ached at the sound of them all around, and he wondered who they were. What they were.

Marja watched Nicolas as they walked. She saw the heaviness in his expression and wondered about the source of it. She wondered, not for the first time, why they were in Italya. She sang to herself often as they walked, a wordless tune she seemed to know from childhood but could not fully remember.

They slept that night in an orchard. The wind—a southern wind, without the bitter ferocity of the mountain gales— moaned in the bare branches above.

The full moon was high in the heavens when Nicolas cried out. Marja was at his side instantly. She stroked his head with gentle hands.

"Hush," she said. "Hush. All is right."

"They are dying," Nicolas said. He reached up and held Marja's hand until she thought he would crush it.

"They are dying," he said again, and lapsed into silence. His grip on her hand lessened, but she did not let go.

A light flickered. She looked up. Peter was sitting under a tree, watching, a match in one hand and his pipe clenched between his teeth. His other hand shielded the flame from the wind.

Marja glanced up to the skies. "It is a full moon," she said. "A night for dreams."

She relaxed her hold of Nicolas's hand until it slipped away from her and came to rest over his heart.

In the morning, the sounds of horses and feet filled the orchard. They could be heard from a long way off. When they had kicked dirt over their fire, Nicolas and Peter lay flat on the ground and crept through the dead underbrush to the edge of the road. Marja was already up a tree above them, hidden by a dense tangle of branches.

Captives came into sight, driven along the road. They were young and fainting from exhaustion and hunger: a ragged cluster of Gypsies. Only three High Police, with one horse between them, accompanied the band. No more were needed.

A foot booted in deerskin landed next to Nicolas's face. He watched as Marja walked out from the trees, stumbled, and joined the troop. A soldier saw her walking apart from the others. "You!" he barked. "Back in line!" Head bowed so that she would not catch his eye, Marja obeyed.

Nicolas and Peter looked at each other. With silent understanding they crept out from their hiding place and joined the stragglers near the back of the line. The soldiers did not see; the captive Gypsies said nothing to give them away. Nicolas took the arm of a limping young boy of fifteen years, face marked by a black cut, and threw it over his shoulder.

Through parched lips the boy said, "Thank you."

The High Police drove the band down the road for miles, past acres of orchards. The soldiers took turns riding the lone horse and drinking from a heavy wineskin tied to the saddle. Those who were not riding walked around the group, making sure that no one escaped. The sound of the brook running next to the road began to echo in Nicolas's mind like a cruel taunt. There was water enough to keep the captives alive, but no mercy to give them access to it.

When they were deep in orchard country—land cultivated but still eerily empty of people—the three soldiers met at the head of the procession and whispered amongst themselves. Nicolas narrowed his eyes and concentrated on them, his ears prickling.

"Captain thinks we're nursemaids . . ." he heard.

". . . could be in Athrom already . . ."

"Kill them all. No one will know."

". . . wait. The time will come."

Peter was farther up the line, helping a woman who had soaked her feet falling through a thin layer of ice. Marja was farther still, near the horse which one of the police had remounted. Suddenly, Marja stumbled and fell. She cried out and clutched her ankle, rocking as though she was in pain. Nicolas slipped away from the boy he had been supporting and moved closer to the soldier nearest him.

The line had stopped where Marja fell. The soldier on horseback pointed the tip of his sword at her.

"Get that one up," he called to one of the other men.

The soldier pushed through the line to the place where Marja crouched, her hands still holding her ankle. "Up with you," he said.

She turned her dirt-smudged face up and met his eyes calmly. "I can't walk," she answered.

"For stars' sake kill her!" cried the soldier near Nicolas. "We can't have cripples slowing us down."

The soldier near Marja reached for his sword, but she was faster. In one fluid motion she pulled the dagger from her boot and sprang to her feet, slashing the soldier across the face. He cried out and reeled back. She snatched his sword from its sheath and drove it into him. He fell to his knees without a sound. She pushed him back with a foot to his chest, and the sword came free.

In the same instant, Nicolas gave a loud whistle and sprang onto the back of the soldier near him. He wrapped one arm around the man's throat and the other over his eyes, kicking the soldier's hand away from his sword. They fell to the ground, and Peter appeared, holding a large rock. He drove it into the back of the man's head. The soldier did not move again.

The last soldier had begun to slaughter the Gypsies around him the instant he saw Marja draw her dagger. He had cut down four of the emaciated captives when Bear, responding to Nicolas's signal, charged out of the orchard bawling like a fiend. The horse reared in terror, and the soldier lost his sword in the struggle to keep his seat. Nicolas ran to join Bear, brandishing the sword of the man he and Peter had killed, but he was not needed. The horse's hooves slipped in the mud, and the animal fell, crushing the rider beneath it.

The battle was over almost before it had begun. The Gypsies stood in silence, staring at their rescuers.

Marja wiped her forehead with the back of her hand, smearing blood across her face. She stumbled, and Peter caught her.

"Some of us will never be enslaved," she said.

* * *

"They rode into our camp in the dead of night. We never suspected danger until they were upon us."

The Gypsy speaker was a young man, not more than seventeen years old. He was called Darne, he said, and he had belonged to a large band. When he began his narrative he had spoken distantly. Now he spoke with a lump in his throat that threatened to choke out his words.

"They killed the littlest children," he said. "They killed them so we wouldn't have any reason to fight anymore. They burned the caravans and cut the horses loose, and drove them through the camp with fire so that our own horses rode down our old men and our little ones. They killed a hundred at least. We who were left were separated into groups. I don't know what happened to the others. I only know what happened to us. They marched us through the mountains and left the dead ones on the road."

"Where will you go now?" Nicolas asked.

"To dig our graves," said the young man.

"No," Peter said. "You are alive. Don't give up so easily."

Darne looked up with anguish in his eyes. "Do you think it has been easy?"

"Dying is easy," Marja said. "But only a coward chooses to do it when the only enemy before him is himself."

"Where can we go? We are dead already. Our bands, our caravans, are gone."

"Go back to the mountains," Marja said. "Go to Sloczka. There is safety in Pravik."

"You will not allow us to die, but you would send us to be buried alive?"

"If you cannot face the underground, then stay above and fight. Only stay alive. Stay free."

The young man hung his head and stared into the blazing fire at his feet. The tree branches above him cast tangled shadows over his dark hair.

"Pravik is far," he said. "And the way is difficult. We have no horses and no food. We cannot go."

"If we bring you horses?" Nicolas said. "If we give you food, and weapons—then will you make the journey?"

Darne looked up and searched Nicolas's face. At last he nodded. "If you will give us the tools, I will lead the people to Pravik while I still live."

The fire glinted on Marja's face as she broke into a fierce smile. Peter put a hand on the young man's shoulder. "Now you speak like a free man," he said.

Nicolas opened a feed bag that he had found on the horse's saddle. The horse had broken its leg in the fall and Peter had killed it, not without a wrench of pain in his own heart. A puff of oat dust filled the air along with the smell of dried oats and hay. Nicolas held the bag up to Bear's nose.

"Your bear eats oats?" Darne asked.

"Bear eats everything," Nicolas said. "But he is not mine anymore than I am his."

"The question is," Marja asked, "where are we going to find horses enough for you? How many are there?"

"Fifteen," answered the young man. His voice dropped. "There were thirty when we started."

"Ten horses should do it," Peter said. "Some can ride double."

"There must be a farmhouse around here somewhere," Marja said. "At the very least we can ask for directions."

"Why do you say that?" asked the young man.

Marja indicated their surroundings. "Someone owns these orchards."

"The Emperor himself owns them," said the young Gypsy. "No one else has owned land around here for decades."

"All the better," Nicolas said. "I might feel guilty about stealing from common farmers."

"Common soldiers or the Emperor Morel himself, you won't find a kind welcome here," Darne said. "This is Italya. We are only a few days' ride from the great Athrom."

"The last place on earth I have ever wanted to see," Nicolas said.

"I would like to see it," Marja said. "I would like to spit on the ground of it."

"How many of you are fit to work?" Nicolas asked Darne.

"There are five of us who can still walk without stumbling."

"Tomorrow we will scout for horses," Nicolas said. "Three of you come with us. The other two stay here, to watch over the weak and forage for food. This is as safe a hiding place as you could ask for, and there is water."

Nicolas turned his head at the sound of the running brook. The water was flowing relentlessly downstream. It would go on, whether or not he followed. It took time away with it—his chance to follow receding ever farther south. He felt like a traitor to the water's call.

But the water had not spoken to him in days, and the Gypsies had.

"I will come back," he whispered.

"What was that?" Marja asked.

"Nothing," he answered. "Talking to myself."

Nicolas sat by the brook late that night, bending a twig in his hands. He threw it and watched as the water caught it, spun it around rocks and over sunken roots, bore it downstream.

"You can't go now, Nicolas," said a voice behind him.

He did not turn to look at her. "I don't mean to," he said.

"Yes, you do," Marja said. She sat down. "If you could you would leave this minute."

"If I could," he said. "But I can't."

"You won't go until these people are on the road to Pravik?"

"I won't go until they have what they need." He took another twig from the ground and twisted it. Snapped it.

"Whatever is down there," Marja said, "at the end of the river—it can wait for you."

"Maybe it can't," Nicolas said. "Maybe I'm too late already."

"What is at the end of the river?" Marja asked. "Where is it leading you?"

Nicolas opened his mouth to answer, but he had no words to speak. He looked to the water for answers, but all he could see was his own reflection.

* * *

They left the little camp in the orchard when the first rays of the sun cut down through the chilled air. Nicolas and the fifteen-year-old Gypsy he had helped in the road headed south; Marja and Darne went west. Peter the Pipesmoker took an older, half-deaf Gypsy man east.

They returned after dark to an orchard where nothing stirred. Not even a sigh of air breathed life into the rows of trees with their tangled branches. There was no smoke, no fire, no sign of life. The Gypsies had vanished.

Darne's face paled as he ran down the row of trees where he had left his people, his eyes searching. For a moment longer silence reigned, and then they appeared, moving like spectres out of the shadows. They spoke in low, smiling voices to Darne, whose relief was clear. They re-lit their fires and settled themselves on the ground, leaning on each other.

"Your lookouts do their job well," Nicolas told a woman, one of the two Gypsies who had been left in charge of the camp.

She smiled. "Disappearing is an old skill."

The three scouting parties met again around the main fire, together with a few of the Gypsies who had stayed in the orchard. Nicolas and his teenage companion had found nothing but an empty barn, its floor strewn with dead autumn leaves and moldy straw, old wagon wheels rusting in its yard. Marja had found even less: nothing but farmland for miles.

Peter listened to their recitals with a twinkle in his eye. When at last attention turned to him, he puffed slowly on his pipe, took it out, and said, "We found a ranch. They're raising horses for the High Police. There's a hundred of them at least, not more than six miles from here. They've provisions enough to send every captive Gypsy on the road to safety in Pravik."

"And likely guards enough to send them all back again," Marja said.

"You are not afraid?" Nicolas asked her, a smile playing on his lips.

"No," she said, and smiled back.

* * *

"I tell you something's wrong."

Inside the guardhouse, the soldier paced the length of the table, ignoring the half-finished game of chess.

"Nothing's wrong," his fellow answered. He took a long drag on a pipe and moved a pawn forward. "Can't the horses get antsy without something being wrong? Most likely there's a storm coming."

In the corral, another horse whinnied. The wind blew a gate loose from its latch, banging it against the fencing. The first soldier took a drink from a bottle on the table and licked his top lip.

"You hear the wind," said his partner. "It's a storm."

An eerie sound floated through the crack underneath the door of the guardhouse.

"What was that?"

"The wind."

"It wasn't." He set the bottle back on the table with a bang. "Don't ignore me. Something's wrong out there."

"All right," said his partner. He stood and took a spear down from its resting place along the wall. "We'll go look. Happy now?"

It had been a warm day, and what little snow lay on the ground had mostly melted off. Mud squelched beneath their feet as the guards made their way to the corral. The loose gate swung and hit the boards of the fence as another gust of wind blew through the ranch. The light from the guardhouse made the gate shine ghostly white in the darkness.

The senior guard made his way to the gate and latched it tightly. Before he had taken his hands from the iron latch, an eerie wail filled the air.

The men looked at each other. A sound in the corral drew their attention. One of the horses was rearing and moving in circles, its ears flat back on its head. The other horses showed similar signs of apprehension.

"I told you something was wrong."

"There!" The soldier pointed into the darkness beyond the fencing. "Something's moving there."

Where he pointed, an almost indistinguishable black shadow was loping back and forth along the fence.

"It's some kind of animal," said the guard, and licked his top lip again. "That's what's worrying the horses."

A wail drifted through the night for the third time. "It's a bloody ghost," said the senior officer.

Behind them, the lights of the guardhouse suddenly flickered and died. The corral was plunged into darkness.

"Get back," yelled the senior officer. "Call the alarm."

They ran for the door of the guardhouse. It was open, as the gate of the corral had been, swinging and creaking in the wind. The light of a single candle ribboned across the floor and out the crack of the door.

The senior officer threw open the door, and his face paled. A ghostly form stood in the guardhouse, candle in hand: an emaciated boy of about fifteen, dressed in rags, a black cut running from his temple to his jaw. The boy looked up at their approach with hollow eyes. He met their stares and did not move.

It did indeed seem to the men that they beheld a ghost, come to bring retribution on those who had caused so much pain to his people. The younger of the soldiers let out a wordless cry and staggered back, but his senior lifted his spear and drew it back to discover whether or not the ghost could bleed.

A strong hand grasped his wrist before he could cast the spear. He cried out in terror. The spear was wrenched from his hand, the shaft driven against the back of his head. He fell to the ground. His partner doubled over as the shaft rammed into his stomach. He caught sight of a slim, fast-moving figure before the wood caught his temple and he crumpled to the floor.

The Gypsy boy took a silver horn from its place on the wall, where it waited to sound the alarm. Together he and

Nicolas slipped from the guardhouse into the night. The boy ran for the back of the corral while Nicolas unlatched the gate for the second time.

In the dim moonlight, Nicolas could see the shadow figures of Marja, Peter, and three other Gypsies as they climbed over the fencing and mounted the horses nearest them, calming the creatures with soothing hands and the commanding air of those who know how to ride, bareback and bridle-less, but still in control.

Minutes later, pandemonium erupted at the back of the corral. The silver horn sounded as Bear crashed through a weak place in the fence and rushed on the horses. They panicked. Their hooves thundered through the mud as the exultant cries of the Gypsies filled the air. The invaders herded the animals toward the open gate. Nicolas launched himself from the top of the fence onto the back of a grey stallion. He clutched its mane, tightened his knees, and held on.

High Police, most half-dressed, ran out of the guardhouses and bunking rooms with spears in their hands. They stood in shock as the stampede poured over the ground toward them. With yells of fright and confusion, they threw themselves out of the way. None saw the women who slipped into the abandoned houses and reemerged clutching sacks of food and clothing.

Riders were dispatched two nights later with messages to the officials in Athrom, explaining that one of the province's finest breeding grounds had been invaded by ghostly riders who drove nearly fifty horses from the corral. Most were recovered the next morning, wandering through farmland and orchards. Only about ten were still unaccounted for. The messages did not mention the missing provisions. The officials at the ranch did not wish to explain what sort of ghosts took bread along with horses.

* * *

They kept the horses in the old barn for a day while Darne consulted with Peter and Nicolas. In the evening, the Gypsies moved out in three groups, each taking a slightly different route through the orchards. Marja had drawn maps showing the way to Pravik—written in symbols that only a Gypsy could understand, and covered with markings to identify friendly wild places where winter berries grew in abundance, red and sweet even through the snow.

Darne and the others thanked their rescuers before they rode out. When they were gone, the barn was left empty and profoundly silent.

Peter took out his pipe and lit it. Marja folded her arms and looked around her at the hoof marks that scuffed the dirt of the barn floor and scattered the dead leaves.

Nicolas closed his eyes and leaned against an empty stall. He sighed, and voices flooded into his head as he breathed in. They piled atop each other, layered, tumultuous. Voices of the dying, voices of the dead; ethereal voices that came from everywhere and nowhere; wind-voices, wolf-voices; and over it all the rushing, rushing, pouring, swirling of water.

The voices overpowered him. With a groan, he sank down to the scuffed dirt and dead leaves. From far away, he heard Marja and Peter asking him what was wrong. He thought he felt hands touching him, but all his senses were engaged in the world of sound.

Come to me, rushed the water. *Come, Nicolas Fisher. Follow the river. No more delay.*

* * *

Adhemar Skraetock had long ago ceased to be a man. Those who thought of him never pictured a face or a figure in their minds—only black robes, long, skeletal fingers, the tip of a white beard, and burning eyes that peered from beneath a cowl. If he had an age, no one knew it.

Not even those who were close to him—which meant only that they were often used by him—had seen the scars beneath the black robes, hundreds of them, small blood sacrifices made to appease the Blackness and increase his own power. Blood, to a burning shell like Skraetock, was a small price to pay. He had spilled torrents of it in his lifetime, and not only his own.

Where Adhemar Skraetock lived no one knew. His students, the followers of the Order of the Spider, met with him in the courts of the Empire. In Athrom, in Pravik, in Londren of the Bryllan Isles. In Ordna.

The black towers of Ordna rose blacker than ever behind Skraetock as he stood in the entrance of the courtyard, watching as chains ground and clanked to life, lifting the iron gate for the riders outside. He watched them enter. The young men of his Order were riding coach horses. They had the girl.

He did not have to wonder what had happened to the detachment of soldiers the Northern Overlord had sent along with them. He could see the answer on the face of the

Nameless One; the exultant flush of fire in his veins. On the face of Christopher Ens, Skraetock saw death.

They did not see him. He turned and disappeared inside the black halls of the fortress as the Overlord's men rushed into the courtyard to greet the newcomers. Soon the Overlord himself—Narald Black-Brow, the Emperor's chosen ruler of the Northern Lands—would come to see what the Order had brought to his fortress.

No doubt he would be pleased.

* * *

Perhaps it was the smell of blood that so agitated the little black mountain pony. They could all smell it. The wolf whined and loped ahead—with its leg it could not run—and the men continued on at their former pace, dread mounting with every step. The pony rolled its eyes and tugged at its rope until Kris spoke to it sharply.

They entered the pass. Michael turned away at the sight, afraid he would be sick. Even Stocky was speechless. The snow was stained red and black around the bodies. The stench was nearly overpowering.

At first Michael thought that the men had killed each other in combat. They were still clutching their weapons, and many of them were wounded. But as they picked their way through the pass, each of the three men thought what not one of them would say: that this mass murder, for murder it must have been, was accomplished at one stroke by one unimaginably cruel power.

Michael's heart beat in his throat as he scanned the bodies. He knew the faces of the High Police, twisted with pain and horror though they were. He had seen them in the village. He unsheathed his sword and clenched it tightly as he passed by, but Miracle was not among the dead. He became convinced that he would not find her, and he relaxed his grip.

They left the pass, but still the pony's eyes flashed and rolled. The wolf raised its head and howled, long and wild. From the cliffs, the voices of other wolves joined in.

A storm came up with little warning, and the men took shelter beneath a dark overhang. The wolf settled itself at Michael's feet. Kris tied the pony to a jutting bit of rock and started a fire. After a time, the pony grew calmer.

Michael fell asleep with the heat of the fire on his face and hands. He awoke when the pony leaped, neighed, and shook her mane, nearly breaking free of the rope. Kris jumped up to calm her. The snowstorm raged beyond the overhang, concealing all around them.

"I've never seen the little girl so troubled," Kris murmured.

"The storm has spooked her," Michael said.

"No," Kris said. "She's not afraid. She wants to get loose."

The wolf lifted its head suddenly, its ears perked forward. Michael and Kris watched as it leaped to its feet and whined. The pony stamped.

"Something's out there," Kris said. Stocky had awakened, and he moved closer to Michael.

A wolf's howl broke out in the white of the storm and echoed off the sides of the pass, but in its notes was not the howl of a wolf only, but the bellow of an elk, the roar of a lion, the scream of a hawk. Michael stood and unsheathed his sword. Kris gripped his axe handle tightly, while Stocky took a sword in each hand and stood, knees bent, eyes watching, ready.

In the swirling snow a shape slowly took form. A wolf it was, white as the moon except for a crimson stripe that began at its shoulders and ran down its back to the tip of its tail. It was easily as big as the pony, and far more muscular. Its mouth was black, and its eyes seemed to burn with a deep fire. One eye was tawny like a hawk or an owl, the other bluer than the eyes of Kris of the Mountains.

As it moved toward them, Michael felt something inside him leap. He understood, suddenly, why the pony had yearned to be free. Inside of him was the same swell of wildness, of raw strength, grace, and a heartbreaking pang for freedom. The very Spirit of the Wild now stood before them, dimming their fire with the power of its presence. The sword dropped from Michael's hand. He heard the weapons of his companions likewise fall to the earth.

The lame grey wolf knelt, its bandaged leg nearly buried in the snow as it touched its black nose to the ground and whined. The pony was silent and still.

The great white wolf touched its nose to the head of the grey, and then it looked into the eyes of Michael, of Kris, and of Stocky in turn. Without a sound it turned and headed back into the storm.

"Follow it," Kris said. The others made no argument. Stocky threw snow over the fire as Kris untied the pony.

They could see nothing of their surroundings in the snow, yet they could always just see the white wolf, like a dream, moving through the blizzard ahead of them. They followed it for what seemed like hours, moving now up, over steep ground; now down, into valleys.

Once Michael looked down at the depths of snow in which his feet were sinking, and when he looked up he saw not a wolf leading them, but a man—a great giant of a man, with long hair and clothing made of skins; and he thought he heard laughter echoing in the air. But in the next instant the laughter was gone. The joy of it had become the sorrow of a wolf's lonely howl, and he was once more looking at the crimson-streaked tail and powerful legs and back of the creature that had come to them by the fire.

The snowstorm cleared up as quickly as it had come. When the swirling curtain of snow was taken away, Michael found himself standing at the edge of a cliff, looking down on the towers of Ordna.

5

Dreams

NARALD BLACK-BROW had spent much of his childhood in Athrom, playing around the throne of the Emperor Lucien Morel. In Athrom, Black-Brow, the Northern Overlord, was a courtier: a man who knew when to speak and when to be silent, what vices to display with pomp and what sins to keep hidden.

In Ordna, the Overlord of the Northern Lands did not care so much for appearances. He ruled as his ancient forefathers had done, who in the Tribal Age were the marauding scourge of the Seventh World.

They sat together at a long table well-laid with haunches of meat and deep cups of dark red drink: Black-Brow, Adhemar Skraetock, and the two young men of the Order of the Spider. It was a strange, silent dinner. Black-Brow kept himself buried in venison while Skraetock only drank. Christopher pretended to eat, but did a bad job of it. The Nameless One watched the Overlord moodily.

He had not always been nameless, this prodigy of the Order of the Spider. He had traded his name away to some creature beyond the Veil years ago, but before then his name had also been Black-Brow. He watched his father eat with thinly veiled disgust. Now and again Narald Black-Brow cast a look at his son that might have shriveled a weaker man. The father hated the son almost as much as the son hated the father.

"Now then, Skraetock," said Black-Brow when he had consumed every piece of meat from the haunch in his hands. "What of this girl for whose capture a dozen of my best men died? You invade my home with your black-robed minions and your mutterings and candlesticks, and send my men roaming all over the country looking for her, and am I not to see her now that she is safely here?"

"She would hardly be safe here under your eyes, Father," said the Nameless One.

"And she is under yours?" Black-Brow retorted.

"Enough," said Skraetock. "She is in my keeping until I see fit to release her. Besides, Narald my friend, surely you had a look at her when your son brought her here?"

Black-Brow's face shone behind the massive bone he still held in his hands. "And one look is supposed to be enough?"

The Nameless One stood abruptly. "Quite enough for you," he said. "Master Skraetock, will she join us? What do you think?"

"I have spoken to her," Skraetock said, and his fingers twitched. There was blood beneath his fingernails. "She does not sympathize with us, but she can hardly resist us." His lips twisted in a smile. "The fire in her is powerful. She has done us some good already."

Christopher started. "What have you done to her?" he blurted.

The Nameless One, still standing, cast a look of scorn on Christopher. The hood was thrown back from his head, revealing a strong, handsome face. He turned back to Skraetock.

"Master, I have served you well, have I not?"

"Without question," Skraetock answered.

"Yet I have asked little of you over the years."

"That is true," Skraetock answered. "You have always been pleased to take what you wanted for yourself." He smiled again. He knew what self-inflicted scars lay under the black folds of the Nameless One's robes—what wraiths likely tormented him in the night.

The Nameless One ignored the jab. "Tonight I ask something of you. Give me the girl."

Black-Brow jumped to his feet. "By rights she belongs to me," he said. "My men arrested her."

"But they did not bring her back," said the Nameless One. A cold smile stretched his mouth and tainted his eyes.

"She is in my home," Black-Brow said.

"It was my home once," said his son. "It may be again."

Skraetock pushed his chair back from the table, its legs scraping across the floor, and rose to his feet. He held a hand in the air. The spider across his palm pulsed in the candlelight.

"Enough," he said. "I have no time to waste with selfish quarrels."

As Skraetock spoke, Narald Black-Brow slumped forward in his chair. His eyes closed; his head bent down and rested on the table. But for the slow sound of his breathing, he might have been dead.

"Then she is mine," the Nameless One said.

"She is not," Skraetock said, "and she will never be. Do you think I would give so much power into your hands? The Gifted will belong to the Order. And I, not you, am the Order."

"You will not deform her," the Nameless One said.

"I will do as I see fit. And you will learn to be grateful for it." Skraetock reached into his robes and drew out a small knife. Christopher closed his eyes at the sight.

"We have finished with trying to convince them. These are days of glory, my children," said Adhemar Skraetock. "When we will at last see what fire may be drawn from Gifted veins."

Somewhere close by, a wolf howled.

* * *

Nicolas came awake with a cry. "No!" he cried. "You're tearing them apart!"

Marja was at his side in an instant, dagger in hand. Her dark eyes scanned the clearing. Seeing nothing, she relaxed her hand and put the dagger away. "What is it?" she asked.

Nicolas sank down on the ground and put his head on his knees. "I don't know," he said.

"Nicolas, you can tell me," Marja said. "What do you hear?"

He met her eyes and shuddered. He looked away.

"I hear voices," he said. "Every day now. I don't know who they are—what they are. But they are dying."

He was quiet. Marja waited in silence.

"Something is breaking through them," he said. "Tearing them. Tearing through the—the Veil, Professor Huss called it.

He said a Veil separated us from dark forces. But the Veil isn't a thing. It's alive."

He looked up, and defiance flashed in his eyes. "There now," he said. "What do you think of that?"

Marja knelt in the dirt beside Nicolas and leaned forward so that her head was almost touching his. "Listen to me, Nicolas Fisher," she said. "You are not crazy. I cannot hear the things you hear, but I believe you."

For a moment he stared at her. The voices were still echoing in his head. So real they threatened to overtake the world he was living in. And yet it mattered that Marja believed him, that someone else might care.

"Thank you," he said, faltering.

* * *

Michael slept fitfully on the cliff. He dreamed of storming the fortress—he, Kris, and Stocky—and seeing its towers fall before them. But even as he dreamed, the presence of Ordna weighed on him. Heavy and stone, real and impenetrable.

He did not know what awoke him, but when he opened his eyes in the darkness of the night, eyes were staring down into his—one blue, one gold. The wolf was waiting for him. He rose to his feet and took up the sword that had lain beside him, sheathing it on his back. The wolf led him soundlessly down a steep path toward the fortress.

It seemed that the path would lead right into the stone walls, but before they came up against the barrier, the path dipped. There was a hole in the ground next to the wall.

Michael climbed in. The top of his head did not quite reach the level of the ground.

The wolf jumped down beside him and began to dig with its massive paws. Michael watched it for a moment, and then the two-coloured eyes looked up at him reproachfully. He fell on his knees and joined the wolf, digging with his hands.

The earth was softer than it should have been, and oddly warm. Even so, the dirt and rocks grated against Michael's hands until his knuckles were cracked and bloody. And then, suddenly, his hands scraped up against iron.

Michael cleared the loose earth away quickly and uncovered an iron ring. He looked up to see what the wolf was doing, but the wolf was not there.

He was alone.

He pulled on the ring, and a trapdoor took shape beneath the last bit of dirt. Michael pulled with all his strength, and the door came away. A dark space opened beneath it.

Michael lowered himself into the hole, growing steadily uneasier as his feet did not touch ground. He gripped the edge of the hole and stretched his legs as far as he could, but there was nothing to stand on. Taking a deep breath, he set his feet against one side of the hole and his back against the other, and slowly descended into complete darkness.

Down the tunnel he went, wondering if he was lowering himself into a well. With every inch he wondered if he might suddenly fall out into nothingness. He wondered, as he went, if he wasn't dreaming this—surely, had he been awake, he would not have done anything so foolish.

After he had gone down several feet, the walls of the tunnel disappeared and he fell. But the fall was short—only three feet or so. He landed on his back on the cool earth, and with hardly a grunt he stood. He could stand with his head and shoulders in the vertical tunnel he had just come through. He moved his feet and found that another tunnel, just big enough to crawl through, led away.

Michael moved awkwardly to his hands and knees and began to push through the new tunnel. If possible, it was blacker than the one he had just descended. It was longer, too. Not until he had begun to despair of its ever ending did he touch paving stones and breathe the cool air of open space.

Blood rushed to Michael's head as he stood, and cramps seized his legs. He stretched and gratefully breathed the air. It was not so stale here as it had been in the tunnel. With his hands and feet, he began to explore the darkness. He was in a little room with nothing in it but a a pile of damp hay in one corner and an empty barrel in another. The ceiling was low. He ran his hands over it and found another trapdoor.

The door opened when he pushed it. A draft of cold air hit him in the face. He drank it in as he clambered out, into a cell where moonlight trickled in from a high window. He caught his breath.

Miracle was there.

She had curled up against the wall farthest from the cell door. She was asleep. Her skin was deathly pale, her mouth and the circles under her eyes dark against her face. One of her wrists was tightly bound with a dirty, bloodstained rag.

Michael crawled across the cold stones to her side. She awoke with a start. He put a finger to his lips.

"Hush," he whispered. "I am here to help you."

"How did you come here?" she asked. Each word sounded as though she had pulled it from some distant place.

"I'm not sure," he said. He smiled, wondering how he could smile in such a place. He did it for her sake. But she did not smile back.

"I don't think I can walk," she said. She was shaking. Michael put his hand over hers. Her skin was damp and cold.

"Then I'll carry you," Michael answered. Even as he said it, he knew it was impossible. There was not enough room below —she would have to crawl through the tunnel in her own strength. Unless he could find another way out.

He stood and looked up at the window, high in the wall. It was barred and too small for anyone but the smallest child to fit through. Perhaps it could be enlarged from the outside.

"Hide," Miracle said. "Someone is coming."

Michael reached for his sword, but Miracle stretched out her bandaged hand to stop him.   "No," she said. "They will kill you."

"I will kill them first," he said. He clenched his jaw as the sound of footsteps echoed on the stones outside the door.

"You can't!" she said, her voice nearly breaking with the effort.

He looked down at her in surprise. Her face was earnest, her hands still shaking.

"You cannot kill them," she said. "You don't know what you're facing."

The footsteps were almost at the door. Michael sheathed his sword abruptly and threw himself down through the floor, drawing the trapdoor shut behind him.

Straw had spilled from the top of it when Michael had come up, and that part of the floor was clean, clearly outlining the door. Miracle leaned heavily against the wall and hoped that no one would notice.

A key turned in the lock.

"In here, my lord," said the guard. "But you must tell no one—no one must know that I—"

The Nameless One interrupted. "Leave," he said.

"Yes, my lord." The guard scurried away. There was silence in the corridor. Miracle closed her eyes as the door groaned on its heavy iron hinges, and he entered.

The room seemed to pulse as he came through the door: a now-familiar pulse that burned in Miracle's head and made her feel sick. She rubbed her arm with her uninjured hand and pushed herself harder against the wall. But she looked up at him, steadily, though she was shaking with weakness and with dread. The Nameless One's skin was flushed. His eyes shone as he looked down at her.

"Have you ever felt the fire in your veins?" he asked. "Felt it as we do? Do you know what power is in you?"

She made no answer.

"All you need do," the Nameless One said, "is give yourself to the Blackness. Give them what they want—blood, worship, sacrifice. In return they will rouse the fire in you till you are greater than you can imagine."

The air quivered with a sound like hornets buzzing as the Nameless One crouched next to Miracle.

"You felt their presence when the Master took power from you. Do you know what they are?" he asked. "They are the

Blackness. They are the true lords of the world—the glorious darkness. And they are coming. With every sacrifice we make, we tear a hole in the Veil that keeps them back. One day soon we will tear a thousand holes in the Veil and rip it to shreds, and they will reclaim their domain."

Miracle shook her head, though the effort took more energy than she had. "We will stop them," she said.

The Nameless One laughed. "Who will?" he asked.

He leaned close, so close that his breath touched her face. The buzzing in her ears grew louder. Dull pain, building up, threatened to overwhelm her again.

"Who will stop us?" he asked. "You? Unless you join us, the Spider will feed on you till you are nothing but a shell. Master Skraetock uses your power to make himself stronger. You are fighting against yourself."

Miracle forced herself to look the Nameless One directly in the eyes. His expression was malevolent and terrifying, but she did not look away.

"It does not matter," she said, struggling for every word. "The King will return."

The Nameless One drew back as though Miracle had bitten him. "So you have heard that lie, have you?" he said. "It has been five hundred years, and still a few pathetic rebels cling to him. He was defeated in the Great War. The Blackness won. *We* won."

"He will come for us, as long as a single heart cries out to him," Miracle said.

"And how many hearts do?" the Nameless One asked. "It was people like you who demanded the King be exiled. Humanity has not learned faithfulness in five hundred years.

They are as treacherous and greedy as they have ever been. They deserve to be slaves. As they will be, when the Blackness breaches the Veil. Only those of us who have allied ourselves with the lords of darkness will rule. It has been promised us. As for you, you will help us reach our goal. Do you think the King will hear you? Why should he save one who would rather strengthen her enemies than save herself?"

The Nameless One drew close and hissed in her ear. "The Spider is hungry for Gifted fire. Master Skraetock will have all you possess, if he must drive you to the brink of death a thousand times over. He uses you to make himself strong." He gripped her wrist as he spoke, tearing at her skin with his thumbnail. Warm blood seeped through the bandage.

"Do you know why he hurts you?" he asked. "It is because if you could fight back, you would be too strong for him. The fire in you is so great that he could not steal it if you were not near death every time he does. But you are a fool who will not take control of her own power, and so others will. And when he has drained you at last, the Master will kill you."

She shrank back from him, from his touch. He was still holding her wrist. The Nameless One whispered now. "But I will not allow it," he said. "I have asked for you, and you have been given to me. Give me all I desire, and I will save you."

"I would not be saved by you," Miracle answered. "Not if the King was dead and all hope was gone from this world."

The Nameless One stood abruptly. The buzzing sound in Miracle's ears abruptly ceased. She rested her hand against the wall, her head on her arm. The dungeon wall was cold against her skin; the bandage warm and wet around her wrist.

In the Nameless One's eyes, hunger and scorn mingled. He looked down on her for long minutes during which she wished she could melt into the stones.

"Cling to your hope," he said. "While you still can."

The prison door opened and shut. Miracle closed her eyes and ached: ached from cold, from pain, from the fear tightening around her heart. Hope—in this place? Her heart cried out for Michael.

But the trapdoor remained closed. Michael did not come.

* * *

The air grew warmer as they journeyed south, and the air was heavily tinged with salt. There were more plants growing, and Bear disappeared on long forages, through fields and orchards and winter-brown vineyards.

The brook grew until it became a small river. It ran west toward the sea. So Nicolas followed it, and Marja and Peter followed him, until they found themselves spending the night in a sea town, with ships in the harbour and sailors in the pubs.

And there, in the sea, the river ended.

Nicolas stood at the place where the river poured out into the wide expanse before it. The coastline was gentle. The land jutted up in rocky places, rough patches outnumbered by sand dunes, rock pools, and salt marshes. Nicolas stood, listened, and heard nothing. He knelt down by the flow of water and whispered to it, asked it to speak to him, to tell him what to do. No answer came.

He had failed. And he did not understand why.

Perhaps he had simply taken too long. He had veered off the path to help the captive Gypsies. The River-Daughter had meant for him to come sooner.

Nicolas stood by the water for a long time. When he lifted up his eyes, he saw the ship coming to harbour.

Marja and Peter saw it, too. Marja had climbed to the top of a dune and was looking out to sea with her hand shadowing her eyes. Peter was watching silently, smoking. Together they watched, wonderingly, as the ship drew closer. Then all together they left the dunes and ran to the town, where the whole harbour was asking what it meant.

The ship's sails were black.

It was driving relentlessly in. The fishermen began to jump into the small boats and head for the ship, seeking to find out what cargo black sails signified and whether or not they wished to let it in. They wasted little time. Fishing boats cast away from the shore every minute. Nicolas ran along a sunny deck and threw himself aboard one of them. The fisherman, a small fellow with a balding head, said nothing.

As they neared the ship, Nicolas could see that its sides were battered, its sails patched. The fishermen together began to cry up to the deck. Nicolas joined in: "Throw down your anchor! Let us aboard!"

There was no answer from the ship.

The fishermen drew alongside the ship and called for ropes to be thrown down, but their only answer was the rocking of the waves and the cries of the gulls over the water.

"Can you get closer?" Nicolas asked the fisherman in his whose boat he was sitting. The man nodded. He brought his tiny craft in so close that it nearly bumped the side of the ship.

Nicolas stood unsteadily as the boat rose and fell under his feet. The shadow of the ship blocked out the sun, so he was able to raise his eyes and look over the wooden side carefully. It was pocked with cracks and holes. Nicolas put his foot into one and his hand into another and scrambled up the side of the ship until he dropped over the rail onto the deck.

The salt air filled his senses, but another smell was mingled with it. At first he thought it was the smell of blood, but quickly realized it wasn't. There was something else— something horrible—in the air.

He looked up into the eyes of a dead man.

The man was lashed to the helm. His hands still gripped the spokes, but his dark head was slumped over and his feet were slack on the deck beneath him. His eyes were open and rolled back so that they looked out at the deck even while his head was bent. There was no one else on deck—no one else on board at all, judging from the silence. It was obvious why this man had not answered the call to lower the ropes and welcome the fishermen of Italya on board.

After a moment Nicolas realized that voices were filling the air again. The fishermen were shouting at him, calling to him to lower the ropes and let them up. He tore himself away from the dead man's stare and grabbed coil after coil of rope, dropping the ends over the side. In minutes the fishermen had boarded the black-sailed ship.

When the feet of the first one touched the wooden deck, Nicolas motioned to the helm and said, "There are no answers here. Only questions."

One man looked up at the black sails. "The wind is

carrying us to harbour," he said. He lifted his voice. "Drop anchor!"

The fishermen rushed to obey. One of them shouted to Nicolas, "Boy, cut the man loose! We'll bury him at sea."

Nicolas drew a knife from his waist and advanced on the corpse. To his surprise, the man's skin was still warm. *He has only just died,* he thought, and then he heard a throaty rattle and realized that he was wrong. The man was not dead at all.

He cut the ropes that bound the man and laid him gently on the deck. "Help!" he called. "This man is still alive! Bring help!"

Nicolas stayed by the man, whispering comfort to him, though he suspected the man's ears were useless. His eyes were jaundiced and glazed. They stared straight ahead without any glimmer of life. The ship rocked as the anchor was lowered. Down the deck, three men opened a hatch and lowered themselves into the hold. The peculiar stench of the ship grew stronger, and Nicolas's stomach lurched. He could taste salt and feel the strong sun on his head and neck.

Scarcely five minutes had passed before the men scrambled out of the hold again. Their faces were pale.

"Burn the ship," one of the men croaked.

Another fisherman, a big, bronzed man with curly copper hair, heard him. He lifted up his voice and called for the men to return to land. Feet slapped the deck as men rushed past. Nicolas reached up and caught the sleeve of the copper-haired man.

"This man is alive," he said. "Help me get him into a boat."

The copper-haired man nodded. Together they picked up

the sailor and carried him to the rail, where they set him down and looked over the side to the waiting boats.

"Tie his hands around my neck," said the copper-haired man. "I'll carry him down."

He knelt on the deck, and Nicolas positioned the sailor on the man's back and tied his wrists with a stout rope. The big fisherman stood and took hold of a rope that snaked over the edge of the ship to the boats beneath. He descended first, with Nicolas right behind him. When they had reached the fishing boat, Nicolas untied the half-dead sailor and laid him in the bottom.

The big fisherman took up the oars and prepared to move out onto the water when a fourth man dropped into the boat and sat down without a word. Nicolas recognized him: the man who had called for the burning of the ship. Panic was in his eyes.

They struck out on the water, a strong wind whipping their hair. Shouts lifted as torches were thrust through gaps in the ship's siding. One landed in the sails and began to smoke.

Nicolas watched the burning ship for a long minute. Gulls circled overhead, calling, although not to him. He thought of Maggie and the ship he had burned to save her. There had been death on board that ship also. He had not thought of Maggie in some time, he realized—somehow her memory had faded a little.

He lowered his eyes from the spectacle as the copper-haired sailor demanded of the man across from him, "Well, what was it? Tell us. What was in the hold of the ship?"

The man looked away. "They're all dead. The whole crew."

He was silent for a moment and swallowed twice. "It stank," he said.

"What killed them?" Nicolas asked. The sailor at his feet still stared up out of unseeing eyes; the last vestiges of life still rattled in his throat. There was no wound on the man, no sign of violence at all.

The fisherman answered at last. "Plague," he said.

The copper-haired man looked aghast at him. "Good stars," he said. "And I've taken the man into my boat?"

The sailor's hair was touching Nicolas's foot. Nicolas looked down at the near-corpse and pulled his foot away as a feeling of revulsion swelled up inside of him. The stink of death was in the man's hair, in his clothing. It was in the yellow of his eyes and the breath that scraped from his lips.

Yet there was something about the man that bound him to Nicolas, as strongly as the cords that had bound him to the helm of his black-sailed ship.

The copper-haired fisherman leapt to his feet and grabbed the sailor under the arms, hauling him off the bottom of the boat. Nicolas caught his arm and held it, his eyes flashing.

"What are you doing?" he shouted.

"Sending the plague into the sea," the fishermen answered. With a strong jerk of his arm, he sent Nicolas sprawling backwards. Nicolas caught his breath as the plank seat caught him in the small of the back. His eyes widened as the man he had rescued was thrown over the side.

He jumped up wildly. The copper-haired man struck out at him, catching him in the mouth. Nicolas dodged the man and dove off the side of the fishing boat. The salt water stung the cut at the corner of his mouth. He kicked his way to the sailor's side and gripped him. In moments both their heads broke the surface, and together they gasped for air. Yellow eyes turned on their rescuer. The sailor was awake and aware. His eyes registered terror.

Instinctively Nicolas struck out for the fishing boat, but a heavy keg landed in the water next his head. The fisherman's shout filled his ears. "Keep away," the man ordered, "or I'll bust your head open, fool of a boy! Drown and be done with it!"

Nicolas drew in a deep breath of air and began to swim toward the shore. It was a long way, much longer than it had seemed when he was safely resting in a boat with wooden planks under his feet and the smell of tar and fishing nets in his nostrils. He struck the water in desperation—aiming for the harbour, though in the back of his mind he knew that no welcome would await him there.

The man in his arms dragged him down and back. His eyes had glazed over again; his limbs were loose in the water. It was a mercy, Nicolas thought, that the man could not struggle. Even if they drowned he would not struggle.

By lengths they drew closer to the shore. Nicolas thought he could see hatred in the eyes of those waiting in the harbour, when a fierce current gripped him and bore them back out to sea. Nicolas closed his eyes and let his head fall into the water as the current carried him. He felt his grip on the sailor relaxing and willed himself to tighten it again. They would both drown, yes—but it would still be wrong to let go.

And then he felt a change in the water, almost imperceptible at first. It had grown warm.

A new smell came to him: the smell of fresh water mingling with salt. The water of the river had reached him.

The current flowed in the wrong direction, back toward the shore. The river fought with the sea and won, and Nicolas and his unconscious companion were surrounded by warm water that flowed between their fingers and through the dark, curling hairs of their heads, pulling them closer and closer to the shore. The current bore them west of the harbour. Soon Nicolas lay on the murky ground of the salt marshes, where the river emptied into the sea.

He knelt in the water and pulled the sailor up so that the sick man's head rested against his shoulder, and for a moment he gave in to exhaustion and relief and let a tear fall. The moment was brief, and Nicolas struggled to his feet. He tried to lift the sailor in his arms, but his strength failed him.

There was a shout and a splashing, and Nicolas turned to see Marja and Peter running through the marsh toward him. A long-necked bird, tall and graceful, burst from the reeds at their approach. It lifted into the air on magnificent wings, and Marja slowed for an instant to whistle a greeting. The bird dipped its wings to her and sailed on to the dunes.

"Help me," Nicolas gasped. "I can't carry him alone."

Peter took the man's feet while Nicolas took his shoulders. They lifted him from the water and carried him while the mud sucked at their feet. Nicolas stumbled, and Marja pushed him out of the way, taking the man from him.

"Walk," she ordered. "You've brought him far enough."

When they reached the edge of the marsh, Nicolas turned his eyes back to the flatland. He stood with his feet ankle-deep in mud and looked out over the reeds and murk to the blue sea.

"Where are you?" he whispered. "Tell me how to find you. I want to free you—I'm here."

There was no answer. Nicolas bowed his head and turned away. He took three more steps toward the sand dunes and turned back once again.

"Thank you," he said. His voice was clear and strong. Marja looked out over the marsh, but no answer met her ears—or his.

The burning ship beyond the harbour sent clouds of smoke into the sky. They mixed with other clouds: a storm was brewing. A cold wind whipped through the sand dunes and made the going harder. Sand coated Nicolas's hair and face and clothing. It clung to Marja's skirt and got into Peter's pipe, even as it closed in around their feet as they tried to walk.

The sailor in their arms continued to breathe and stare, but gave no other sign that he was alive.

They made it underneath a pier before the storm broke. There, they rested on the wet sand left behind by the tide. Marja and Peter laid the sick man down on the highest part of the ground. Nicolas stretched out and fell promptly asleep.

Peter looked down on them and shook his pipe ruefully. Grains of sand retained their stubborn residence and kept him from lighting it. Marja sat down by Nicolas's head and let her eyes rest first on one of the sleepers, then on the other. Her fingers moved to Nicolas's hair, and she flicked grains of sand from it while rain drummed on the pier overhead.

"Odd, isn't it?" Peter asked.

"What?" Marja asked.

"Look at them," Peter said. "They could be the same man. A boy beside his future."

Marja shivered. "No," she said. But she saw it as well as Peter did. The dark, curly hair—jet black in the one, greying in the other; the lanky form, the set of the jaw. The lines in

Nicolas's forehead were only deepened in the older man.

She noticed, suddenly, that the sailor's lips were moving. He was talking to himself deliriously, and she leaned closer to hear what he was saying. She grew pale at his words, but had no time to think over them before Peter grunted and fell to the sandy ground beside her.

A voice said, "Stand up slow, Gypsy. You're under arrest."

6

Under and Around

In Pravik, under the ground, it was cold and numbingly grey.

Maggie sat by one of many small fires and warmed her hands through worn wool gloves, her fingers poking through at the tips. She followed the smoke with her eyes as it curled up through cracks in the ceiling, drawn out to the world above. She was thinking, as she often did. There was little else to do.

Pat was stretched on the rock beside her, twisting a piece of string around her fingers. She looked up and regarded her friend.

"Penny for your thoughts."

Maggie looked up from the flames. "Hmmm? Oh, it's nothing."

Pat sat up and drew her long legs underneath her. "Don't give me that. What are you thinking of, Maggie Sheffield? Fields of posies and hills of green?"

Maggie laughed. "No."

"Are you thinking about him?" Pat said. Her voice was gentler now.

Maggie nodded and covered her mouth with the heel of her hand, resting her fingers against the side of her cheek. When did she ever not think of him? Jerome had created a new place in her and then left it empty. Empty, aching, and daily more confused.

"You have to let go someday," Pat said.

"Of what?" Maggie asked. "I don't even understand why I loved him—if love is the word. He wasn't just a man to me. He was—all this."

Pat raised an eyebrow. "Dark, cold places underground?"

Maggie smiled. "You know what I mean. All these changes —this colony—the fight against the Blackness. He was going to change the world." Her voice grew very soft. "I was going to help him."

"We'll change things yet," Pat said. "They won't keep us underground forever. I know, though—that doesn't mean it doesn't hurt when some dreams don't come true."

Maggie was still looking at her hands. Dreams. She'd had a dream once—a dream in which Jerome had left her behind, had left her to fall back into the darkness while he flew to the light. She bit her lip. She wished there had been more to the dream. Some sign for her waking hours—some pathway to the light.

"Maybe they'll come true yet," she said.

Pat drew herself closer so that the firelight brought colour to her face and played in her short dark hair. "When the King comes?" she said.

"Yes. Or when we go to him."

"'Beyond the sky,' is that the phrase? The professor always uses it. It's very poetic."

"That's the one," Maggie said.

"The professor's been quiet lately," Pat said. She picked at the string in her hands. "I don't think he's well."

Maggie tilted her head up and looked at the solid grey ceiling above her. "The ground weighs on him. On everyone." She sighed. "Sometimes I don't believe the sun is up there at all anymore."

"Of course it's up there," Pat said. "But it's lonely for us, I'll bet. Up there all it has to keep it company is the Emperor and his minions."

Maggie chuckled. "What a terrible thought."

A young boy appeared in the light of the fire and bowed. His voice was hoarse from the cold, and he spoke with the accents of an Eastern farmer.

"A message from Professor Huss," he said. "He wishes to see you at the Upper North Gate."

"We'll come at once," Maggie said.

* * *

The Upper North Gate was not a gate at all, but a maze of tunnels near the surface of the ground. The rebels knew the way through to an entrance on the hillside, outside the wall of the City of Bridges. It was the usual entrance of the refugees and adventurers who had come to join them since the Battle of Pravik. The Ploughman had posted guards in the maze to see to it that friends found their way in and enemies did not. With High Police patrolling the mountains, the Ploughman had forbidden his people from going all the way outside.

Maggie and Pat joined Jarin Huss at the entrance to the Gate. An intoxicating scent tugged at Maggie's senses as she reached it, the smell of *outside*—of people whose hair and clothes still smelled like snow and wind and mountains, of horses, mud, and sweat.

The Gate was full of ragged Gypsies. One of them was deep in conference with Professor Huss. Huss smiled as Maggie and Pat approached. He held out his arms to them and greeted them like daughters.

"This young gentleman has told me a very interesting story," Huss said. "It seems that he and his people were rescued by an extraordinary young man and two Gypsy companions."

Maggie's heart jumped, and she fought to keep a smile from her face. It was no use smiling until she knew for sure.

"Nicolas?" she asked.

"I do not doubt it," Huss said.

"And his companions?" Maggie asked.

"A young man and a young woman," said a voice from the shadows. The Gypsy leader called the Major stepped into the torchlight. His eyes were dark in his bearded face. His shoulders had lost nothing of their broadness; his stature nothing of its height. Even so, the Major was paler and thinner than when Maggie had first met him. Life underground was not easy on anyone, but of the community of rebels and refugees who lived under Pravik, the Gypsies suffered most from their deprivation.

The Major clapped a big hand on the young Gypsy's shoulder. "Darne here says the young man smoked a pipe and the young woman was very reckless and beautiful." He winked.

"Nicolas likes to be alone, but it would seem that our friends have found him."

Maggie stopped trying to hold back her smile. "Then Marja and Peter are also alive?"

"And wandering the roads of Italya," the Major said.

"Italya?"

"Yes," Huss said. "Nicolas has gone south."

"How is that other fellow coming along?" the Major asked. "The one you think Nicolas rescued and sent to us by the strange doctor."

"He is well," Maggie said. "The wound was a bad one, but Libuse's tendings have kept infection away. He'll be whole again before long."

The Major inclined his dark head. "We are much indebted to the Ploughman's Lady for the care she takes for our people."

"They're not just your people, Major," Maggie said. "Down here we all belong to each other."

Her eyes strayed to the refugees huddled in the Gate. They were thin and filthy, and their Italyan clothes did little to keep out the cold.

A rustle in the tunnel announced a new approach, and Libuse entered the Gate. Her clothing, once fine, was drab and ragged, but her carriage was nothing less than regal. Rich brown hair hung down her back in a thick braid. She inclined her head to the young Gypsy leader, who bowed.

"Princess," said the Major, "this lad is Darne. He led the band you see here."

"He has done well," Libuse said. "You are welcome here, with all who seek refuge from the Empire."

Darne lifted his eyes. "Thank you, my lady."

"Now," Libuse said, "it looks as though some of you could use bandaging after the tender care of the High Police. Major, you will take them to the northwest cavern for me?"

"Right away, my lady" the Major said.

"I'll be off to the kitchens," Pat said. "I'm willing to bet that by the time you're finished binding up their wounds, they'll be more than ready for a bite to eat."

Darne roused his entourage to their feet, and the Major led them away through the tunnels to the northwest. Libuse followed behind them, with Maggie and the professor at her side. Pat disappeared in the opposite direction. A young rebel carried a torch before them.

"The Ploughman returns soon, I believe?" Huss asked.

"I hope so," Libuse said.

"These excursions are necessary. If we continue to bring in refugees, we will soon outgrow our refuge."

"I know," Libuse said, managing a smile. "But there is a knot in my stomach every time he leads our men deeper into the ground. It is so dark here. Sometimes it seems that all that stands between us and nothingness is the torchlight. The Ploughman takes his torch, and descends where I cannot see him—and then I wonder if he is there at all, or if he has truly disappeared." She laughed a little. "I know that sounds ridiculous."

"No," Maggie said. "Not at all."

They went on in silence until the tunnel widened into a stone hall, and then into a high-roofed cavern. Torches blazed in the walls, lighting numerous makeshift cots where the sick and injured lay. They smiled and reached out for Libuse as she passed by. She stretched her own hand out and touched their fingers gently, whispering comfort.

A stout woman greeted them as they entered. "Here, Princess! Maggie!" Mrs. Cook said. "Look who's walking!"

A thin Gypsy, his chest and shoulder swathed in bandages, approached slowly with a wan smile. Libuse smiled back and took his hand in hers.

"It is healing nicely," she said. "The Major will be pleased to hear it. He has been wondering how long it will be till he has you on his task force."

The man stood a little straighter. "I'll be ready to work in no time," he said.

"I'm sure you will." Libuse turned and kissed the stout woman on the cheek. "Is this your doing, Mrs. Cook? I'm sure I said he wasn't to be out of bed for another three days at least."

"That you did," Mrs. Cook said. "You were wrong, and don't tell me you're not tickled pink to know it." Mrs. Cook surveyed the other two sternly. "Maggie, how is your cold?"

"Fine," Maggie said. "My throat still hurts a bit."

"Cup of tea would fix that," Mrs. Cook said. She sighed. "Why no one brought tea down with them I'll never know," she said. "My own stash is nearly gone. I'm saving it for emergencies. Professor!"

Professor Huss stood up straight, startled.

"You look pale."

He smiled. "I imagine we're all a good deal whiter than we used to be."

"True," Mrs. Cook said. "But you look worse than most of us. Are you eating?"

"Very well," Huss said.

"See that you keep it up," Mrs. Cook said. "We're not out of food yet."

"Thank the King, no, we're not," Huss said. A shade crossed his face as he spoke. They yet lived on the stores brought down by the farmers of Pravik and the spoil looted from the city after the battle, but no one believed it would last forever.

Other women, once the mothers, wives, and daughters of farmers and tradesmen, now themselves warriors in the fight against cold, dark, and death, were already tending to Darne and his people. Libuse watched them for a minute and hurried to help when a child began to wail. Mrs. Cook slipped her arm around Maggie's waist.

In a moment there was a clatter in the tunnels, and a voice carried down the stone passages: "The Ploughman has returned!"

* * *

They sat together around a low table in the Ploughman's alcove, using cloaks as cushions on the rock. The Ploughman dipped a hunk of brown bread into his watery soup and ate with evident satisfaction.

"The caverns and tunnels below aren't as extensive as they are on this level," he said, "but they will offer us relief from the cramped spaces here. The men have mapped out a good portion. On our next trip down we'll begin to make the caverns ready for occupation. It shouldn't take more than a few days."

"Then you'll be leaving again soon?' Libuse asked.

"Soon enough." He put down his food and looked at Huss, seated next to Maggie on the other side of the table. His voice lowered. "Professor," he said, "are you aware that there is another level below the one we just explored?"

Huss blinked. "No," he said. "I was surprised to discover one below this."

The Ploughman nodded his head. "I thought as much," he said. "But it's true. We uncovered more than one passage leading down through the mountain. I don't know how far they go. When I am peering down them, it seems to me that they might go on forever."

"That they might," Jarin Huss said. He frowned. "I'm not sure I like the thought."

"That is not all we discovered," the Ploughman said. "There is evidence that we are not the first colony to settle underground."

"What?" Libuse asked.

"Carvings, stairways, sconces," the Ploughman said. "All of them very old. In a few places there are words carved into the walls that must date before the Empire, for they are not written in our language."

"Fascinating," said the professor. "I should very much like to see that."

"You shall," the Ploughman said. "Come with us on our next journey."

Huss took a drink from a clay mug. "Perhaps I will."

"More refugees came today," Libuse said.

"Gypsies?" asked the Ploughman.

"Yes. Fifteen of them. Six are in the sick ward. The others are under the Major's care."

"It is good we went deeper when we did," the Ploughman said. "We'll be needing the extra space very soon."

His face looked drawn and severe. Maggie's heart moved for him. Once a farmer, then a warrior, the Ploughman belonged in the open air with the sword of freedom in his hand. But he had buried himself here for the sake of his people, his ever-growing colony. Under the leadership of the Ploughman and Libuse, the underground city had become a refuge for the oppressed, a place where all men were given a voice. Pravik was the capital city of a whole new world, born of one miraculous battle, out from under the thumb of Athrom and everything that was wrong in the Empire.

Maggie remembered a discussion among the leaders one night shortly after they had gone underground.

"We are everything Athrom is not," Huss had said. "You must be everything the Emperor is not—a leader who leads out of compassion and conviction."

"But what good can we do here?" the Ploughman had asked.

"All the good we can do. If Athrom is a place of darkness in the sun, then Pravik must be a place of light in the darkness. It is not our surroundings that matter now, my friend. New worlds are born in the hearts of men. Look to your heart—to all our hearts."

And he had, Maggie thought. The Ploughman and his lady had given the people hope and freedom. Yet, the underground was no place for brave hearts. And she remembered Huss's final words.

"The time will come. We will go above again."

They would have to, Maggie knew. Food would run out. Space would grow too tight. And then—well, who knew what would happen then?

The Ploughman stood and turned his back on the company. "Excuse me," he said. He began to move toward the door, but the others stood and vacated the alcove before he could. Maggie cast a compassionate glance on him as she left.

Libuse, who had not gone, stood and touched his hand gently.

"What is it?" she whispered.

"We cannot burrow forever," he said. "I have no wish to bury the people alive, Libuse."

"There is nothing else you can do," she said. "We are waiting, that is all. Waiting until something changes, as it will —as it must. Strengthening our hearts. In the right time you will lead us up again."

The Ploughman covered Libuse's hand with his long fingers. His ruby ring glinted deeply in the torchlight. He closed his eyes.

"I am not enough for them, Libuse," he said. "I am not enough for any of you."

Libuse began to protest, but he stopped her. "Huss and Virginia are right, with all their mystic dreams. We need the King. He must come again."

Libuse hesitated. "Are you sure that he exists?" she asked.

He looked at her for a long time, the gentle love in his eyes making his worry-lined face less severe. "I am not sure of anything," he said at last. "Only of our need."

* * *

Maggie walked alone through the underground passageways. Her feet passed over lit stone and stone plunged in darkness, but she hardly noticed the difference. She walked through tunnels where the walls glistened with water and the roar of the river could be heard close by. The black waters of the Vltava flowed on the other side of the rock walls. The lights of fifteen bridges sparkled on it. The longing to see it was nearly overpowering, and Maggie leaned up against the wet wall for support.

"You're a long way from the others," said a voice. Maggie looked up in surprise. As her eyes adjusted to the darkness, she made out the form of Virginia Ramsey a few feet away, her green eyes looking out at nothing.

"So are you," Maggie said.

"I am often alone," Virginia pointed out. "You are not." She took an unsteady step forward, her hand on the wall. Her other hand reached out for Maggie. Maggie took it in her own.

"What are you doing here?" Maggie asked.

"Dreaming," Virginia said. "As you are."

"Yes," Maggie said with a rueful smile. "Why else would I seek out the darkness?"

"Is it dark here? More than other places?" Virginia asked. "I suppose it must be."

Virginia took Maggie's arm, and they walked back through the passage, away from the rush of the river. Maggie watched the Highlander at her side, wondering about her. Everyone wondered about Virginia Ramsey, for no one really knew her —not even Mrs. Cook, who held the blind girl in a sort of affectionate awe. Virginia's wrists were still scarred from the iron of the High Police. Her bearing was still haunted by ghosts and visions no one else could even begin to imagine. And her dark hair still smelled of the wind.

Maggie thought of the day she had first met the blind seer of the Highlands. On that day, they had buried Jerome.

She drew a deep breath, and Virginia stopped walking.

"What's wrong?" she asked.

"When is the King coming?" Maggie asked. "Have you seen that? How long until the Seventh World is free?"

"Soon," Virginia said.

"Yes," Maggie said. "That's what the professor says. When people ask me, it's what I say. But the truth is I don't know. When I heard the horn of the Huntsman over Pravik, and the Golden Riders came and fought our enemies, I thought the King would come then. But he didn't."

Pain lay stark in Virginia's face. She laid her hand on Maggie's, and the touch was achingly gentle. "What are you afraid of, Maggie?" Virginia asked.

Maggie bit her lip. "Have we done something?" she asked. "Is he waiting for us to—to do more, to bring him back somehow? I fear that he no longer desires to come. We are all discouraged. Even the professor doubts. I've seen it. Yours are the only clear eyes in this new world of ours, Virginia. Can you tell me the truth?"

Virginia hesitated. Slowly, she said, "My eyes are not as clear as they once were. You cannot rely on me, Maggie. You must not. I may not always see."

Maggie stared at the seer. "But—Virginia, you are our eyes. Professor Huss says so. Without you we are blind!"

"No," Virginia said. "Without me you have to trust. Trust is not blindness. It is the truest sight. Trust disregards illusion and holds fast to truth. What do you know, Maggie Sheffield? What have *you* seen?"

Maggie swallowed. "I saw the Huntsman begin his chase. Begin to rout evil. I saw the King's deliverance in the battle."

"Cling to that," Virginia said. She smiled. "We all must cling to something, and what you have seen is no small thing."

"I wish that Nicolas was here," Maggie said. "Or at least that he had come to believe before he left."

"Do not fear for him," Virginia said. "I think—I think I have seen that he is well."

"You think?" Maggie asked.

Virginia nodded slowly. She began to walk again. They moved silently through the dripping corridor. Torchlight fell on their path as they entered more commonly traveled paths.

"The King has not forgotten us," Virginia said suddenly. "He has not forgotten you, or any who have been faithful. The earth is awakening even now. That much I *know* I have seen."

And Maggie felt a chill in her spine, for as she listened to the words it seemed to her that the wild scent of the wind was stronger about Virginia than ever before.

* * *

Marja stood slowly. Her dark eyes flashed as she turned. There were five men; too many to fight. Her fingers itched to draw the jeweled dagger from beneath her skirt, but wisdom prevailed. She could not overcome the men now, and the dagger would be needed later.

The men were rough in appearance and dripping from the rain. There was not a single soldier among them.

"By what right do you pretend to arrest me?" Marja demanded.

"By the right to reward," said one of the men, a short stocky fellow with two days' stubble on his chin. "A silver coin for every Gypsy brought in."

Marja arched an eyebrow. "Is that all?" she asked. "Life is cheap these days."

Peter groaned and raised himself to his knees beside Marja, holding the back of his head with one hand. Behind them, neither Nicolas nor the stranger stirred.

The man who had spoken gestured to his fellows, and they moved forward. Two hauled Peter off the ground and held his arms while another grabbed Marja's wrist. She wrenched it free with a quick motion, and the man flushed.

"Don't touch me," she snapped.

The fifth man had approached Nicolas and the sailor, and now he stood up with a pale face. "Something's wrong with this 'un," he said.

"Right you are," Peter said, his voice groggy. "He's sick."

"What do you mean, sick?" said the leader of the men.

Marja smiled and sidestepped the man who lunged for her arm again. "Plague," she said.

The men holding Peter looked at each other nervously. The man who had attempted to grab Marja took a step away from her. "You ain't sick, are you?" he asked.

She sidled closer and breathed in his face. "Wouldn't you like to know," she said.

The feverish sailor groaned. Marja turned to see that Nicolas had risen to his hands and knees. He looked somehow smaller than usual; frailer. He crawled forward and fell with his face to the ground, inches from the men who held Peter. Both men let go and scurried away.

The leader cleared his throat. "Enough of this," he said. "No more foolery. You're coming with us."

One of the men, the one who had tried to take Marja captive, shook his head. "They ain't worth it," he said. "Count me out." He turned and ran from the pier.

The two men who had held Peter inched closer to their leader. Suddenly, Nicolas rose to his knees again and launched himself at one of them. He caught the man by the ankles and began to kiss his sandy feet.

"Please help me," he groaned. "Doctor . . . take me with you!"

The man tried to jerk his feet away, but Nicolas held tight. His companion looked wild-eyed at their leader.

"Let's go!" he said.

"Four silver pieces!" said the leader.

"And we'll all die!" said the man who had just succeeded in wrenching free of Nicolas.

Marja's eyes glinted. "Life is cheap," she said.

The men looked at each other, and the two subordinates bolted away. The leader looked back, his face angry and red, and his eyes widened to see the dagger Marja now held in her hand. She twirled the blade through her fingers. The man stood for a moment longer before he turned and chased after his companions.

Marja threw herself into a cross-legged position on the ground and applauded.

"Magnificent performance," she said.

Nicolas grinned and bowed his head, spitting a bit of sand from his mouth. "It was nothing," he said.

Peter was still standing, watching the horizon where the men had disappeared. "That was close," he said. "Why would they look for us here?"

Marja shrugged. "Likely they only wanted shelter from the rain. They must have felt lucky."

Peter smiled and stuck his pipe in his mouth, frowning when he remembered it was still full of wet sand. "Until they found out we had pestilence on our side."

Peter sat down, and they grew quiet.

"Do we?" Marja said finally. "Or will that be us in a few days?" She gestured at the sick man. "If it is plague, the odds are . . ."

"Maybe we should leave him." Nicolas spoke the words abruptly. "He's going to die, that much is obvious. Perhaps it's best we leave him here. The tide will usher him out of this world with more courtesy than the plague will."

"Could you leave him?" Marja asked.

Nicolas shook his head and looked down. "No."

"Then maybe we should start digging our own graves," Peter said.

"We're practically dead already," Marja said. "A piece of silver each—stars, what a world we live in!"

"Don't tell me you're ready to give up on it," Nicolas said. "You haven't saved your people yet."

"It will take something far greater than me to save our people," Marja said.

Nicolas closed his eyes. That song was in his head again—

vague and faint and tantalizing. "It would take the King," he said.

Marja was drawing circles in the sand. "He is the sun-king, the moon-king, all-the-stars-king," she said in a sing-song voice. "And he shines like them all together."

"That's from one of your old stories, isn't it?" Peter asked.

"Mmm," Marja said. "The one about the birds."

"You know," Nicolas said, opening his eyes, "some people think the 'all-the-stars-king' is more than a myth."

Marja gave him a long look. "I hope he is," she said. "Because we could use his help."

"Maggie thinks he's real," Nicolas said. "She thinks he's coming back."

"Do you think so?" Marja asked.

"I don't know," Nicolas said.

Marja shook her head. "You astound me," she said.

"What do you mean by that?"

The sick man suddenly cried out and twisted in pain, and in the midst of his groaning they all heard the words.

"My son, my son. Nicolas, my son."

* * *

When the rain stopped, Nicolas left the little group under the pier and went into the town. He skulked in shadows and hovered in doorways, listening, and watched with great satisfaction as a wagon driver sat in a tavern and drank himself into a stupor. His wagon, roofed and sided, was full of hay. Nicolas rushed back to the pier and gathered up the others. Peter tied the sick man's arms around Nicolas's neck, and they crept through the scant afternoon population in the town and into the hay wagon.

It took only a short time for Marja and Peter to unload much of the wagon's cargo into the feeding troughs in the nearby stable. The horses which would draw the boxed wagon were happy to help dispose of it. Once they had made room for themselves, Nicolas and his little band burrowed toward the back of the wagon and heaped up hay next to the door. If the wagoner opened the door to check on his cargo, he would see nothing amiss.

It was hot and stuffy in the wagon. Hay dust settled in their noses and irritated their skin. Marja took off her head scarf and covered the sick man's mouth with it so he wouldn't breathe too much dust. Peter lay back in the hay with a sigh and went to work cleaning his pipe. Nicolas drew his knees to his chest and looked up at the wagon's dusty ceiling, through the cracks where a few rays of sun managed to shine.

"Where are we going?" Marja asked. She cleared her throat from the dust.

"Further south," Nicolas said. "Into vineyard country."

"What do you hope to find there?" Marja asked.

"Shelter," Nicolas answered. "It's winter; the vineyards must have outbuildings that aren't occupied in the off-season. We'll find one and stay in it."

The sick man groaned and stirred, displacing the scarf from his mouth. Marja repositioned it.

"He's becoming very active," she said.

"Maybe he'll wake up soon," Peter said.

"Maybe he'll die soon," said Nicolas.

They heard the sound of muffled voices and so fell silent. The wagon rolled forward slightly as the horses were put into the harness, and the companions relaxed into the hay as the wagoner shouted a command and they moved out.

They didn't speak as they journeyed. There was little risk of the driver hearing them; the clatter of the wheels and the muffling of the hay would drown out their voices. Still, they did not wish to take a chance. So they went in silence. The faint sunlight through the cracks painted golden stripes on the hay and on the passengers; it illuminated the dust that never quite settled. Peter finally managed to light his pipe, and he lay in the hay smoking it thoughtfully. Nicolas watched the sick man as they went, and Marja watched Nicolas; and not once did their eyes meet.

Nicolas wasn't sure when he fell asleep, but there in the closeness of the wagon he began to dream. In his dream he saw men and women, but they were unlike any human beings he had ever seen. The beauty of their faces made Nicolas want to cry. The grace of their movements was like the grace of the stars, tracing their dances in the sky. They wore clothing of all the colours of the rainbow: long, flowing, shimmering gowns and robes; and in their faces was a golden joy, a peace and innocence that brought Nicolas's heart to its knees, although he did not physically kneel—he was asleep, unable to wake himself up and unwilling to do so.

When they spoke, he knew their voices. He had heard them before: the dying, mourning voices of the Veil. Only now, in his dream, they were not dying. They were strong and beautiful as they had been long ago. He watched them as they moved together in a sort of dance, their robes flowing a

122

rainbow behind them. They spoke to each other, and he understood the words, but could not hold them—one moment they were in his ears, and he knew what they meant, and the next minute the words were gone and he could not recall them.

But then they turned to him, and one of them, a man with long silver hair and eyes like crystal, with a thousand glimmering colours held within his gaze, spoke.

"You must learn the Song of the Burning Light, child of man," he said.

"I can't hear it," Nicolas heard himself answer. "It is too far away."

"It grows closer," said the man. "Open your heart to it. Let the song fill you."

"I can't," said Nicolas.

A woman spoke, the grandest lady Nicolas had ever seen, with shining black hair and a long shimmering gown of white. "The enemy wants you," she said. "You must learn the song before they reach you."

Nicolas wanted to speak, but words stuck in his throat. The man spoke again.

"You have a task to finish," he said.

"I couldn't do it," Nicolas said. "I looked for her, but I could not find her. I have already failed in the task."

"You have not failed," the man answered. "The River-Daughter is kept in a far, deep place. She will not be freed until the Song of the Burning Light calls to her. You must be cleansed by fire and brought to the water."

"I don't even know what you mean," Nicolas said. "Please, I cannot do this."

"The River-Daughter has led you wisely thus far," the woman said. "Now you must use the gifts she has given you. They will awaken the song in you."

"Will you help me?" Nicolas cried.

The beautiful ones looked at one another. Infinite sadness marked their faces.

"We can no longer be of any help to the children of men," they said. "Our last sacrifice wanes even now."

"You are dying," Nicolas said. "I have heard it."

"We are fading away," said the woman. "We are no longer as you see us—we are not what we once were."

"What were you?" Nicolas asked.

"We were called the Shearim," said the man.

And Nicolas woke up.

Marja was asleep. Her black hair cascaded down to touch the face of the sick man.

There was a song, terribly faint, in Nicolas's ears. He strained to hear it, but it only seemed to move farther away. *Open your heart,* they had said. *Use the gifts you have been given.*

"How?" he asked aloud. "What gifts?"

But there was no answer.

7

Choosing Sides

KRIS OF THE MOUNTAINS awoke with a start when a boot prodded his stomach. He reached for his sword, swallowing a shout at the sound of Michael's impatient voice.

"Hush," Michael said. "I need your help."

Kris sat up. Stocky was already awake, blinking away sleep and fingering his sword hilts. The lame grey wolf lay with its head on its paws and its eyes wide open, seemingly listening to Michael.

"There's a tunnel into the dungeon," Michael said. "Miracle is there. I've seen her."

"How did you find it?" Kris asked.

"The white wolf led me," Michael said. "I am not sure what happened—but he did. They've done something to Miracle. She's too weak to get out through the tunnel. We can go in that way, but we're going to have to find another way out."

Kris rubbed his bearded chin. "Perhaps if we disguise ourselves," he said.

"As what?" Stocky asked. "Traveling tinkers?"

"Soldiers," Kris said. "We could ambush a few and take their uniforms."

"We would be recognized," Michael said.

"Do you have a better idea?" Kris asked.

Somewhere below, a twig snapped. They fell silent, every muscle tense.

"Someone's down there," Stocky whispered.

"Now might be a good time to put our plan into action," Kris said.

"Unless they're coming to ambush us," said Michael.

"If they are, they've failed," Kris said.

The three men drew their swords and crept away from their small camp. The grey wolf rose and limped after them.

Michael split off from the others and made his way down a natural stairway to the base of the cliff. Even in the darkness, a black figure stood out starkly against the snow. The man in black did not seem to hear him, and Michael rushed forward suddenly and pressed the tip of his sword into the small of the man's back.

"Do not move," he whispered.

"Keep quiet," said the black-robed man. "I am your captive."

Michael moved around his prisoner so that his sword pointed at the man's heart. Their eyes met. Michael recognized the younger of the black-robed men who had taken Miracle. His eyes were strangely calm.

"You do not need your sword," said the man. "I will go with you willingly."

"How do I know that?" Michael asked.

"Because if I was not a willing prisoner," the man said, "you and your friends would already be dead."

Kris and Stocky appeared out of the night, the grey wolf with them. Kris cast a questioning look at Michael.

"Let's take him to the camp," Michael said. "I want to talk to him."

The man smiled coldly. "You are very kind," he said.

They made their way back up the cliff through a lightly falling snow. Michael kept his sword pointed at the black-robed man's back, but the prisoner paid no attention to it. He showed not a shade of fear.

When they reached the small camp on the cliff, the black-robed man looked around him. "You have done well to find this place," he said. "It is well-hidden and off the road; I cannot think how you did it."

"Sit," Michael said.

"You do not need to play captor," said the man. "I am here willingly. Remember that." He sat down next to the remains of the campfire. "You have come to free the girl. I will help you."

"Why?" Michael asked.

"Because I owe her a debt," the man answered. His voice grew low so that Michael could barely hear it. "And because she does not belong here."

"Who are you?" Michael asked. "I will not work with a stranger." He held out his strong hand. "I am Michael O'Roarke, chief of the Clann O'Roarke of the Green Isle."

The black-robed man looked at Michael's hand for a long time before taking it. "My name," he said, his tongue faltering, "is Christopher Ens."

"And I am Kris of the Mountains," said Kris. He stepped closer to the fire, his battle axe in his hands.

"Stephen O'Roarke," said Stocky, inclining his head. "Stocky."

"Well then," said Christopher, "now that we are known to one another, let us get to work."

"Wait," Stocky interrupted. "Where's our proof that you're our friend?"

"I am not," Christopher said. "The Order makes no friends, only pawns for its own use. But I want to use you to get Miracle out, and I do not think you object."

"There is a way into the dungeon," Michael said. He silenced Stocky's objections with a look. "A tunnel. We can go in that way, but not out—Miracle is too weak, and there is no room to carry her. We thought we might disguise ourselves as soldiers. Get out of the stronghold that way."

Christopher shook his head. "It would never work," he said. "The soldiers in Ordna know each other well. A stranger would never get past the gates. Besides, if you all go in through the tunnel, you will simply give us three more prisoners. You need a way to open the cell door, and that is no easy task."

"Then what do you suggest?" Michael asked.

"I will arrest you," said Christopher, looking at Michael as he spoke.

"Are you out of your mind?" Michael asked.

"Not at all," Christopher said. "I will arrest you and escort you to Miracle's cell. Your friends will be waiting there, having come up through the tunnels, and together the three of you will overpower the guards—and me, as it must not look as though I helped you. You will take the girl and run for the gates."

"And we will not be opposed on our way out?" Michael asked.

"Of course you will," Christopher said. "You must move quickly. The guards may be too slow to act. If not, you must fight your way out. But I will see to it that the gate is opened for you. You will be outnumbered, but with speed and surprise you may well succeed. Once you are outside the gates, I have ways to make sure you are not found."

There was silence as the companions thought it over. Michael looked to Kris.

"I do not see any other way," Kris rumbled.

"Aye, Michael," said Stocky. "I'm willing."

Michael clapped Stocky's shoulder. "As ever," he said. "And I am willing. We will trust you, Christopher Ens."

The young man in black nodded. "You may be sorry you did," he said. "But I will do all I can for you. I have only one demand."

"What is it?" Michael asked.

"Even if the battle overwhelms you," Christopher said, "do not play the coward. Do not surrender. Get Miracle out. If you fail, you will answer to me."

Michael smiled. "Your demand does you credit," he said.

Christopher Ens stood and pulled his black cowl over his head. "When the sun has risen there," he said, pointing at the sky, "come down unarmed to the frozen stream near the gates of Ordna. I will arrest you there. You two must go to the dungeon at the same time, through the tunnel. See that no one discovers you before we arrive."

Kris nodded. The lame wolf whined. Christopher turned and disappeared in the snow.

"We're crazy to trust him," Stocky said.

"We have no choice," Michael said.

"We have one choice," said Kris. "We could give up."

"No we couldn't," Michael said. His eyes flashed. "Never that."

Kris smiled. His blue eyes were hard. "Good," he said. "I wanted to be sure we were all together in that."

Stocky was the only one of the three who managed to sleep more that night. Kris spent the late hours of the morning sharpening his sword on a bit of flint, and Michael spent it staring into the embers of the fire and listening to he knew not what. The sun had nearly risen to the place Christopher had pointed out when a distant wolf howl filled the air. The lame wolf lifted its head and answered the call. The sound rose and fell eerily in the camp. Stocky sat up and met Michael's eyes.

"Time," he said.

"Aye," Michael answered.

They stamped out the last of the fire and rose to go. At the bottom of the cliff, they separated. Michael took his sword from his back and handed it over to Kris. The lame wolf stayed above. It lay at the edge of the cliff and watched the men.

* * *

Michael's legs felt weak as he knelt by the frozen stream. Inwardly he cursed himself— now was no time for weakness! The clearing was silent except for the faint tinkle of water beneath the ice. Michael closed his eyes and drew a deep

130

breath of the cold air. He should not have sent both Kris and Stocky away. One of them should have stayed to guard his back. Christopher Ens might well be a traitor.

No, Michael thought. *He is no traitor. He is a strange friend, but a friend nonetheless.*

Michael turned at the sound of footfalls in the snow. Christopher Ens was coming. A torch burned in his hand.

But no—there was no torch. As Christopher drew nearer, Michael could see that the fire burned in his bare hand. Michael began to rise, his hand half-raised in greeting, but then his eyes met Christopher's. The look of hatred there halted him.

Michael tensed to spring, sure that he had been betrayed, when Christopher clenched his fingers and flung them open. A bolt of fire slashed Michael's face from the corner of his mouth to his temple. Michael staggered at the pain. He covered the wound with his hand. Blood ran through his fingers, but the slash was hot, still burning. Beneath his fingers, the blood staunched, and the skin around the wound became crusted and black.

Christopher closed his hand, and the fire went out. When Michael met his eyes this time, there was nothing in them. They were utterly blank.

"Now we have proof of a struggle," Christopher said. "Come. They will not suspect us."

Michael rose warily, resentful of the word "us"—he was not pleased to be joined with such a man. He allowed Christopher to bind his hands and place a hand on his shoulder. The heat of Christopher's black-stained palm burned even through Michael's thick winter cloak and shirt.

Christopher shoved Michael forward, and the young chieftain staggered as he walked. The wound on his face still stung, and he winced at a blast of icy wind. They reached the gates of Ordna within minutes.

"Open for the Order!" Christopher called.

Michael heard the sound of men hurrying to obey. The wooden gates swung open. Chains rattled as the iron grid was pulled up, and High Police surrounded the men as they entered the courtyard. Michael glared at them, but said nothing. A man wearing a captain's insignia reached out to take Michael's arm.

"Leave him," Christopher snapped. "He is a prisoner of the Order."

"Another one?" one of the soldiers called out. "And here we've hardly had a look at the last one!"

The soldiers jeered and laughed. Michael hung his head for a moment, inwardly seething. In that moment, the voices of the soldiers died out as if they had been choked. A chill ran through Michael's veins. He lifted his head and found himself looking at another man, whose face, shadowed though it was by a black hood, he would have known anywhere. It was the cruel face of the man who had led Miracle's arrest.

"Well, well," said the Nameless One, stepping closer to Michael. "What have you brought us, little brother?"

"Surely you remember him," Christopher said.

"Indeed," said the Nameless One with a smile. "Amazing that he should have followed her all the way here. What do you think? Shall we kill him in front of her so that she might know how dearly her freedom was lost?"

Michael tightened his jaw, but said nothing.

"I have reason to believe he may be of use to us," Christopher said.

The Nameless One gave Christopher a searching look. There was a clatter in the yard as a big, dark-bearded man approached. Christopher turned and bowed his head slightly to the newcomer.

"My lord Black-Brow," he said.

"Another prisoner?" Narald Black-Brow demanded. "And what do you plan for this one?"

"Only the best," said a new voice. An old man in a black robe, his face all in shadow except for the tip of a white beard, stepped up beside Black-Brow. "We will dine with him tonight. We are old friends, Master O'Roarke and I."

* * *

Miracle lifted her head as a scraping sound met her ears. As she watched, the trapdoor lifted. A head emerged, followed by a pair of massive shoulders. Miracle stiffened when she realized it was not Michael—but in the next instant recognition flooded her. She hardly noticed the smaller man who followed as Kris rushed to her side. She held out her hand to him. He took it in his rough fingers and kissed it.

"Kris of the Mountains," she said. "My old friend."

There were tears in Kris's blue eyes. He bowed his head and shook his grey mane. "You are not well," he said.

"I have been better," she said with a weak smile.

Stocky came up beside Kris and bowed awkwardly. Kris thumped him on the back. "This is Stocky," he said. "A good companion. We're here to get you out."

133

Miracle smiled, but her face was pale under the smile. "Where—"

"Michael is coming," Kris said. "Soon. And when he arrives, we are all leaving."

* * *

In the hall of Narald Black-Brow were tables enough for fifty warriors. So the silence of the stone room as Michael was left alone was all the more ominous. Under the direction of Master Skraetock, two soldiers took Michael from Christopher and brought him to the hall. They cut the rope that bound his hands and left him alone in the cold darkness. Michael could make out the shapes of high windows, but all were covered to keep out the light.

Michael sank into a chair at the head table and stretched his hands and wrists. He touched the warped skin on his face and tried to swallow back a sense of panic.

After a minute there was a sound in the hall, and Master Skraetock appeared—out of nowhere, it seemed. He glided to the table and sat down, bringing a goblet of wine to his lips. He poured another and offered it to Michael.

"No," Michael answered.

"You need not be afraid of it," said Skraetock. "Or of me. I mean you no harm."

Michael did not answer.

"Do you know who I am?" asked Skraetock. Once again, Michael made no reply. Skraetock hardly seemed to notice his silence. "My name is Adhemar Skraetock," he said. "I am the Grand Master of the Order of the Spider."

"What do you want with me?" Michael asked.

"I want your help," Skraetock answered.

"And what makes you think I would help you?" Michael asked.

Skraetock smiled as one would smile at a child. "I think, from your manner, that you have been misinformed, Master O'Roarke," he said. "You seem to think I am your enemy."

"How do you know my name?" Michael asked.

Skraetock did not answer. Michael could feel the hooded man's eyes burning into his face.

"You look very like your father," Skraetock said at last.

Ice pricked up Michael's spine. He suddenly knew himself to be caught in a far greater trap than he had anticipated.

"We were friends, your father and I," Skraetock said. "In the days when he explored the mountains, many long years ago. He could trust me. I alone knew what he was."

Michael did not meet Skraetock's eyes. He felt short of breath as he groped for the right words to say.

"Did you come here to seek your father, Michael O'Roarke?" Skraetock said. "To discover what it was that Gifted him and set the fire in your family's veins? The mountain heights will not give answers. Only I can do that."

"You lie," Michael said.

"Do I?" Skraetock said. "You have seen my men near your home. We have been looking for your family. You are in danger. I have never forgotten your father. I want to help you."

Michael's eyes blazed as he lifted them to the Grand Master's face. "Was it not your men who caused my father to die?" he asked. "And my mother, and all the rest of their

135

generation? You left us orphaned and alone. What help can you possibly offer us?"

"The Order did not kill your family," Skraetock said. "You are mistaken."

"But they were in the village," Michael choked.

"Do you want answers, boy?" Skraetock asked. "Then cease casting blame without foundation and ask me for them. More than that—help me find the answers. The Gifted are the key to the mysteries of this world. The clann children are Gifted as your father was. He was the first—the very first. I was his guardian, but he did what you are doing: he believed lies and pulled away from me. You need me. Without my protection, you will lose the children as you lost your parents."

Michael looked away again. He was still trying to breathe; to think.

"Bring the little ones to me, Michael," Skraetock said. "Let me teach them. Let me protect them as I could not protect your father and mother."

"And who must you protect them from?" Michael said. "Miracle?"

"Miracle is greatly deceived," Skraetock said. "I have brought her here for her own good."

Michael shook his head. "I saw her," he said. "I know what you've done to her."

"No," Skraetock said. "I very much doubt that you do."

Michael had a sudden desire to see the face beneath the cowl—to know what expression it held. But the shadows were too deep. They thwarted his vision even as Skraetock's words thwarted clear thought.

"Tell me," Skraetock said. "Do you know what your father encountered in the mountains?"

Michael closed his eyes. A picture arose before him, brilliant and blazing for a moment only: a vision of a fire that swept across the world but did not destroy. He saw it as his father had described it to him, as he had imagined it a thousand times in boyhood.

He opened his eyes. Skraetock was watching him intently. "Keep your secrets, if you will," Skraetock said. "But beware, Michael O'Roarke, for you are keeping secrets that will consume you if you are not careful. There are two opposing forces in this world, my young friend. You are in danger of falling in with the wrong one."

Michael felt suddenly dizzy. "I don't know what you're talking about," he said.

Skraetock's voice lowered. "They say *he* will come back," he said. "But he is nothing. Throw your lot in with him and you fail."

Michael looked at Skraetock, his mind straining to comprehend, his eyes empty of understanding. The Grand Master sat back and sighed a little.

"You do not know?" he said. "You do not understand. Well. I am glad that you are not entirely eaten up by their lies. Join me, Master O'Roarke. I will make you understand."

Michael closed his eyes. The slash on his cheek burned. His tongue felt heavy in his mouth. Confusion overwhelmed him. But then, somewhere deep within, he reached for the anchors he had always known. The children. The memory of his father. And to them he added Miracle—Miracle, so weak, and so wounded by this man who claimed to have answers.

Michael felt a sudden revulsion. His stomach lurched and his throat burned. He jumped to his feet and moved away from the Master of the Order of the Spider.

"I do not know you," Michael said, "but I know that you lie. Whatever your side is, I am not on it."

Skraetock stood and cast a long, sad look on Michael. "So be it then," Skraetock said. "I will call for you again, Michael O'Roarke. When the day comes that you see your error, my arms are open to you. Until then, you must be my prisoner. For you *will* help us. You have no choice but to help us."

Skraetock moved backward. Michael watched as the old man seemed to fade away—to become one with the shadows. He was gone. The doors of the hall opened. Light came in, accompanied by the boot tramps and calls of soldiers.

Two soldiers pressed their spear tips against Michael's back. Without a word they took his arms and marched him out of the hall and down a long corridor. He did not protest. He felt shaky; weaker than he had ever felt. He tried to fight the weakness down and regain his bearings—to remember why he was here.

His alarm grew as the soldiers opened a door and led him up a flight of steps. The dungeon was beneath the castle. *He was not being taken to Miracle.* Urgency burned in his throat. He had to do something, anything, or he was a prisoner, and Miracle was no closer to freedom!

Before he could gather his thoughts, Christopher Ens stepped out of the shadows, into the soldiers' path, and halted their ascent. His face was flushed. His eyes flashed, not with fire, but with the hardness of diamond.

"Take this man to the dungeon," Christopher ordered. Michael choked back a cry of relief. He nearly smiled, but when he looked in Christopher's face, the young man cast such a look of hatred and disdain on him that he lost all desire to smile.

"We have orders to keep him in the tower," one of the soldiers said.

"Idiot," Christopher said. "How dare you question me?"

The soldier bit back a retort. "I have my orders from the— from Master Skraetock himself," he said.

"Do you think I don't know the wishes of my own master?" Christopher demanded. "I have just come from him."

He stepped close and wrenched a spear from the hand of an unprepared soldier. "Now get out, all of you," he said. "I'll take the man down myself."

The soldier who had spoken before looked inclined to argue, but a scathing glare from Christopher silenced him. He and his two companions turned and left, their boots echoing down the long flight of stone steps.

Christopher grabbed Michael's arm and half-dragged him down the stairs without a word. They followed twisting corridors until they reached a nail-studded door that led down a damp, crumbling passageway, illuminated only by the sickly light of a single torch. They followed the passageway to a flight of steep, winding steps, ancient and encrusted with lichen. The stairway led them deep beneath the castle to the dungeon.

The dungeon-keeper was startled by their sudden appearance, but Christopher propelled the man ahead of them without a word of apology. They reached a high oak door, and Christopher stopped.

"Open it," he ordered.

"This is the girl's cell," the dungeon-keeper stuttered. "I have orders . . ."

"Don't lie to me, man," Christopher snapped. "You've opened this door to others, despite orders. I am come from the Master himself." He smiled. "Do as I say."

The dungeon-keeper swallowed, searching for words to defend himself. Thinking better of it, he turned to obey. The door swung open to the heavy iron key. Christopher shoved Michael forward. As he stumbled inside, his eyes met the welcoming faces of Kris of the Mountains and Stocky. He saw flashing steel and heard Christopher cry out.

Michael rushed in and lifted Miracle in his arms. She buried her face in his shoulder, her bandaged hand rested by his neck. Wondering at her trust, Michael carried her out of the cell. Stocky slammed the door behind them, locking the hapless dungeon-keeper inside. Christopher had fallen to the dungeon floor, seemingly unconscious. Kris and Stocky leapt over him.

They ran together: Kris and Stocky before with their weapons drawn, Michael behind with Miracle in his arms. They mounted the ancient steps with concentrated speed, bursting out of the door at the top. A lone soldier in the corridor yelled before Kris took him down. They kept running, through the corridors, running blindly, trying only to reach the sun before opposition reached them.

The few soldiers in the halls fell quickly beneath the blades of Kris and Stocky, but the commotion did not go without notice. Michael heard shouts and the blowing of a horn. The alarm was sounded. They were discovered.

Kris kicked open a door, and they spilled out into the
courtyard. Michael drank in the sight of the mountains and the
smell of fresh air, holding Miracle more closely to him. And
then the attack. Soldiers rushed at them from every direction.
Stocky moved behind Michael as they raced for the outer gates,
but by the time they reached the center of the courtyard, they
were surrounded. Michael set Miracle on her feet and moved
in front of her. He took the sword Kris handed him. They stood
together, breathing hard, in the midst of their enemies.

Narald Black-Brow pushed through the ranks of High
Police, a huge sword in his hands. His eyes gleamed at the sight
of his catch: Stocky, crouched, with a slim sword in each hand;
Kris of the Mountains, huge hands gripping an axe; Michael,
sword drawn; and Miracle, leaning against Michael's back, pale
and beautiful.

"They are mine," Black-Brow growled. "They should have
been mine from the start." He pointed to a few soldiers. "Take
the girl," he commanded. The soldiers started forward. Kris and
Stocky leaped at them. Blades clashed; the soldiers fell. Stocky
returned to his place, a wound running blood in his shoulder.
His mouth twitched with pain, but he still clutched his swords
tightly. Kris stayed where the soldiers had fallen, tense and
ready.

The police charged forward. Michael brought up his sword
to meet the attack. Kris and Stocky were nearly overpowered
on either side of him. A soldier slipped past the men. He
grabbed Miracle's arm roughly, and she cried out.

"Desist!"

The order came from a corner of the courtyard, where three men in black walked swiftly into the midst of the soldiers.

"Black-Brow, withdraw your men!" Adhemar Skraetock commanded.

"I am the Overlord of the Northern Lands," Black-Brow began.

"You are an old fool," said the Nameless One. "Do as the Master says."

Black-Brow motioned with his hand. His soldiers moved away, leaving the small group intact. The guards stayed in a circle around the little group, spears leveled.

"You will not play your bloody games with my captives," Skraetock said.

"Your captives tried to escape," said Black-Brow, spitting out the words.

Christopher Ens smiled. "Yes," he said. "And they nearly succeeded, thanks to your poor defenses."

Narald Black-Brow sputtered but did not retort. Master Skraetock crooked his finger to summon several soldiers and strode toward the captives. He stopped in his tracks as a wild scream split the air.

The eyes of every man in the courtyard turned to the high west wall. Over it loomed the cliff where Michael and his companions had spent the night. An enormous spotted mountain cat, eyes glittering and claws gleaming white, crouched atop the wall. The creature screamed again. The sound carried primal fear into the courtyard.

Thunder rumbled in the mountains.

The cat leaped from its place on the wall, landing on the stones of the courtyard. A soldier raised his spear, hand trembling. The cat turned and leapt too quickly for him. The soldier went down under the mountain cat's claws, screaming for help. The silver-tipped spears of the High Police took flight toward the animal's silken hide, but the cat only leaped again, and each spear missed its mark.

The thunder grew louder, and then it was no more thunder, but the wild echo of hoofbeats, the power of hoof and hide striking against the gates. The gates burst open, and the mountain ponies streamed through, neighing, lunging, and shaking their manes. Kris recognized even his little pony in the midst of them. And at the head of them all came a great white wolf.

Behind the ponies came the wolves, a pack of thirty at least, howling and baring their teeth. Wild mountain deer and goats rushed in behind them, sharp-hoofed and sharp-horned. White owls soared in over the walls, and little birds, hundreds of little house-birds, dove into the fray.

Michael caught Miracle up again and ran for the open gates, Kris and Stocky behind them. They reached the gates and passed through. Michael took a last look back as he ran, and he saw that even Adhemar Skraetock was fighting. But it was no wolf or antlered fiend he fought. It was a great man, dressed in skins, who pressed the Master of the Order with laughter and filled the air with a war cry that made the mountains tremble.

They made camp that night in a small cave deep in the mountainside, some ten miles from Ordna. They would have gone further, but Stocky was steadily losing blood from his shoulder, and Kris insisted on stopping to bandage the wound. Miracle helped to tend the wound—with help of the most ordinary kind—until her own strength gave out and she lay down on a bed of dry pine needles. Michael sat near the entrance to the cave, the wound on his face burning.

Long after midnight, Michael sighed and turned his face away from the entrance of the cave. The huge shape of a stranger was sitting in the shadows across from him.

Michael reached for his sword, but the man put out a hand to stop him.

"Do not you recognize me?" the man said, with a smile like a laughing wolf.

Michael was about to reply when he saw the man's eyes: one blue, one gold.

The white wolf.

"Who are you?" he asked.

"I am Lord of the Wild Things," the stranger said. "Gwyrion, of the Brethren of the Earth."

"You led the attack on Ordna—you saved us all today," Michael said.

"At great cost," Gwyrion said. He looked down at his hands, which, in the darkness, were faintly striped. "Ah, but it is good to run again. Too long did I sleep."

For a moment Michael felt again the confusion that had assailed him in Skraetock's presence—the sense of being deep in something he did not understand. But in Gwyrion's presence was such a pulsing power and rightness that the confusion abated before it. Michael still had no answers, but anticipation grew in him.

"I came here to seek a mystery," Michael said. "I did not expect to find you."

"What mystery?" Gwyrion asked.

"My father—" Michael's voice caught in his throat. "Many years ago, my father saw something in these mountains. A great fire—a light that swept over the whole earth and did not destroy, but purified all that it touched. It changed him. It was his great hope that what he saw in the mountains might become reality all over the Seventh World. And there was a man, who was not a man—"

"It was not I," Gwyrion said. In the shadows his eyes gleamed like a wild cat's.

Michael swallowed his disappointment. "I see."

"Your father met with the King," Gwyrion said quietly.

Michael looked up. "With who?"

"With the one for whom I fight," Gwyrion said. "The one for whom the Earth Brethren now awake."

"Why do you fight?" Michael asked.

"Because we are at war," Gwyrion answered.

"I am not," Michael said.

Gwyrion looked at Michael piercingly. "For one who is not at war, you fight hard against the enemy."

Skraetock's words came back to memory: *You are in danger of falling in with the wrong side.* Michael looked down suddenly. "I do not fight for any man's cause," he said. "I fight for love. For love of my family, for love of . . ." His voice trailed away.

"Love *is* the King's cause," Gwyrion said. "Fight for it, fight for truth, and you fight also for the King. As Gwyrion of the Wild Things fights for him. As she fights for him."

145

Michael did not have to ask who he meant. He looked into the shadows of the cave where Miracle still slept. She was weak and faint, but had not breathed a word of complaint. Nevertheless, Michael could see traces of fear and suffering in her eyes. She was no soldier, whatever Gwyrion might say about wars.

"She can't stay here," Michael said. "They will come after her again."

"So you will take her home?" Gwyrion asked. He did not wait for answer. "And I will also go with you."

Michael was silent for a few minutes. He bowed his head and said, "My father's belief in . . . the King . . . was the strongest thing about him. But he died, and no great power came to rescue him."

He looked down at the floor of the cave. "I came here to seek refuge for my family. And now I go home, bearing more trouble for them. Bearing this war of yours."

"The whole world is troubled," Gwyrion said. "Meet evil head on, fight on the right side, and you will overcome it. Your father saw the truth. The Burning Light will come and purify the world again. It has already begun."

Michael looked up at Gwyrion again. A sudden image of home came to mind. He saw the thatched cottage, the stone hearth, the faces of those he loved—his sister and cousins, Grandmother, the children.

"I must go home," he said.

"Yes," repeated Gwyrion. "For that is your place. And I will also go with you."

8

Father-Song

THE AIR IN THE VINEYARD smelled of salt and mud. The one-room
hut, made of mud and thatched with twigs, was round and
damp. Still, it was shelter. It kept the wind out, though the
melting snow trickled through the roof. An iron stove in the
center, stuffed with dry grape vines and any other fuel Peter
could find, kept the hut warm.

Marja had carried a load of hay on her back all the way
from the wagon, which they had quitted in the middle of the
night while the horses rested, and this she fashioned into a bed
for the sick man.

Marja started a fire early each morning while Peter left the
vineyard in search of food. Nicolas wandered listlessly—
through the hut, until Marja lost patience with him and
ordered him out, and then through the long brown rows of
grape vines. When he returned, he said very little. Sometimes
he ate the food that Marja thrust at him. Other times he sat
against the wall and stared up at the twiggy ceiling and the
light that slipped in through its cracks. Only rarely did he even

look at the sick man. The man was kept clean and fed; Nicolas assumed that Marja was taking care of him.

Marja left the hut late on the night of the third day. The air was cold. She wrapped her red coat tightly around herself and walked up the slope of the ground. Clouds wreathed the moon, but it still shone brightly enough to show the way.

Nicolas stood at the top of the hill, the north wind blowing in his face, looking over the vineyard with his back to the hut.

They stood together in a long silence while the wind whistled through the grape rows.

"You have to *do* something," Marja said at last. "You'll go crazy if you stay idle."

"I'm homesick," Nicolas said, swallowing.

"You can't go home now. You know that."

"I miss Bear."

"Stop making excuses!" Marja stepped in front of Nicolas. He did not look at her face.

"Why won't you tend him?" Marja said. "You brought him here; now you abandon him."

"He's taken care of," Nicolas said.

"He needs you."

"He doesn't!" Nicolas turned away. "He needs real care. We'll take him into town. Find a doctor."

"He's dying, Nicolas. No doctor can change that."

"Well, I can't change it!"

"Go talk to him."

"He's delirious."

Marja's voice lowered with urgency. "He's your father."

Nicolas snapped his head around and looked into Marja's eyes so suddenly that she caught her breath.

"He's not!" Nicolas shouted. "He's no father at all."

"Then why won't you go to him?" Marja asked.

Nicolas's voice was half-choked. "He left me," he said. "I was four years old. Not even four years old. He left me, and he left my mother, and she died, and I needed him! And he wasn't there."

"Do you remember him?" Marja asked gently.

"I've always remembered his face," Nicolas said.

"And the man in the hut?"

Nicolas nodded.

"You look like him," Marja said.

"I hate him," Nicolas whispered. "I don't even know why."

"I do," Marja said. "You hate him because you won't go into that hut and love him. Love is a choice, Nicolas Fisher. Love is the decision to be there when you're needed. You haven't even looked at him since we got here."

"He wasn't there when I needed him," Nicolas said.

"Do you want to be like him?" Marja asked.

Nicolas looked down. "No."

Marja reached out and touched Nicolas's arm. She smiled and stepped back. "I'll see you in the morning," she said.

* * *

"There's a good stand of reina trees a few miles from here," Peter said, his teeth clenching his pipe as he talked. "I'll strip enough bark to keep us eating for a few days."

"Good," Marja said. "If you can bring me another rabbit, do. We'll all start to look like reina bark by the end of the winter if that's all we eat."

"Brown and stringy?" Peter asked with a grin.

Marja pretended to smack his head. "Yes. Now get going."

The door of the hut swung open just as Peter stood, and Nicolas entered. He did not look at either of his companions. His eyes were on the hay cot across the room.

Marja moved close to Peter as they watched Nicolas kneel by the bed. The sick man's eyes were open. They heard his voice, weak and raspy. "Water?" Nicolas's voice was quiet, but they heard him, too. "Here," he said. "It's here. I'm here." He took the cup that rested by the cot and lifted it to the old man's lips.

Marja hugged Peter's arm and whispered, "Bring me two rabbits, Peter-cousin. We'll celebrate tonight!"

Nicolas heard whispering behind him and the swish of Marja's skirt as she busied herself at the stove, but his attention was fixed. The old man finished his water and rested his head back. Nicolas put the cup back on the dirt floor. "How do you feel, Father?" Nicolas asked, wincing at his own awkwardness.

The old man closed his eyes and did not answer.

Peter returned a few hours before dusk, bearing a load of reina bark, two rabbits, and a grouse. Marja skinned, chopped, and boiled until the smell of stew filled the hut. Peter sat outside the door and smoked his pipe, and Marja and Nicolas joined him with steaming bowls of stew when the cooking was finished. The stars were just beginning to come out in a clear winter sky.

"Bless the man who left us pots and bowls to go with the stove," Marja said.

"Not to mention that broom," Peter said. "Did I see you

sweeping again when I came down the hill this evening? How many times can you sweep a dirt floor?"

Nicolas took a bite of stew and looked up at the sky. The hot broth warmed his throat. A shuffling noise issued from the hut, and the old man called out, "Nicolas! My son!"

Nicolas shoved his stew into Peter's hand and bolted through the door. It was dark inside, except for the glow inside the iron stove, but Nicolas could see that his father's eyes were open. One frail, thin hand reached toward the door. Nicolas went to his knees beside the hay cot and took the hand. His hand tightened almost involuntarily around his father's.

"It is you?" said the old man. "I am not dreaming?"

"No," Nicolas said. "You are not dreaming."

"I was coming to find you," said the old man. "To tell you. I was sailing to find you . . ." He brought his other hand out from under his makeshift blankets and covered the exposed part of Nicolas's hand with it. There were tears in his bloodshot eyes. "So many years I longed to see you," he said. "I fought for my freedom so I could see you again."

"Your freedom?" Nicolas asked.

"We were trapped in the islands of the south . . . there is evil there, too." His words were laboured. "Evil. We fought. We thought we had killed it. But one of the men brought it with us."

"Brought what?" Nicolas asked.

"The serpent," said the man. "It bit me—all of us. You see it?"

His hand shook as he spoke, and Nicolas looked down. To his horror he could see two tiny marks near the joint of his father's thumb, like pinpricks—or a snake's bite.

"We killed it that time," said the man, "but it got us first. Poison."

Nicolas bowed his head and lifted his hand so that the father's fingers rested against the son's forehead. "I'm sorry," he said.

"I came to tell you," said the old man. "You have to take sides. There is real evil in this world—I never believed it when I was young." He stopped and closed his eyes, his chest rising and falling. "There is a King," he said. "He is coming with fire. Look for him. He will overcome evil, and you must fight with him. And there are some—the Gifted—who need protection. I know it sounds crazy . . ."

Nicolas leaned forward and said, "I know a little of what you say, Father. I am Gifted."

The wrinkled hands tightened, and a tear slipped down the old man's cheek. "My son. Do you follow the King?"

"I don't know," Nicolas said.

"Decide!" said the old man, drawing himself up for a moment. He fell back on the hay with a deep sigh of exhaustion. "It is war. You must decide. Don't run. I ran for so many years."

"Ran from what?"

"From the truth. From the King himself, though I didn't know it then. I thought I was a wanderer. I didn't want anything to tie me down. My freedom was all that mattered. It was no freedom at all."

Nicolas swallowed a lump in his throat, but said nothing. His father cried out suddenly and then began to sob, his emaciated frame shaking with every breath. "I'm so sorry," he said. "Oh my son, I'm so sorry . . ."

Nicolas began to cry too, and he bent down so that his head rested on his father's shoulder. Even as he did, the faint strains of a song began to play in his ears. Through his tears, wonder tugged at him. The river had led him here. Straight to the black-sailed ship—straight to his father.

Open your heart, the Shearim had said. *Use what the river has given you.*

When the old man had ceased crying, he tapped Nicolas's shoulder. "I am sorry I took so long," he said, his words clipped with pain.

"It's all right," Nicolas said. "Just rest."

The old man looked up at his son with pain-filled eyes. "I did not come to rest," he said. "I came to fight evil. I wanted to do it with you by my side."

The old man's body convulsed, and he lay still until Nicolas began to grow alarmed. He was about to call for Marja when the old man spoke again. "It is over so quickly for me," he said. "I wanted to fight in this war. To make others see the truth"

Nicolas swallowed. "There are others to spread the word," he said. "This war has begun. I have seen it. I have seen evil defeated. Some in the Eastern Lands believe in the King. I have friends among them."

"But you are not one of them?" the old man asked.

Nicolas hung his head. "I did not want—"

"To be tied down," said the old man. "You must decide, Nicolas. You can't remain a loner forever. I know what it is to be snared by your own foolishness. Open the trap, my son. Set yourself free—truly free."

Nicolas began to say something, but the words caught in his throat as a song broke out in the hut. The music filled the little room as waves fill a drowning ship. It was a wondrous song, indescribable in its strong, comforting beauty. As Nicolas raised his shining face and drank it in, he realized that no one else could hear it. But he could, and he heard, too, the name of it. He thought perhaps the voices of the Shearim named it for him.

Hear the Three-Fold Song, the Song of the Burning Light! Heed the Father-Song, son of light.

* * *

In Pravik, the move deeper underground had begun.

Teams of workers began by installing sconces for torches throughout the lower corridors. Men cleared debris while women came behind them and cleaned. On the higher level, the explorers explained maps and drilled the men, women, and children in the twists and turns of their new home.

Maggie and Pat pushed carts of food and supplies down the long corridors until they were ready to drop from exhaustion. They had just finished stocking the shelves of an underground pantry when the Major stuck his dark head in the door.

"Time for a break," he said. "Come join us."

Maggie and Pat needed little urging. They left the pantry, gathering with a tired, dirt-smeared group of Gypsies in a torch-lit cavern. Three carts had been overturned and pushed together to form a long table, which was laden with salt pork, dry bread, and water collected from the damp corridors near the river.

"Whatever else the inconveniences of underground life," Pat said, making a face as she tore a piece of pork from a large hunk, "you can't say the food isn't great."

"All right then," said the Major. "I won't say it."

Darne's eyes laughed as he bit into a piece of bread. He was still too new to underground life to complain about it, even in jest. Only veterans had that right.

Pat sighed deeply and looked up at the high stone roof. "Lovely weather today, isn't it?" She sat up. "Enough. I'm going crazy down here. Darne, tell us the story of how you got your horses from the Emperor's ranch in the middle of the night."

Darne smiled. "It sounds to me as if you already know the story," he said.

"Of course I know it," Pat said. "I want to hear it again."

Darne launched into the tale. Maggie rested her chin in her hand as he spoke. She closed her eyes and pictured Nicolas heading up the raid. When the story was over, she opened her eyes again. "That will make a wonderful tale for Marja to tell around the campfires," she said.

"There are precious few campfires left for storytelling," the Major said.

A tall dark man in fine clothing, who had sat quietly through the story, spoke up. "Does the Ploughman mean to sit here and do nothing while the High Police enslave the Gypsies? I had heard that he was a man who fought for freedom."

"He's not doing nothing," the Major said. His dark eyes seemed troubled. "He has a home to provide for all these people. He is doing his best."

155

The tall man sat forward, and the torchlight fell on his thin face and amber eyes. Asa, the strange doctor who had come to Pravik with a wounded Gypsy. He had worked diligently with the others since coming to the underground colony, but Maggie had never felt comfortable around him.

"I came here to seek strength," he said. "But I have found only people in hiding. There is too much weakness here."

Pat's face clouded over. She opened her mouth to answer when an eerie howl filled the cavern. The company sat in silence until the sound died away.

"What was that?" Maggie asked, shivering.

"Only the wind in the caverns below," the Major said.

"They say there are untold levels down there," Darne said.

"They say there are strange creatures down there," said Asa.

"It is only the imaginations of the explorers," said the Major. "Long days alone in the dark will play tricks on your mind."

Asa sat back, a smile on his face. "Have it your way," he said.

An uneasy silence fell over the company. Pat replaced her hunk of pork on the cart tables. She stood and stretched. "I'm going back to work," she said. "Maggie, are you coming?"

"In a minute," Maggie said.

Pat left, and Darne and Asa got to their feet. The Major stood and offered his arm to Maggie.

"Walk with me?" he asked.

She nodded. "Thank you."

They walked together out of the cavern, down a long stone passageway. "Something is bothering you," the Major said.

"I'm worried," Maggie confessed.

"About?"

"I don't know. Everything. I suppose it's just the waiting. Virginia says we must cling to what we have seen and trust that the King has not forgotten us, but . . . it is not easy."

"You have been talking to the seer?" the Major asked.

"Yes."

"She doesn't talk to many people."

"I know," Maggie said. "She is—there is something dark in her as well. I am a little afraid of her."

"What else did she tell you?"

"That Nicolas is well."

The Major raised his eyebrows. "That is good to know."

"Of course, that was days ago," Maggie said. "The way things are, he might not even be alive today."

The Major grunted. "It is a dangerous thing to be a Gypsy —even a half-Gypsy—in the world today."

They said nothing for a few minutes, then Maggie said, "Do you think he's right?"

"Who?"

"Asa. He thinks we ought to be doing something more than just sitting here."

"And what could we do? Storm Athrom?"

"Maybe," Maggie said. "We won the fight in Pravik."

"With the help of Heavenly Warriors, they say," the Major said.

Maggie stopped walking, but she still clung to the Major's arm. "That's what troubles me," she said. "Yes, we won—and then the warriors disappeared, and we went underground. And now Pravik and the mountains are overrun with soldiers looking for us, and we're hiding in the dark. Is this what the King wants from us? To bury ourselves until he comes back?"

"I wish I could answer you," the Major said. "But of all of us here, I know the least about this King of yours. What does the professor say to your questions?"

"Professor Huss says very little," Maggie said. "I haven't asked him. Lately he seems so troubled."

The Major started to say something, and bit his tongue. A moment later he spoke, slowly. "I do not know what is required of the Ploughman," he said. "I think it is right that he stays here. If he tries to go above now, his colony will be destroyed, and all of my sheltered people with it. Too many people here are still reeling from their wounds. It will not hurt them to stay below and rebuild before the time comes to go above. But I will not stay underground much longer."

Maggie looked at him in surprise. "What do you mean?"

"I am going to find Nicolas," he said. "Since I have been here, Nicolas seems to have made it his business to rescue our people from their enemies. I mean to join him."

"But your people are safe here," Maggie said.

"My band is here, yes, all except Marja and Peter. And I have stayed as long as I have because I felt that the Major's Gypsies needed their leader. But no more. They are settled here now. The Ploughman governs his cavernous kingdom well, and I trust him. They don't need me. Our people outside do."

"But you could be killed out there," Maggie said.

"So could Nicolas."

Maggie shivered. "Don't remind me."

"The truth is, little one, I go for Nicolas's sake as well as for my own peace of mind. I bear some responsibility for him."

"He once told me that your mother had raised him, after he ran away from his home."

"Yes, that is true. Although some would say he ran *to* his home, not away from it."

Maggie spoke hesitantly. "Nicolas always said that even the Gypsies did not fully accept him; that his only real home was the forests. But he longed to belong with other people."

"He belonged with us," the Major said, "but he would never stay. He drove himself out."

"But—" Maggie began.

"Nicolas has never accepted himself," the Major said. "Perhaps because his father left him. Perhaps because he was Gifted. But we never drove him out. He did that himself."

"It is good of you to make yourself responsible for him," Maggie said.

"It is no more than I am bound to do, by blood duty." The Major smiled ruefully. "I used to wonder that Nicolas told you so much about himself. He does not normally open up to anyone. But now I don't wonder. You are a good listener."

Maggie smiled at the compliment, but she couldn't help asking. "What did you mean by blood duty?"

"I told you that Nicolas did not run away from home so much as he ran to it," the Major said. "He thinks that he found my mother. The truth is, she found him. We came to the city to take him away with us so that his mother's family could not send him to the orphan house after she died."

159

"But why?" Maggie asked. "Nicolas made it sound as though he had never seen any of you before he joined the band."

"He hadn't," the Major said. "But that doesn't change the truth. Nicolas is my brother's son."

* * *

Marja slept with her back against Peter's, huddled next to the stove. Melting snow dripped through the roof and ran through her black hair, now and then hitting her face like an icy tear. A drop of water collected on her eyelash, and she blinked and opened her eyes as the cold stream ran down her cheek.

Nicolas and his father were whispering together.

Nicolas was talking. Marja watched him as he told his stories. He lifted his hands and moved as he spoke, all of his energy poured into the telling. Only his voice was subdued, kept low so the others could sleep. Marja saw Nicolas's father smile and try to laugh, and another stream of water ran down her cheek—but this was a real tear, hot on her skin.

She smiled as she closed her eyes, letting the whispers surround her. She had worked so hard to keep the old man alive, bringing all the skill of her people and the training of her mother to bear as she tended him. It was for this she had done it. And Nicolas's desire to know his father, coupled with the father's desire to know his son, had done wonders for the old man's health. He would live longer than she had first thought.

But he would not live forever. She brushed her cheekbone with the edge of her thumb, smearing the tears across her face.

He would not live forever.

And when he died, where would Nicolas go?

Marja was a true daughter of her people. Never once had she ever desired to put down roots—her roots were in the sky, ever winging over the roads and the forests of the Seventh World. Her desires, her passions, soared as well—she longed for freedom for her people. She wished for vengeance on their enemies.

But now, as she fought back tears in the salty darkness and listened to the whispers of two men, she wished for the first time that things might never change.

* * *

Professor Jarin Huss held his torch close to the rock face. For the first time in weeks, his eyes were bright. His forehead furrowed as he studied the characters carved in the stone.

"What do you think, Professor?" asked the Ploughman. He stood behind Huss, arms folded.

"Fascinating," said the professor. He turned to look at the tall rebel leader. "The language is very old, but it is not one I recognize—and I can read some of the oldest languages known to the Seventh World."

"The carving is that old then, do you think?" the Ploughman asked.

"It dates from before the time of the Empire, at least," Huss said. He turned back to the stone and traced one of the old letters with his long finger. "Fascinating," he said again.

They stood in a deep place, below the now-occupied second level of tunnels and caverns. Both men turned at the sound of boots tramping down the corridor toward them.

A small company of men entered the cavern. Their leader, a one-time farmer whose face was pale but still weathered, bowed his head to the Ploughman. "Reporting from below," he said. "You wanted me?"

"Your men are refusing to go deeper," the Ploughman said. "So they say."

The man coloured slightly. "Only to the west."

"Do they have a reason for going against my orders?" the Ploughman said.

The leader of the company seemed uneasy. "Voices, sir," he said.

"What?" said the Ploughman.

"They say there are voices in the deep western part of the caves," the man said. "Forgive me, but they are afraid. I hate to make them keep going."

The Ploughman frowned, then laid his hand on the farmer's shoulder. "You have all worked hard since we came here," he said. "Perhaps it is time your men are given a break."

The leader smiled. "It might help with the voices, my lord," he said.

"Yes, I expect it will," the Ploughman said. "Withdraw your men. We'll put a new company of explorers to work."

The farmer looked at his leader with affection and nodded his head. "Thank you."

The men left the cavern as Libuse entered with a small retinue. She went to the Ploughman, who bowed and kissed her hand. Professor Huss smiled wryly and turned back to the wall.

In a moment Libuse's voice pulled him away from his examination once again. "Will you come with us, Professor?" she said. "The Major has asked for a meeting. I don't know for sure, but I believe he means to say good-bye."

* * *

They met in the Ploughman's quarters: old friends and new. Maggie and Pat stood on either side of Mrs. Cook. Virginia sat apart from the others, listening with her head bent. Darne shuffled his feet and hung his head, embarrassed, it seemed, to be counted with such a company. Professor Huss poked the young Gypsy occasionally in an effort to make him stand still. Libuse and the Ploughman sat together, while the Major stood before them, in the center of the company, and spoke of his desire to serve his people outside of the city.

"I cannot continue to sit in the darkness while the enemies of freedom persecute my people," the Major said. Libuse watched the Ploughman uneasily as the Gypsy leader spoke, but his face did not betray how he felt.

When he had finished, the Ploughman stood and took the Major's hand in his own.

"We will miss you," the Ploughman said. "You are right to do as you do. Know that all you send to us will find refuge."

"I know it well," the Major said.

He turned to go when the voice of a young woman, tinged with the accent of the Bryllan Highlands, spoke.

"Major," Virginia said, rising slowly to her feet, "you may find the darkness above ground harder to bear than the darkness here. But do not lose hope. There is light in the world yet. One day soon it will burn back the darkness."

* * *

Shannon O'Roarke let the waves wash over her feet and soak her thin shoes. The salt wind was cold; it blew through her chestnut hair and made the edges of her shawl dance. The rising sun painted the horizon cream and blue, green and purple, and behind her a cock crowed.

Shannon watched the sun rise until at last she turned away. She sighed as she started back up the path to the cottage, where peat smoke smudged the sky above the thatched roof and thorny rose bushes. Vines lay dead and brown in the chill of winter. A cow lowed in the yard, and Shannon heard the creak and rattle of chains as a bucket was brought up from the well.

The water crashed behind her. A far-reaching wave lapped at her ankles, and she turned back to the sea one last time.

There was something on the horizon.

Shannon lifted her hand to shade her eyes and gathered her skirts as she dashed back into the waves, running as though she meant to run across the sea to meet the longship.

It was Michael. She was sure of it.

Shannon turned and ran for the cottage, shouting at the top of her lungs.

* * *

They saw the children first, dancing and leaping in the sea foam on the shore. Michael shouted and waved, and the four little ones clapped their hands and waved back, their voices drowned out by the crash of the water. Stocky grinned and whooped.

"Eh, Michael! That's a welcome, isn't it?" he said.

Behind the men, balancing carefully in the rocking ship, Miracle smiled and stood. Kris steadied her with his hand. They peered at the shoreline where young men and women were gathering now, waving, shouting, capering in the waves like children themselves.

"It's been a long year since," Kris said quietly. "And Michael says my roses still bloom!"

Two of the younger men struck out in the waves as the longship drew close, bearing ropes. They attached the ropes to the ship and pulled it to shore, laughing and calling to Michael and Stocky as they worked.

When the bottom of the ship scraped sand, Michael jumped down into the embrace of a young woman who bore a striking resemblance to him. Stocky hurled himself over the side and nearly landed on a small child, whom he chased with a bellow and good-natured threats.

Kris stepped into the ankle-deep water and approached Michael and his sister.

"Shannon O'Roarke," he said. "How you have grown!"

Shannon held out her hand with a smile. "Michael promised to bring back a deed to land from the mountains," she said. "He said nothing about bringing back Kris of the Mountains himself!"

"Do you remember me, miss?" Kris asked.

"I would know you anywhere," Shannon said. "But whether I remember you or whether it is my mother's many descriptions of you that make me think I do—that I cannot say."

Michael left Shannon's side and waded back to the boat. Miracle looked down at him with a gentle smile. He took her in his arms and carried her to shore while the people of Clann O'Roarke walked before and behind them with many a curious, badly-covered glance.

Michael set Miracle down on the dry ground. He took her hand and joined it with Shannon's.

"My sister," he said. "Shannon, this is Miracle. She is going to stay with us."

Shannon nodded and smiled. "Welcome," she said. "I'm sorry we could not come out to greet you properly. My brother hardly gave us fair warning. The real celebrations will have to wait a while!"

Stocky appeared on the horizon, surrounded by four children who somehow made a crowd. "Do you smell the stew, Michael?" he shouted. "We're home!"

"Aye, Michael," Shannon said, laying her head on her brother's shoulder. "Welcome home."

They walked together, Shannon, Michael, and Miracle. Shannon looked behind her and gasped.

"Michael, what is that?" she asked.

Michael turned and eyed the creature on the beach with the strangest of smiles. "Another new companion, Shannon," he said. "Don't worry your head about him. He doesn't look it —but he's safe."

The white wolf followed them to the cottage door.

166

9

Unexpected Meetings

SPRING CAME EARLY to Italya. It came in whispers on the warm wind and crept through the ground, where roots drank it in and began to wake.

Nicolas stepped out of the hut one morning and looked around him with clouded eyes.

"The vines are budding," he said. His voice was thick. "The first buds of spring."

Marja looked up from the coat she was mending. She stood and laid a hand on Nicolas's arm. "Has he—?"

Nicolas looked away and nodded quickly.

Marja stepped back and nudged Peter. "Come then," she said. "There's work to do."

Peter put out his pipe as he stood. He stuck it in his pocket as he followed Marja into the hut.

Nicolas stayed outside, alone. He let the clouds over his eyes burst and send rain down his cheeks as he surveyed the long rows of grape vines, taking in every tiny green bud. He ran his eyes down the rows to the horizon, where the morning haze had come in from the sea, and he looked for a place to dig a grave.

They buried Nicolas's father in the bright sunlight of midday, at the top of the hill overlooking the hut. Peter and Nicolas brought a stone to lay on the grave, and Marja carved it with the curious markings that only Gypsies could read.

"His name, Nicolas?" she asked. "What was your father's name?"

He looked at her for a long moment, as though he did not understand, and said, slowly, "His name was Lucas Barrington."

Late that night Nicolas awoke to the sound of footsteps and voices. There were men coming. They were yet a good way off, but they were headed for the hut. Nicolas heard them as plainly as if they had been standing next to him.

"I tell you," said one voice, *"I've seen smoke from the hut more than once over the winter."*

"We've had squatters before," said another. *"Won't take long to drive them off. Not if my sword-arm has anything to say about it."*

Nicolas rolled over and tapped Peter. He squirmed in his sleep, and Nicolas tapped him harder.

"Ow," said Peter. "What's that for?"

"Wake up," Nicolas whispered. Across the floor, Marja lifted her head.

"Our stay here is over," Nicolas said. "The vineyard-keepers are on their way."

It didn't take long to vacate the hut. Peter folded their small store of reina bark and rabbit meat into his coat while Marja and Nicolas gathered the few things they had collected over the winter. The hut was empty in less than half an hour.

Only some scattered straw on the floor and a few warm coals in the stove were left to say that anyone had ever been there.

* * *

"O where shall ye go,
   and where shall ye go,
and where shall we go,
   O wanderer?"

Marja sang as they walked, twirling a willow branch in the air. The muddy road sucked at their boots and filled the air with a rank smell, but even Nicolas felt a certain exhilaration in the wind on his face as he watched the road pass by underneath his feet.

"We shall go with the road,
   where'er the road goes,
there we shall go,
   O wanderer!"

Nicolas smiled as he listened. He turned his head to watch Marja as she moved. Peter said something and laughed, but Nicolas didn't catch his words. Other words were ringing in his head: his father's words just before he died, words Nicolas had not shared with his companions.

Suddenly even the memory of his father's voice faded out, replaced by others. He stumbled in his surprise and nearly landed face down in the mud.

"What is it?" Marja asked.

"I heard—I'm not sure," Nicolas said, "but I think the Major's on the road ahead of us."

They met together hours later in the warm spring sun, up to their ankles in mud, and laughed with the joy of meeting. Indeed, the Major was on the road—had been, he said, since late winter. And he was not alone. Bear had joined him only three days before and startled him very badly.

Whether Nicolas was happier to see Bear or to see the Major was not easy to tell. But when they had gone a few miles down the road together, Nicolas ducked his head shyly and said, "It *is* good to see you, Uncle."

The Major stopped in the squelching mud. "And you, Nephew!" he said. "But I think you must have a story to tell me."

"I do," Nicolas said, but the story had to wait. In the time it had taken the Major to say his few words, he had become stuck fast in the mud, and it took nearly half an hour to get him out again.

It rained—a warm, sparkling, spring rain. The companions climbed a tree by the side of the road and let their sodden boots hang down. Bear walked circles beneath the branches while the Gypsies talked. Nicolas ended his story with the burial of his father. For a while they let it hang in the air, as uncle and nephew each became lost in his own thoughts.

After some time Peter spoke, from a branch above the Major's head.

"And what of you, Major?" he asked. "Last we knew you were on your way to Pravik."

"I have been in Pravik," the Major said. "Most of the winter. The band is settled there. The Ploughman rules a good camp. Our people are safe."

Marja's eyes flashed. "Some of our people," she said.

"Yes," the Major answered. "That is why I left. In midwinter we were joined by a ragged band of refugees led by a young man named Darne."

Nicolas looked up in recognition.

"Earlier in the year, a Galcic vagabond they call Asa joined us, bringing with him a badly wounded Gypsy. From the accounts of both Darne and Asa, we learned that you have been very active."

"And that is why you came above ground?" Nicolas asked.

"I couldn't very well leave you three to do all the work yourselves," the Major said.

"So you came to find the saviours of the Wandering Race," Marja said. "And all the time we have been hiding in a mud hut."

"Not a bad idea," the Major said. "The persecution of the High Police seems to have eased over the latter part of the winter. Now that spring is here, it is time to come out of hiding again."

Bear grunted beneath the tree.

"Yes," Nicolas said, "and it is high time you came out of hibernation as well."

In the quietness of the day Nicolas leaned against the trunk of the tree and closed his eyes. He could *hear*—spring was possessed of a thousand voices, and he heard them all. He heard the birds calling to each other, heard the scrape and hurry of small animals as they emerged from their winter dens and established homes for the coming seasons. He heard Bear thinking to himself, talking in his peculiar bear-voice. And through it all, woven through it all, he heard the Father-Song.

He heard other music as well. Still so far away that he could not distinguish the notes were the second and third strains of the Three-Fold Song.

He thought of the River-Daughter and wished to hear her voice again. He had come so far in obedience to her call. It had been so long—he still feared that he would fail her before he finished his task. But excitement and anticipation also filled him now. In some way, the journey itself would teach him the song that now sang just at the edges of his hearing.

He whispered the words as the sun streamed through the tree-branches and bathed his head with warmth. "I am trying. But I still can't hear it all. Stars help me—help me hear the song."

* * *

Pat stepped close to Maggie and whispered, "I didn't think it was possible for it to get *darker.*"

"You wanted to do this," Maggie whispered back.

Behind them, Darne said aloud, "Now I understand why the explorers thought they heard voices."

The Ploughman, holding a torch at the head of the small procession, turned and looked down the narrow corridor at Darne. "The darkness has a thousand tricks to play," he said. "The deeper you go, the more true that is."

Professor Huss tucked Maggie's arm into the crook of his own. "Lead on," he said. "We are curious to see what is ahead."

"Yes," said Asa, who was directly behind the Ploughman. "Lead on."

The Ploughman lifted his torch high. They continued down the dark tunnel when a sudden whoosh of air whistled past their ears. The torch went out. The tunnel was plunged into absolute blackness.

"Is it too late to make a decision?" Pat said. "I don't want to do this anymore."

"We're not far from the Hold," the Ploughman said. "Some of the men are there. They will have light. Join hands and follow me."

Pat, Maggie, Professor Huss, Asa, and Darne obeyed. They were in the deepest part of the Ploughman's excavations, not far from a place he called the Hold—an enormous fortified cavern which he planned to use for defence in case the underground colony finally clashed with the forces of the Empire.

Maggie held the professor's wrinkled, thin hand in front of her and felt Pat's tight grip behind as she stumbled through the dark passage. The Ploughman led in silence, and the others followed suit. The only sounds were the cautious shuffle of footsteps on rock and the occasional moan of wind. From what the Ploughman had said, Maggie thought they would have reached the Hold in minutes, but time—if time even existed in the dark—seemed to have slowed. They went on and on, and no one said anything.

A gush of wind brought with it the smell of camp smoke, mingled with the scent of fish and bread, and Maggie breathed a sigh of relief. She wondered where the Ploughman's men had come by a supply of fish, but before she could ask, the line in front of her stopped.

Her heart beat painfully in the stillness. She knew why they had stopped; why no one dared speak a word.

She had heard it, too.

There were voices in the darkness.

For an instant she dared think it was only the wind, but then she heard them again: whisperings, mutterings, now alone, now speaking all together. The voices came from above and behind and all around. And then another sound: blade sliding against leather as the Ploughman drew his sword. The quiet chatter intensified. The Ploughman's voice cut through it.

"Show yourselves," he said. "If you are friends or foes, let us see you."

A voice answered. "The Sunworlders' eyes are weak. We can see *you*." The words were spoken in the language of the Empire, but the accent was strange to Maggie's ears.

There came a scrambling as someone moved from a perch above and settled directly in front of the Ploughman. A dim blue light came on suddenly behind the smudged glass of a lantern held in a thin, pale hand. It illuminated the face and outline of a man.

He was small in height and in build. His dark eyes, enormous in a gaunt, small-boned face, glimmered. His head was white and hairless except for one dark, bound lock that began at the top of his head and fell to his shoulders, and a glittering band of fish scales circled his brow. His other clothing was dark in colour, but here and there the light picked up a strand of gold in the weaving. He wore a sleeveless tunic that reached his knees, cinched at the waist by a braided belt. His shoulders were bare; each arm covered to the wrist with a sleeve of tight braids. His legs were covered with the same material from his knees to his ankles, and his feet, which were large and pale, were bare.

The Ploughman dropped his sword as other members of the man's strange race stepped into the ring of lantern light, pointing double-pronged short spears at the line of intruders. The light did not reach far enough to show Maggie what was behind or beside her, but she knew from the scuffle of feet and the whisper of voices that she and her companions were surrounded.

The Ploughman looked above him as though expecting salvation to drop from the cavern roof. "I led in the wrong direction," he said, half to himself. "We took the west passage . . ."

"You will come with us," said the lantern-bearer. "All will come with us."

"Why?" asked the Ploughman. "We mean you no harm. Why not let us go?"

"You are the leader," said the man. "We have watched you. We know. You will lead your people right into our homes if we do not stop you." Air escaped through his teeth in a long hiss. "You are trespassers."

"We only seek shelter," the Ploughman said. "We did not know anyone was here."

"Do not tell me your excuses," the lantern-bearer said. "You will tell them to the Majesty."

The Ploughman bowed his head in submission and asked quietly, "May I know who takes us captive?"

The lantern-bearer seemed pleased. "I am Harutek, Sixteenth Son of the Majesty."

The Ploughman motioned to the sword that lay at his feet. "I have laid down my weapon," he said. "I will go with you willingly, Harutek, son of the Majesty. Only tell your men to lower their spears. Neither I nor my people are a threat to you until you show plainly that you are a threat to us."

Harutek nodded. The men beside him pulled the forked ends of their spears up to their shoulders in one swift motion. Maggie heard the rush of air as the men all around did the same. She had not realized that she was holding her breath, but she let it out now.

Harutek held his lantern higher, and his lips curved in a smile. "Follow," he said, and turned his back.

As he did so, other dim lamps flickered to life on every side. Maggie clearly saw the pale, expressionless faces of the men who flanked their prisoners. She could see the cave better now, too. They were in a high-roofed passage. Ledges on either side provided plenty of space for guards to sit above and watch those who passed below. Her eyes widened, and she nudged the professor; he looked up and quickly saw what she had seen. The edges of the passage were intricately carved with strange letters and shapes. The writing was unintelligible to Maggie, but amidst the carvings she recognized stylized pictures of fish, spears, rivers, and people, often surrounded by twisting braids. For a moment Maggie allowed her eyes to drift up to the ceiling of the passage, and there she saw carvings of another sort, flickering in the shadows of blue lantern light: here were carvings of the sun, moon, and stars, of trees, and horses, and mountains.

The walls of the passage swept out to either side, and the ceiling rose higher. They began to descend a twisting staircase carved in the rock, down into an immense cavern lit by hundreds of fires and lanterns—on the floor, in caves, and on ledges all down the sides. The cavern smelled like fish and smoke and oil, and in the dim light Maggie could see the forms of people, some still, some busy. The voices of the colony echoed in the cavern, mingling in fleeting whispers. The voices were too quiet, the accents too strange, and the echoes too jumbled for Maggie to understand anything said, but she whispered an exclamation herself. Darne, Pat, and the professor all did the same. Their voices joined the echoes.

The staircase took them past dwellings in the side of the cavern, and large eyes peered at them from the dark holes. A half-naked child—head completely shaved—darted out of a small cave below and stared up at them until the procession had nearly reached it. Then he dove back into the shelter of the cave again.

When they reached the floor of the cavern, silent forms watched them from every side. Led by Harutek, they tramped down a street through the middle of the colony. Women carrying baskets stopped their work to watch the strangers pass by; old grandmothers looked up from their fires. Children ran alongside them and then huddled behind the legs of their elders. Men sharpened forked spears as they watched, bowing their heads to Harutek.

The people of the colony were alike in a few particulars. Their skin was pale and their eyes large. They were small of build, and their hair—what little of it there was—was dark. The men were dressed after the fashion of Harutek. The women's attire was much the same, except that instead of tunics, they wore sleeveless dresses that brushed the tops of their bare feet. And men, women, and children were all shaved, but for a single braid worn by the women. In the younger women this braid was short; in some of the older, grey-haired women, it reached the ground. Harutek's one lock of hair was unique among the men.

The shadow-licked street led them through the colony to the far side of the cavern, where a high arched door, lined by carvings of stars and twining rivers, led into another cave. At the highest point of the arch was a carving of a man wearing long robes, whose crown was made of seven stars.

They passed through the doorway and entered a long, low-roofed cavern. Lanterns hung from hooks down the length of the cavern, casting a blue, flickering light over the white stone floor. Between the lanterns, guards stood immobile, double-pronged spears at their sides. The guards bowed their heads as Harutek passed and did not lift their eyes again until the procession had gone by.

At the end of this cavern, three smooth steps led up to platform of rock. A man stood at the top of the platform. He wore a helmet and wristbands of fish scales. As the procession approached, he raised his hand in salute.

"Hail Harutek, Sixteenth Son of the Majesty," he said.

Harutek saluted in return. "Hail Ytac, Captain of the Guard."

"Your father will see you now," Ytac said. He turned, and his braided cape swished behind him, and put strong hands to a pair of white doors. They swung open, revealing the throne room of the Majesty.

It was a round, white room, draped with tapestries of the same dark and gold cloth that formed the underground people's clothing, with here and there a weaving of dark red or fiery orange. When these colours occurred, they were almost invariably woven in the shape of a burning sun. In one tapestry, dark red cloth formed hundreds of tiny red flowers on a golden background. In the center of the tapestry was a crown, woven in black, with seven white stars over it.

Below this tapestry stood a dais, and on the dais a throne, carved of black stone and adorned with jewels. An old man sat on it, his single lock of hair snowy white and his dark eyes still bright and sharp. Twelve lampstands glowed along the back of the dais, six on either side of the throne.

Four men and two women sat on the dais around the throne. Their appearance contrasted sharply with everyone Maggie had yet seen. They wore long robes. Their wrists, ankles, waists, and necks were encircled by dark red braid. Most striking of all, their hair was long and full. The hair of the men was bound with a single cord at the neck and fell past their waists; the hair of the women was worn long and reached nearly to their ankles.

Harutek ascended the steps of the dais and fell on one knee before the throne. The white-haired Majesty laid his hand on his son's shoulder.

"Rise, Sixteenth Son," he said.

"My father," said Harutek as he stood. "The leader of the intruders has come to speak with you."

The Ploughman stepped forward and bowed low. "Majesty," he said. "I am honoured."

"The tongue of the intruder is gentler than his chisel, that carves a home out of realms that belong to others," said the

Majesty. "Gentler than the tramp of boots he leads down into my earth."

"Majesty," the Ploughman answered, "we meant no intrusion. Today we have learned of your existence for the first time. We only sought shelter."

"Yes," the Majesty said. "As others sought shelter below the ground, long ago, and found it. My forefathers carved a refuge from this rock. If you have come to take it from us, we will fight."

"We have not," the Ploughman said. "I do not mean to make the underground a permanent home, nor do any of my people. When the time comes that we may go above safely, we are more than willing to leave your possession to you."

"He says he will leave it," the Majesty said, half-whispering the words. "He will leave it as he found it. Doesn't he know the damage he has already done?"

The old king stood, revealing a back and shoulders bent with age. He straightened himself as far as he could and said, "I am the Majesty, Lord of the Darkworld: Nahtano, son of Tebazil, son of Haiso; Sire of Seventeen Sons; Keeper of the Black River; Guardian of the Holy Priesthood. My forefathers carved this kingdom far away from the Sunworld. And now, in my day, the Sunworld has come down to us. How can I believe that things will ever be the same?"

He remained standing for a moment, his eyes looking away: to the past, perhaps, or to the future. Then he shuffled back a step and sat down in his throne of black rock. With a white hand he gestured to his left.

"Come, my son, Harutek," he said. "Sit with me."

Harutek moved to the place beside his father and sat down.

Once more the Majesty indicated a place beside him, this time on his right. "And you, leader of the Sunworlders, come."

The Ploughman bowed his head again and stood. He mounted the smooth steps of the dais and sat on his cloak beside the king.

For the first time the Majesty seemed to see the others. "These," he said, motioning toward them. "What shall we do with these?"

One of the long-haired men, who was taller than most of his people and whose hair was black as the Vltava River, bowed his head near the old king's ear.

"If you will, Revered Guardian," he said, "allow my brethren and myself to minister to our guests."

"It is well, Divad," said the Majesty. "Do with them as seems best to you."

Divad bowed again and gracefully descended the steps of the dais. His five companions followed him, seeming to hover over the ground rather than walk on it.

Divad approached the Sunworlders, who had broken their line to huddle together. He bowed with his hands spread apart, the dark red braid around each of his wrists glinting in the lantern light. When he looked up, his eyes were calm and welcoming.

"Come with me," he said. "The Holy Priesthood will do all we can to comfort your spirits while our leaders commune."

"Thank you," Professor Huss answered. "I think I should like a chance to speak with you."

Divad smiled. "And I with you," he said.

The long-haired priests now gently broke up the huddle formed by their guests. Divad stepped close to Professor Huss and began to lead him away, while the other priests each chose a particular guest to make their own. A young priestess, whose ankle-length hair was bound in hundreds of tiny braids, took Maggie's arm.

"I am Rehtse," she said in a low voice. "Welcome to the Darkworld."

Maggie smiled and murmured her thanks. She could hear the others giving their own names in equally low, calm voices. "Nahtan." "Haras." "Hazrit." "Annan."

The small company glided out of the throne room and through the long, lantern-lit chamber, but they did not reenter the enormous cavern. Instead, Divad led them through a narrow doorway and up a steep flight of stairs. At the top, they entered a round room with a low ceiling. A blue fire burned in the very center of the room. Smoke rose through a cylindrical hole above the fire.

Maggie looked around her with a keen sense of wonder. The chamber was carved—floor, walls, and ceiling—with thousands of intricate scenes and symbols. Firelight deepened the carvings and made them stand out starkly against the pale stone. There were all the symbols and pictures that Maggie had already come to recognize as somehow sacred to these underground people: suns and moons and stars, mountains and trees and flowers, and the crown with seven stars. There were also the symbols of fish, rivers, and two-pronged spears. Braided strands twined all around the other carvings.

Rehtse led Maggie to a cushion by a low table near a fire. "Sit," the priestess said. "You are tired. Sit and be at ease."

Maggie sank onto one of the cushions. Her legs were shaking. Perhaps Rehtse was right: the strange ordeal had exhausted her more than she realized. Pat dropped down onto a cushion on one side of Maggie, and Darne took his seat on the other. The professor was seated across the table with Asa beside him.

The priests made sure each of their guests was comfortable before sweeping from the room, leaving the Sunworlders alone.

"Fascinating," Professor Huss said, his eyes dancing along the shadowed carvings. "Even when the Ploughman first found carvings beneath the city, I never dreamed that anything like this could exist."

"I have known many things in my lifetime," said Asa. "But this—no, this I did not know."

Darne spoke up hesitantly. "Are we—do you think—are we safe here?"

"I have known Divad for less than ten minutes," the professor declared, "but I feel I would trust him with my life."

"You are, you know," Pat said. "Trusting him with your life. If his Majesty wishes to dispose of his guests, how better to do it? Make them comfortable, welcome them with open arms —"

"Hush, Pat," Maggie said, unable to resist smiling a little. "You're going to frighten Darne."

"He's already frightened."

"Well, you don't have to make it worse. Besides, I think Professor Huss is right. I don't know about the Majesty, but I think we can trust the priests."

"The Holy Priesthood," Pat said, looking up. "Who live in absolute darkness and surround themselves with pictures of the sun."

"Yes," Professor Huss said. "And more significant still: the seven-starred crown."

Maggie lowered her voice. "What does it mean?" she asked.

"Suppose we ask them," Professor Huss answered, motioning toward a low door through which the members of the priesthood were already returning. They held steaming platters of fish and flat bread in their hands, and these they lay before their guests, along with stone mugs full of clear liquid.

Maggie raised a mug to her lips and took a swallow. The drink was cold, but it burned in her throat. Rehtse smiled and nodded, and Maggie took another swallow. When the burning subsided, the liquid made her feel stronger.

Divad sat down at the head of the table. His four companions stood behind him, their hands folded, calmly attentive. The black-haired priest raised his cup and smiled before drinking.

A few minutes passed in relative silence as the hungry company devoured their food. The appetites of Darne and Pat especially seemed enhanced by their surroundings. But Professor Huss only picked at the platter before him. Long before the others were finished eating, he pushed his food away and looked eagerly to Divad.

"We thank you for your hospitality," he said.

"We are only too pleased to give it," Divad answered. "In the throne room you indicated that you would like an audience with me. Please, the hour is yours. Say whatever you like."

"With an invitation like that," Huss said, "how can I refuse? Tell me who you are. You are a priest . . ."

Divad nodded. "I am the High Priest of the Holy Priesthood of the Darkworld. These are my brothers and sisters in the faith. In the past there were more of us. The people of our cavern world do not esteem faith so highly as they did in years gone by."

"And what faith?" Huss asked. "What faith do you minister, here under the ground? In the world above, only one faith is allowed—faith in the Emperor's ability to do what is best, even if he kills us."

Divad cocked his head. "Does the Empire still rule?" he asked. "The Empire of Lucius Morel?"

"Indeed it does," Huss said, "though Lucius himself has been dead half a millennium. Lucien Morel is ruler now."

Divad shook his head. "To think both our civilizations have existed so long." He stopped himself. "But I am a poor host, and a poor priest. You asked what we believe."

The four long-haired priests behind Divad bowed their heads as he spoke. "Many long years ago," he said, "the Great War was fought between the King of the Seven-Starred Crown and a rebel who called himself mankind's friend and salvation. Morning Star was his name; long and bloody the conflict. Many turned to Morning Star, but our fathers stood with the King and fought faithfully beside him."

As Divad spoke, the markings on the walls seemed to come to life. It was all there, etched into the rock—the story of the Great War, of the final battle. It seemed to Maggie that she could hear swords clashing, voices breaking, horses pounding over the earth. Even the smells of the fight seemed to reach her. She realized that she was studying her hands and looked up, into Asa's face—but his face was so dark and clouded that she had to look away again.

"The day came," Divad said, "when it was clear the King would lose the war. Mankind had sided against him. Few remained true to their allegiance. In that day, our fathers sent messages to Morning Star, offering their service to him. They pretended loyalty and rode into battle with the King once more, and there on the slopes of the Eastern Land they turned and slaughtered their old comrades.

"They were right. The King lost the war. He sent himself into exile. But something happened. Even our oldest stories cannot explain what. The Blackness—Morning Star and his warriors—disappeared. A barrier came between them and mankind, as though a curtain had fallen through the world. Left to themselves, the people of the Seventh World formed tribes and bands, killing, stealing, and burning in a desperate attempt to keep themselves alive. Our fathers among them. But unlike the others, who grabbed power joyfully, our fathers mourned. Some were driven mad with grief. With guilt.

"After many years a cruel conqueror began to unite the tribes. Lucius Morel. He demanded loyalty. The black-robed ones who were his shadow demanded loyalty. And our fathers would not give it."

Divad looked up, his eyes burning. "The King would come back. They believed it. We believe it. They would not betray him a second time by pledging fealty to the conqueror who ruled by dark powers and sorcery. We resolved to throw ourselves on the King's mercy and judgment. He may slay us when he returns. It is his right, and we will bend our knee to it.

"Our fathers led the people underground. Here we were hidden from Morel and his evil. Here we determined to wait and to offer our services to the King once more. When he returned, we would go forth ahead of him. We would turn the world back to him."

Divad looked up to the low ceiling of the chamber, where blue firelight flickered on the carved sky. "Our people struggled below ground. Many died of sun-sickness. Others were driven mad by the darkness. In those days of hardship the Holy Priesthood was formed to care for the weak—and above all, to keep our people in remembrance of the King. So that is the faith we hold, Sunworlder. We wait for the return of the King, hoping that he will look on the fidelity we have shown him these five hundred years and forget that we once betrayed him."

"Tell me," Professor Huss said. "Do your people still hope to return to the Sunworld and make the Empire ready for his return?"

For the first time since he had begun his story, Divad averted his eyes. "That is for the Majesty to decide," he said. "For me, I think as my predecessors have thought. The world above is enslaved to the darkness that worked in Lucius Morel and surely works in his descendants. To go above would only mean death for us and would not offer help for others."

Huss looked troubled. "Perhaps you are right," he said. "But I fear the King will leave us in darkness as long as we are content to stay there."

"What do you know of the matter?" Divad asked earnestly. "Tell me, teacher from the world above: have you the faith of the King in the Sunworld also?"

"Some have," Huss said. "Some have. I suppose we have come underground for many of the same reasons you did." The professor smiled wryly. "The ancient war has begun again, Divad. My eyes looked on the first battle between the King and the Blackness to be fought in centuries. Hardly a season ago, a force of rebels, led by the very man who is now speaking with your King, attacked the Empire's men in the city directly over our heads. We would have lost the battle, but Golden Riders joined us—only to disappear after the battle. Truth to be told, I still sometimes wonder if I really saw what I did."

Divad looked around the table. "And these?" he asked. "Were they also there?"

"I was," Maggie answered.

"And I," Pat said.

"This happened above our very heads," Divad said. "And we knew nothing of it."

Maggie smiled at the tone of loss in Divad's voice, suddenly wanting very much to comfort him. "If you'll allow me," she said, "I can sing you the story of it."

Professor Huss opened his mouth to answer, but Divad beat him to it. "Do so, please," he said.

Maggie closed her eyes and felt the song welling up deep within. She let the words and melody pour forth, as she had done before. She felt, as always before, that she was not singing the song so much as the song was singing her. She sang the story of the Battle of Pravik as it had sung itself in her dreams every night since: the story of farmers and townspeople who stood against powers of darkness, the story of Nicolas and Jerome, of the Ploughman and his lady, of the mystery that was Virginia.

In and through the song a theme wove itself: *awakening.*
In her spirit as she sang, Maggie felt the darkness around her
like a weight, like a heavy sleep. Her song called to the sleeping
world to raise its head and come to life again.

When she finished singing, Rehtse and Annan had turned
away; Hazrit, the other woman priest, was lost in tears. Divad
himself seemed lost in a deep reverie.

The soft voice of Haras broke the spell. "Hail, Harutek," he
said.

Maggie turned to witness the entrance of the Sixteenth Son
of the Majesty.

10

Lover-Song

HARUTEK SMILED BROADLY and spread out his hands. "The Majesty has sent me to announce peace between our people," he said. "Your leader has found favour in his eyes. The guests of the Darkworld Kingdom are to join in the celebrations of this year-night, as a sign of our goodwill."

Divad stood, and the others at the table hastened to do the same. "This year-night is a sacred time in the Darkworld," he explained. "With your presence, we will make this year one to be remembered always, should our people remain underground yet another five centuries."

"Let us hope you do not have to remember it that long," Huss answered. "We are honoured, son of the Majesty."

"Well then," said Harutek. "The preparations for the night are nearly finished. Will you see that our guests are properly tended to until the celebrations begin, Divad?"

"Of course," the priest answered.

Divad turned to his fellow priests and uttered a few commands in a strange language. The professor leaned forward at the sound of the words, and Maggie felt a deep excitement.

Not since the reign of Lucius Morel had more than one language been spoken in the Seventh World—but here, deep under the ground, another race had lived out five hundred years beyond the reach of the Empire.

In obedience to Divad's instructions, Hazrit and Rehtse came forward and led Pat and Maggie out of the chamber. From the corner of her eye, Maggie saw Darne, Asa, and Professor Huss leave the chamber with the male priests.

Rehtse and Hazrit led Pat and Maggie down innumerable long corridors and through many carved chambers. They were empty—it seemed to Maggie that they had once been designed to house many priests, but so few held that office now. They descended a flight of stairs and came out in a high-walled room where lanterns glowed blue on the walls while water splashed down a splendid waterfall and collected in a sparkling pool surrounded by smooth grey boulders.

"The water is quite warm," Hazrit said. "There is soap here," as she reached into a crevice near the waterfall, "and these robes are for drying. Please, take as long as you need. The celebration will not begin for another hour at least. We have clean clothing if you wish it, though you may find your own garments more comfortable."

Maggie smiled at the dubious way in which Hazrit said this. "We would be grateful for a clean change of clothes," she answered. "I feel as though I've been wearing these since the Battle of Pravik."

Hazrit smiled and left the high-walled chamber, followed by Rehtse. Pat laughed out loud when the priestesses were gone.

"Did you see the way she looked at our clothes?" she asked.

"She's probably not used to seeing a woman in trousers," Maggie said, looking at Pat. Pat grinned and ran her hand through her short dark hair. "Nor one with such short hair . . . but what am I saying? These people have less hair than I have ever seen."

"No wonder," Maggie said, lifting the edge of one of the robes Hazrit had indicated. "I think their clothes are made of it."

"What?" Pat exclaimed. "Of human hair?"

"What else?" Maggie asked. "They can't grow anything here, or hunt anything besides fish."

Pat joined Maggie in examining the closely-woven robe. "You're right," she said.

Maggie smiled. "I knew I was."

Pat pulled one of her trouser legs up and stuck her toes under the waterfall. "And Hazrit was right," she said. "This water is *warm*."

"I haven't been warm since we moved underground," Maggie said.

"Mmm," Pat said. "This is going to fell heavenly. Oh, bless those long-haired priests. They know how to make a guest feel welcome."

Hazrit returned twenty minutes later with long dresses made of woven brown hair, adorned with rich golden highlights. She and Rehtse helped Pat and Maggie dress, surrounding their waists with thick gold braid and covering their arms with sleeves of the same colour. The clothing was rich, not like that of the common people, and both young women were conscious of the honour with which they were treated. Rehtse did Maggie's hair up, handling the auburn locks carefully.

"Your hair is beautiful," she said as she worked. Hazrit smiled her agreement as she combed Pat's hair with a comb made of shell. The older priestess hesitated a moment, then said, "Your song was beautiful also. You have a gift."

"That is more true than you know," Maggie said. "I never sang before last fall, when the songs began to come to me. They are a gift—from the King, I believe."

Hazrit rested her hands at the back of Pat's neck. "Yes," she said. "When you sang I felt that he was here, and our long waiting was over."

"I've been told that waiting is the hardest thing in the world," Maggie said with a smile. "And I believe it, after one season spent so doing. And you have been waiting your whole lives!"

"Sometimes I do not know which is worse," Hazrit said. "The agony of the wait, or the dullness that comes when that agony subsides."

"At least when we feel the pain of waiting," Rehtse added, "we know that we are alive, and that we really do believe. Your song made my heart ache, and I thank you for it." Rehtse laid down her combs and looked at Maggie, smiling. The young priestess held out her hands. "You are beautiful," she said. "Come now. The Majesty and his sons wait, and the patience of the Darkworld rulers is the stuff ballads are made of."

Maggie took Rehtse's hands and stood, while Hazrit linked her arm with Pat's. Together they left the waterfall chamber and followed a dizzying maze of tunnels until they came out in the long cave before the throne room of the Majesty. The cave had been transformed. When Maggie had last walked through it, it was empty except for the guards who stood between the lanterns on the walls. Now long tables lined it, loaded with whole fish, flat loaves of bread as big as dinner plates, and pots of a steaming green vegetable. The clear brew which burned and revived so effectively was also abundant, along with three or four other drinks.

On the platform that led to the throne room doors, a long table had been set. There, in all his glory, sat the Majesty. He was dressed all in white, with glittering adornments of white, pink, and purple fish scales. The Ploughman sat between Harutek and the Majesty, and Divad was already seated on the king's other hand with Professor Huss beside him. Darne and Asa sat alongside the seventeen sons of the Majesty. Each of these wore one lock of hair, like their father and Harutek. The other priests—Haras, Annan, and Nahtan—were also at the table. Ytac and his men, wearing fish-scale armour and long capes, guarded the table with their arms folded across their chests.

Rehtse and Hazrit led Maggie and Pat to their places. They found themselves sitting at nearly opposite ends of the table. Maggie sat between Rehtse and Darne, who kept moving his hands—from his lap to his sides to the table and back again—as though he wasn't sure where to put them. Maggie laid a reassuring hand on his arm.

"I'm glad you're here," he whispered.

"Relax," Maggie answered.

On Darne's other hand, a young prince, who could not have been older than nineteen, was talking energetically with

Asa. Their voices were low, and Maggie strained to hear them, but could not catch more than a word here and there.

Rehtse saw her watching them and said, "Caasi, Seventeenth Son of the Majesty, is a young man of strong passion."

"And our Asa is . . . strange," Maggie said. "He has been with us since early winter, but we know little about him."

"They seem to enjoy each other's company," Rehtse said.

Just then Caasi turned his head and looked at the young women. Rehtse blushed and turned her eyes down. Maggie bowed her head to the young prince. He nodded back and resumed his conversation with Asa.

The hall filled until there was not an inch of space left at the tables, its sides lined with people who stood against the walls. Beyond the open hall door, many others gathered in the cavern. The excitement of the gathering was palpable, although the clamour seemed somehow hushed: subdued by the walls and roof of rock. When the hall was full, the Majesty stood. His sons raised their hands together and clapped three times. The sound echoed in the hall, and the crowd fell silent.

"Welcome, my people," the Majesty said. "This night we celebrate with greater than usual joy, for seated with us is the leader of the Sunworlders who have encroached on our territory."

A ripple of whispers ran through the hall, and the Majesty held up his hand to silence them. "We have met and spoken together," he said, "and we have found these Sunworlders to be men of honour. We have their promise that no harm will result from their coming."

There was a cheer, and the Majesty added, "Nor do they plan to stay." The cheers seemed even louder this time, and Maggie looked down the table at Pat, who raised an eyebrow and choked back a laugh.

"Now, my people," said the Majesty. "Now we celebrate the Night of the Warm Waters. Good feasting!" The Majesty raised his cup, and all in the hall did the same, thundering out the words: "Good feasting!"

"Good loving!" proclaimed the Majesty, and the hall echoed him. "Good loving!"

Then the seventeen sons of the Majesty stood to their feet, and all together they shouted, "Good hunting!"

Maggie lifted her own voice in the refrain, smiling as the enthusiasm of the response drowned her out. The seventeen princes each took up a loaf of flat bread and broke it, and the gathering fell to the feast.

Despite the meal they had just eaten with the priests, the Ploughman's people had little trouble putting away fish, bread, and steaming green vegetables with the hungriest of the princes. Darne especially seemed to drink vats of the cold, clear drink, and he lost much of his shyness and discomfort as the meal went on, punctuated by shouts of laughter throughout the hall. Servants carried baskets full of fish and bread to the great cavern beyond the hall, rolling caskets full of drink to the crowd. The noise outside the hall was greater, if possible, than it was within.

Maggie had just decided that she could not eat another bite when a high-pitched sound subdued the noise in the room. A small troupe of musicians emerged from a door into the hall, playing an eerie tune on flutes of bone. They danced as they entered, their feet moving faster as the music picked up pace. As the flutes reached a climax, the hall erupted with a shout. The people clapped and stomped their feet as the music played.

The song ended on a long, haunting note, and the musicians bowed to a hall that had fallen completely silent for the first time that night. Now Divad and his priests, Hazrit and Rehtse among them, stood and descended the steps of the platform. They were joined on the floor by other men and women in uniform—not priests, but ready to fulfill some special role.

The flutes began to play once again, a slow song that promised hope, with notes of tragedy woven throughout. As the music played, a score of young women stood from the tables where they had feasted and approached the priests and their helpers in the center of the room. They knelt before them, and Divad and his companions poured a golden substance from small vials onto the heads of the kneelers. Then the priests and their fellows knelt also, whispering in the young women's ears. The music shifted tone slightly, and the priests stood and stretched out their hands to a table of young men.

The young men stood and went to the priests. A slight stir arose from the head table, and one of the Majesty's seventeen sons joined the group on the floor. The priests took each young man by the hand and led him to a woman, laying the youths' hands on the waiting heads. In response to song, the priests lifted their hands and spoke in the strange language Maggie had heard Divad use. The young men touched their knees to the floor and then rose, pulling their new brides up with them. The faces of the young couples glowed with joy, and one of the

197

flute players let out a whoop. The flutes flung the hall into a dance, and the newly joined men and women danced to the thin piping with smiles and blushes and obvious delight.

The dance continued for some time, while the onlookers shouted their approval and downed more of the clear drink. At last Divad, who had regained the platform, raised his hands for silence. The flute players ended their song and bowed respectfully, and the rest of the hall followed their example. The brides returned to the tables while the men stood to their feet. For the time, Maggie realized that every man in the hall held a two-pronged spear.

"This is the time of the Warm Water," Divad said. "Tonight we are blessed with fish and good hunting. May the Seven-Starred King go with you. May he protect you and fill your hands with bounty. Go and drink of the waters of strength; return, and drink of the waters of love."

The priests bowed their heads low when Divad finished. The hunters—or fishers, for it was certainly fish they went to slaughter—left the hall quietly, respectfully. Shouts greeted them in the cavern and echoed strangely in the hall, as though they came from far away.

Maggie watched the last of the men leave. She turned to say something to Rehtse when Pat grabbed her hand. "Come on!" she said. "You're not going to miss this, are you?"

The rest of the night passed in a blur. They followed the hunters out of the hall to a place where long ladders stretched up the sides of the cavern. These they climbed until their hands and feet were nearly numb, and at last they came out in the open night air.

Maggie didn't quite believe it at first. Surely they had not stepped outside! The lights of a single bridge in the nearly-abandoned city of Pravik, reflecting on the black water, told her that it was true. They had left the underground. She gulped the air with tears in her eyes, hardly noticing the astringent smell or the taste of smoke in the air. The air was cold, but it was the gentle cold of spring and not the bitter freeze of winter. The Darkworld hunters dived into the river again and again, staying under the water far longer than seemed possible, and returned with fish—huge, gasping fish that were loaded into baskets and sent back through the tunnels to the great cavern to be smoked and salted or cooked and eaten right there.

Maggie's recollection of the evening was fuzzy, made so by the blurring of her eyes and the lurch of her stomach, which she supposed was caused by drinking a little too much of the cold liquid at the feast. The only thing she felt clearly—and still felt clearly, sharply, the next day—was the heady sense of freedom in knowing there was nothing above her but sky and stars and the glorious moon. The moon was not to be seen, and the stars were blocked by clouds, but it hardly mattered.

Maggie was in tears when the tide of humanity carried her back underground; she was silent and morose when a young man—it might have been Caasi—carried her down the ladders to the lair of the priests. She hardly heard the low voice of Rehtse as she conferred with Maggie's benefactor—now she was certain, it *had* to be Caasi—and she was asleep before Rehtse made her comfortable in a simple bed in the priestess's own chambers.

Her dreams were invaded by music, the song she had sung for the priests mingling with the dream-shout of voices, the clash of swords, and the high, thin, haunting sound of flutes.

Maggie woke up sometime the next day and staggered down a familiar corridor toward the sound of water. She found herself in the waterfall chamber and availed herself of the soap and water before putting her own clothes back on. They had been washed and dried and hung over a rock in the waterfall room. Maggie's head ached as she dressed, and there was a taste like silver in her mouth.

Hazrit appeared in the door of the chamber once Maggie was dressed. She smiled gently. "Breakfast," she said. "This way."

Maggie followed her down the corridors to the circular room where the priests had first led their guests the night before. The others were there, all except Darne, and all were dressed in their own clothing again. Pat seemed glad to be back in trousers, though Maggie caught the looks on the faces of Rehtse and Hazrit that said they did not entirely approve.

Maggie eased onto a cushion next to Pat and took a bite of hot bread. Pat was stripping a last bit of fish off its bones.

"Try the fish, Maggie," she said. "It's fresh today."

"Did it happen?" Maggie asked, obediently taking a piece of fish. "All the—celebrations . . . and did we really go outside?"

Pat nodded. "Imagine," she said. "These people have been going out to the river once every year for five centuries, and no one has caught onto their existence yet."

Maggie mumbled something about it being amazing, but she felt a pang when she talked of the world above that hurt too much to aggravate it by continuing the conversation. Darne staggered in and to the table, led by an amused Haras. He sat down and slurred an apology for being late. He ate very little. Maggie noticed that only water was poured at the breakfast table.

They returned to the court of the Majesty when they were finished eating. The Darkworld king and his sons, who were all in attendance, welcomed them warmly, presented them with gifts—Maggie was given a necklace with a woven image of the sun for a pendant—and bade them farewell.

They did not go alone. The young priest Haras accompanied them, along with Ytac, the captain of the guard, and the prince Harutek.

* * *

Lucien Morel, the man who ruled the world, stared at the ceiling of his ornate bedroom and trembled. Sweat poured down his face, drenching his feather pillows and lately-clean sheets. He pointed a shaky finger at the shadows, punctuating his speech with it.

"I *told* you to go! I told you I would take care of things. They are a plague, I know; but I will stamp it out."

Nothing moved or spoke in the darkness. Yet the Emperor's fear refused to abate. He had awakened, sweating and terrified, from a dream in which the river had flooded the world. He had tried to sit up, to calm his pounding heart. Images from the dream kept flashing at him. Gypsies dancing on the water over him, even as he drowned. A great red dragon wrapping its long tail around his waist and dragging him down, its eyes gleaming like jewels. And the Gypsies laughing.

His finger twitched violently. He had tried to calm his pounding heart upon awakening, but that was before he felt it.

The Presence.

He had never told anyone about the Presence. They thought he was mad, after all. He was not mad. He was *haunted.*

The Presence swathed his heart like grave clothes. Instead of pounding, it nearly stopped. The Emperor gasped for breath.

"I told you!" he screamed into the shadows. "I've done it! My soldiers are everywhere, rounding them up. I bring them here; they're caged like rats!" He stuck his finger in the air again, trying to find the eyes whose glare he could feel but never see. "*You* . . . you leave me alone. I'm doing it."

In the shadows, words impressed themselves on the Emperor of the Seventh World.

It is not enough.

Lucien Morel's whole body shook with fear, laced with a desperate rage that alone kept him breathing. All he wanted was to rule his Empire in peace. He had not slept through the night in months—sometimes it seemed like years.

"It will be," he said. "I will do enough. I will do all that is needed."

The Presence faded. He felt its warning as it left. It would return. It would not trust him. It would haunt him till the promise was fulfilled. Till he had done everything in his power to rid the world of the plague called Gypsies.

Lucien Morel tried to sleep, but he feared too much what might lie on the other side of his eyelids. Somewhere in the palace he could hear water running. Nightmarish sound. He rose instead, and passed the night in pacing.

* * *

As the weeks passed, the persecution of the Gypsies
resumed in full force. Those bands which had before escaped
were rounded up, decimated, herded toward Athrom. But now
a counter-fear dwelt in the roads, striking the hearts of the
High Police. The Gypsies were fighting back. The dirt of the
roads covered over deep stains of blood.

The name of the Major was whispered among the refugees
and captives. Many waited for him to rescue them, and the
Major and his small band did. Others grew tired of waiting and
struck back at their captors themselves. In some cases they won
their freedom. In other cases they won their deaths.

The High Police began to devote larger troops to the cause
of rounding up the Wandering Race. They tramped the roads,
heavily armed and watchful. The renegade bands of Gypsies
who attacked the police—for others took up the example of the
Major and his young allies, forming vigilante groups
themselves—risked more and more every time they fought for
their freedom.

But they kept fighting. And everywhere, carved on rocks
and tree trunks and fence posts, the markings of the Gypsy race
told tales of battles and suffering. They promised vengeance
and encouraged hope. The weary captives who passed by the
writing felt their blood quicken at the knowledge that great
things had been done where they stood.

It was a bright day, full of flower-perfume, when a young
scout brought the message to the Major and his fighting band
of fifteen Gypsies. "Captives driving over the fields, half a mile

west of the north road," he reported. "They look to be in bad shape, and there aren't many guards."

"Aren't many?" the Major repeated. "That's not how I've taught you to scout, boy."

The scout coloured. "There's not much cover in the fields," he said. "I couldn't get close. But I counted four guards, sir. No more."

The Major smiled through his thick black beard. "Good boy," he said. "Well, Nicolas: and how are we to handle these four guards in the open fields where there is no cover?"

Nicolas smiled. "I say we walk up and reason with them," he said.

The Major nodded, and the scout's jaw dropped. "But—" he started to say.

Nicolas stood and knocked the scout's cap down so it covered his eyes. "Never question your elders," he said. "Now, look up and see what I mean."

The scout took the cap from his head, exposing a head of wild curls, and his jaw dropped for a second time. He nearly shouted the alarm, but the soldier in black and green who now stood before him removed his pipe from his mouth and grinned.

"The Pipe-Smoker," the boy stuttered.

"In the flesh," Nicolas said. "We captured a few uniforms in the last skirmish down by the vineyards. Now, exactly which way are our friends heading?"

The scout described their course in detail. Nicolas and the Major nodded with satisfaction. The police and their captives would soon be within eyeshot of a dilapidated old barn.

The Major's band moved fast. In less than twenty minutes, Marja had led most of the fighters to the barn. The Major, Nicolas, Peter, and the young scout dressed themselves in the stolen uniforms and went out to meet the enemy. They removed their earrings and head scarves, preferring the decoration of thickly smeared mud and red berries, crushed and smeared on their faces. From all appearances, they'd lately had the worst of a fight.

They had barely reached the field when they saw the captives. It was a large group, some thirty of them, in bad shape as the scout had said. Most were men, but they staggered as they walked, and some fell. Nicolas's face burned as he heard the shouts of the High Police and saw the butt of a spear fall on the head and shoulders of a Gypsy too weak to resist.

Swallowing his rage, Nicolas tore the sleeve of his uniform a little more and began to run, limping slightly as he went. "Stop!" he shouted. "There is danger!"

Two soldiers were leading the procession. They reined in their horses as Nicolas approached. Nicolas grabbed the bridle of one of the horses and gasped for breath.

"What is it?" one of the High Police said. "Speak, man!"

"Treachery," Nicolas gasped out. "The Gypsy murderers are on the road close by. They attacked us as we brought captives to Italya. They have scouts everywhere—they will set upon you when you least expect it."

"Indeed," said the rider whose horse Nicolas had latched onto. "How big is this band?"

"There are twenty at least," Nicolas answered. "All armed and healthy. You are no match for them—not here in the open."

"Then what shall we do?" asked the other front rider.

"There is a barn back that way," Nicolas said, pointing in the direction indicated. "Take your prisoners there. Then you can fight with the barn wall to your back. And if things turn to the worse for you, you may fire the barn and keep the prisoners from escaping." Nicolas's eyes glinted as he said this. The memory of a past fight was still fresh in his mind.

The lead soldier nodded. "You are right," he said. "And can we count on your sword and that of your friends?"

Nicolas nodded. "Of course," he said.

Half an hour later, the barn door creaked and groaned as Nicolas pushed it open, and the soldiers herded their captives in.

"Quickly," Nicolas said, even as the Major, Peter, and the scout slipped in through the door. The soldiers had just finished herding their prisoners together when the Major slammed the barn door shut. The only light came in through cracks in the door and the walls, painting dusty streaks in the dirt and hay and casting shadows on an overturned wagon.

"What is the meaning of this?" the lead soldier demanded, drawing his sword.

"Three guesses," Nicolas said. "One, you're caught. Two, you're too dull to recognize an enemy when he's staring you in the face. Or three, you're caught."

Marja and the other members of the Major's band appeared from behind the wagon and out from under the straw. A few jumped down from the loft overhead and landed on the packed earth. All had their swords drawn and waiting.

"You can surrender now," Nicolas said softly.

The soldier lowered the tip of his sword. "Actually," he said, "I don't think so."

There was a sudden cry from above as one of the Major's Gypsies hurtled down from the loft. He landed on one of the captives with a shout of "Fake!" The next instant he was dead—killed by a long knife drawn from beneath the clothes of a blood-smeared Gypsy.

The soldier lunged forward. Nicolas barely had enough time to jump out of the way. Their swords clashed, but Nicolas proved faster than his adversary. He cut the man down with one swift thrust. In the next moment his sword rang again, this time crossed with that of a man dressed in the colourful, dirty rags of the Wandering Race. The man's sword slashed Nicolas's uniform but missed his flesh.

The barn rang with the battle. Nicolas's compatriots, outnumbered two to one, fought like cornered wildcats. Bear roared out of a stall and knocked the enemy over with his furious strength. But the men in disguise—mercenaries or High Police, whichever they were—had the advantages of training and surprise.

Nicolas had defeated two more men, one with Peter's help, when he found himself battling a giant. A quick flip of his wrist at just the right time wrenched the huge man's sword from him, but Nicolas dropped his own in the action. A moment later the wind was knocked out of him as the giant charged into him. They burst through the barn door and into the dusty field.

The man's hands closed around Nicolas's throat, and he fought for breath. Spots danced across his vision as he pulled his legs up and rammed his feet into the giant's stomach. The man's hands loosened as he let out a startled puff of air. Nicolas dragged air into his lungs and choked on the dust. The man's hands tightened around his throat again, and a massive knee drove into his stomach.

Strains of music passed wildly through Nicolas's mind as his eyes lost sight. He heard the Father-Song, loud and furious, and behind it the harmonies—the two other strains needed to make up the Song of the Burning Light. Voices danced through the music. He heard the lament of the Shearim, dying their long death in the air all around him; the River-Daughter calling him; Marja screaming his name. Then the Major's voice: *"Marja, come back!"*

His eyes had grown dark. He heard the grass growing, the thoughts-that-were-not-thoughts of the worms in the dirt under his head, the dirt that was soaking up his life.

Help me, he thought. Or maybe he said it—though how a plea could escape his lips now he did not know.

He woke up, and he was not dead. Marja was with him. Marja was cradling his head in her lap, and her hair was falling over his face. His body jolted. He heard the clatter of wheels. They were passing over the ruts in a road.

"Where are we?" he asked, but the words did not come out as words, only as a groan.

"Hush," Marja said. He heard tears in her voice and felt them on his face.

"Where are we going?" he asked. This time, half the words came out the way they were supposed to.

"To join our brethren," she said.

"Where are—" he started to ask.

"Oh, would you hush?" she answered.

"No," he said. "Where—"

"The Major and Peter are safe," she said, sobbing as she said it. "They got away. No one else."

"We didn't?"

"No, Nicolas, we didn't. We were taken."

"Bear . . ."

"I don't know," she said. She bent her face close to his so their foreheads touched and her tears ran over his face. "I'm so sorry."

Nicolas was still fighting for comprehension. His whole body hurt—his throat when he talked screamed at him to stop. But he couldn't. Not yet.

"You came back for me?" he asked. "I heard the Major call to you." His words were coming out almost normally now, even though Marja could barely talk from crying.

"Yes, I came back," she said. "What if I did?"

He closed his eyes and remembered her telling him, *"Love is a choice. Love is the decision to be there when you're needed."*

He opened his eyes again and surveyed her face. She had stopped crying, and the look on her face was as brave as it could be, defensive against him. He smiled a little. Of course, he knew now—the river had led him to her, just as surely as it had brought him to his father.

Marja was a part of the song, too.

"You came back because you love me?" he asked.

"Yes," she said.

"Will you marry me?" he asked.

She sobbed with her face next to his. "Yes."

He kissed her forehead gently. And he heard it then: the second strain of the Song of the Burning Light. He heard it clearly and beautifully there in the prison wagon, as they bumped over the ruts in the road. The bruises on his neck hurt, and he could smell Marja's hair. It was the Lover-Song, and it was beautiful.

11

Gifted

IT WAS MID-SPRING, and the Green Isle was living up to its name.
Shannon O'Roarke balanced a shepherd's crook across her
knees as she watched the play of children and lambs on the
mountain pastureland that swept down to the sea. The air
smelled sweet with new green shoots, and a coquettish breeze
blew the sounds of surf and laughter up the mountainside to
the stone where she sat, absently tearing pieces of grass into
her skirt.

She had gone with the four clann children, who had
abandoned their task of sheep watching in favor of romping in
the grass. Two black and white dogs played with them, and the
white wolf—whose presence Shannon had at last come to
accept, as she accepted Miracle's, without question or fear.

Miracle returned from wandering higher on the
pastureland and sat down in the grass. Hours in the rose
garden had perfumed her hair and skin. Shannon couldn't help
breathing a little more deeply when Miracle was beside her.

"They grow so fast," Miracle said, the northern accent in

her voice still strong. "They were much smaller when I came, weren't they?"

Shannon looked out at the children and smiled. "The sea air grows them fast here," she said.

"It grows roses well," Miracle said. "I have twice the response from them here as I do in Fjordland, and with half the work."

"You have a special touch with the roses," Shannon said. "I'm sure they've never bloomed so early before."

"Children and roses," Miracle said. "Both will grow for a hand that loves them." She smiled up at Shannon. "I'm sure that's why the children grow so well here."

"Aye," Shannon said. "The O'Roarkes have always loved their children. And now we have Michael and Stocky home to protect them, and Kris to spoil them, and you to make the little boys go weak at the knees when you smile."

Miracle laughed. "No, they don't," she said.

A barking dog launched itself up the hill into Shannon's lap, and a dark-haired boy, eleven years old but small for his age, limped up to Miracle and brought a handful of purple flowers out from behind his back. He held them out.

"Are these for me, Kieran?" Miracle asked.

"Aye," Kieran said softly, with his eyes turned down. "I picked them for you."

"Thank you," Miracle said. She pried his fingers from the prickly stems with one hand, taking the flowers in the other. "They're beautiful."

Kieran opened his mouth to say something, but turned and ran instead. Shannon laughed merrily.

"I told you," she said.

Miracle watched the boy as he hobbled back down the hill with the dog on his heels. The white wolf loped up to greet him, and the boy stumbled and fell, rolling until the wolf stopped him.

"Why does he limp, Shannon?" Miracle asked.

"He fell under a carriage when he was learning to walk," Shannon said. "The driver tried to stop, but it was too late—the wheels only rolled back over his leg when the driver pulled back on the reins."

"I'm sorry," Miracle said.

"Eh, so am I," Shannon said. "I was there. I should have been watching him, but I was distracted. It nearly killed his mother when she saw him. She thought her baby had been crushed. That was the worst of it all—knowing how she felt." Shannon's eyes grew distant.

"But he lived," Miracle said.

Shannon nodded. "He did that. And his mother knew that he would live, before she died herself." Abruptly, she stood and whistled. The children, far down the hillside, turned their heads to look at her. She waved for them to come up.

"Archer!" she called. "Take back your crook. I resign."

Archer, the oldest of the children, was a handsome, golden-haired boy of thirteen years. He took the staff from Shannon while the others crowded around him.

"Cannot you stay a little longer, Shannon?" one of the boys, a red-headed scamp called Seamus, asked.

"Only if you don't want any dinner," Shannon answered, shaking her skirt as she stood. Bits of grass rained down. "Get along with you. Archer, bring the sheep in before dark. There's rain blowing in from the sea."

213

"Yes, Shannon," Archer said. He turned and ambled down the hillside. The other children reluctantly followed him.

Miracle stood and walked with Shannon. Stocky waved at them from the middle of a field he was ploughing. The air was beginning to smell like rain.

They smelled the roses before they reached the cottage. Shannon left Miracle in the garden. She brought a bucket of water in from the pump and poured it into a pot on the stove. As she bent over to stoke the fire, a pair of fingers poked into her sides.

Shannon jumped and whirled around, nearly smacking Michael in the head. "Are you trying to frighten me out of my wits, Michael?" she demanded.

He grinned. "Never."

Shannon turned back to her soup pot. "How went the day?" she asked.

"Well enough," Michael answered.

"Did the old man agree to up Archer's wages?"

"I didn't ask him."

Shannon turned around and shook her wooden spoon reprovingly. "Michael . . ."

"He wasn't in a good mood. I'll ask him tomorrow."

"Where's Kris?"

"Walking."

"Miracle's in the garden." Shannon took a cutting board from a peg on the wall and slapped it onto the counter. "Give me those potatoes, and go talk to her."

Michael obediently lugged the bag of potatoes from the corner to Shannon's side. "Why should I go talk to her?" he asked. "It's nice in here."

Shannon shot him a withering glare. "Because you can't drag a girl here from halfway round the world and ignore her," she said.

"I haven't ignored her," Michael answered.

"I've noticed," Shannon said. "So go talk to her."

"And what do you want me to say?" Michael asked.

"How about, 'Will you marry me?'" Shannon said, chucking a board-load of potatoes into the pot and splashing hot water in all directions.

There was a long silence. Then, "That's not funny, Shannon."

"It's not supposed to be," she said. She turned and looked at her brother. "What did you bring her here for, if it wasn't because you love her?"

"I've never said that," Michael said. "I brought her here because she needed help."

"*And* because you love her," Shannon said. "Anyone can see that. Miracle especially. It's not fair to pretend you don't."

"I'm not pretending anything," Michael said. "It's not that simple."

"What's so complicated?" Shannon asked. She moved closer and sat down, wiping her hands on her apron. "You and Kris and Stocky have been hiding the truth from me—all of us —since you got here. And if I start to hint at what happened in Fjordland, Miracle gets a look in her eyes that makes me afraid to ask further. But you've never kept secrets from me, Michael. Tell me what happened."

Michael looked away for a long time. "I can't," he said finally.

Shannon stood and returned to her soup pot. "All right," she said.

* * *

"The soup's getting cold." Jenna, a teenaged girl of the clann, placed the lid back on the pot and looked at Shannon. Rain pattered on the dark windows.

"Let it," Shannon said. She closed her eyes. "Where *are* they?"

An old woman, grey hair piled on her head, stood from her rocking chair with a creak and began to pace the room.

"Sit down, Grandmother," Jenna said, approaching the old woman. The woman called Grandmother—the only surviving member of the older generation of O'Roarkes—shook her head. "No, no," she said. "Let me walk it out. It's so much like . . ."

"Hush," Shannon said sharply. "Don't say it."

Thunder crashed, and all of the women jumped. Jenna's older sister Cali let out a long breath of air and rubbed her pale cheek.

"Grandmother, *do* sit down," Cali pleaded. "You're making me nervous."

Grandmother O'Roarke stopped for the moment and jerked the door open. Rain blew into the cottage in a cold blast.

"Do you see anything?" Grandmother called out, shielding her eyes with a hand. A voice called back from the yard. "Nothing."

"I wish she'd come in," Shannon muttered.

"She's in a tree," Jenna said. "The rain won't pelt her so hard under the leaves."

"I know she's in a tree," Shannon answered. "Safest place to be in a lightning storm."

"Oh . . ." Jenna paled under her freckles.

Grandmother O'Roarke shut the door and sat back down in her rocking chair. She lowered a wrinkled hand and smoothed Miracle's hair away from her face. The northerner was on the floor beside the rocking chair, knees hugged to her chest, staring away at nothing.

"Well," Jenna quavered, "I'm going to eat something."

No one answered her.

Jenna had just succeeded in maneuvering across the crowded floor with a bowl of soup in her hands when the door blew open and a flash of lightning outlined a dripping figure. Cali screamed, and Shannon leapt to her feet, only to sink back into the rocking chair an instant later, breathing in fast, shivering breaths.

"Don't scare us like that, Lilac," she said.

Lilac O'Roarke wrung out her skirt on the doorstep and brushed a lock of dark, curly hair out of her eyes. "Someone's coming," she said. Her face was pale.

"Is it Michael?" Shannon asked. "Has he got the children?"

"No and no," Lilac said. Stark fear lit her eyes, though courage tried to rise up and meet it. "It's a man in black, on horseback. I wouldn't have seen him if it weren't for the lightning."

Miracle was on her feet before anyone else had time to react. She threw her dark cloak around her shoulders and flung the door open. She was too late. The horse outside the door neighed, and the man in black looked down through the open door into the firelit room. Miracle stood frozen in the doorway.

Shannon appeared on one side of Miracle, and Lilac stood on the other. "Leave us alone," Shannon said. "You have no business here."

The man declined to answer, instead throwing back his hood. Miracle gasped slightly. "Christopher?" she said.

"That is my name," he answered. His face held no expression. "I've come to tell you to run. All of you. Where are your men?"

"Searching for the children," Miracle said.

"They won't find them," Christopher answered.

"Where are they?" Shannon demanded.

"Did you hear what I said?" Christopher asked. "Run. Get out now."

"We can't leave until we know what's happened to the children," Miracle answered.

Christopher pounded his horse's neck in frustration, and the animal stamped its foot. "I will come to you later," he said. "I'll tell you what you need to know then. For now you have no time."

Miracle turned to Shannon. "We can trust him," she said.

"The sea-caves," Shannon said, looking bravely up at Christopher. "Come to us there."

Christopher nodded and drove his heels into the horse's side. Thunder rolled as horse and rider disappeared into the black night. When Shannon, Miracle, and Lilac turned back to the room, Grandmother O'Roarke had Cali in her arms. Both were crying.

"Is it happening all over again?" Cali sobbed.

Shannon wiped a tear from her own eye. "Get up," she

said. "Bring cloaks, blankets—a little food. Nothing else. We'll come back for the rest."

The wind had increased to a gale when they quitted the cabin. It blew against them as they trudged over the fields toward the sea. A flash of lightning illuminated a hillside to the left, outlining the silhouettes of ten men. Shannon waved and jumped, shouting through the wind.

"Michael! Here! Come to us here!"

It was doubtful whether the men could have heard her voice through the storm, but the lightning that had revealed the men to the women also revealed the women to them. They ran down the hillside. Michael gripped Shannon's hand with one hand and Miracle's with the other.

"What are you doing?" Michael shouted through the lashing rain. Another flash of lightning etched the pale faces in the darkness.

"The Order is here," Miracle answered. "Christopher warned us to get out."

"To the sea-caves, Michael!" Shannon said.

Michael opened his mouth to say more, but a thunderclap drowned him out. He nodded and waved for the men to follow. Together, the rain-drenched group of refugees headed for the shore.

* * *

The fire crackled brightly inside the dry cave. Shannon held her hands over it as she listened to Michael speak.

"The black-cloaked men—the Order of the Spider—were

in Fjordland when I arrived. They were looking for a Gifted one. Miracle." Michael closed his eyes. "I know I should have turned for home the moment I saw them there, but I couldn't come back and tell you I had failed. I went out to retrace Father's footsteps—to find his hope for myself, and perhaps his power." He grimaced. "But I was a fool. I fell and broke my back. I should have died."

Michael looked up and met Shannon's eyes, though he spoke to them all. "Miracle came to me in a tavern and healed me. When she left the tavern, the Order was waiting for her. I couldn't let them take her without trying to help. Kris and Stocky and I followed them to the fortress of Ordna, and we got her away. The man who came to our door is one of the Order, but he helped us for Miracle's sake. He betrayed his own kind to do it."

"And now he has come to rescue her again," Shannon said. "Or does his benevolence reach *all* who are Gifted?"

Michael hung his head. "I don't know," he said.

"We have to tell her, Michael," Shannon said. "Our secrets have not kept anyone safe."

Michael said nothing. It was Grandmother O'Roarke who took up the tale of her clann, addressing herself to Miracle.

"We were always a small clann," she said. "But a special one. And there was no more special man than my nephew— Thomas O'Roarke, the father of Michael and Shannon. He was what some call 'Gifted.' Some said he worked magic, but we knew it was a Gift given to him. He married a beautiful girl."

"Molly Sullivan," Kris said.

"Yes," Grandmother O'Roarke said, nodding her sage head. "Molly. She looked like you, Shannon."

Shannon smiled, but did not look up from the fire.

"Thomas left us before his marriage to make a journey to the north," Grandmother O'Roarke said. "He returned with this grey-haired menace, Kris of the Mountains—and he returned changed. Gifted, as I said. He married and started a business in the town. It went well—those were good days for us. But then, as people came to recognize Thomas's Gift, they became hostile to us. We could never understand it. True, Thomas could be unnerving. He always seemed to read a person's thoughts. But he was a good man and never used his gifts to harm anyone. And then one day *they* came. The black-cloaked ones. They spoke to Thomas, and when he came home that day he was angry. He said they had wanted him, and he refused to join them."

Grandmother O'Roarke's voice cracked. Jenna and Cali were quietly crying in a corner. Lilac was stirring the straw around with the end of a stick, a stricken expression on her face. Jack, Andrew, and Patrick, the younger men of the clann, guarded the cave entrance and paced far from the fire. They said nothing.

Grandmother O'Roarke regained control. "One night—during a terrible storm—the villagers came to our homestead. They burned it down, trying to get at Thomas. Our brave men and women would not give him up, so they were killed: every last one of them. Only Michael and the other young boys escaped, with Kris."

"And you, Grandmother?" Miracle asked.

"I was here," she said. "In this very cave. With the girls and the babies, the tiny children. When the night was over, Michael had become our chief."

"We thought it was over then," Michael said. "Kris and my father had brought roses from the north. We tended them as a memorial, and as a sign that Kris would stand by our family so long as the roses bloomed. They would not die, for Father had planted them—and something of him was in them. Kris told me to come to him in Fjordland if we ever needed help. Then he left us, and we rebuilt our lives."

"Why did you come to the north again, Michael?" Miracle asked.

"Because our children are Gifted," Michael said. "All of them, we think. The villagers begin to see it. And for a few days last fall, there were black-cloaked men in the village, asking about them. Asking about Father; about us. We have always believed it was they who caused the villagers to attack us. They left, but I knew it wasn't over. I went to Fjordland to seek protection. You know what I found there."

* * *

Rain pelted the window of the train car. The children of Clann O'Roarke huddled together in a corner. The old man who sat across from them, thin hands resting on carved wooden armrests, smiled from under his black hood. But his smile, Archer thought, was as unnatural as a flying serpent.

The man's eyes were boring into him, but Archer refused to meet the stare. He tightened his arm around Moll. Her face, framed by curly hair, was streaked from crying. She had cried the entire way across the Channel—a weird voyage that Archer remembered in colours of green and grey. The pitching of the waves still thumped in his stomach. The smell—strange, bittersweet, sorcerous smell—was still in his nose. Moll had kept him busy comforting, busy being a leader, so he had not given in to fear during the journey. Fear wanted to overwhelm him, but he kept it at bay. It lay low behind his eyes and gave him a headache. Moll lay curled up against him now. His head still ached. He kept his eyes on the little one's curly head and avoided the old man.

"Tell me your name, boy," the old man said. "We should not be strangers."

Archer met the man's eyes for an instant. "I am Archer O'Roarke," he said.

"A strong name," the old man said. "It suits you. I am Master Skraetock. And now that we know one another's names, we are friends."

"I'm Moll," piped up the little one under Archer's arm. Archer pinched her, but Skraetock was already nodding.

"Moll," he said. "Your aunt's name. They must have named you after her."

"Did you know her?" Moll asked, awe sketched across her face.

"We were good friends," Skraetock said.

"You're a liar," Archer said, as much to make Moll stop talking to the man as to confront him. "If you were a friend, you wouldn't have brought us here."

"There you are wrong," Skraetock said. "I have brought you here to protect you from those who fear you. They would destroy you if they could."

"Why?" Archer said. He heard his own voice quaver.

Skraetock smiled again. "Come now," he said. "No secrets. We all know that you are not normal children." Something under Skraetock's cloak moved and yowled. He reached inside and drew out a black cat. Moll and Seamus smiled and exclaimed despite themselves, ignoring Archer's fierce scowls in their direction.

"This is Nowl," Skraetock said. "I brought him to keep you company—I had almost forgotten, can you imagine that? I must be getting very old indeed."

Skraetock set the cat down. It padded across the floor to the children, holding its long black tail in the air. It jumped up on the seat and looked around it with green eyes, suffering in silence while Seamus petted it and scratched its ears.

Moll pulled free from Archer and leaned over to pet the cat. Archer reached out to stop her. He touched her shoulder. The cloth of her shirt felt like smooth stone. There was no warmth, no sign of life. Archer blinked in astonishment. The children, the cat—even the smells and noises of life in the train —had become as wax, frozen and silent. Only the sound of the train wheels still met his ears.

And then the voice of Master Skraetock.

"They are children," he said. "Young and innocent. You are nearly a man. It is with you that I must speak, so I have taken this moment of privacy. You do not mind, I know."

Archer turned his head slowly and looked at the black-robed man. Skraetock had leaned forward. His thin hands were clasped in front of him.

"I should have come to you a long time ago," Skraetock said. "I should have made myself known so you would not fear me now. I am not taking you from your family, Archer O'Roarke, whatever you may think. They will come after you. I am taking you all home."

"Our home is in the Green Isle," Archer said. An image of the little homestead filled his mind, and to his shame he found himself fighting back tears.

"Do you remember Thomas O'Roarke?" Skraetock asked. "Your uncle and chieftain."

"I was little when he died," Archer said.

"He was a good man," Skraetock said. "A great man. The first of the Gifted."

Archer was silent.

"I see you know what I mean by that word," Skraetock said. "Of course you do. You are also Gifted. I am guardian of all who are like you. They come to me for protection and training. Your uncle did not. He wished to remain in the Green Isle. I urged him to reconsider but did not beg him—how since his death have I repented of that! The shadows of death are gathering around your family again, boy. I have come to keep my promise of guardianship over you. It is time you learned all that you are."

"Where are we going?" Archer asked.

"To a secret place," Skraetock said. "Where you must fulfill your destiny."

Archer's stomach fluttered. His headache pulsed to the rhythm of the train, to the pounding of grey-green waves. *Destiny.* The word echoed in his mind. His eyes moved desperately to the wax-figure images of his cousins, but they gave him no help. He turned his gaze back to Master Skraetock. One of the old man's hands slowly opened.

"Do you see this, boy?" he asked.

Archer shuddered at the sight of the black spider. "It is a symbol," Master Skraetock continued. "The symbol of great

225

power. I am more than just the guardian of the Gifted. I am the guardian of all the Seventh World. I am head of the Order of the Spider. We alone keep the people of this world safe from powers that would enslave them—great powers which the Gifted alone can stand against."

The spider was so ugly. Archer felt that Skraetock's words must be lies. He closed his eyes and tried to picture Michael and Shannon, Grandmother and Lilac, Jack and Stocky. Miracle. They would not listen to this man. They would not sit and talk with him. They were strong and good, and he was something black and terrible.

But he could not hold their images in his mind. The rushing of the train drowned all else out, and then the voice of Master Skraetock again, drawing him.

"You must join us," the Master whispered.

A moment later the wax melted. The scene was alive again. When Archer looked up, Master Skraetock was gone.

* * *

"It's too late," Christopher told them. He had appeared at the mouth of the caves, as promised. "They're gone."

"But they can't have left the island!" Shannon exclaimed. "In a storm like this?"

"It makes little difference," Christopher answered. "There are powers greater than any storm."

"Why have they left you behind?" Michael asked.

Christopher looked up at him with a face devoid of friendship. "To wrap up a few little details," he said. "Like burning your homestead down."

"You didn't!" Shannon said.

Christopher looked away from her. "I can't blatantly disobey orders."

"But the rain . . ." Stocky said.

Christopher's mouth twisted into a smile. "Rain cannot put out Covenant Fire," he said.

Miracle looked at Christopher's hands. The tips of his fingers were grey as with soot. The spider tattoo had grown blacker than ever. She shuddered.

"Where have they gone?" Michael asked, his voice tightly controlled.

"Athrom," Christopher answered. "They will take a train once they reach the mainland. They should be in the capitol in three days."

Michael stood. "Then there is no time to lose," he said. "We'll salvage what we can from the ruins and then head for the mainland ourselves. Christopher—" he stopped. Christopher's place by the fire was empty.

"He left when you stood," Miracle said.

"Thank the stars," Shannon muttered.

"How could he leave?" Michael demanded. "We still need his help. He could tell us—"

"We cannot count on him," Miracle said. "If he would renounce the Order, we could trust him completely. But he is still ruled by evil. You must have seen it in his eyes, Michael. In his hands."

"Aye," Michael said.

Kris stood and laid a massive hand on Michael's shoulder. "If our enemies have crossed the sea already, we don't have time to lose," he said.

"The longship is not big enough for all of us," Michael said.

"No matter," Lilac told him. "There is a ship in the harbour that will take us."

"On a night like this?" Michael asked.

"On any night," Lilac answered. "I know the boatman. He will ferry us across."

Michael looked at Lilac long and hard, and she met his gaze. The slightest of smiles twitched in the corner of Michael's eyes. Lilac dropped her eyes and blushed. She turned and busied herself with putting out the fire.

"Let's go then," she said.

Thunder and surf roared in their ears as the Clann O'Roarke followed the coast to a harbour nestled in a tight valley some miles away. The ships in the harbour danced on the water as wind and rain lashed at them. Lilac strained her eyes in the darkness.

"There!" she called, pointing to a small ferry that strained at its moorings. "*The Lady Chance.* That's her."

They clambered over the slippery dock but found no way to enter the ship. Lilac began to shout the name of the boatman, and the others of the clann joined in, their voices swamped under the swell of the storm.

"He's not here," Michael said. "He's wetting his throat with something other than rain, if I know anything about sailors. Stocky, Jack, Kris—come with me. The rest of you wait for us here. What is the rogue's name, Lilac?"

"Jonathan Flynn," Lilac answered.

Michael and his small party turned and disappeared through the pelting sheets of rain, following the wet glimmer of tavern lights. The others made their way off the docks, which were bucking underfoot, and stood waiting on solid ground.

Michael burst through the doors of the first tavern he reached. It was a low-roofed, orange-lit place that smelled of beer and mutton stew. The men inside turned as one to face the newcomers. Jack glowered at them, and Kris folded his arms so his muscles bulged, but the men were not threatening, only curious. The clann men relaxed.

"We're looking for Jonathan Flynn," Michael said. "Can you tell me—"

He hadn't time to finish before the bartender interrupted. "It's Jonny Flynn you're wanting, is it? Well, he's not hard to find. He's sitting there, plain as the nose on your face."

The bartender pointed his mutton knife to a table in a corner, where a man was slowly rising to his feet. Jonathan Flynn was a young man, but battle-scarred from his lifelong war with the sea. A long scar snaked from his right ear down his cheek, across his chin and down his neck. He wore a patch over one eye.

"What do you want with me, eh?" Flynn asked.

"We need the services of your boat," Michael said.

"What?" hooted a man from Flynn's table. "Tonight?"

"Yes, tonight," Michael said. "You're not afraid, are you?"

Jonathan Flynn drew himself up. "I'm no more afraid of the sea than she is afraid of me," he said. "But we both know who's the stronger. Respect, that's what she needs."

Michael reached into a pouch at his waist and drew out a bag of coins. He threw them to Flynn, who opened the bag and examined its contents. He looked up and handed the bag back.

"Very nice," he said. "But I don't care much for money except as it buys me comfort, and no amount of silver can calm that storm."

"Even so, we hoped you'd help us," Michael said. "We were told you would not refuse."

Flynn raised an eyebrow. "And who told you that?"

"My cousin," Michael said. "Lilac O'Roarke."

Michael nearly laughed at the look that jumped into Flynn's scarred face. "And would you be Michael O'Roarke?" he asked.

"The same," Michael said.

"And do I ferry you, or Lilac?" he asked.

"Both," Michael said.

"You're mad to take her out on a night like this," Flynn said. "You'll risk her life."

"It's risked," Michael said. "If I could tell you everything, I would—but this is not the place."

Flynn stepped forward and took Michael's arm confidingly. Michael noticed that the sailor's left ring finger was missing. "Then let's go find us a place where you can talk," he said. "My ferry's like to be noisy tonight, but there will be no unwanted ears to listen."

A clap of thunder broke over them the instant they stepped out of the tavern door, and the rain came down in renewed fury. Jonathan Flynn shouted to his new companions as they made their way to the dock, but no one could make out his words. They found the rest of the clann waiting for them, and Flynn led them all down the dock to the ferry.

It was a struggle, but in the space of an hour they were all sitting on board. Most of the young men stayed on the broad deck while the women entered the small cabin.

No one heard what Michael said to Jonathan Flynn, or what Flynn said back to Michael, but before long they were away from the dock, headed into a raging sea. Lilac emerged from the cabin long enough to stand by Flynn at the helm and say something in his ear. He looked back on her sternly.

"Don't tell me that," he said. "I can see enough that things here aren't canny—I'm helping you for my own curiosity's sake. I may not come back alive, but if I do I'll tell this tale for the rest of my life!"

The tale told by Jonathan Flynn in later time was a strange one indeed. He spoke of the waves that threatened but did not kill; the storm that raged but stopped short of murdering those who ventured out in it. He told of the northern girl who left the cabin to stand on the deck and let the wind tear through her long pale hair, and of the men of the clann who fought the storm valiantly with him, but most of all he told of the strange giant he had somehow missed seeing before—a great man who stood with his long hair streaming, who threw back his head in the midst of the storm and howled like a wolf.

They reached Galce in the thick of darkness. The wind had blown them farther south than they had planned. Jonathan Flynn refused the money Michael offered him, and he stood on deck for a long time and watched the soaked figures of his passengers disappear in the shadows of the continent.

12

Visions of Darkness and Light

THERE WAS SOMETHING WRONG about Nowl the cat. No, there was nothing wrong *with* it—it could see, hear, and yowl as well as any other cat. It treated the children with legendary feline disdain. But there was something wrong *about* it. Something that made Kieran cry when it came near him and prickled Archer's skin when it curled around his feet. So Archer watched with deep displeasure as Moll scooped the cat up and carried it off to play with her, under a shelf in the baggage car.

Archer wandered through the train cars, stopping now and then to watch the beautiful Galcic forests rush past the windows. He wondered again how badly it would hurt if he threw himself off—but he couldn't go without the little ones, and who knew what would happen if they tried to jump? Moll might catch her skirt on the train and drag—Kieran might cripple himself worse—they might be killed.

He would not admit to himself that something else held him back. *Destiny. You must join us . . . join us . . . join us.*

He didn't look up as he pushed his way into a nearly-empty passenger car—not until he heard voices. The man called the Nameless One was talking to Seamus. His hand was full of blue fire.

"Touch it," he purred. "Hold out your hand. It won't burn you."

Seamus stretched out his fingers and let the flames lick at his hands. The tips of his fingers turned black, but he did not pull away. His eyes widened in amazement, and deep within them hunger kindled.

"It is a very hot fire," the Nameless One said. "The hottest fire in the world. It does not burn you because I do not let it. I am the master of the flame. You also carry fire within you, Seamus O'Roarke. You can learn to master it. You are special."

"Don't touch it, Seamus," Archer said.

The Nameless One looked up. His eyes narrowed. The lines of his face—a handsome face—were sharp and cruel. "Why shouldn't he?" he hissed.

Archer wasn't sure where the words came from, but they stumbled out of his mouth before he could stop them. "Master Skraetock wouldn't like it," he said. "He wants to teach us first."

The Nameless One stood. "Master Skraetock is an expert at creating puppets." He looked down at Seamus. "Is that what you want to be? A puppet on a string? Yes, boy, Master Skraetock would teach you. He would teach you rules. He would tell you what is forbidden. But nothing is forbidden to me. I have embraced freedom."

He held out his hand, and the flame kindled again. Seamus reached his fingers out. Archer stepped forward swiftly and knocked the Nameless One's hand away. "Stay away from us!" he shouted.

The Nameless One's face twisted with anger. He struck
Archer, knocking him to the ground. He turned back to
Seamus. "Give me your hand," he commanded.

Seamus looked down at his blackened fingers and cast a
glance at Archer, who was still stunned. A look of shame
passed over Seamus's face. He hid his hands behind his back.

"No," he said.

The Nameless One seemed very close to striking Seamus as
well, but he restrained himself. Instead, he turned and glared at
Archer. "Idiot boy," he said. "What does the Master tell you?
That you are powerful and great? Already you dance on the
end of a string. Dance, boy, dance!" His voice grew dangerously
quiet. "The dance will soon be over. I will speak with *you*"—he
looked at Seamus—"later."

Seamus knelt by Archer and tried to help him up, but as
Archer regained his senses, anger flooded through him. He
jumped to his feet and ran for the back of the car, pushing aside
door after door until he reached the car where Nowl the cat
was purring, purring. The cat sounded like the Nameless One
when he talked to Seamus.

Archer grabbed the cat by the scruff of its neck and yanked
it from Moll's arms, ignoring her cry of protest. He held the cat
against him as Moll pounded his back with her fists. He stepped
out of the car onto the platform at the end of the train, where
the rain still pelted down, and he lifted Nowl and threw him
from the edge.

The cat screamed, but not a cat-scream. It turned itself in
the air and flew back at Archer, flapping ragged wings. Claws
raked Archer's face, and blood ran in his eyes and over his

cheeks. He heard Moll screaming and crying, and he crumpled
on the platform and forgot everything.

* * *

The Clann O'Roarke battled through the darkness and rain
until Michael realized that he could hardly see the hand in
front of his face.

"Stop!" he called, letting the others pick up the call so it
would carry through the lashing storm. "Stop. We'll never find
them this way."

Lightning flashed overhead, illuminating thick forest
across the cold, soaked sand of the shore. Kris pointed to the
dark mass. "Take shelter there!" he roared.

With the white wolf at his heels, Michael forged through
the wind and rain. The ancient trees kept some of the water
out, though their branches lashed in the storm. In another flash
of lightning, Michael spotted a dark hole beneath the roots of
an enormous oak. The white wolf beat him to it, turning to
look up at him with eyes that summoned him to come.

Michael slid into the shelter, relieved to find it mostly dry.
The others were likewise finding places to hide from the fury
of the night. Michael watched them with his head half-out of
the hole, making sure no one was left behind. Miracle was
passing, and Michael reached up and grabbed her hand.

"Here," he said. "There is room."

Gratefully, she slid into the shelter. The wolf sat up,
pushing its head up so that Miracle's arms surrounded its neck.
She closed her eyes, soaking up the wolf's warmth and

235

presence. Michael watched her with a deep pleasure he could not express, even to himself.

The storm ceased sometime before sunrise. Michael had not slept. Weariness battled the urgency within him. He doubted the Order had been forced to hole up in the ground. Who knew how far they might have gone by now?

Forest creatures began to stir in the still, rain-washed air. Michael's legs were cramping, and he pushed himself out of the hole and stood beneath the ancient canopy of the oaks. High above, branches moved despite the lack of wind. Michael could hear them rustling and see the slight movement against the higher canopy of stars. In a moment a warm, gentle breeze brushed his face.

The breeze seemed to call to him. He followed it, wandering paths that were hardly paths. They kept him close to the tree line. The sea murmured not far away. But then something changed. On the breeze came ashes and the stomach-turning smell of death.

Michael broke into a run. The sun was beginning to rise, just enough to illumine a nightmare. A settlement, in a hollow along the shore. Still burning. He could see the dead through the hazy light. On the other side of the hollow, a great white rock overlooked the little village.

Across it, huge and black, was the mark of a spider.

Michael stared at the scene. He did not tear his eyes away even when he heard the others coming up behind him; some running, some trudging. All drew to a stop as they came close. He heard gasps and quiet exclamations. A hand slipped into his —Shannon. Miracle approached on the other side, the wolf beside her. The great white creature growled, low and angry.

"Why?" Shannon asked.

"It is a warning," Kris said from just behind Michael. "A warning to us to follow no further."

"The villagers . . ." Shannon began.

"We cannot help them now," Michael said.

He closed his eyes. Fear rose starkly before him in the shape of a spider. Could they help anyone now? Even the children— In the smoky air a warning throbbed, almost at the edge of hearing: *Turn away. Turn back. You can do nothing now.*

"Kris, Miracle," Michael said. "Tell me. How great is their power?"

There was a moment's silence. Miracle answered, "Greater than you can imagine."

Jack heard the words Michael didn't speak. "But we can't turn back!" he said. "They have the little ones. We don't have any choice."

"Don't we?" Michael asked. "I would go and die for them. But the rest of you—"

"Are no less heroes than you are, Michael," Shannon said.

Michael turned and looked at the faces of his beloved clann. The last of the family. The survivors of that first attack so many years ago. Young men and young women. How could he take them into the power of the Spider?

"Christopher told us that they would take the children to Athrom," Michael said. "The heart of darkness. It may be we have no hope."

"You are wrong," Miracle said. Her confidence surprised everyone. They turned to watch her speak. The white wolf moved close to her. "You forget—theirs is only the power of death. We have the power of life in our hands."

Michael smiled. "Well . . . you do."

"We all do," Miracle said. "We do not go alone to Athrom, Michael. A greater power goes with us."

"Years ago," Kris of the Mountains rumbled, "your father came to Fjordland and saw a vision. A fire that burned across the world, purifying but not destroying. A fire that ended the rule of the Blackness and brought new life. It was the fire of the King—the Burning Light. The same fire is here, in Miracle. In your children. In all the Gifted. And the one who lights the fire is watching over us. I have long believed it to be true."

"And why should we believe that?" Jack asked.

"Because you have to," Kris answered. "For the sake of your children. For the courage to go on. The whole world may disbelieve, but we are going to challenge the ancient Blackness, and we must have light on our side. Your father saw the light of the coming King and believed. So did your mother. They were sure the King would come. Don't let their belief die out with you."

Shannon cast down her eyes. She remembered. Remembered the things her mother had told her in secret; remembered the name she and Thomas had invoked as the embodiment of hope. Molly Sullivan's last words—the last her daughter ever heard from her mother—had been a prayer. Shannon still remembered them.

But to remember was one thing, to believe quite another. After all, she who had prayed the words was dead.

"Who is he?" Lilac asked quietly. "This King."

It was Miracle who answered. "I hardly know," she said. "I do know that he is the source of my healing Gift—that his power flows through me to give life. I feel his presence then, and I feel it around me in creation. In growing things—in everything alive. In roses. He is life. In the north, some few have always believed in him. They were too few for the Empire to bother with. My father believed in him. He told me that the King hears those who call upon him. He gives strength to the weak. He will stand by you, Clann O'Roarke, if you will stand by him."

"He did not stand by my father," Shannon said. "Or my mother."

"You did not see him," Kris said. "That does not mean he was not there."

"But . . ." Shannon began. And stopped. For something was happening in their midst, and Shannon could not speak in its face.

The white wolf had begun to glow with all the colours of a sunset. His thick white and crimson fur fell away in silky layers until a giant stood before them, gazing at them with the eyes of the wild.

"Do you still doubt?" he asked with a voice like a stirring in the leaves, like a slap on the water. "I am Gwyrion of the Earth Brethren, Lord of the Wild Things. All my allegiance is to the King, the Life of Heaven and Earth. You did not see me, yet I have been with you."

Behind Gwyrion, the village still smoldered. The black spider still defaced the rock. Shannon looked at them both. She looked at Miracle and Kris, who stood a little ways apart, believing as Thomas and Molly O'Roarke had believed. She swallowed and turned to Michael.

"We are going to face the Spider," Shannon said. "If there is some good power in the world, then we should not go without it."

Michael smiled at his sister. He reached out and took her hand. The clann gathered around them, leaving the others on the outskirts.

Shannon smiled, her eyes shining with tears. "Do you remember Mother's prayer?" she asked. She did not wait for an answer. On the hill overlooking the burning clearing, under the black glare of the spider, Shannon O'Roarke dropped to her knees. Michael knelt beside her. The others slowly lowered themselves to the ground.

Shannon raised her face to the sky. Hot tears slipped through her eyelashes. "King of Ancient Days," she began, "hear us now. Watch over our children. Hide us from evil, beneath the shadow of your wings. Fill us with the Burning Light."

Her words caught in her throat as the memory of her mother's voice filled her ears. "Guide our footsteps, and make us truly free."

Behind Shannon, the long-haired giant with one gold eye and one blue lifted his own voice. It burst from his chest like the bell of a stag, clear and keening as the cry of a hawk.

"Come!" he called. "Come to your wakened lord!"

Before his voice had died away, the sky darkened with wings. Birds circled overhead in great numbers, over the clearing in the Galcic wild where the Clann O'Roarke stood.

They landed on Miracle's outstretched hands and arms, on her shoulders and head. They perched on every available part of Gwyrion's massive body. They came to rest on the tentatively offered hands of the clann.

"Go find the children," Gwyrion ordered. "Find them and watch over them, all of you. Send messengers back to me when you find them."

* * *

When Archer woke again, Kieran was whispering in his ears.

"Now you know why the cat makes me cry, Archer, because you know it isn't a cat. You can't hear me but I have to tell you, because I've been wanting to tell you and I was so afraid before . . ."

Archer opened his eyes but saw nothing through the bandages on his face. He moved his hand until it found Kieran's, and he gripped the younger boy's hand as hard as he could without hurting him.

"Oh, can you hear me, Archer? Oh I'm glad; I'm so glad." Archer felt tears on his hand. Kieran was crying again. Archer had always been irritated with Kieran for crying when he was getting so old, but now he couldn't feel irritated—only fond of his cousin, and protective.

"But good has come of it," Kieran said, "because Moll won't go near the cat anymore. She says it grew wings and flew back to the train and it was no cat at all. I didn't see it grow wings, but I know it's no cat. I wish I knew what it was. It's like him —the Nameless One. They make me very afraid."

"Don't be afraid, Kieran," Archer said. "Michael is coming after us. I know he is."

"How can he come? There was such a storm when we left," Kieran said.

"The rain wouldn't stop them," Archer answered. "The rain isn't our enemy. Not like the fire."

"Seamus keeps playing with the fire, and it turns his hands blacker and blacker," Kieran said. "Moll might touch it too. I try to tell them no, but they don't listen to me. It pulls at them so."

"Why?" Archer groaned. "Why can't they leave it alone?"

"The Nameless One says he can make us powerful," Kieran said. "He says there is fire in all of us. He's trying to make us want to wake it up."

"He's lying," Archer said.

"No, he's not."

They were quiet for a long time, and then Archer said, "What?"

"There is fire inside me, Archer. Sometimes I can feel it. When the Nameless One plays with his fire, it makes me want to learn how. It could make us strong, Archer. It's hard not to try it. So hard."

Archer sought for words, but he could find none. Kieran's confession both scared and excited him.

Kieran continued. "Maybe if we learn and become powerful, we'll be strong enough to get away. We won't be children anymore. We'll be older. And strong." His voice was quiet, and it shook a little as he spoke.

"Think of Michael," Archer whispered. "Think of Shannon and Grandmother. If we play with the fire, it will hurt them."

"I know," Kieran said. "That's why I stay away from it. I will run away from it if I can."

Archer fell asleep again without trying to. Kieran watched his cousin and thought that he didn't like the way Archer's face glowed beneath his bandages. He was dreaming, Kieran knew —dreaming of deep and raging fires.

* * *

Adhemar Skraetock met the Nameless One coming back from the end of the train, where the children had the run of five or six cars.

"What were you doing?" Skraetock demanded.

"Helping you," the Nameless One told him. He held up his tattooed palm. "We were playing with fire."

"I wish you to leave the children to me," Skraetock said.

"Wish as you will," the Nameless One answered. "And I will do as I wish."

Skraetock bridled. "You are stepping beyond your limits."

"I have no limits," the Nameless One said. "Not like you."

"I am the most powerful man in the Order," Skraetock said.

"No," the Nameless One said. "You are the most influential man in the Order. Raw power exists that you have never dreamed of."

"You will unleash the Blackness on us too soon," Skraetock said.

"They cannot return soon enough."

"You are a fool," Skraetock said, dropping his voice. "If they come now they will eat us alive."

"That is your mistake," the Nameless One said. "You seek life and power. I seek only power."

They stood in the narrow aisle of the empty passenger car and looked into each other's eyes, and the Nameless One deferred his gaze first. Yet Skraetock was shaken. The younger man had not looked away out of fear, but to avoid conflict for his own reasons.

Adhemar Skraetock had lived many years and stored up great power. Never had anyone challenged it. The Emperor himself did not challenge it.

"Let me handle the children," he said. His voice rasped.

"Very well," the Nameless One said. He bowed and turned on his heel. In a moment, the Master of the Order of the Spider was alone.

An hour later, a guard in his employ told him about Archer. Master Skraetock nearly choked on his anger. The Nameless One was responsible for this. Skraetock had not wished the children harmed. No one could be as ruthless as the Master in tormenting those who would not join him—those like Miracle and the blind girl, Virginia Ramsey, who clung to their desperate loyalties—but these were children. Still able to be twisted.

He went to visit the boy. Archer lay on a cot with his face swathed in bandages. He was awake. The Master sat beside Archer and laid a hand on his.

"I am sorry for this accident," Master Skraetock began, but Archer cut him off. The boy was quivering with anger.

"The Nameless One listened to you once, didn't he?" Archer said. "I will never be like *him*."

Skraetock leaned close. "Awaken the flame in yourself, Archer," he said. "Teach the other children to do the same, and you may *kill* the Nameless One."

Archer moved, trying to think on the words Skraetock had just spoken. But the words ran away from him, like sand through an hourglass: there one minute and then gone. Archer was left blinking. Had the Master said something?

"You must join us," the Master said. "There are great things for you to do. It is your destiny, boy-who-are-a-man. It is time to leave childhood behind and take the future into your own hands. Let us teach you to awaken the flame in yourself. Join me."

Archer made no answer. Master Skraetock slipped silently from the car—but he smiled as he went.

* * *

Feeling lost after Archer fell asleep, Kieran wandered from the car. He looked furtively around him before stepping from one car to the next, trying to avoid the black-cloaked ones who so terrified him—who frightened him because they drew him. Because he wanted so badly to be one of them, to let the fire in his veins burn free. His heart beat faster as he realized that his hands were heating up.

He broke into a run, racing toward the last car and the open air. He pushed open the door and stepped onto the platform where Archer had thrown the non-cat. He gulped in the fresh green air. It cooled him, baptized him like water. He held out his hands to the forests and said, very quietly, "Save me. Please."

And something in the forests answered him. The tree branches bowed to him, reaching for him even as the train sped past. Deep in the woods, Kieran heard something rustling and moving. His heart leaped.

* * *

The train stopped shortly after entering Italya. The delay angered the Master, who had ordered that the journey be without pause. There was no help for it, the driver argued nervously. Something inexplicable had happened. Where there should have been open fields, the forest had grown up over the tracks.

Master Skraetock left the train and stood amidst the tangled jungle that obstructed the tracks. The fall of the guards' axes sounded distant in his ears. The growth made him uneasy —but as he stood, his unease shifted to horrible fear. He returned to the train and sat in a dark car with his head in his hands, muttering until the fear left him and the train started again.

Christopher Ens boarded the train while it was stopped. He reported his job done. The Clann O'Roarke was destroyed, their home burned to the ground. Skraetock commanded that the matter be hidden from the children. The Nameless One demanded to know what had become of Miracle, and Christopher could not say. She was not there, he told his companion. She and the mountain man of the north were gone.

When the train pulled out again, no one noticed that Kieran was no longer aboard.

* * *

Gwyrion's birds left in a rush of wings, leaving the clann subdued in wonder as feathers drifted down through the air. The young women twisted them into their hair, and Gwyrion did the same. Kris wore one in his braided beard, while Andrew and Patrick festooned them in their clothing. The sun was climbing in the morning sky as they stood and gathered themselves for the journey.

Michael stood at the edge of the clearing, looking down on the destroyed village. The voice in the air still urged *Turn back.* But with Shannon's prayer and his clann's support, he had challenged the voice.

Miracle walked up beside him, hugging herself. He saw the strained expression on her face. Death was raw in the air, and it touched the heart of the healer.

"Couldn't we at least bury them?" Miracle asked.

Michael shook his head. "There is no time," he said. "I know. I want to help them too."

They ate—the young men had slaughtered a few rabbits— and Michael held council. "How can we catch up with them?" he asked the few who gathered around a fire with him. "We can't go on foot."

"Take the straightest route," Gwyrion said. "That which they also have taken. Go by the iron serpent."

"You rule a great kingdom, Spirit of the Wild," Kris said. "But an iron serpent I have never seen."

Gwyrion laughed a silent wolf-laugh. "No!" he said. "The iron serpent is no subject of mine, but of man."

Shannon smiled. "We should take a train?" she asked.

Gwyrion laughed once more. "Indeed," he said.

"Yes, well," Michael said. "We'll simply find a train and hand the conductor all our money."

There was a long silence, while Gwyrion's quick eyes darted from face to face. Stocky spoke first.

"I suppose we could drive a train ourselves," he said. "How hard can it be?"

Kris picked up the idea immediately. "No harder than stopping a train—and if we can do one, we should certainly do the other."

"Are you suggesting that we hijack a train?" Michael asked.

"Of course," Kris said.

"A train powered by our efforts would be sure to reach Athrom faster than anything else," Stocky said.

"Aye," Michael answered. "And my brave relations have already figured out how to do this thing, I suppose?"

"It can't be harder than getting a ferry in the middle of a storm," Shannon said.

"No," Michael grumbled. "We shall just have to send one of the girls off to flirt with a conductor first." Lilac, who was seated a few feet behind the council, choked back something indignant. Michael stood and stretched, turning on his heel to face the eavesdroppers.

"Perhaps Jenna could promise her hand in return for a good stock of coal?" he asked. "Or Cali might promise a lock of her hair for every train car we make off with."

Grandmother O'Roarke waved a stick at Michael. "Sit down, young man," she said. "Or you'll see how much power feminine wiles can have."

Michael grinned. "I already know on your account, Grandmother," he said. "My backside could never forget."

"Well, it'll get a memory boost if you don't stop this and lead us like a leader should," Grandmother said.

"Right," Michael said, turning his eyes to the young men of his clann. "Are you ready for a hunt, boys?"

"What are we hunting, Michael?" Patrick called.

"An iron serpent," Michael answered.

* * *

The underground was at once a lonely place and a crowded one. There were stone ceilings, walls, and people everywhere, yet Maggie usually felt out-of-doors. No place under the ground could truly be called "home." The knowledge that an ancient colony dwelt just under their feet made Maggie feel even more estranged.

The nearest thing to a homey spot in all of underground Pravik was a little alcove that overlooked a wide thoroughfare. The Ploughman had made it his private quarters. Woven rugs lay on the floor, given to the Ploughman and his lady by farm wives, with a low table in the center of them. In the far wall was a sort of fireplace. The alcove was always open to the little circle of the Ploughman's friends. Maggie resorted to it each time she felt alone, oppressed, or dreamy.

Today was a dreaming day, a day when the haze of underground fires curled in the black corridors before drifting through chimney-cracks in the rock. Maggie sat by the low fire in the alcove and hummed a song. The tune brought images to her mind, and now and then she sang words. It was a ballad,

249

about an ancient warlord who commanded golden forces. It had come to her, as all songs did, unexplained and unannounced.

Haras, the Darkworld priest, was listening to her instead of to the others. He had come to the alcove with Harutek and the Ploughman. Libuse came on their heels, Professor Huss with her. They talked in low, serious voices. When they first arrived, Maggie stood to excuse herself and was told to stay. She could have joined the conversation but didn't care to. Even so, their words intruded on her song.

"I don't know what to offer in return," the Ploughman was saying. "Some of my people brought money below ground with them, but it would do you no good. We have little left in the way of provisions to trade."

"Which is why you need our help in the first place," Harutek said. "Perhaps we can use your labour. Your time for our fish?"

Maggie looked into the fire and concentrated on her song. If it would come clearer she could sing it for her friends at dinner. In her mind's eye she could see golden warriors, long hair streaming in the sun, row upon row on horseback. She closed her eyes for a moment and thought she could feel the sun on her face.

Something broke her concentration. She turned her head and saw Virginia standing in the entrance to the alcove. Mrs. Cook stood behind her, concern written on her matronly face.

The party at the table had just noticed Virginia. They fell silent before her presence.

"Who is here?" Virginia asked.

Mrs. Cook answered her. "The Ploughman and Libuse; Professor Huss, Maggie, and the Darkworlders."

Virginia nodded and said, "I have seen."

Mrs. Cook rushed to guide Virginia as she stepped down into the alcove. Room was made for her at the table. Maggie moved away from the fire and slipped into the circle next to Haras. The priest acknowledged her with an uneasy smile and nod of his head, but his eyes did not leave Virginia's face. No one's did.

"I have seen the future," Virginia said. "A terrible future. The Blackness will come here. They will destroy us."

Libuse uttered an exclamation. Virginia continued. Her voice was strained, hiding great emotion no one could touch. "I have seen the Veil torn and the Blackness coming through."

"We fought them once before," the Ploughman said.

"What you fought was nothing," Virginia said. "Only a pittance of their strength."

"How can they come through?" Professor Huss began.

"The Veil will tear," Virginia said. "It is fading now—wearing thin to the breaking. It is meant to be so. That is not what frightens me. I have seen a violent tearing—something not meant to be, something wickedly forced before its time." For a moment she stopped and struggled to regain control of her voice. "They will do a great evil and unleash the Blackness too soon. Somehow you must stop them."

She reached out until her fingers found the Ploughman's hand. Gripping it, she said, "You must fight them before the Veil is torn, or it will be too late for us."

"What can I do?" the Ploughman asked. "I am only a man."

"Fight them with the power of the Golden Riders," Virginia said.

"Where are they?" the Ploughman asked. His voice twisted. He stood, tearing his hand from Virginia's grasp. Libuse stood also, looking for some way in which she could help him.

"They left me after the battle," the Ploughman said. "All my life they have been with me. I have sensed them with me, but no longer. Now I am only a man, and I cannot fight."

"Then all will be lost," Virginia said. The strain had returned to her voice. "But you may be wrong. I know what it means to distrust a Gift. Perhaps you must go farther—trust the King."

Someone cleared his throat. Every head turned at the sound. A guard was standing in the entrance to the alcove.

"Forgive my interruption," he said. "Someone is approaching the Upper North Gate."

They left the Ploughman's quarters, all of them—not because it was necessary for any one of them to go, but because Virginia's words had shaken them. Not one of them wished to be left with only silence and imagination for companions.

Maggie approached the Gate with Mrs. Cook behind her and Virginia on her arm. There was light in the passage—real light, filtering through the mass of branches that blocked the Gate from sight. Maggie could smell green things growing beyond it. She breathed in deeply and heard the murmur of voices outside. Branches swished; she caught the smell of pipe smoke; and a ragged figure stepped into the passage. Libuse saw the look on Maggie's face and asked, "Do you know him?"

"Yes," Maggie told her. "He's one of the Major's Gypsies." She took a step forward, into the stripy, filtered light. "Peter."

Peter seemed just as surprised to see Maggie. "It's good to see a familiar face," he said.

"Are you here alone?" Maggie asked.

Peter bowed his head. "The Major is a day behind me on the road, helping a few others along," he said. "I need to speak to the Ploughman."

The Ploughman bowed his tall head. "I am he," he said.

"I have a message from the Major," Peter said. "He told me how to find you. We need your help."

Libuse took the Ploughman's arm and said, "Perhaps we can speak elsewhere?"

"Yes," the Ploughman said. "It is not safe here, so close to the surface."

"Are you hungry, Peter?" Maggie asked.

"Very," he replied.

"I'll feed him," Mrs. Cook said, hurrying past Maggie. "You walk with Virginia."

Mrs. Cook disappeared down the passage. The others followed more slowly. They went back to the Ploughman's quarters. Peter sat down with Maggie on one side of him and Virginia on the other. He looked over the low table at the Ploughman.

"I've been told that you have a great army here," Peter said. "They say you beat the High Police and—others—in the Battle of Pravik."

"We weren't alone," the Ploughman said. "There were others with us then."

"However that may be," Peter said, "we need your help. We, the Gypsies."

"We've sheltered as many as would come to us," the Ploughman said.

"Yes," Peter said, "and we are grateful. But many couldn't come. Many were taken by our enemies before they could. It's on their behalf that I'm here. We've lost two of our own now. The High Police have taken Nicolas and Marja."

A cry escaped Maggie's lips. The professor looked white.

"Nicolas fought with us in the battle," the Ploughman said. "We'll help him if we can."

"To help him you must help all of us," Peter said. "The High Police are taking them to a place—a prison camp— in the city of Athrom itself. We heard the soldiers say so. All of our people are there—the hundreds who have been taken from the roads. "

"What do they want with them?" Libuse asked. "Why imprison hundreds of Gypsies?"

"They will kill them," Virginia said.

There was silence, and then she spoke again. "They will sacrifice the Wandering Race and tear the Veil open."

"A great evil," Maggie said, echoing Virginia's earlier words.

"Even they wouldn't dare do such a thing," Libuse said. She closed her mouth and looked away.

The Ploughman looked at Virginia. "That is what you saw? Why did you not tell us?"

Her head was bent, as it had been throughout the conversation. "I am not always sure of what I see at first. Now I am."

"And what can we do?" he asked.

"You must take the battle there," Virginia answered. "Or they will bring it here."

"If the Veil tears now, everything we've hoped for is lost," Libuse said.

Haras, the soft-spoken young priest of the Darkworld, spoke up. "We have waited far too long to lose all now."

The Ploughman stood. "Professor," he said, "will you walk with me?"

"Of course," Huss answered.

The two men left the alcove and walked down the dark thoroughfare. Professor Huss waited for his companion to speak, and at last he did so.

"How great is the danger?" the Ploughman said.

"If it happens as Virginia has seen," Huss said, "we will all die. And the world will be enslaved again before the King returns."

"Why does he not come now?" the Ploughman asked.

"I only wish I knew," Huss said.

"You know many things," the Ploughman said. "There are many who seem to think you know everything. Tell me, Professor—do you know who I am?"

Professor Huss stopped and looked up at the younger man. "A great leader," Huss said. "A man chosen for a difficult hour."

"Chosen," the Ploughman said. "By whom?"

The professor did not answer, and the Ploughman began to walk again. His eyes swept the rock, the floor, walls, and ceiling, and flashed to Huss's face. "I have fought evil all my life," he said. "I protected my tenants, my farmers, even as a boy. I raised a militia. I taught them to fight when the Empire

255

came to their doors, asking a greater price than any man should have to give. But I was never alone. The Golden Riders were always with me. As a child I could almost see them. They gave me strength. They taught me to fight. And now they are gone, and how can I move against the Empire without them?"

"Perhaps you can't," Professor Huss said. "But at the same time—can you remain here, buried away from the world, for the rest of your life? Even if Virginia is wrong and the Blackness never comes, can you allow the Empire to slaughter a whole race of people while you hide here?"

The Ploughman leaned against the wall. "I don't know," he said. His voice was raw. "I don't know what to do."

"You asked me how great the danger is," Professor Huss said. "But perhaps I have answered you wrongly. I told you once that you must be everything the Emperor is not. That Pravik must be a place of light in the darkness. Perhaps the greatest danger is that a free people will be enslaved and destroyed—and we will have done nothing."

The Ploughman looked up at his mentor. Conflict and deep concern showed behind the surface of his eyes. He was listening.

"Perhaps it will not take the Blackness to put out Pravik's light," the professor said. "Perhaps we will do it ourselves."

The Ploughman lifted his hand to his chin. His ruby ring seemed to glow, deep, dark red. "Do you know, all my youth I suspected myself of being insane. I was trained by warriors no one else could see. But now it all comes together—and I realize that none of this is my plan. Someone else has directed every step of my life until now. Virginia tells me to trust the King, and I wonder how I can. But maybe—maybe I cannot do anything else."

"Did the Golden Riders teach you so that you could use them as an excuse not to fight?" Professor Huss said.

The Ploughman was silent for a long time. "No," he said at last.

"Then do what they trained you for," Huss said. "So you are only a man. Be a good man."

"Advise me," the Ploughman said. He stepped away from the wall and folded his arms. He seemed to have grown in stature; a decision had been made.

"Pick out the leaders among your men and meet with them," Huss said. "Find the fastest route to Athrom."

The Ploughman nodded, but sadness lined his face. "My men fought for their families," he said. "They did not want this."

"Let them choose," Professor Huss said. "Let them make the same choice you do."

"And if none will go with me?" The Ploughman smiled. "I know. If none will go with me, I will ride on Athrom myself and behead the Empire singlehandedly."

Professor Huss chuckled. The men turned together, and Huss's laugh died in his throat.

Virginia stood behind them, alone, her hand on the wall. She looked toward them but not at them; her green eyes unseeing.

"Take me above," she said.

"Above—" the Ploughman began.

"Take me into the city," she said. "I have something to show you."

The threesome passed through the colony with uneasy steps. No one saw them leave. They made their way up stairs and through layers of rock until they reached a familiar passageway and descended one last, well-known flight of steps. Then the Ploughman found a triggering mechanism. The rock above them lifted, and they stepped into a burned-out courtyard in the fading light of dusk.

The professor looked around him with watering eyes. "My old home," he said. "Sad that no one has been to repair it."

The city was empty of civilians, a ghost-haunt of blackened stone and ashes. The smell of smoke lingered in the air. The only sounds were the distant tramp of a High Police battalion and the rush of the Vltava under the fifteen bridges that spanned the river. The Ploughman stood in the street and looked down at the Guardian Bridge, where the old statues still stood. Soldiers stirred among them.

"Do you think they have other watchposts, or is the bridge the only place in the city they hold?"

"I don't suppose they're eager to make themselves at home here," the professor answered. "What happened in this city is a mystery to *us*—imagine what it is to them."

They ignored the watchmen on the bridge and entered the unwatched ruins of Pravik Castle. Together they climbed to the highest parapet, and there they stood, Virginia closest to the edge, with the wind in her face and a light in her eyes.

"Now," she said, turning to the Ploughman. He started when she turned, because there was recognition and focus in her eyes; she could see him, for the moment. She smiled at his fright and said, "Now, see what I see."

And the Ploughman turned back to the city. The streets beneath him were full of warriors, of great golden giants, armed and silent and watchful. Their white horses stamped their feet and moved through the streets.

"You do see them?" Virginia asked after a moment.

The Ploughman nodded. "Yes," he said. His eyes filled with tears, from emotion or from the thin wind in his face.

"I envy you," the professor said. "I see nothing. Except . . . there is something glowing in your cloak."

The Ploughman looked down. "It is Libuse's thread," he said. "Maggie gave it to her."

"Thread from the Huntsman's cloak," Professor Huss said.

A great golden giant with hair like a lion's mane rode to the parapet and reined in his horse. He looked to the Ploughman and bowed his head.

"We cannot ride against men to destroy them," the giant said. "The hour for that has not come. But we can go with you and lend some measure of strength."

"Have you been here all this time?" the Ploughman asked.

The warrior smiled a lion-smile. "We are ever where we are needed," he said. In an instant the vision was over. The Ploughman looked out over an empty city, even as his heart soared above it.

13

Hope Lives

THERE WAS A COLISEUM in Athrom, a great oval chamber where thousands could sit and look up at the open sky. But little could be seen in the sky but grey clouds. The skies of Italya were bright blue when the world was right, and sometimes crossed with cotton-wisps of white, but the world now was wrong—so wrong—under the leaden sky.

The people in the coliseum were listless in their dusty, ragged clothing: shawls, skirts, scarves, and vests that had been bright and gay once, but now were only shrouds. The people who wore them looked little better: hollow-eyed, gaunt-cheeked, and thin, they sat by their fires and stared, or else they wandered—paced and hopped like crippled birds.

The Empire kept the Gypsies alive. Every day an armed contingent of soldiers came into the coliseum, walking straight forward like superstitious children walking into a graveyard, whose only hope of escape is to deny that the ghosts are there. They came armed, as though the weakened people of the Wandering Race were a threat to them, and they served something hot and sludgy, sometimes green but usually grey, from an iron pot they brought with them. Some days they gave out bread. Usually they brought water.

Every day Marja tried to collect two bowls of sludge, and every day they only gave her one. Sometimes they hit or shoved her so that her one bowl spilled out onto the sand. On those days, both she and Nicolas went hungry. When the soup wasn't spilled, only Marja did. She would carry the soup carefully to the place where Nicolas lay on a pile of burlap sacks under a bench up one side of the coliseum, and she would tell him that she had eaten hers already because she couldn't carry two bowls at once. He believed her and ate the soup, and it was good—because if he hadn't, he might not have recovered from the beating the High Police had given him before sending their captives to the great theatre with all the others.

Marja didn't starve, because an old Gypsy woman saw what she was doing and saved a little for her every day.

The Gypsies of the Seventh World were a people of song, but there were no songs—or stories, or even laughter—around the fires in the coliseum. So Nicolas grew stronger and Marja grew weaker, and the Wandering Race died by degrees under the leaden sky.

* * *

The Ploughman stood before his people in the great cavern he called the Hold. A ladder, fashioned in the Darkworld, leaned against one wall. The Ploughman climbed it so that he could be seen and heard by all. He looked down on the sea of faces, turned up to him in waiting. They were lined faces, grey

261

and pale in the flickering torchlight, yet there was hope in their eyes.

Many of these men had stood with the Ploughman since his boyhood. They were his tenants, farmers from his land. He had long ago sworn to be a brother to them and not a lord. For that, they loved him. Some were old, some young. Women stood at the far end of the cavern, listening anxiously. Gypsies stood in family clusters, flashes of colour in the darkness. On the left, pale, large-eyed faces looked up: the faces of the Darkworlders. The Majesty's seventeen sons were there, and the priest Divad, and others. And at the foot of the ladder, Libuse stood.

The Ploughman's voice caught as he looked out at his people. He looked down to Libuse for strength. She smiled up at him. The torchlight brought out the gold in her light brown hair. The Ploughman took a deep breath and looked over the Hold again.

"My people," he said. His voice faltered. He forced it back to compliance. "Over a season ago, many of you faced a threat to your families and to your lives. You stood with me, and together we overcame that threat. We determined to build a life for ourselves, and so you have done. You have carved life out of rock. None but you could have done it so well. Now there is a new threat. Once again I must ask you to fight with me. Once again we must take the battle to the enemy."

He looked to the far end of the cavern. His eyes found Virginia's. She stood in a dark doorway. Her eyes did not see him, though her face was turned to the sound of his voice.

"Have the High Police come?" a farmer asked. "We'll beat them again. We'll drive them out of the city."

"My friend," the Ploughman said, "I only wish it were that easy." He heard himself continue. "In the battle above us, many of you saw creatures that were not of this world. Many of you lost brothers and fathers to their power. That Blackness is coming here once more, unless we cut them off before they can enter our world. To do that we must go to the place where the breach will be made and stop it. We must go to Athrom."

There was silence for the space of a minute, and then voices clamored. The Ploughman held up his hands, but before they quieted, another voice rang out above them all. The lean form of Asa stepped out from the crowd.

"Tell the truth!" he said. His face was dark with storm clouds. The Ploughman met his eyes with difficulty. Something frightening burned in Asa's amber eyes—something almost inhuman.

"Tell the truth," he demanded again. "This isn't about our colony. You have no proof any creature of Blackness will come here—only one woman's word. This is about Gypsies." Asa turned and faced the people in the Hold. "Word has come that the Gypsies are imprisoned in Athrom," he said. "So the Ploughman will have us leave everything, leave our loved ones, just to save them."

The Major stepped forward dangerously. "I wasn't aware that you *had* loved ones, Asa. Sometimes I doubt if you even have friends." The Gypsy leader raised his voice. "It is not merely that an entire race has been imprisoned. They are to be slaughtered. Can you leave them to that fate?"

"One woman tells you they will die," Asa snapped back. "You are quick to believe her—a freak of nature who hardly believes herself. We cannot fight the High Police in Athrom.

The Gypsies may not die if we leave them—*we* will certainly die if we don't!" He faced the Hold and called out to the people, "What are the Gypsies to us? Why should we die to save them?"

Farmers and Darkworlders took up the call, shouting the questions like a battle cry. Gypsies in the crowd yelled back. The two groups seemed about to converge.

"Enough!" the Ploughman shouted. "Enough. Is it not enough that they are a people? That they are women and children and men, that they are hopes and dreams, that they are a generation descended from countless generations? If we let them pass from this world, then it is *we* who are less than human. Can we call ourselves men if we allow such a thing without even trying to stop it? I will not force any one of you to join the march on Athrom. It is a choice I leave to you. But I am going, if I have to go alone."

In the momentary quiet created by his words, the Ploughman spoke again. "We have begun to build a new world here. Moments like these determine what sort of world we are building. Is this a place where mercy and brotherhood will rule? Or do we create for ourselves another Empire?"

The Darkworlders had pushed their way to the fore. Harutek spoke. "What proof have you that the Blackness will come here?"

The Ploughman looked down at the prince. "The word of a prophet," he said. "And the testimony of my own heart. That is all."

"We have long believed in prophets." Divad, high priest of the Darkworld, stepped forward. "Such a threat is greater than your colony. If the Blackness comes here, they will destroy us as well. We have long waited for the day the Great War would begin again, for we wished to be on the right side. This would seem to be our chance to declare allegiance."

"You have waited for the King," the Ploughman said quietly. No one could hear him but those who stood close by— the Darkworld leaders and the Ploughman's few friends. "But I fear he is not coming. At least not now."

"It does not matter," Caasi, Seventeenth Son of the Majesty, said. His face was impassioned. "We will fight with you."

"Caasi, hold your peace," Harutek answered. "Our father . . ."

"Must agree," Caasi said. He turned back to the Ploughman. "Ride into Athrom, Sunworld leader. I will go with you, and an army of Darkworlders behind me."

"No!"

Caasi turned to see Asa coming toward him. The dark man's face held more than anger now. Fear was etched across it. "No," Asa repeated. "The Blackness is great and powerful. You will be destroyed. If you cannot stop them . . ."

"Asa, my friend," Caasi said. "When we sat in my father's chambers you spoke of great and noble things. Why this change?"

"Indeed, Asa," the Ploughman said. He descended the ladder and stood before the men. "You have never opposed me before—not openly. You have worked alongside us. And I have even heard you say that we are cowardly to remain here without acting. Do your opinions always change so quickly?"

Asa cowered before the rebel leader. Before he had always been tall; now he seemed to shrink into the ground. "You do not know," he said. Even his voice was changing. He sounded unlike the man they had known—unlike any man at all. "You do not know what the Blackness is."

The Ploughman took a step closer. "Do you?"

Asa made no answer. The Ploughman stretched out his hand. "Take my hand, Asa, and pledge faith to me. I will not force you to fight, but what I see in your face disturbs me. Proclaim allegiance, and I will trust you. If you do not, I cannot allow you to live freely here."

"My lord, that is harsh," Caasi said. "He may be a coward, but to imprison him . . ."

"No one forced him to come here," the Ploughman said.

They were interrupted as the crowd parted. Virginia approached on Maggie's arm. The seer's green eyes were fixed on Asa. She walked forward slowly, fingers outstretched. The strange man towered above Virginia, yet he shrank from her. For a moment it seemed that he would bolt, but his feet stayed where they were. She reached him and touched his face with her sensitive fingers.

"He feels like a man," she said to herself. "What is your name, you who have questioned my sight with so much fear?"

Asa crumpled to his knees. His voice was quiet and craven. "Undred the Undecided," he said.

"You must choose," Virginia said. "Creature of light or creature of darkness. Take allegiance, Undred. Your time has come."

For a long time Asa remained frozen on the ground, staring up at Virginia with eyes full of conflict. Her fingers were still on his face. He stretched out one hand toward her and held it in the air, shaking.

"My friend?" Caasi asked.

Asa's eyes shifted to the Darkworld prince and back to Virginia. Virginia let her hand drop to her side. Asa turned to face the Ploughman. He shook his head. "You don't know," he said, his voice a rasping half-whisper. "You don't know what you're asking."

The Ploughman spoke quietly, but his voice carried to his men. "Take him away," he said. "Lock him up."

Two ex-farmers stepped forward and took Asa by the arms. He hissed, a strange sound that echoed in the cavern and caused the lines of concern on the Ploughman's face to deepen. The leader held up his hand as the men began to take Asa away. "Treat him kindly," he said.

Caasi turned to the Ploughman, about to speak. Harutek stopped his brother with a hand on his shoulder. "Later," the prince told his younger brother.

The Ploughman turned back to his people. "As long as the Empire has existed, the Gypsies have been free. They are imprisoned now in Athrom, and the Emperor will kill them if he can. We have been warned that such an evil will destroy us also, and I believe it is true. But even if it is not—I fear that, if we do not go, our hearts will be destroyed."

Silence answered him. Libuse's eyes were filled with tears, but she made no move to go to him. The Ploughman scanned the crowd, the faces that he loved and admired. Faces that looked to him to lead them.

"I go to Athrom," he said. "Make no decision now. If you will come with me, make yourself known by tomorrow."

He turned away, bowing his head so that no man could catch his eye. His stride was as strong as ever—stronger, perhaps, than it had been of late. As he left the cavern, he stopped to take Virginia's hand.

"I have heeded your warning," he said.

That night, the Ploughman brooded in his alcove, alone with his thoughts and his lady. She sat in silence, watching him, simply being the strength he needed. She shared his worry, his deep concern for his people, yet as she watched him, she smiled to herself. His strength had returned. It seemed she could almost see the old golden power hovering in the air around him.

So many things to worry about. The people—the decision they would make. The future of the colony seemed to lay in that decision. And then, if they did what was right and chose to go with their leader, the very real possibility of dying in Athrom.

A righteous death, Libuse thought. Golden. One her ancestors would be proud of.

The Ploughman said nothing, yet she could almost read his thoughts. He thought of the Darkworld, of the Majesty; he wondered what that aged ruler thought of his sons and their hasty allegiance. He wondered if Caasi's promises were empty, or if he had become the catalyst the Majesty feared. If the Darkworld went to Athrom, it would truly change them forever. He worried about Asa—Undred the Undecided, locked away as the first prisoner of Pravik.

Outside of the alcove, a man cleared his throat. The Ploughman looked up, firelight glowing on his face. Libuse stood and moved to the door, drawing aside the curtain that separated them from the rest of the colony. A burly man, more pale and thin that he had been above ground, but still like an oak in his stature and manner, bowed slightly.

"My lady," he said, his voice deep and quiet. "Will you give this to the Ploughman?" He held out a piece of paper, rolled tightly and bound with string.

"Of course," Libuse said.

The man bowed again. "Thank you, my lady."

She let the curtain fall, handing the paper to the Ploughman without a word. He took it and unrolled it in the light of the fire. His eyes scanned the parchment quickly, then returned to the top to read it again. He smiled. When he looked up at her, she could read relief in his eyes.

"They will go with me," he said. "All."

Libuse felt her heart leap, but she only smiled. "Thank the King," she said.

* * *

Moll and Seamus stood on either side of the bed where Archer lay. Master Skraetock held out his bony hand. Archer took it. With Skraetock's help he stood and took three steps through the train car. The children grinned at him with delight. He smiled back, and the smile tugged at the deep scratches on his face.

"Easy now," Master Skraetock said. "Don't overdo it. The infection may come back again."

Archer nodded and looked around him. The slight smile on his face faded. "Where is Kieran?"

The children's expressions changed in an instant. Moll started to answer, but Master Skraetock did first.

"He is gone, Archer."

Archer looked around vainly, scanning the faces that
looked at him, searching the shadowed nooks of the car.

"Gone?" he asked.

"He disappeared," Seamus whispered. "The same day you
got hurt."

Archer pulled his hand away from Skraetock and wheeled
on the Master. "Bring him back," he said.

"I can't," Master Skraetock said. "I don't know where he
is." But Archer heard the undercurrent in the Master's voice—
the unspoken meaning. They understood each other, the
Master and Archer O'Roarke. They knew the truth.

The Nameless One had done it.

"What has he done?" Archer said, a sob welling in his
chest.

"Children," Master Skraetock said, "go now. Leave us alone
for the moment."

The two children who remained turned and left the car.
Moll was crying, and Seamus held her hand as they left. When
they were gone, Skraetock shut the door behind them and
looked sadly at Archer.

"There was nothing I could do," he said.

"Why?" Archer asked. "What would he want with
Kieran?"

"I am not sure what you mean," Master Skraetock said, in
that veiled way that meant he knew exactly—that he knew the
Nameless One was behind it all; that he had—had killed
Kieran.

"I will take revenge," Archer said.

Skraetock had his hand on the door; his back turned to Archer. "You are a child," he said. "What can a child do?"

Archer closed his eyes, fists knotted. A tear slipped out. He remembered Kieran's words.

Maybe if we learn and become powerful, we'll be strong enough to get away. We won't be children anymore. We'll be older. And strong.

The voice in his mind changed. It hummed the anthem Archer had heard every night since it was first spoken. *Join us. You must join us.*

"If . . . the fire . . ." Archer whispered.

Master Skraetock turned slowly. "What did you say, boy?"

"I want to be a man," Archer said. "Like Michael and Kris of the Mountains. I don't want to be a child anymore. Can the fire make me a man?"

In an instant the room was aflame. The fire was blue. It licked up the car all around Archer, but it did not burn. He shrank from it and heard Master Skraetock say, "The fire will make you anything you want to be."

Inside of himself, Archer felt another fire rising to meet the one that blazed around him. It was not quite strong enough to reach the surface.

But that, he knew, could be changed.

* * *

The iron serpent roared over the tracks. In the engine room, amidst the coal and the heat, Michael, Stocky, and the others knew only sweat and heat, glare and backache, but they shoveled coal, and the engine screamed with power. Andrew's

271

lip split in the heat; Patrick's face turned brown. Their eyes shone with determination.

Around them, the forests of Galce gave way to the open fields of Italya. The roads were quiet, yet a dark spirit seemed to hover over them—a spirit of sorrow and loss. In the heat of the engine room, Michael suddenly shivered.

"Are you cold, Michael?" Stocky asked incredulously. "Go sit down, man."

In answer, Michael picked up a shovelful of coal and threw it into the fire. "We have to find them," he said.

* * *

The day came that Nicolas could walk, if he limped a little; and his voice was strong enough to do what he wanted it to.

"Is there no one in this entire place who can perform a wedding?" he demanded of a greying old leader.

"No one who will," returned the Gypsy. He looked on Nicolas and Marja, who was propping Nicolas up, with scorn. "To marry now is to mock us all. We're dying, can't you see that?"

"I can see that you've chosen to roll over like dogs in the dirt and give up on life," Nicolas said. "You are your own murderers."

"We are trapped here!" said the man.

"Your bodies are trapped here!" Nicolas said. "But you kill your own spirits."

"Now there, boy, calm yourself," said another voice. Nicolas spun around. He found himself looking into the smiling eyes of a small, middle-aged Gypsy on crutches. The Gypsy's green stocking cap was perched oddly on his head, and he looked up with a crooked smile. "I'll marry the two of you," he said.

"You can perform a wedding?" Nicolas asked.

"You've never heard of Caspin the Cripple, have you?" the Gypsy said. "I am the pride and fame of my Gypsy band—most of which is here, scattered around the fires."

"I have not heard of you," Nicolas said. "But I think perhaps I've missed out."

"Indeed," the cripple said, laughing to himself. "But if you want a wedding, boy, there'll be a wedding."

Nicolas smiled, and relief washed over him. He felt suddenly dizzy and nearly fell, but Marja's arm under him held him up. "I'm much obliged," he said.

* * *

The summons came unexpectedly, born by two guards in gleaming fish-scale armour: the Ploughman was called before the Majesty. He went at once, descending into the strange world below with a sense that he was passing through time. He took only a small entourage with him; some of his oldest farmer friends. The guards took him straight to the throne room.

He entered to find the Majesty seated at a long table spread with maps. Harutek, Caasi, and four of the Majesty's other sons were arrayed on either side of him. They all looked up, and the Majesty raised a regal hand in greeting. His eyes were accusing as he said, "Welcome, Sunworlder, beloved of my sons."

The Ploughman bowed. "I thank you, Majesty."

To his surprise, the Majesty withdrew, seating himself on his throne. The priests were silently seated in their usual places, and they looked to their king as he sat amongst them. He waved a hand. "My sons will speak with you now."

The Ploughman looked to Harutek and Caasi. "Word has reached us that your men will go with you," Caasi said. "They show courage and spirit. May it never be said that the Darkworlders were not equal to their guests."

The Ploughman tilted his head.

"Yes," Caasi said. "My brother and I will lead a contingent into battle alongside you."

"Now," Harutek said. "What do you plan to do?"

The Ploughman cleared his throat. "We will leave the city in small bands, under cover of night," he said. "The High Police are arrayed around the city, but we know paths they do not. We will reconvene once we are beyond their reach and march to the city, entering it secretly if we can. We mean to find the coliseum and find a way to get the Gypsies out."

"Without the Emperor noticing?" Caasi asked.

"We are not eager for a battle," the Ploughman said. "This is a matter of rescue, not of aggression."

"Indeed," Harutek said. "But your plans will not work. You cannot take a large enough force into Athrom without being noticed, nor can you spirit the Gypsies out."

"We have to try," the Ploughman said.

"Undoubtedly," Harutek answered. He tapped his pale finger on the map before him. "If the maps we have are accurate, you will never reach Athrom on foot before your enemies come to you, in greater force than you can withstand. Even if you manage to get past the troops outside of Pravik, you will be discovered and slaughtered before you reach Italya."

"What do you suggest?" the Ploughman asked.

Harutek looked down suddenly, and Caasi spoke. "Go underland," he said. "Take the rivers. You and your people will sail to Athrom. You will come up in the middle of the city like a volcanic fire, unlooked for and great in force."

The Ploughman looked to the Majesty, seeking some confirmation from the king of the Darkworld. But it was Divad, the high priest, who spoke.

"It must be as the princes say," he said. "The Darkworlders will lead you. We know our way in the darkest of places. You can bring the Gypsies back the same way, into the hidden paths you have prepared for them."

"And if the Emperor sends his men after us?" the Ploughman asked. "Will not the rivers lead them to your doorstep?"

Here the Majesty smiled. "You underestimate us, Sunworlder," he said. "Do not assume we are so easy to find. Without my sons to guide you, you would never find your way to Athrom. Nor would you ever come back."

The Ploughman turned back to the princes, aware suddenly of the enormity of the trust he was being asked to place in them. He found that he could give it. In Harutek was wisdom and knowledge; in Caasi a fire that burned as truly as any in the Ploughman himself.

* * *

Virginia Ramsey passed through the corridors of underground Pravik, listening to the sounds of men preparing for battle. She could hear water lapping against boats, the clink of swords and armour, the calls of men who worked together to ready themselves. A sense of urgency filled the sounds. There was no time to waste.

She wandered alone, the sounds growing more distant and bouncing off the corridors in disorienting echoes. Alone, but not without purpose. She smiled as she heard the voices of the two she was seeking. The young voice of Caasi, seventeenth son of the Majesty, Darkworld prince. And the eerie, disinterested voice of Undred the Undecided.

She stopped, hidden in the shadows, and listened as they spoke to one another. Caasi pleaded with the man he called "friend," seeking out some understanding. But Asa would give no explanation. His voice was human again, but Virginia knew its tones were deceptive.

"Let me out," Asa said suddenly.

Silence answered him. Then, "Are you mad? Asa, if you would prove your allegiance, I would let you out in a heartbeat. But I am no traitor."

"You don't know," Asa said. "You don't know what lies under Athrom. I do."

"What are you talking about?" Caasi's voice held a growing edge of frustration. "Tell me, man."

"Take me with you," Asa said.

Boots scraped against rock as Caasi stood. "You will not be moved? Has nothing I have said changed your mind?"

"I am no fool," Asa answered. "The Ploughman is not strong enough. You are not strong enough."

"We have the right on our side," Caasi said. "The King's right. That is strength enough."

Asa only laughed bitterly. Virginia listened as Caasi's footsteps moved away in the darkness. She stayed where she was, unmoving, until Asa called out, "Who is there?"

Still she did not move. "What lies under Athrom, Undred?" she asked.

He chuckled, a desperate, empty laugh. "Death."

"And why are you so eager to face it?" she asked.

"I do not die," Asa said. "I am only set free."

Virginia nodded. She took a deep breath, stepped forward, and pulled out a key from her sleeve. Without a word, she unlocked the door. She felt him move past her with a sensation of hot wind brushing by. He hissed his thanks.

She said nothing.

* * *

The Emperor Lucien Morel, Lord of the Seventh World, bid the newcomers enter. The Grand Master of the Order of the Spider bowed before the Emperor, and the Emperor inclined his head in return. Adhemar Skraetock presented a boy before him. The Emperor laid his hand on the boy's head and blessed him, though inwardly he disdained anything so marred—the boy's face was slashed with white scars.

Lucien Morel nodded his head to the man Christopher Ens, and to the un-man, the Nameless One. The Emperor watched them leave his throne room. His eyes fixed on the back of the Nameless One, and his little finger twitched.

Just before the doors of the throne room closed, the Nameless One turned his head. His eyes met the Emperor's, and he smiled.

The Emperor's finger jerked. Why did the Nameless One's smile make him think of voices, of hauntings in the night? The rushing water of a nearby fountain made him suddenly nervous.

Adhemar Skraetock and his party slipped unseen through the city of Athrom. In late afternoon they stopped to drink from a clear spring, and a bird flew down and landed on a branch in front of Archer.

The boy looked at the bird and studied its feathers and its dark eyes. The bird lifted its wings, and Archer's heart leaped. So small, so frail, the bird—and yet so free. No traps held the tiny creature. It had no power and no fear.

Archer felt other eyes on him. He turned his head and saw Master Skraetock watching him. The Master lifted a hand and moved his fingers. The bird fell dead into the stream.

* * *

Dusk fell as the Gypsies gathered and formed circles within circles. Nicolas stood in the center and looked up. He smiled, because for the first time since he had come to the coliseum, stars were shining.

And the women began to sing, a soft, lilting song; sung for hundreds of years by the Wandering Race whenever two of their people made the ancient promise of fidelity—that they would wander together, not apart, forever until the end.

* * *

Black water lapped black rock under flickering torchlight, and the men of two worlds bowed their heads as Divad raised his hands and spoke.

"Blessed be the King of the World, who teacheth our hands to war," he intoned. "Blessed be those who lay down their lives for the right."

The Ploughman listened with his eyes fixed on the cavern ceiling, searching beyond the rock for a glimmer of light. Golden light. He was not alone. He knew that now.

In a boat behind him, a tall man sat with his limbs pulled in, his face shadowed by the hood of his cloak. His eyes were fixed on the leader of Pravik, the one who had tried to force him to choose allegiance. Asa had chosen his allegiance, though no other knew it. He listened to the words of the high priest with distaste, feeling only the slightest of pangs as he remembered what it felt like to believe in something greater than himself.

* * *

The lilting song ended and the circle parted. Marja entered. An old woman held her left hand and another old woman held her right, and a tiny child stepped solemnly before them. Nicolas lifted his own hands and stretched them out to her.

The old women let go and stepped back, and Marja put her hands in Nicolas's.

* * *

"Blessed be those who hope for the King's return," Divad said.

"May he come soon," said his five attendant priests. "And may he look kindly on us."

"May he forget our betrayals and remember this day," Divad said. "May he look kindly on the warriors of the Darkworld who go forth to join his army."

* * *

Marja spoke with all the warmth of her race in her voice, her eyes lately marked by suffering but alive despite it all. "This promise I make to thee, Nicolas Fisher, that where you wander I will go; that where you fly I will follow."

He spoke with the same warmth back to her, aware that every word was his choice. His choice to love. His choice to run no longer. "And this promise I return to you, Marja of the Sky, that where I wander I will shelter you, and where I fly I will soar with you."

* * *

"The journey is nearly over," Kris of the Mountains said.

"We failed to catch them," Michael said. "They are already in Athrom."

"Have you thought what we will do when we reach them?" Kris asked.

"We will get our children back," Michael answered.

"And we will make the spider tremble!" Gwyrion said, and his eyes flashed like the lightning in a wolf's eyes.

* * *

"In the sight of these many witnesses are these hands joined," said Caspin the Cripple. His voice dropped as the ceremony ended, and he smiled. "Hope lives!" he shouted. "There is yet a future for the Wandering Race! Do not stand there in silence, cousins. Rejoice!"

* * *

"Go forth with courage, my sons," said the Majesty. "My people. Let the Sunworld know the valour of those who have lived hidden lives."

"And my people," said the Ploughman, standing in his boat. "You who have fought well and hard with me. I see you now, and I am grateful to be one of you."

All but Asa's eyes looked back to the Ploughman with a quiet solidarity that took their leader's breath away. Pravik had chosen—to follow him. To do right.

The water stirred as the long river boats pushed away toward the south, and the current caught them and swept them forward.

* * *

The Gypsies joined hands and danced in circles within circles. They sang, and the crippled hearts took flight once more.

Archer closed his eyes and concentrated on the burning inside him, and the iron serpent journeyed ever farther south.

The darkness rushed past a hundred river boats in the deepness of the earth.

The Nameless One smiled over his own secrets.

A full moon rose, and Gwyrion threw back his head and howled.

14

Through the Veil

IRON WHEELS GROUND against the track in a sparking screech. The train lurched to a stop and settled, hissing. The Clann O'Roarke descended from the train cars and gathered around the still-smoking engine.

"This is far as she takes us," Michael said. Below them, city lights glowed in the night. "Athrom. The end of our line."

Miracle drew her cloak around her shoulders and shivered in the night air. A dove fluttered down from the train and came to rest on her shoulder.

"All those lights," Jack said. "I never knew a city could be so big."

"How will we ever find them?" Jenna echoed.

"We will," Stocky said. "They are there. Somewhere."

Shannon shook her head. "Are they?" she asked. "How do we know? Those men could have taken them anywhere, and we wouldn't know it."

"No," Miracle said. "They have gone to the city. I am sure of it."

Her voice was faint. Kris put his hand on her shoulder. "Are you well?" he asked.

Miracle nodded and attempted to smile. "As well as I can be, Kris of the Mountains," she said. The look on his face said that he didn't believe her, but he stepped ahead to join Michael and left Miracle by herself.

"Kris of the Mountains," Miracle repeated quietly. "Will I ever see those mountains again?" The white wolf appeared at her side and pushed his head up under her hand. She stroked his silvery fur and looked to the horizon again.

"As well as I can be," she whispered. "Better. I know now what I must do."

Half an hour's debate yielded the decision to camp for the night. Michael sat with Kris and the young men around the fire, making plans. Shannon and the younger girls leaned against each other and tried to sleep, and no one noticed when Miracle left the camp with a tread so light it would not have wakened a mouse. Nor did anyone notice when the white wolf raised its great head to look after her, and then stood and glided into the darkness behind her.

Two miles from the camp was a stand of birch trees, much like those that grew in the north. Miracle stopped beneath their rustling leaves, letting herself imagine for a moment that she was at home again. She felt rather than heard the footsteps approaching behind her.

"Do I do right, Spirit of the Wild Things?" she asked.

The answer was a deep growl that changed timbre until it became a rich voice. "Only you can know."

"Then yes," she said. She turned so her eyes could take in the strong form behind her. "There is no other way."

"There is one," Gwyrion answered.

"And I want to take it," Miracle said. "But I cannot allow myself to run. What sort of person would I be if I could allow them to sacrifice themselves when I can prevent it?"

"You would be a weak human being," Gwyrion said.

"I *am* a weak human being," Miracle answered. "But I withstood the Order once, though they nearly killed me—and they may kill me yet. I believe it was the King who gave me strength."

Gwyrion looked up through the break in the trees. His eyes reflected the moonlight. "The King is the great giver of strength," he said. "I have been called the bounding step of the deer, the running strength of the wolf, the leaping power of the salmon. I exult in strength. I rejoice in power. But all that I am, I am because the King lives. He is the heart of the world."

"You speak the truth," Miracle said. "Of that I am sure."

"It is not really strength you need," Gwyrion said. "That you have in abundance, for I will go with you. What you need is love."

Miracle turned and looked in the direction of the camp. "I have that," she whispered.

"Then you will not fail," Gwyrion said. "Love holds fast and never fails."

She couldn't go on just then. She walked the two miles back to camp in the moonlight. Gwyrion stayed near, but he did not show himself again. Miracle walked until she reached the crest of a little hill looking down on the dying campfire and the clann clustered around it. Her eyes searched the faces of the sleepers, traced the suffering and determination in their expressions. She smiled sadly. And then a twig cracked. Her

285

heart jumped and pounded in her throat, and she turned to face Michael.

"I frightened you," he said. "I'm sorry."

"I couldn't sleep," she said.

"You've been gone a while," Michael said. "I was about to go looking for you."

She smiled. "No need. I wasn't lost."

Michael looked at her curiously, but didn't pry. She was looking at the camp, not at him, and he followed her gaze.

"It is good that they sleep," he said. "Tomorrow will be a long day in the midst of long days."

"You should also sleep," Miracle said.

He smiled. "It is my watch. And who gives you the right to wake in the middle of the night if I should sleep? Who do you think is the chieftain of this family?"

His smile disappeared when he saw the look on her face. "You're crying," he said. "What's wrong? Did I say something to . . ."

"Of course not," she said.

He moved close to her. She backed away—one step and no further, turning her back to him. Hesitantly he moved closer and put his arms around her. She stiffened, but then she relaxed and leaned against him, leaned into the protection of his arms.

"I wish you didn't ever have to let go," she said.

"I don't," he whispered.

"Yes, you do," she said. She pulled away and turned her tear-stained face to him. He moved toward her again, desperation written across his face.

"I don't," he said. "Tell me that you want me to stay with you, and I'll never leave you. I'll never let go. I love you, Miracle."

She closed her eyes and commanded her breathing to be still. "Oh, Michael," she said.

"Yes?" he asked.

She shook her head. "You should never have fallen in love with me."

And that was all. She turned and walked away. Michael was left empty-handed, staring after her. A sob broke loose from his chest and came out in a strangled cry. He turned to the fire and his sleeping people.

"I told her, Shannon," he whispered. "I finally got up my courage and told her. Aren't you proud of me?" His face twisted. He staggered away from the camp in search of a place where he could be completely, bitterly, alone.

When Michael O'Roarke awoke with dew on his skin, his head hurt and his fingers were clenched in a fist. He stretched them out and winced. Around him, the Clann O'Roarke prepared to leave for the city of Athrom.

Patrick pulled his tall boots on his feet and looked over at Michael's strained face. "Don't worry," he said. "We'll find them."

"I know," Michael said, but he was unable to smile.

Shannon approached and set a bucket full of creek water on the ground. "Where's Miracle got off to this morning?" she asked.

Michael started. "Isn't she here?" he said.

"No," Shannon said. "Don't look so frightened, Michael. She's gone off to be alone, I expect. She'll be back."

* * *

"You're a liar, little brother." The Nameless One spoke the words inches from Christopher's ear. Christopher's skin crawled as he turned to face his fellow. Around them, crumbling stone walls cast a deathly pall over the tiny corridor.

"I don't know what you're talking about," Christopher said.

The Nameless One smiled. "The healer," he said. "You told Master Skraetock that she had left the Green Isle. The truth is, she's coming here."

Christopher's eyes narrowed. "You don't know any such thing," he said.

"I do know it," the Nameless One said. "I saw her."

"You used a Seeing Spell," Christopher said. "The Master forbids anyone but himself from—"

"The Master," the Nameless One crooned. "The Master, the Master. The Master is fallen, little brother. He is only an acolyte now, and I am the Master of the Order of the Spider."

Christopher jerked away. "You are speaking treason," Christopher said. "You could die for those words."

"Who would kill me?" the Nameless One demanded. "Skraetock may pretend to control the Order. He pretends to control the Blackness itself. But he is an old fool, isn't he? Isn't he? Say it!"

"I want nothing to do with you," Christopher said. "Or your rantings."

The Nameless One tilted his head. "I am the Master now," he said. "I am the Master now. I am the Spider. I will suck them all dry, and bring all the Blackness into myself."

"You're mad," Christopher said.

The Nameless One grinned. His handsome face was hideous. "Yes," he said. "I am."

Christopher turned away and walked down the stone corridor. His footsteps echoed in the darkness as he climbed the twisting stairs to the room at the top of the tower. When he burst the door open, Moll gave a little shriek.

"Nothing to be afraid of," he said. His stomach twisted as he said it. "It's only me."

"Have you come to make us ready?" Archer asked. His golden hair was dull in the grey light that came in through the tower windows. The salt air seemed to coat his eyes so that they stared like wax. One of his arms was around Seamus's shoulders; the other held Moll to him.

"Yes," Christopher said. "Calling up the fire for the first time can be dangerous. We can protect you with a spell, but you must be willing to receive it."

"We are willing," Archer said.

"Good boy," Christopher said. He knelt and put his hand on Archer's head. His tone was bitter. "And you will serve the Master faithfully, won't you? He has been good to you."

Archer's dull eyes filled with an expression Christopher could not decipher, but it seemed as though it might take form in tears. "He can make me a man," he said. "That is all that matters."

* * *

A foul wind wafted up the stairs of the tower through cracks in the door of the Master's study. Adhemar Skraetock shivered and stood. He did not turn to see who stood behind

289

him. He did not need to. "You have been in the Pit," he said.

The Nameless One's voice came from the open door behind him. "Yes," he said.

"The Pit is forbidden without my permission," Skraetock said. "You have no right to commune with the Blackness without my knowledge and involvement."

"Your knowledge," the Nameless One mocked. "You knew I was there. You were too afraid to stop me."

"The Blackness will not commune with you again," Skraetock said. "I have spoken with the great powers beyond the Veil. They are displeased with you, for I am displeased with you." He turned now.

"They have betrayed you," the Nameless One said. "They are overcome by the smell of blood."

"What are you talking about?" Skraetock said.

"You are a hypocrite," the Nameless One said. "All your life you have worked to guard the supremacy of the Blackness. Why? So that, as our Oath says, 'they may one day tear the Veil and take their place in the world.' And here you are, terrified that it will happen soon. Frightened to death that your masters might come and displace you."

"You do not understand the nature of the Blackness," Skraetock spat.

"I understand it far better than you do," the Nameless One said. "You hold it at bay. It has consumed me."

"What do you plan to do?" Skraetock said.

"I will kill all the Gypsies," the Nameless One said. "One great sacrifice."

Skraetock paled. "That will tear the Veil."

"Yes," the Nameless One answered. "It will."

"You cannot," Skraetock said. He took a menacing step forward.

"In three nights' time the smell of my sacrifice will rend the heavens," the Nameless One said. He laughed. "Did you really think it was the Emperor who brought all the Gypsies to Athrom? Did you really think he did it out of spite?"

Skraetock had gone white with anger. Though he tried to answer, nothing came out of his mouth.

"I told him to do it," the Nameless One said. "He doesn't know it, but I told him."

"You will not remain supreme long," Skraetock said. "The children of Thomas O'Roarke are strong. When they have joined me, I will destroy you."

"Do you think so?" the Nameless One said. He smiled, a long, purple, insane smile. "I told the Emperor to bring the Gypsies," he said, sing-song. "I told you to bring the children. And you did it. You both obeyed me."

"Why?" Skraetock said, his long fingers clenched.

"I want the girl," the Nameless One said. "And she's coming for them. The whole world dances when I sing."

"Not anymore," Skraetock said. He lunged at the Nameless One. His long fingers closed around the younger man's throat —and the Master's eyes widened with shock as the Nameless One closed one hand around his elder's neck and lifted him high in the air. The Master's eyes bulged as the Nameless One tightened his grip.

"Now give to me," the Nameless One said. The Nameless One closed his eyes and opened his mouth to breathe great gasps of air as life drained from the one-time Master of the Order. Skraetock groaned and tried to cry out as he felt power flow out of him, sucked out by the Nameless One's grasp. He knew now, too late, what his acolyte had been doing in the Pit. He had enacted the Rite of the Spider. Only one man had ever possessed that power—the power to drain another, to claim another's life force for his own. That man was Adhemar Skraetock.

That man died in the grasp of his former student. The Nameless One loosened his grip and let Skraetock's body fall to the floor. He took a step backward, reeling with the shock of energy and life.

"He *was* strong," the Nameless One said. "I didn't know—" He began to laugh. "He was right," he said, laughing hysterically. "He could have killed me. He was that strong, but I didn't believe him."

He stopped laughing abruptly. His chest heaved as he sucked in great breaths of air. The power he had taken even now threatened to overwhelm him: to slay him even after the Master himself had been slain. For a moment the Nameless One teetered on the edge of death, but the moment passed. He stood straight.

"Now I *only* am strong," he said.

He moved to the window of the study and looked out on the swampland that surrounded the tower. The sky was grey; the air salty.

"Dance, world," he said. "The Nameless One is singing."

* * *

"There must be some way out," Nicolas said.

"You must want escape badly enough," Caspin the Cripple told him. They stood at the high extreme of the coliseum, at the very top of the wall.

"Has no one escaped?" Nicolas asked.

"Some," Caspin said. He motioned to the city below them, its lights beginning to glimmer as the night drew near. "They jumped."

"Then they died," Nicolas said. "No one could survive that fall."

Caspin shrugged. "They wanted escape. They took it as they found it."

"Death is not an option for me," Nicolas said.

"Why not?" Caspin asked.

Nicolas looked down. "There was a time I didn't care if I lived or died," he said. "I lived because it was more interesting. That's changed now—and you of all people should *know* why."

Caspin smiled, a sad, thoughtful smile. "I lost my wife here, you know," he said. "She died of illness contracted on the road to Athrom."

"I'm sorry," Nicolas said. He closed his eyes for a moment, struggling to keep emotion back. "I never thought I'd want so badly for there to be another tomorrow."

"Family has a way of doing that to a man," Caspin said.

"This is no place for a family," Nicolas said. "For any family, even one as small as mine. Marja is weak—weaker than she ought to be. I think she has deprived herself to feed me."

Caspin cast a glance at Nicolas's thin, still faintly bruised frame. "You needed it."

"And besides that," Nicolas said. "There is something I must do. Something I never finished."

293

"Then find a way out," Caspin said.

"There *is* no way out," Nicolas said. He brought his fist down on the wall. The stone scraped his skin.

"If you need a way badly enough, you'll find one," Caspin said. He winked. "That's all the wisdom I have left."

The Cripple took his crutch and hobbled away. Nicolas slid down with his back against the wall. The stone felt cool on his back; the air heavy and hot. He looked down at the arena, the floor of the coliseum where his people had formed circles and danced for him not long ago. Marja was down there now, with the older women fussing over her. She was not well.

She had given him so much, he thought. She had given him love and joy—together they had given joy to the whole colony of refugees, if only for a night. She would have come with him to find the River-Daughter. She would have stayed with him till they changed the world.

He had to find a way out.

Had to.

He closed his eyes, and his lips formed words.

King of the World, he prayed. *You, who Maggie believes in. You, who my own wife tells stories about—Sun-King, and Moon-King, and All-the-Stars-King. If you can hear, listen to me! Surely your hearing cannot be worse than mine. I am Gifted, they say; and you are the Giver of gifts. So if I can hear, can you not hear me?*

He swallowed hard and continued. *Can you not hear all of us? We need you! We need help! They say you're coming back. Why not now?*

There was no answer but silence. He put his head on his knees and began to cry, racking sobs that ached and tore at

him. He was so helpless, and this trap where he lived was so
without hope.

*It's your song, isn't it? The Song of the Burning Light. You
are the Father who sings the Father-Song. Then why don't you
save us? Aren't we your children? And if you are the Lover of
the Lover-Song, then why do you leave us alone?*

When he opened his eyes, a man was sitting across from
him. He was a young man, Nicolas thought—but then, no—he
was not old, but he was somehow ancient. Nicolas blinked. The
man—a young man, he decided—wore a homespun robe, and
his feet were bare. His face was grave, but something about it
spoke of a great shouting gladness just below his solemnity.

"You have never been alone," he said.

"You heard me?" Nicolas asked. Something inside him was
swelling, as though his spirit would burst through its shell to
meet this man.

"Did you think I couldn't?" the young man asked. "You
should know better."

"Will you get us out of here?" Nicolas asked. "Save us?"

"Yes," the young man said. "Through you."

"What must I do?" Nicolas asked.

"Finish your task. Free the River-Daughter."

"From here?" Nicolas asked. "I am trapped here. I cannot
even reach the river."

"Have you not learned yet?" the young man asked. "The
true path is often hidden until the time comes to take it. You
have been called, Nicolas Fisher. We have not released you
from that call."

"Where are you going?" Nicolas asked, alarmed. Before his
eyes, the young man was beginning to fade.

"Away," he answered, "and not away. I will see you soon. You are never alone, Nicolas Fisher."

He was gone in the next instant. Nicolas shook his head in wonder and frustration.

"I don't understand," he muttered.

"Nicolas?" It was Marja. She looked amused as she climbed up to the level where Nicolas sat. "Is there some reason you're talking to yourself?"

Nicolas jumped up. He took her in his arms and kissed her suddenly. "I'm leaving," he said.

She looked down and nodded. "Where?" she asked.

"I'm going to find a way out," he said.

"Is that even possible?" Marja asked.

"He didn't tell me," Nicolas said, looking up.

"Who?"

Nicolas knew the answer. "The King," he said.

"You spoke with him?"

Nicolas looked in her eyes and smiled. "I think I did."

Marja smiled back and stepped away. "Hurry back," she said. "I'll be waiting for you."

The sun was beginning to set, and Nicolas felt a sudden urgency. He took Marja's arm. Together they descended the side of the coliseum to the floor, where Nicolas found Caspin the Cripple and pulled him aside.

"I am leaving," he said. "Take care of her."

Caspin nodded. "I'll do my best."

"Thank you."

"Find what you are looking for, Nicolas Fisher," Caspin said. "We have no hope left but you."

Nicolas turned away, tearing his eyes from the old man and the woman he loved. He climbed back to the top of the wall, stood on the edge, and looked out on the city of Athrom. A breeze blew from the purple, sun-streaked west. Nicolas's legs shook. He imagined the hopelessness of those who had found escape by jumping. From this very height. Perhaps from this very spot.

Far away in the west was a break in the clouds. Nicolas watched the edge of the dark orange sun dip below the horizon. It was gone, and the air smelled of dusk. The purple in the skies blended with the dark of the coming night.

The air shifted and changed, and a heavy-silk voice spoke in Nicolas's ear.

Close your eyes, Nicolas Fisher.

Nicolas obeyed. For a moment he wondered if he had lost his balance—if he was not now falling from the height of the wall—escaping, but escaping alone. Through closed eyes he saw a flash of rainbow colours and what might have been the sorrowful faces of the Shearim. Then the voice spoke with a hundred other, quieter voices, all of them sounding at once in his ears—*Open your eyes and see.*

His pulse quickened. He opened his eyes.

Behold a world divided, said the voices.

Before him and above him—everywhere he looked—stretched the Veil. It was clear like water and shot through with rainbow colours that changed and swirled in misty patterns before his eyes. It was not cloudy—it was most like a very clear mountain stream—yet he could not see through it to the other side.

Here lies the path before you. We bar the way to a part of the world you have never seen before. You must step through, said the heavy-silk voices. The Veil shimmered with the sounding of them. It was true, Nicolas realized, what he had told Marja. The Veil was not a thing, it was a Being. A thousand Beings, knitted together. The Shearim.

He had forgotten all about the long fall before him, had forgotten everything except the moment. He stretched out his hand, and his fingers touched the Veil. It rippled under his fingers like water and sounded like harp strings. Rainbow colours swirled around the spot where his fingers touched. The Veil was cool to his hand. He pulled away.

You must step through, the voices said again.

Nicolas swallowed and touched the Veil again. This time he pressed against it, and his fingers slipped through. He gasped and pulled them back. Silvery rainbow tendrils tightened gently around his fingers and spread over his hand. He stretched his fingers; bent them; played with them.

He looked up once again, nodded his head, and stepped off the edge of the coliseum.

Nicolas gasped as the Veil closed around him. This was no fall, no plummet from the coliseum edge. It was a passing from dimension into another. Instead of darkness he saw misty light. The coolness surrounded and supported him. He breathed in, and with his breath came air that was not air: that was spirit, that was life. Life tingled and burned in his veins, like a fire leaping up to greet the air. He heard voices but could not understand the words; he heard harp strings that were also voices, wondrous and heartbreaking. The closest to him sounded thin and pained, like something being torn apart. And then he was through.

It was dark on the other side of the Veil. Dark in this second dimension—in this world within the world.

Nicolas turned to look back and stumbled backward in shock. The Veil here had none of the shimmering beauty of the other side. It was beautiful, yes, but the beauty was terrible and frightening. It was black, shot through with lightning. A barrier.

Nicolas crawled to the Veil's edge and reached out to touch it. Pain stung his fingers. He pulled his hand close and cradled it. He could smell burned flesh. His own flesh. He began to look around him. The ground where he sat was scorched, black, and cold. He touched it, and when he lifted his fingers they were covered with inky soot. He stood and shivered.

The sky was low and dark, and the horizon glimmered with distant orange light. There was no vegetation anywhere, and no water. The ground was flat. It stretched away forever in every direction. To the north, black mountains spiked the rim of the visible world. The air smelled burned and sweet, a strange sweetness that was pleasant for a moment and then revolting. And there was sound: a constant, distant noise that defied concentration. A sound that might drive a man crazy before he had ever learned to describe it.

Nicolas took a tentative step to the south and stopped. He could see no one anywhere.

"I don't—" he said, stopping to clear his throat. "I don't know which way to go."

The answer came from his memory: *Follow the river.*

Come for me. I am the prisoner River-Daughter, yearning to be free. Set me free, Nicolas Fisher. Your journey is not over yet.

"Follow the river," he repeated. Only the distant roar answered him. "There is no river!" he said, and then looked to his right.

It was there. A dry river bed.

Nicolas forced himself to put one foot in front of the other along the place where a river had once run. How long he walked he could not tell. The darkness and distant noise swallowed up time. He talked to himself as he went, narrating his own actions, just to give himself some clear sound to cling to. Never had his ears been so without anchor.

He dove for cover in the river bed at the sound of a distant, blood-chilling howl. He had heard such a thing before. He lay on his back and looked up as shadows fell over him and the creatures passed by. He could just see them over the crust of the earth.

The hell hound came first, its green eyes glowing and its green breath marking the air. The stench of death fell over the river bed and nearly choked Nicolas. He squinted his watering eyes and swallowed hard. The hound snuffled and whined. It opened its mouth to reveal massive teeth. They were real, those teeth, real and solid and deadly, and yet there was something about the whole body of the hound that was not quite *there*—its edges were frayed, its lines not entirely static. Nicolas thought it might dissolve its shape at any moment and become something else, because its true shape was not that of a hound but that of a spirit.

This, too, he had seen before. The ravens that had attacked the Major's Gypsies long ago in search of Maggie had changed shape and become one great bird. The Gypsies had killed it. Marja had wounded it, he remembered. He wanted to close his eyes and think only of her, but fear kept his eyes open and riveted on the passing creatures.

Behind the hound came a skeletal man, too long and too tall, with limbs that seemed to drift over the ground and trail behind him and a head far too big for his body. The skeletal man turned his head as he passed. Nicolas saw his face: it was a carved, grinning mask, with nothing but blackness where the eyes and nose and mouth should be. Nicolas bit back his own fear till he could taste blood.

The creatures of shadow passed by and disappeared over the horizon, but it was a long time before Nicolas could move.

He clambered cautiously out of the river bed. His hands shook as he lifted them and placed them on the ground again, crawling. After a while he was able to walk.

There was no sun or moon in the burnt sky. Nicolas turned to look at the Veil, and in its dark surface he saw the Gypsy camp. He saw Caspin and he saw his wife, and then it all faded away. He saw a golden-haired child with a scarred face. The boy seemed to be staring straight at him, and Nicolas stared back. Fear for the child gripped him. And then that vision, too, faded away.

He forced himself to keep walking.

After some time the riverbank crowded over with bare, black, thorny bushes, many of them. They threatened to choke out the path and obscure Nicolas's sight of the river. He knew that if he tried to go around them he would lose his way, so he stepped down into the river bed and walked inside it.

In the distance he saw something bright—a white light, unlike the orange glow on the horizon. He kept walking toward it until he could see it flickering, steadily burning. A fire. As he drew near, he shielded his eyes with his hands.

When he reached it, he saw a great bush on fire, taller than he was and wide enough to fill the river bed. It stood directly in his path. It was brighter than most fires, so that he could not look directly at it. He began to climb out of the river bed, seeking a way around it, when a powerful presence fell over him, arresting him. It weakened his limbs so that he slid back down the bank. Slowly, he turned to face the bush.

It was gone. In its place, standing in the center of the flame with his eyes and hair shining white, was the ancient young man in homespun.

"Would you learn the Fire-Song?" the King said. "Then come. Pass through the fire to me."

15

Fire-Song

"I CAN'T," NICOLAS WHISPERED. His mouth was dry. The fire grew as he looked at it, grew till it seemed to him great enough to swallow the world—yet it was still there, still contained in the river bed. Instead of casting light on the desolate land, it seemed to draw the darkness in around it. It burned like the very center of the world, terrible, white, and deadly.

And there was something else about it—Nicolas felt afraid in its presence as he had never before felt afraid. This was not like the fear of evil. It was instead the fear of good—great, infinite good. It made him know how small and full of blackness he himself was.

"Are you afraid?" the King asked.

"Yes," Nicolas said. He did not say what he felt with all his heart. *I cannot come. The fire will destroy me.*

"I have led you here," the King said. "Will you turn away now? You have heard two strains of my song and known their beauty. The Fire-Song is greatest of all, for it is the song of my spirit. Tell me, son of the earth. Will you come?"

"I cannot," Nicolas answered. "You know I cannot."

"You could not if you faced the fire alone," the King said. "But I am here."

"What if I do not come?" Nicolas asked. His whole body, his whole spirit, was shrinking back from the flames. Yet the King's eyes kept him riveted to the spot, drawing him—drawing a deep part of him.

"You feel the blackness in yourself?" the King asked.

"Yes," Nicolas whispered.

"If you do not come," the King said, "that blackness will destroy everything you love."

Nicolas lifted his tear-stained face and looked through the flames at the face of the King. "You will help me?" he asked.

The King in homespun nodded and smiled. The gladness Nicolas had sensed below the surface of the King's face sparked now in his eyes. "Yes."

"Then I will come," Nicolas said.

The King held out his hands. They reached beyond the fire to Nicolas, themselves alight, strong hands white like star fire.

"Take my hands," the King commanded.

Nicolas did.

* * *

They stood in the streets of Athrom, Michael O'Roarke and his family. Straight up the main road, overlooking the city, rose the golden walls of the Emperor's Palace. They were dull under the clouded sky.

Michael hardly saw any of it.

Kris of the Mountains laid his hand on Michael's shoulder. "We'll find her," he said.

Michael shook his head. "She's not here," he said.

"She told us we would find the children in the city," Shannon said. "If you're right that she's gone to try to free them herself, where else would she be?"

"She lied," Michael said.

Shannon started to answer and bit her lip instead. He was right. She knew that.

"Gwyrion's with her," Shannon said. "She'll be all right."

"Where are they?" Michael breathed.

The sound of beating wings filled the air, and suddenly birds were all around, landing on the hands and heads and shoulders of the clann. The birds called and sang, demanding attention before they lifted up again.

"Follow them!" Michael shouted. "They've found the children!"

* * *

The white wolf pushed against Miracle's leg as they looked down at the swamp and the tower that stood in its center, a short but treacherous distance away.

"It's an ill place," Miracle said. "Everything here is sick."

She took a deep breath and stepped forward, down the hill to the swampland. At the base of the hill, mud sucked at her boots and weighed down her skirt. She stumbled as she walked. The wolf pushed ahead of her and whined. She looked up and saw that he stood on a solid piece of ground. She picked her feet up and struggled to reach him.

The grass on the solid ground was sharp. It cut at her ankles as she moved through it. She stopped and brushed a lock of hair out of her face, streaking her cheek with mud.

"Where am I taking myself?" she asked. Her eyes filled with momentary tears, but she willed them away. The distant cry of a carrion crow fell through the darkness.

A light glowed in the top of the tower, and she followed it. The white wolf went ahead of her, testing the ground, leaping over pools of filth. She followed. The weeping branches of a gnarled tree brushed across her face and shoulders, and she lost her step for an instant, plunging one foot into deep muddy water. She cried out and pulled her foot back again. A pale snake had wrapped itself around her ankle. She felt its fangs sink into her leg.

The white wolf was at her side in an instant. His jaws snapped at the serpent, his teeth so close they nearly grazed her skin. He severed the snake's body, and its coils loosened and fell. Miracle pulled up her skirt to reveal two perfect fang marks, dripping blood and poison.

Already her head was spinning. Pain shot through her eyes, and her fingers felt clumsy. She bowed her head and placed her hands over the wound.

"Not for me," she whispered. "Not for me, but for the children, bring healing through my hands."

She closed her eyes and let the heat in her veins rise and flow through her fingers. In a moment the pain subsided, and her head began to clear. She opened her eyes and removed her hands, watching as the fang marks closed and left her skin streaked with blood—but whole.

She lifted her head and said, "Thank you."

The white wolf nudged her arm, and she held onto his shoulder as she pulled herself to her feet. She took three more steps and stopped—she could not go on quite yet. Not until she had left a mark of her own in this place.

Miracle took the rose from her belt and knelt on the earth. The smell of the swamp filled her senses and in a moment nearly overwhelmed her. She fought back the sickening feeling and fixed her eyes on the rose. She said something inaudibly, only her lips moving, and the rose began to change. From its stem roots grew. She dug with her hands in the dirt and planted the rose in the center of the swamp.

"Grow," she said. "Grow and heal this place. May the land remember me kindly."

For a long time she stayed there, hushed, while the swamp around her crawled and skittered with the sounds of the night. At last she breathed in deeply and stood, turned, faced the light in the tower, still some distance away. Time to go on.

* * *

The Black Tower, ancient stronghold of the Order of the Spider, was guarded by nothing more than a single oak door on one side. No one knew who had built the foreboding structure. Legend said it had grown there, like the drooping trees in the swamp. Sometimes it did seem alive, its black stones quivering, the vines that wrapped around its height growing from the tower itself and not from any root in the ground.

In the highest part of the tower, a candle burned orange. And in the deepest part, in the Pit far under the ground, another fire burned blue.

Christopher Ens spoke solemnly to the children in a room just above the tower's base. They listened with serious eyes. Moll clung to Archer, and Seamus stayed just behind him. Christopher wanted to tell them to run, get away, before it was too late—but he couldn't. The Oath of the Covenant controlled his lips now.

He hated himself for it.

"Fire dwells within all of us: within every human being. Most can never call it up or control it without the help of the Blackness. When the Blackness joins its strength with ours, we become more than human. Their power and ours, joined together, is Covenant Fire: the greatest power in existence. The spell I place over you now will protect you as the Blackness falls over you for the first time. Without it, you would die."

Moll was sniffling. Archer held her closer. "Hush," he said. "It will soon be all right."

Christopher heard himself say, "Yes. You are children. You do not understand everything that will happen today. But the Blackness will accept you into itself, and it will make you great."

"Greater even than you," Archer said. "We are Gifted, and you are not. Is that not true?"

Christopher stared at the child. Earnest eyes looked back at him, determined to do evil that good might come. For an instant Christopher could speak his own words, without the Blackness controlling his mouth. "It is true," he said.

A single ghost ray of moonlight fell across the floor from a high thin window. Christopher looked up at the sickle moon. "Close your eyes, children," he said. "While I speak protection over you."

The guttural words that flowed from Christopher's mouth, a spell born of Covenant Fire, fell over the children like black water. Archer felt something deep in him burning in response. His heart beat faster.

"Come," Christopher said.

Together, they descended the staircase one after the other, down through the floor of the tower. They turned a corner and saw the blue fire burning far below them. They stood at the edge of a great pit, its sheer black walls plummeting thirty feet on every side. Carved stairs wound down the side of the wall.

Tall, twisting candlesticks formed a path along the floor. At the end was a deep circle in the ground, blue fire roaring within it. Beyond that sat a high throne. Christopher Ens approached the edge of the circle and dropped to his knees. He looked up, the word "Master" on his lips—and froze with shock.

The Nameless One sat on the throne, gloating. He stood with a swish of black robes and raised his tattooed hand.

"Where is Master Skraetock?" Christopher demanded.

The Nameless One looked at him for a long moment. "Who?" he asked.

Christopher felt his throat tighten. "Don't play games with me," he said. "Where is the Master?"

The Nameless One smiled. His tongue behind his teeth was blood red. "I am the Master now," he sang.

"No," Christopher said, shaking his head. He took a step back, toward the children. He had to protect the children.

"Have you brought new recruits, little brother?" asked the Nameless One. "A shame—the Order of the Spider is no longer accepting acolytes."

"What are you talking about?" Christopher said.

"They are not needed," the Nameless One said. "I am going to tear the Veil. You—all of you—are no longer necessary. After tonight the Order will cease to exist."

Archer's voice was small in the firelit darkness. He pushed Moll and Seamus behind his back. "What are you going to do with us?"

The Nameless One brought up his tattooed hand, clenched in a fist. He looked at it as though it didn't belong to him, turning it, surveying it. Slowly, he began to uncurl his fingers. As he did so, he spoke, vomiting out strange, guttural words.

Christopher let out a cry of defiance and sprang at his one-time companion—but he stumbled and sprawled on the hard floor of the Pit. His feet were tangled in a pale, sticky web.

Behind him, Moll started to cry.

* * *

When Nicolas stepped into the flame, much that had always defined him died.

The fire was hot—excruciatingly hot. It grew hotter still, white hot, melting down his soul till it was white and malleable as glass, and then shaping it: crystallizing it till it became something new and strong and silver inside of him. Nicolas's transformed soul was awake, alive, full of the young spirit-man in homespun, full of his courage and love and freedom, so pure and sweet it hurt.

The song overwhelmed him, coursing through his veins, beating through his heart. Fire-Song.

The fire died away. Nicolas found himself on his knees, song and fire still searing within, his heart beating as it had never beaten before. He felt as though, for the first time, he was what he should always have been—as though his whole life he had been made of stone and not of spirit, and he had not known it until now.

The King stood before him. Nicolas looked up into his eyes. The depth of the world was in those eyes. The vastness of the star-filled heavens, the stillness of the forests, the jubilation of the seas. Heights and depths of love. Nicolas bowed his head. The fire within him was still free, still dancing, still rejoicing. And then it calmed and left him full of silence.

When he stood, the King was gone. Nicolas was still in the desolate land, but its roar was gone—swallowed by the song within him. The Veil still flashed with lightning and twisted in the darkness. The dry riverbed stretched on for miles.

Nicolas turned and looked at the bush that had burned. It was still there—unconsumed. But it was not what it had been, either. It was the colour of fire.

Could Nicolas have seen into his own eyes, he would have seen the same living colour there.

* * *

The white wolf whined as they passed through the swamp, and the wild things answered. They rose from the water and scurried down from the trees; swooped in from the air and crawled out of the dense tangles like phantoms. They were ugly and small, many of the creatures of the swamp. Yet the white wolf's eyes shone with pride in their allegiance to him.

311

An emerald green snake passed between Miracle's feet, and a little marsh owl sat on her head as she walked, spreading its wings in protection. Swamp cattle, thin and bony, plodded through the water and mud, their wide hooves splashing in the darkness.

They reached the mound of earth where the tower stood, and Miracle turned and knelt. She threw her arms around the white wolf's neck. "Thank you," she whispered. "Don't forget me."

The wolf whined, and Miracle brushed a tear from her own face. "I have to go alone," she said. "You know that." Miracle stood and raised her hand to the door. Her face filled with pain, and she turned back with a motion so sudden that a crow squawked and flew into the air to avoid the arc of her skirt.

"Gwyrion," she said, "tell Michael—tell Michael that I love him."

* * *

In the Pit, the captives lay bound and helpless, captives of the Spider's web. The Nameless One stood over them and smiled cruelly. The fingers of his tattooed hand opened and closed spasmodically as he surveyed Christopher.

"The Rite of the Spider is a powerful thing," he said. "Shall I drain you dry before the Blackness comes? Feed on your fire as I did the Master's? Did you ever think it would come to this, Christopher Ens?"

Christopher's mouth was bleeding. The webbing held him fast. "What will you do with the children?"

"I could do with them much as I will do with you," the Nameless One said. "But I won't. I wish to bargain with them. I will, if she doesn't disappoint me."

Christopher felt his heart sink further. He opened his mouth to reply, but Miracle answered first. Her voice rang out in the pit. He turned his head and saw her standing in the midst of the twisted candlesticks, beautiful in the firelight, and the smell of roses reached him.

"I trust I have not disappointed," she said.

A moan escaped Archer. "Miracle . . ."

Her eyes flickered away from the Nameless One to the place where the children sat together, back to back, trussed tightly. Christopher saw her flinch at the sight.

"It's all right now," she said softly. "I'm here."

"Yes," the Nameless One hissed. "You are."

"Let them go," Miracle said.

The Nameless One took a step away from the fire, toward the corridor of candlesticks. "Not for nothing," he said.

"I'm here, am I not?" Her voice shook almost imperceptibly. "I am making a trade. That's what you wanted."

The Nameless One looked at the children. The webs around them dissolved with a hiss and floated into the air in tendrils of steam. Archer stood uncertainly and helped the others up.

"Where is Kieran?" Miracle asked.

Archer sobbed once. "Dead," he said.

Miracle bowed her head and struggled for composure, then lifted her violet eyes to the children. "Go," she said. "The white wolf will watch over you and take you to your family. Do not turn back."

Moll buried her face in Archer's chest. He held her close to him and shook his head wordlessly as he looked at Miracle.

"Go," Miracle urged.

Archer's chest heaved. He gently parted Moll from himself. "Come on," he said to her, and looked at Seamus. "Let's go."

They went, scampering down the corridor of candles to the stairs. Their feet scratched on the floor like mice. The Nameless One walked closer. Miracle held up her hand for him to stop.

"Let him go also," she said, nodding at Christopher. The Nameless One's face darkened.

"You don't want him," the Nameless One said.

"You are right," she said. "He helped betray the family I love. I don't want him." Christopher bowed his head at her words. He swallowed a painful lump in his throat. "Even so," Miracle said. "I gave him his life back once. I wish to do it again. Release him."

The Nameless One said nothing. He entered the corridor of candles and ran his hand through a strand of Miracle's hair. She closed her eyes as he circled her. He motioned to Christopher, and the web that bound him dissolved.

Christopher raised his head slowly and brought his free hands up where he could see them. He stared at them, disbelieving.

"Run away, little brother," the Nameless One said. "Run with your tail between your legs, and remember that you are so helpless you had to be saved by a woman."

Christopher stood slowly, deliberately. The palm of his tattooed hand grew hot as fire kindled there. It took shape and crackled in the air. He stared down the corridor of candles straight into the eyes of the Nameless One.

Warning curled in the lip of the Nameless One. "No," he said.

"Oh yes," Christopher said. He moved so fast that there was no time for the Nameless One to react. Christopher flung the fire at his enemy and howled, following it, throwing his weight against the man he hated and bearing him to the ground. He grasped at the Nameless One's throat and bit at his face.

There was a sound like metal sliding through metal, and Christopher grunted and fell back. He rested on his knees. His face was pale, and blood trickled from his mouth. He looked at Miracle with pleading eyes.

"I am sorry," he said.

She shook her head, tears running down her face. "I cannot save you this time," she said.

Christopher's eyes widened at a sight no one else could see. He reached up one hand and shielded his eyes, although the Pit was black as ever. He swayed, and his eyes began to cloud over.

"Have mercy on me," he whispered, and fell dead.

The Nameless One stood and looked down on his fallen companion. When he turned back to Miracle, his face was flushed. "You should never bargain with the Blackness," he said. "I could have killed him in a much more useful way." He stepped close, and she tried not to shrink away. Tried not to show fear. "But it doesn't matter, does it?" he said. "You will serve me far better than he ever could."

He hissed through his teeth and moved forward, but he was stopped by a loud thud. He spun away, an arrow quivering in his shoulder. The Nameless One cried out, his voice more angry than pained.

Miracle whirled around and looked up to the edge of the pit, where Stocky and Jack and the others had fitted new arrows to their bows. A battle cry echoed through the Pit.

"Michael," she said.

Michael O'Roarke fairly flew down the stairs into the Pit. He ran down the corridor, seeing nothing but her. His sword was drawn; his face twisted with fear and rage and love. He nearly reached her, but the Nameless One was there first. A black arm circled Miracle's waist and pulled her against him. His tattooed hand hovered near her face. Michael watched in horror as the skin of the Nameless One's fingers stretched and buckled, and his nails grew until they were claws—long claws, razor sharp. He rested them on Miracle's throat and tapped them lightly against her skin.

"Come and fight," the Nameless One said. "What are you afraid of?"

"Let her go," Michael choked.

"That sounds familiar," the Nameless One said. "Michael O'Roarke, isn't it? The one my old master so wanted to join the cause. You should have listened to him. He might even have shared her with you."

"What do you want?" Michael said. "I'll do anything."

"You can't give me what I want," the Nameless One said. "All you can do is amuse me."

"Then I challenge you to a game," Michael said. "A contest of skill."

"Winner takes all, I suppose?" the Nameless One said.

"Winner keeps his life," Michael said.

"Tempting stakes," the Nameless One answered. "But not tempting enough. I already have my life. I've already taken all.

You, on the other hand, are about to die. So why should I play your game?"

Michael lowered his sword and tried to answer, but no words came out.

"Here then," the Nameless One said. "Say goodbye."

He let go of Miracle and shoved her across the floor. She fell into Michael's arms.

"Miracle . . ." he said.

"I love you," she said.

He buried his face in her hair. "You do?" he asked.

The Nameless One's voice rang out, cruel and final. "Enough!" he said. "It is over."

He raised his tattooed hand in the air and screamed in a guttural voice, bringing his hand down to point his clawed fingers at Michael. And then he screamed again, this time in shock and pain. He fell forward.

Kris of the Mountains stood behind him, still clutching the hilt of the sword that was buried in the Nameless One's back.

From above came a deep, wild voice like the belling of a stag. The voice laughed and boomed in the darkness of the Pit. "You can kill many things, scum of the earth," Gwyrion said. "But you cannot kill love."

The creatures of the swamp soared, scurried, and scaled their way into the Pit. The hulking shape of Gwyrion, glowing with moonlight even though the moon could not be seen, appeared at the head of his army. The young men of the Clann O'Roarke stepped forward with the wild things, arrows still ready, swords drawn. The children came behind them, Archer with the young men.

A hush fell over the Pit. The only sounds were the roar of the blue fire and the gasping, scraping breath of the Nameless One. He lay stretched on the ground. Kris put a foot on the Nameless One's shoulder and pulled out his sword. A crow cawed.

The Nameless One stretched out one hand and clawed his way across the floor, until he lay gasping at Miracle's feet. Michael held her closer to him.

"Heal me," the Nameless One rasped.

Miracle looked away and buried her face in Michael's shoulder. A clawed hand reached out and grasped her ankle. "Heal me!" the Nameless One begged.

"Let go of her," Michael said. "Die like a man."

The Nameless One looked up. His eyes flashed. "I am not like a man," he said. "And I do not mean to die yet."

Michael kicked the Nameless One's arm aside, knocking his fingers free. "You can't save yourself now," he said.

The Nameless One rolled over onto his back, and a hideous light came into his eyes. He began to flex his fingers and chant under his breath. In the palms of his hands a fire began to burn. The great blue fire behind him roared up.

Moll screamed.

Michael whirled around and saw Moll suck at her fingers desperately, while Seamus held back sobs. Archer fell to his knees, clutching his middle. His eyes pleaded with Michael to help him. Smoke began to rise from his body.

"Stop it!" Michael commanded. He drew his sword and whirled to face the man on the ground.

The Nameless One laughed. "They should know not to play with fire," he said. "In the end it always burns." His bloodshot eyes moved to Miracle. "We made a bargain. You broke it, not I."

"Release them," Miracle said. She left Michael's side and stepped forward before he could react.

"No!" Michael cried. The Nameless One stood uncertainly and wrapped his arm around Miracle's neck. He leaned on her, shrieked three words, and ran backwards.

Through roaring heat and macabre shadows, Michael saw them fall into the great blue fire.

Behind him, Archer groaned. He heard the voices of his clann and the cries of Gwyrion's creatures. He heard the wolf's howl that could only belong to Gwyrion himself.

But he could not tear his eyes from the place where Miracle had disappeared. The emptiness inside him threatened to swallow him—to plunge him into a deep, tearless darkness.

But then, somehow, he knew.

"She's not dead," he said.

Archer stumbled forward and grabbed Michael's hand. "The Nameless One is going to Athrom," he said, his voice thick with pain. "He said he wanted to kill all the Gypsies."

"So great an evil will wreak terrible things," said the deep voice of Gwyrion. "It cannot be allowed. The whole earth would cry out against it."

"Then I am also going to Athrom," Michael said.

"Not alone," said Kris of the Mountains. Stocky and the others echoed.

"Nor on foot," Gwyrion said. "You would never reach the city in time."

Michael turned. The eyes of the Spirit of the Wild Things were deep and burning wild. Gwyrion threw back his massive head and began to bell. He leaped up the stairs of the Pit, three and five at a time. The swamp creatures lifted their voices and joined their lord. The cacophony was deafening.

"Now run!" Gwyrion roared from the high edge of the Pit. "Speed awaits you on the edge of the swamp. Run to meet it!"

* * *

Nicolas saw the Veil warp and twist, and he heard the Shearim scream. Blue fire licked through the surface of it. In a blur, he saw a man and a woman falling together. The man was nearly indistinguishable from the darkness around him, but the woman shone as brightly as a star. She was in pain. Nicolas reached out as though he could save her, but the vision vanished before he reached the surface of the Veil.

A sound began to pull at his ears—a sound like running water. He quickened his steps. The thorny black bushes were thinning out around the river bed. The landscape was changing.

Nicolas tripped and fell, the ground turning his hands and knees black with soot. He picked himself up and started running. The voice of the River-Daughter sounded in his head, clear and rippling and flowing in every part of him like a rushing stream. The Fire-Song played a wild, free harmony all through the call.

Faster, Nicolas Fisher! Set me free!

16

Golden War

THEY SAT IN A CIRCLE on the floor of the Majesty's throne room, deep in the Darkworld. Candles flickered all around, filling the chamber with an oily smell. They held one another's hands. A map lay on the ground before them with lines like veins drawn across it. Divad traced a thick line with his pale finger and tapped a spot in the south.

"They will reach the city soon," he said.

"They must hurry," Virginia said.

The Majesty's face was tight and drawn in the darkness. The priests especially seemed aware of it; attuned to their king in a special way, they watched him with concern.

"You have done right, Majesty," said Rehtse. Maggie held the young priestess's hand tighter than before.

"The lives of my sons are at stake," the Majesty said.

"The lives of many are at stake," Libuse said.

The Majesty turned hollow eyes on the map. "Is it worth it?" he asked.

"Yes," said Jarin Huss. "Prince Caasi was wise in his words to you."

Divad stood and placed his hand on the Majesty's head in comfort and blessing. "It is as it should be. As it must be," the high priest said.

Rehtse looked at Maggie with eyes that betrayed the conflict within her. The young priestess's mind might agree with Divad, but her heart only wanted to know that Caasi would be safe. Maggie's heart moved for her. She remembered how it felt.

"It will not be easy," Virginia said. "More awaits them than they know."

"Will they win?" Rehtse asked.

"That," Virginia said, "I do not know."

* * *

The riverboats scraped against sand in the darkness beneath the city of Athrom. A winding staircase, wide and older perhaps than the river, led up into the inky silence. The Ploughman stood at the base of the stairs while his little army left their ships and assembled behind him, lanterns in their hands. His heart had beaten strong as the river while the boats traveled south, but now, facing up a passageway that seemed to lead through the ages, it quailed. Surely he only imagined the foreboding presence he felt in the dark.

A low voice at his shoulder said, "The men are assembled, my lord."

The Ploughman turned his head and nodded. "Thank you, Ytac." He looked up the dark staircase and steeled himself, drew his sword and raised it high. The air whistled behind him as four hundred and fifty swords were held aloft. The men raised no battle cry. They were below Athrom now, and had no wish to alert the enemy of their coming.

The Ploughman took a step upward. The edge of the stair crumbled slightly. He heard the crunch of stone as his men followed him, wordlessly, step by step, higher and higher. In the darkness ahead, something moved.

Fragments of stone showered down on the step in front of the Ploughman. He stopped and held his sword ready. Listening.

More stone fragments tumbled over the steps with a sound like dry rain. An animal whine sounded through the passageway. The men stood frozen. Not one said a word. The Ploughman stood alone at their head and stared into the unknown.

There was a movement at his elbow, and a man slunk forward, stepping ahead of the Ploughman. With a shock, the Ploughman recognized Asa's lanky form. The strange man cast amber eyes on the Ploughman and whispered, "Be pleased, mighty leader, that I am with you. You do not know what awaits beneath Athrom. I do."

Asa looked into the darkness, his eyes a slit. "Come now," he said in a high, cajoling voice. "We know you're there."

In answer came a crack like thunder or the beat of enormous wings, and the darkness was lit by a burst of flame that revealed a terrifying visage of red scales and white eyes, teeth, claws, and wings.

"A dragon," the Ploughman whispered.

Pebbles rained down as the dragon moved into the lantern light. Its front legs, clawed and terrible, rested on a step not twelve feet from the Ploughman. Its long body disappeared in the darkness. It opened its mouth and hissed. The inside of its mouth was the burnt red and orange of a furnace. Its teeth were long and sharp.

Before the Ploughman or Asa could move, one of the men shouted and let an arrow fly. It bounced off the dragon's neck. The creature's head snapped forward, and the Ploughman leaped backwards down the stairs while arrows and spears whistled around him and clattered off the dragon's scales onto the stone. Asa stood his ground, daring the dragon to come near him.

The Ploughman grabbed a spear from the hand of one of his men and let it fly. The dragon turned its head an instant before the spear would have pierced its eye. Asa turned his head, looking at the Ploughman and his soldiers. "Fools!" he cried. "You cannot destroy it! The beast is too great for you!"

A young Darkworlder sprinted forward, sword held high, aiming for the creature's throat. "For the Majesty!" he cried. In an instant his cry died along with him. The dragon snapped its jaws around his body and flung him through the air. The young man's sword flew, and Asa caught it. He held it high, letting out a strange battle cry, high and unearthly. The men watched in horror as the dragon loosed a stream of flame that caught Asa in mid-stride and engulfed him. They could see his body, black in the midst of the fire, and they heard him scream.

Yet he did not fall.

The dragon drew back its head. Asa still stood before it, still engulfed in flame. His skin shone bright amber and seemed to fall away. Beneath it appeared a new skin, the colour of the sun. Asa's eyes glowed a deep crimson. The men stepped back, awed and terrified, as Asa shed his form as a snake sheds his skin. He stood before them as something older and greater and more terrible than man.

Asa raised his fist and shouted. He threw himself up, into the air, and flew for the dragon's neck. Into a soft spot at the base of its skull Asa drove his sword, and the dragon screamed and writhed. It shook Asa from his place. Smoke and fire filled the stairway, blinding the Ploughman and his men, but they thought they heard the snap of jaws and saw the flash of teeth. And then a wind blew past them, leaving an impression of amber in their minds.

The smoke thinned and the fire ceased to burn. The Ploughman stepped cautiously forward. The dragon was dead.

"My lord," Caasi said.

The Ploughman turned. Caasi stood two steps back, over the body of the man they had called Asa.

"We will take him home for burial," Caasi said, his voice tight.

"Yes," the Ploughman said. They would bury Asa. But the Ploughman knew—they all knew—that a being called Undred the Undecided yet lived, and he would not be buried with Asa's body.

The men followed the Ploughman onto the body of the dragon. They clambered over its long tail and glistening red scales, up toward the city of Athrom.

* * *

Thick black clouds rolled over the city of Athrom, and a wicked streak of blue lightning snaked across the sky. Cold rain began to fall on the city. In the coliseum, the Gypsies shivered.

325

Marja tightened her arms around the shoulders of a toothless old woman and looked up at the gathering blackness. "Hurry, Nicolas," she whispered.

* * *

The High Police stood in long rows beneath the shadow of the Emperor's Palace. Lucien Morel himself inspected their ranks. They stood tall and strong, faces implacable beneath the grey onslaught of rain.

The Emperor's voice was strained in his own ears. "On my orders you rid the world of an ancient pestilence," he said. He grimaced, but beneath his distaste, exultation held quiet sway. This would rid him of the haunting. The one who had tormented him—who had appeared in his court that very day, at last revealing himself—would never come again.

Behind the dull eyes of the soldiers, thoughts flashed. *There is nothing honourable in killing captives.*

"They have overrun the world for centuries, spreading sedition as rats spread filth."

Nothing right in slaughtering Gypsies.

"You cannot show pity."

Nothing good in murdering Gypsies.

"You have laboured and died to bring them here. Do not shrink from finishing what you have started. It is an honour to serve your Emperor in whatever he may ask." Morel hesitated, then strengthened his voice. "Finish it before the sun rises! Salute me!"

Dead eyes turned to regard their emperor. *We who have lost our souls—salute you.*

Thunder clapped as a thousand black-gloved hands snapped in a salute. Two thousand dull grey eyes followed their Emperor as he returned to his palace. One thousand hands tightened around one thousand spears.

The night was still young.

Lucien Morel, Lord of the Seventh World, stopped in the shadowed gateway of the palace. His bodyguards waited a respectful distance behind. Morel turned eyes full of hate on a dark figure in the doorway, a man in black who stood with a fainting girl behind him.

"They will march on the coliseum, as you have desired," the Emperor said. His little finger twitched sharply.

"It is good," hissed the Nameless One.

"It is good if it earns me your promise," the Emperor said. "I will not see you again?"

The Nameless One smiled. He tightened his grip on Miracle's wrist. "After tonight," he said, "I will never bother with you again."

* * *

Nicolas stepped beyond the fringe of black vegetation, and the river bed disappeared. He stood in a flat plain. The black earth was soft under his feet. He looked out on an endless horizon: a dry ocean.

He swallowed. The air in his throat and in his nostrils was hot and scorched, though his heart was still leaping from his encounter with the King. His feet sank in the soft black earth, and the sand burned as though it had been years too long under the sun. He pulled out one foot and then the other, sinking as he walked and then pulling himself back out.

He looked up and saw a familiar ship on the black ocean. His heart jumped in his throat. He said the word before he had time to think: "Father!" But he blinked, and the ship was gone. Tears stung his eyes. The voice called again. *Hurry! Set me free!*

He nearly tripped over a sword. It was half-buried in the sand, only its sooty hilt visible. He took it and pulled it free of the earth. It was a beautiful sword, finely made and perfectly balanced. The hilt where his fingers rubbed away the soot was gold and marked with the sign of a seven-starred crown.

As he made out the symbol, Nicolas thought he heard voices. Ancient voices, crying ancient battle cries.

And then there was nothing.

Nicolas held the sword in both hands reverently. He looked up at the orange horizon. It seemed to pull him toward the vast expanse before him. Filled with a sense of terrible significance, he reached the edge of the sea-that-was-not.

She was there. The captive River-Daughter.

She lay at the place where the river should have emptied into the sea; where, on the other side of the Veil, it did. She was asleep.

In wonder, Nicolas fell to his knees before her. He still held the sword in his hands. "Wake up," he whispered. He hardly understood the emotions filling him now. If he tried to speak any louder than a whisper, he would not be able to go on. Sorrow, ancient sorrow and fear for the future, would choke him. "Wake up, please."

She did not stir.

He had never seen anyone like her. Her skin was blue-pale and her hair deep gold, and even in the dryness and the stillness she seemed to flow. Her hair, her dress—green and blue, pink and sun-sparkled—her fingers, and everything about her was fluid. Hers was beauty that did not belong to the human race, that did not belong to anything but the rivers and the seas.

But she was still sleeping. He had come for her, but he could not wake her.

He knelt in the black sand with the old sword balanced across his knees. His shoulders bowed, and his head fell. He closed his eyes.

Stillness.

The world had never been so still. So still and so silent. And in him, fire still burned.

Up from the stillness the song arose. Nicolas sang it softly. The notes were uncertain. He was not a singer. He whispered the words. But they came.

He sang the Father-Song, Lover-Song, Fire-Song. The Song of the Burning Light.

And when he was done, he opened his eyes and she was looking into them. Her eyes were no colour he could describe: they were the crystal of the clearest stream. She did not smile at him. The expression on her face was a deep pool under dark pines in the farthest north—still, solemn, and ancient.

She spoke. He knew the voice already. It rippled and flowed, a dozen little swirls running up and down in the current of her speech. "There is work to be done," she said.

The voices of the Veil cried out in pain when Nicolas and the River-Daughter passed through to the other side, but there was peace and a blessing in the pain. Nicolas carried the old sword with him, brandishing it like a warrior.

He meant to use it.

* * *

The lookouts, perched high on the wall of the coliseum, saw the soldiers first. They shouted warnings, wailing in fear and hopelessness as the soldiers marched. On the floor of the great prison, old women and children picked up the wail. Through their own cries, they heard the *tramp, tramp, tramp* of boots and the jangle of swords.

For a few minutes Marja tried to comfort the old woman who rocked and moaned in fear, but her efforts were more than useless. She stood, brushed off her skirt, and began to move through the crowds of her people to the coliseum gates. She went to meet the death of the Wandering Race with courage. Those who watched her go whispered with admiration.

She had never felt more alone.

A hand touched her arm, and she whirled around. "Wait for him," Caspin the Cripple said. "Hide in the crowds. Live as long as you can. Maybe he will get you out."

"Not alone," Marja said. "We live together—all of us—or we die together."

"Child of the Sky," Caspin whispered. "You cannot save us."

"Come with me," Marja said. "Come and meet our enemies boldly."

"A bold cripple and a brave woman," Caspin said. "What a pair we make." He tried to smile, but his face twisted with grief. He nodded his head too quickly and began to hobble ahead.

The crowds of weeping Gypsies parted for Marja and Caspin the Cripple. Some ceased to weep as they passed and held their heads high instead.

At last Marja and Caspin stood between their people and the doors. They waited.

* * *

The Ploughman led his men forward, toward the place where Caasi's maps promised they would find a way up. His mind went over their plans again: wait for the night. Ascend in silence. Take the coliseum guards when they do not expect it; spirit the Gypsies out. Battle—he steeled his jaw. They would fight if every other choice was lost to them. But he knew well enough the odds of their winning.

Another step forward, and the Ploughman stopped. His heart pounded—expanded, swelled to the presence of something else in the darkness. Something good, this time.

Something golden.

With a sound like falling sand, a bright light appeared in the corridor before him, shaping itself into a giant on horseback. The Ploughman smiled at the gasps behind him; they all saw it. But his smile faded quickly. The horsemen appeared for war, and the Ploughman did not want to go into battle now.

"Are you ready?" the Rider asked. "It is time to go above."

"Here?" the Ploughman asked.

"They need you now," the Rider answered. "Prepare yourselves for battle."

* * *

The High Police approached the coliseum in a long column, the foremost of them falling beneath its shadow. Great wooden doors barred the way before them.

They halted.

A muscle twitched in the jaw of their commander, but he hardened his face and raised his sword. When he brought its tip down to face the door, all would be over for the Gypsies.

He hated the word *massacre.*

But then, he had never liked the Gypsies.

He brought his sword down, and the ground erupted before him. The High Police fell back before the thrashing hooves of a horse, dazzling white and shining like the sun, half as tall as the doors of the coliseum when it reared on its hind legs.

On the horse's back sat a great golden warrior. Bronze eyes looked down on the High Police, who stood frozen in shock and fear.

The Rider raised his fist and said, "Let the battle begin."

In a moment the Rider was gone, but the fissure he had opened in the ground was crawling with men. Farmer-soldiers and Gypsy men rushed from the earth alongside pale, hairless warriors whose battle cries shook the air.

"Darkworld!"

"The Majesty!"

The Ploughman led his rebels as they charged the ranks of the High Police, shouting, "For Pravik!"

"The King and Pravik!"

"The King!"

Two armies, both small and unprepared for battle, clashed before the gates. The noise of their meeting carried over the walls.

"What is it?" breathed Marja.

"It can't be . . ." said Caspin.

"Nicolas," Marja breathed. "Hurry."

* * *

"They come out of the ground," the soldier said. "Their battle cry is *Pravik*. Forgive me, your excellency. They are slaughtering your men."

"How can they have come here?" the Emperor demanded. He bit the nail from his little finger and spat it on the tiles of the floor. "Call out every soldier in Athrom. We will destroy them. From this day forward there is no rebellion in Pravik!"

Lucien Morel strode out of the throne room and turned on a sickly shadow in the hall. "What of your plans now?" the Emperor snapped. "Get out of my sight. You have brought this upon me!"

The Nameless One drew himself up. "You do not know who you are talking to," he said.

"I know what I am talking to," the Emperor answered. "I am talking to a dead man."

Lucien Morel stalked away, and the Nameless One whirled on Miracle. She leaned against the wall behind him, pale and worn. He had stolen too much life from her already—taken it from her as a spider drains its prey. They had fallen through Covenant Fire, and its effect made her too weak to fight him.

"Heal me," he shrieked.

She met his eyes and did not look away. She said nothing.

"It does not matter," he said. "I will be healed. The sacrifice will bring the Blackness into the world, and I will be found within its shades. I am immortal!"

Her strength began to drain from her again. She fought to remain conscious. His voice rang in her ears even as darkness darted through her eyes. "I will make the sacrifice myself. I will drink death as the Blackness drinks it. I will live . . ."

Lucien Morel, Lord of the Seventh World, did not hear the Nameless One. He threw a purple cloak over his shoulders as he rushed down the hall, calling for his attendants. "Make my coach ready," he commanded. "I must leave Athrom."

Morel's men scrambled to obey as their emperor stood and looked out on the city. He could see and hear the upheaval of battle around the coliseum. His finger twitched. He breathed short, nervous breaths. They were here. The rebels were here. Perhaps they would win, and the Gypsies in the coliseum would come for revenge. But no, they couldn't win. He was sending out his army. The whole army of High Police would destroy the Pravik rebels forever.

But then again . . .

"Hurry!" Morel shouted, not caring if anyone was near enough to hear him. "I must leave the city!"

* * *

The Ploughman cut a wide swath with his sword as he sprinted for the heap of rubble around the fissure in the ground. He climbed the broken blocks of stone and looked down on the battle. His men had driven into the ranks of the enemy. The sheer surprise of the attack, rising like a whirlwind from the ground, had driven the High Police back.

But they would not lose ground for long. Over the turmoil of the battle the Ploughman could see a dark river of men moving through the streets toward the coliseum. More soldiers. He closed his eyes and ducked his head for a moment as numbers swam in his head. They were outnumbered—how greatly? His spirit refused to give him an answer.

A contingent of High Police, spears lowered, drove through the rebels, straight for the gates of the coliseum. The Ploughman thought he heard a child sobbing over the sound of the battle: a Gypsy child behind the gates. He raised his horn to his lips and blew.

"Form ranks!" he shouted. "Guard the gates!"

His men picked up the call. Horns that had once belonged to farmers blew the signal, and the men regrouped before the high wooden gates of the coliseum. Many fell before they reached their comrades. The High Police rushed forward. The Ploughman heard himself shouting, "Stand your ground!" His men stood with their backs to the coliseum. High Police surrounded them on three sides. They had no choice but to stand their ground—though they die trying.

Swords clashed as the High Police reached the rebels. A high, wailing blast sounded on a horn made of bone and scales: the Darkworlders broke ranks and charged forward, led by Harutek and Caasi. The battle surged around the heap of rubble

335

where the Ploughman stood. He leaped down and drove his sword into the nearest soldier. He pulled it out and whirled on another. Beside him, Harutek screamed a shrill battle cry.

A silver horn blew, and another rank of High Police charged the gates.

"Hold!" the Ploughman screamed as he ran to join the men who guarded the coliseum. Eyes that had known him since boyhood followed him as he sprinted the length of their ranks. "They must not break through!"

A volley of arrows rained down on the rebels. Men cried out and sank to their knees as silver-tipped arrows struck, driving through the rebels' leather armour and burying themselves in the thick wooden gates.

"Shields up!" the Ploughman cried. He turned his head to see that his orders were obeyed. His men crouched under battered shields. The wailing cry of the underground warriors rang in his ears; they were shieldless, yet still they drove into the vanguard of the enemy.

The Ploughman felt and heard an arrow drive into his shoulder. He cried out and fell. His knees slammed into the smooth pavement, and for an instant the world swam before him. Then he rose again to his feet and made for the heap of rubble. He climbed with clenched teeth as arrows rained behind him and swords rang and clashed all around.

From the top of the heap, he watched the archers draw once more and let fly. Too many of his men fell beneath the volley. The enemy foot soldiers were waiting now. When the bowmen had weakened the rebels' ranks beyond endurance, the High Police would charge again. It was clear enough: the rebels had to take the archers down.

"Caasi!" the Ploughman called. The young prince of the Darkworld felled two men and turned to face the Ploughman above him. He saluted, his pale skin streaked with blood.

"The archers!" the Ploughman said. "We must defeat the archers!"

"We have no protection!" Caasi answered. "Our fish scales cannot withstand their silver."

"Scales," the Ploughman repeated to himself. Light filled his eyes. "Scales!" he shouted.

Understanding glimmered in Caasi's eyes. He whirled on his heel and raised a horn to his lips. The high blast called his own men to him, and the Darkworlders disappeared into the ground beneath the Ploughman's feet.

They needed time now. That was all. The Ploughman turned his head to those who still huddled beneath their shields at the gate. He blew a charge on his horn. The men raised their heads and shields and ran forward, into the ranks of the High Police, where arrows could not kill them without taking down their own men as well.

But there was no one now to guard the gate. The commander of the High Police saw through the confusion to his chance. He sounded a battle cry and led the march toward the doors of the coliseum.

The Ploughman leapt from his place and ran over the slick street to the gates. Power flowed through him as he ran. His face glowed golden; his hair blew wildly in an unearthly wind. He raised his sword and lifted his voice, and the Riders came to his aid. Hooves pounded the ground around him. The battle cry of the heavens resounded through the earth. Twelve golden warriors arranged themselves before the gate, and the High Police drew back in fear.

You have come, the Ploughman said to them, in wordless thanks.

We cannot kill men, the lion-haired captain said. *This you know.*

I do not ask you to kill. Only guard the gates.

"March!" the commander of the High Police shrieked. His men surged forward and drove into the Golden Riders, whose horses reared and slashed down with their hooves. The blows passed through the bodies of the High Police, bearing them to the ground but not wounding them. Arrows arced through the air to the gates once more, sticking in the golden warriors. The horses whinnied in pain. High Police surged in, around and under the giants.

The archers all aimed at one Rider. He gave a cry of anger and pain as their arrows drew blood. Three arrows, expertly aimed, pierced his horse's right eye. The animal fell to its knees. The Golden Rider dismounted and drove into the High Police, but now foot soldiers swarmed over him. The Ploughman watched in agony as the High Police brought the giant warrior down. High Police stood atop the Rider's shoulders and screamed victory to the air, even as a gentle breeze turned the warrior's body to sand and bore it away.

Strength and fury filled the Ploughman, and he rushed forward. Twelve men were dead at his hand before he became aware that he was fighting. There was fire in his veins, golden fire. The arrow wound in his shoulder grew hot, and the heat seared through his arm and hand, but it was the heat of a forge. It made him stronger even as it burned. The golden sands of

the Rider's body swirled around him as he fought, flecking his
skin with glints of gold. He threw back his head and roared like
a lion.

The Ploughman raised his sword, and three arrows hit
him. One drove deep into his already-wounded shoulder; one
pierced his armour and lodged in his thigh; one slashed
through the skin of his left arm. His leg buckled beneath him,
and he fell to the ground, racked with pain. He looked through
a haze of blood at the battle.

The ground was trembling. Hooves. The High Police were
sending horsemen.

The rebels were still fighting, but they could not hold
much longer. The Golden Riders alone stood between the High
Police and the coliseum—but they could not kill. The
Ploughman cried out in frustration. The heat of battle-joy left
him. They were losing the fight.

Darkness started to drift across his eyes. But then he heard
a high wailing horn, and Caasi rushed from the ground with
his men at his back, armoured in the flashing red scales of
dragon hide.

They charged through the enemy, leaving dead men in
their wake. They charged for the archers. The Emperor's foot
soldiers scattered before them. Arrows rained down on them,
only to bounce off the scales. The archers broke ranks and
turned to run—too late. Caasi and his men shrieked and wailed
as they bore down on the enemy.

The skin at the corner of the Ploughman's mouth cracked
as he smiled. He felt strong arms behind him, helping him up.

"My lord," Harutek said.

"I am all right," the Ploughman said. His leg nearly buckled. "I will live."

His hand shook as he raised his horn to his lips and blew the signal for the men to form ranks. Farmers, Gypsies, and stable boys withdrew from the melee and formed tight ranks again, though their numbers were thinned. Protecting the gates.

The Ploughman leaned on Harutek as he heard other men shouting the words that had been his: "Stand your ground! They must not break through to the gates!"

Harutek led the wounded leader to the fissure in the ground and began to descend with him. "You'll be safe down here," the prince said.

"No," the Ploughman answered. "I want to see how the battle goes. I want my men to see me."

Harutek nodded, though there were tears in his eyes. "Yes," he said.

Together they struggled up the heap of rubble until the Ploughman could see. The Emperor's horsemen were in the rearguard, preparing to ride down on the gates. The rebels could not stand against them. The Ploughman looked up to the Golden Captain.

The horses, he said.

Aye, the captain answered. He raised an ornate gold horn to his lips and blew a charge, and the eleven remaining Golden Riders charged forward, knocking down men and riding over them. Army horses lost their nerve before the Riders and bolted. Some charged forward, High Police riding with their lances leveled. A group of them knocked a Rider from his horse and bore him to the ground, lances deep in his chest. The

Ploughman closed his eyes and felt a breeze around him; felt sands in the air.

He did not ask Harutek to tell him what he knew already. Though they fought bravely, though they had already beat enormous odds, they were losing the battle.

Horsemen, regrouped and determined, charged for the gates.

* * *

Miracle lay on the stone edge of the coliseum. Wind whipped at her hair as the world spun around her and the rain lashed down. The Nameless One stood beside her and shrieked strange, harsh words into the black sky. He thrust his hands to the clouds. Lightning, blue and terrible, sliced the air around him.

Miracle rolled over and fought darkness as her stomach lurched. She could see people far below, pelted by the rain, huddled in little groups. She could hear them crying.

Her eyes went to a figure who stood before the doors of the coliseum. A young Gypsy woman. The young woman turned and looked up, and her eyes met Miracle's.

The battle raged on the other side of the doors. Who could say what side was winning?

But it didn't matter who won, Miracle remembered. The man at whose feet she now lay dying would kill them himself. He could do it. She had seen him kill.

And to think, he had pleaded with her to heal him.

As though she would ever help him.

He was too far given to evil to help. He was hardly human. He was sick . . .

Lightning danced in the Nameless One's eyes as he spit the last words of his spell into the dark air. He felt Covenant Fire in his fingertips; felt it crackling through him. This was life. This was power. He was a god.

He jerked his hands down, and the Gypsies began to die. Old ones and children first.

Before the doors of the coliseum, Marja fought to stay on her feet as pain racked her body. Dark faces and grinning masks flashed before her eyes. She lifted her eyes to the cloaked figure on the wall.

"No!" she cried. Thunder drowned her out. The raindrops were black and hot and heavy like tar.

The High Police succeeded in breaking through the guard before the gates. The doors of the coliseum burst open, and the battle spilled in. The Gypsies were past caring. Some were past knowing.

A wolf's howl split the night, strong with rage, and a stag leaped through the battle with a man on its back. Michael jumped down from the stag's back and began to climb up the wall. He could see her.

He had to reach her.

Miracle saw him, too, but she forced herself to tear her eyes away. Slowly, painfully, she raised herself to her knees. Then to her feet. She took a step nearer the Nameless One. He did not see her. He was laughing, and his face was changing. He was a skeleton: a mask with nothing behind his eyes except deepest black.

But then she touched him. She stood behind him, raised her hands to his face, and held him; and his laughter turned to screams.

"What are you doing?" he cried.

"Healing you," she said.

The Nameless One fell to his knees as power drained from him. Miracle fell behind him. She cried out and looked to the sky, but still she held on.

The death throes of the Gypsies were changing. They were only weeping now—and only the living can weep. The rain was rain, and it was not black, or heavy, or hot.

The Nameless One seemed to fold in on himself. He lay on his face and whispered for her to stop, to let go. But she would not, not until she had driven the pestilence from him. She would not stop until he was human again.

That would kill him, he reasoned with her in his mind. There was not enough left of him to live—he had lost it all to the Blackness.

The voice of Michael O'Roarke echoed in Miracle's ears. She turned to see him leaping the steps and the seats of the coliseum. Kris of the Mountains was behind him, the white wolf following. And Archer: Archer, bless him, he was coming for her too.

She let go.

The Nameless One groaned wordlessly and rolled so that he could look into her face. She leaned on her hands, bent over him, breathing hard. She hardly recognized him. He was emaciated and afraid, nothing like the man she had known.

"Now you are healed," she said.

She could not take her eyes from his face, so she didn't see him pull a dagger from beneath his cloak. Not until the other hand grabbed her throat. His face twisted with hatred as the dagger stabbed.

Michael shoved Miracle aside and killed the man before the dagger pierced her skin.

The Nameless One was gone.

Michael knelt on the edge of the coliseum and took Miracle in his arms. She clung to him, shaking with weakness and pain, and they wept together. Kris of the Mountains stood over them and looked down on the coliseum as the skies cried rain.

"The battle is lost," Kris said.

"No," Gwyrion growled. "Can you not smell the change in the air? It is just beginning."

* * *

The Emperor had elected to leave on the eastern road, where the entrance and exit of the city was bordered by the high walls of two aqueducts. Now he regretted it.

Lucien Morel emerged from his coach red with anger. "Why are we stopped?" he demanded.

"Your excellency," the coachman faltered. "Look, your majesty . . ."

Lucien Morel failed to hear the man's voice. He could see nothing but the water that was pouring over the road—his road—blocking the way out of Athrom. Water was pouring over the edges of the stone aqueducts.

The water began to gather around his feet and swirl in angry currents. Lucien Morel turned white as death and scrambled for the safety of the coach. A swift current in the water knocked him from his feet. He landed on his face, and water poured into his mouth and nose. He pulled himself up onto his hands and knees and crawled through the mud, crying in terror.

The river had come for him.

He heard the incredulous cries of men and women somewhere in the streets, spreading the news that had even now begun to reach the city.

"The river has turned back on itself! It flows inland from the sea!"

* * *

The Ploughman watched from his vantage point as the battle streamed past him through the open doors of the coliseum. A soldier in black and green leapt up the rock and charged at him, and he calmly watched him come before Harutek cut him down. He looked down at the dead soldier's face, and the sounds of battle rang in his ears. Battle, and screams—the screams of women, children, Gypsies.

The forge inside him flared to life once more. He felt the searing heat through his wounds and the strength that came with it. A strength not his own; a strength born of greater powers. For an instant his eyes flashed gold, and he leaped down from the heap of rubble and into the fight. He cut, slashed, whirled, lunged, and soldiers fell before him—ten, fifteen. Thirty.

Sand swirled around him. Three men charged him and he cut them all down. Five more came. Two before him; one to the left; one to the right; one behind.

He moved faster than any human being should move. One was dead; two, three, four. He could not move fast enough to kill the fifth. He whirled around to face the man charging him, knowing it was too late, knowing he would die now; and then a blur of red passed in front of him and made a sound like a wounded animal as the soldier's sword drove into it.

The Ploughman killed the soldier and knelt by the body of Caasi, Seventeenth Son of the Majesty, clothed in a makeshift cape of dragon hide. The sword had found a rift in the cape and driven home.

Caasi groped for the Ploughman's hand and gripped it tightly. The young prince's eyes were racked with pain, but he gripped harder and licked his bloody lips.

"We have fought well, have we not?" he asked.

The Ploughman bowed his head. "Yes," he said. "You have done proudly."

Caasi looked up, past the Ploughman. "I am glad," he said, "that it was done under the sky."

Caasi's eyes closed, and the Seventeenth Son of the Majesty slipped away.

The Ploughman bent his head low over the young man's body. Sobs racked his frame and made the pain of his wounds come back. His face was wet with tears, every other inch of him wet with blood. But there was more—a new wetness, a new warmth around his feet as he crouched on the ground. He opened his eyes and saw clear water washing the blood from Caasi's face.

In the distance there sounded a roaring as of a river broken loose.

* * *

Soldiers in and around the coliseum froze with their swords in mid-stroke as the sound reached their ears. The Gypsies turned wondering eyes to the gates.

The seven remaining Golden Riders sent up a shout that echoed through the streets of the jewel of Italya. The rebel army, streaked with blood and dirt, turned their faces east.

The river swept into Athrom. Waves crashed down over the High Police as currents picked up the rebel fighters and carried them up in the warm embrace of the water. It washed away the blood and gore and made even the dead clean. The Ploughman held the body of Caasi in his arms as the river cradled them and carried them away. He closed his eyes and let the warm waves wash his wounds and cool the fire in his soul.

Marja stood with tears pouring down her face as the water swirled around her feet and lifted her up. She saw Nicolas coming to her, riding in the arms of a creature more beautiful than anything she had ever seen. The River-Daughter swept Nicolas into Marja's arms and carried them away together.

The rain and the river mixed together until all of Athrom was under the floods, and the people fled their city for higher ground in the country.

When they returned, the Gypsies and the rebel soldiers were gone.

The River-Daughter carried her refugees back to Pravik, but this time the rivers they traversed were above the ground.

The Darkworlders drank in the sun as it sparkled on the water around them. When they reached Pravik, the Majesty and Libuse and Divad and Maggie and all of the people were waiting for them. The River-Daughter had sent word of their soon arrival by sweeping acres of water lilies into the caverns under the City of Bridges, filling the sunless world with the smell and sight of hope.

The Clann O'Roarke went home to the Green Isle and set about rebuilding their home. They mourned the loss of the child Kieran and celebrated the marriage of Michael and Miracle. Kris of the Mountains disappeared the morning after the wedding, and a north wind blew down from Fjordland in farewell. The white wolf was gone as well.

The Gypsies took to the roads in caravans of crimson and purple and brilliant yellow. They danced and sang and told stories, and the people of the Seventh World feared them.

And when their caravans rattled over bridges and past marshes and ponds, the water laughed.

Epilogue

GOLDEN LEAVES RAINED DOWN on the wagon, unseen in the moon-light.

Nicolas Fisher lay awake in the dark. Crickets chirped in the forest, and the sound of his wife's breathing filled the wagon. He thought he could listen to such sounds all night and never need to sleep.

Even so, when he first began to hear the voices, he thought he was dreaming. They were so far away—so thin. But he knew them, these silk rainbow voices, and he sat up a little and tried hard to hear them.

The Veil grows thin, said the voices of the Shearim. *We are passing from the world at last.*

Tears filled Nicolas's eyes and he whispered, "But—"

Soon anyone will be able to put a hand or a foot through the Veil, and then there is no telling what may happen.

"Why are you telling me this?" Nicolas asked. Marja stirred beside him.

For this last moment we have voices. It is good to talk with a friend.

"Thank you," Nicolas said. "For everything."

Marja sat up and strained her ears in the darkness. But

there was no answer. The voices were gone—and always would be.

"Nicolas?" Marja asked, settling down again.

Nicolas leaned over and kissed the top of his wife's head.

"Is something there?" Marja asked.

"No," answered Nicolas.

He closed his fire-coloured eyes and went to sleep.

One last voice broke through his dreamless slumber. The voice of his son.

He had told Maggie, long ago. *Sometimes I can hear a baby talking when it's still in its mother's womb.*

What do they say? she had asked.

They dream, and they wonder, and then they go back to sleep.

Nicolas smiled and joined his child. They dreamed. And they wondered.

"Nicolas?" Marja asked, her voice groggy in the pillows.

"Mmm?" he asked.

She smiled and took his hand. "Go back to sleep."

Did You Enjoy This Book?

Do you know someone who would enjoy reading it? SPREAD THE WORD! As a small press, we value the power of READERS to decide what is worth reading. We believe that a book's true value cannot be measured in marketing dollars. The worth of a book is in the impact it has on YOU. If you have seen value in this book, we encourage you to let others know.

It's simple:

- Spread the word!

- Give a copy as a gift.

- Leave a review on Amazon.com or BarnesandNoble.com. Then email us a copy so we can post it on our Web site.

- If you write a newsletter, ezine, blog, or print column, consider letting your readers know about this book! Write a review, host an author interview, or hold a contest.

- Send us an email: publisher@littledozen.com

Visit the author at
http://www.rachelstarrthomson.com

The Adventure Begins with Little Dozen Press

Worlds Unseen
Book One of The Seventh World Trilogy

When she learns the terrible truth about the Seventh World, Maggie Sheffield is sent on a journey that will change her forever. Along with the Gifted gypsy Nicolas Fisher, who hears things no one else can, Maggie joins with the last surviving members of the Council for Exploration Into Worlds Unseen and a group of eastern rebels to discover the truth.

It won't be easy. The Seventh World has long been controlled by the Blackness, and its monstrous forces are already on Maggie's trail.

Worlds Unseen can be purchased in trade paperback or downloaded as a free ebook.

For more information, visit

www.rachelstarrthomson.com

Free Fiction from Little Dozen Press

Taerith

by Rachel Starr Thomson

http://www.rachelstarrthomson.com/books/taerith-a-novel/

Second born of the outcast Romany family, Taerith finds new purpose in the kingdom of Corran, where he befriends a persecuted queen, defends a beautiful slave, and serves a bitter prince at the crossroads of good and evil.

"Devastatingly beautiful... I am amazed at every chapter how deeply you've caused us to care for these characters. " - Gabi

"Taerith updates are the absolute highlight of my RSS feed moments. Deeply satisfying." - Kapezia

"Wow. I am not one to be lavish in my praise, but this is a really amazing story. I printed it out and read it this weekend and now... I want more!" - Danielle

"It had me on the edge of my seat (literally!). Your descriptions are amazing; I can picture every scene. You are developing the story so well and interweaving the characters. I love the way you use dialogue, like flavoring it's just enough." - Elizabeth M.

"You are an artist, Starr. Every chapter is like a painting. It's beautiful." - Brittany Simmons

"Great rhythm to your writing. The pace never abates and it keeps me engaged. I am hooked and totally invested in this tale." - Kappa

"Vivid and intriguing!" - Marsha